Beyond the Barrier Reef

The Navy Cadets

C.R. Cummings

Also By
CHRISTOPHER CUMMINGS

The Green Idol of Kanaka Creek

Ross River Fever

Train to Kuranda

The Mudskipper Cup

Davey Jones's Locker

Below Bartle Frere

Airship Over Atherton

Cockatoo

The Cadet Corporal

Stannary Hills

Coast of Cape York

Kylie and the Kelly Gang

*Beyond the Barrier Reef

Behind Mt. Baldy

The Cadet Sergeant Major

Cooktown Christmas

Secret in the Clouds

The Word of God

The Cadet Under-Officer

Through the Devil's Eye

The Smiley People

Barbara at her Best

Beyond the Barrier Reef

The Navy Cadets

C.R. Cummings

DoctorZed
Publishing
www.doctorzed.com

Published 2018 by DoctorZed Publishing

DoctorZed Publishing books may be ordered through booksellers or by contacting:

DoctorZed Publishing
10 Vista Ave
Skye, South Australia 5072
www.doctorzed.com

ISBN: 978-0-6483871-0-7 (hc)
ISBN: 978-0-6484096-9-4 (sc)
ISBN: 978-0-6484096-8-7 (ebk)

National Library of Australia Cataloguing-in-Publication entry

Author: Cummings, C. R., author.
Title: Beyond the Barrier Reef/ Christopher Cummings.
ISBN: 9780648387107 (hardcover)
Series: Cummings, C. R. The navy cadets.
Target Audience: For young adults.
Subjects: Adventure stories, Australian.
Military cadets--Queensland--Fiction.

Cover image © Joanne Weston | Dreamstime.com
Cover design © Scott Zarcinas

Printed in Australia, UK & USA

DoctorZed Publishing rev. date: 21/11/2018

Dedication

**The Officers of Cadets and Instructors of Cadets
of the Australian Navy Cadets**

This book, while a work of fiction, is respectfully dedicated
to all the Officers of Cadets and Instructors of Cadets of the
Australian Navy Cadets who have done such a magnificent
job in preparing young people for life as good citizens.
By being good role models and by delivering such useful
nautical training, and by mentoring and inspiring young
people to be useful citizens of Australia, you have provided
a magnificent volunteer service.

Thank you.

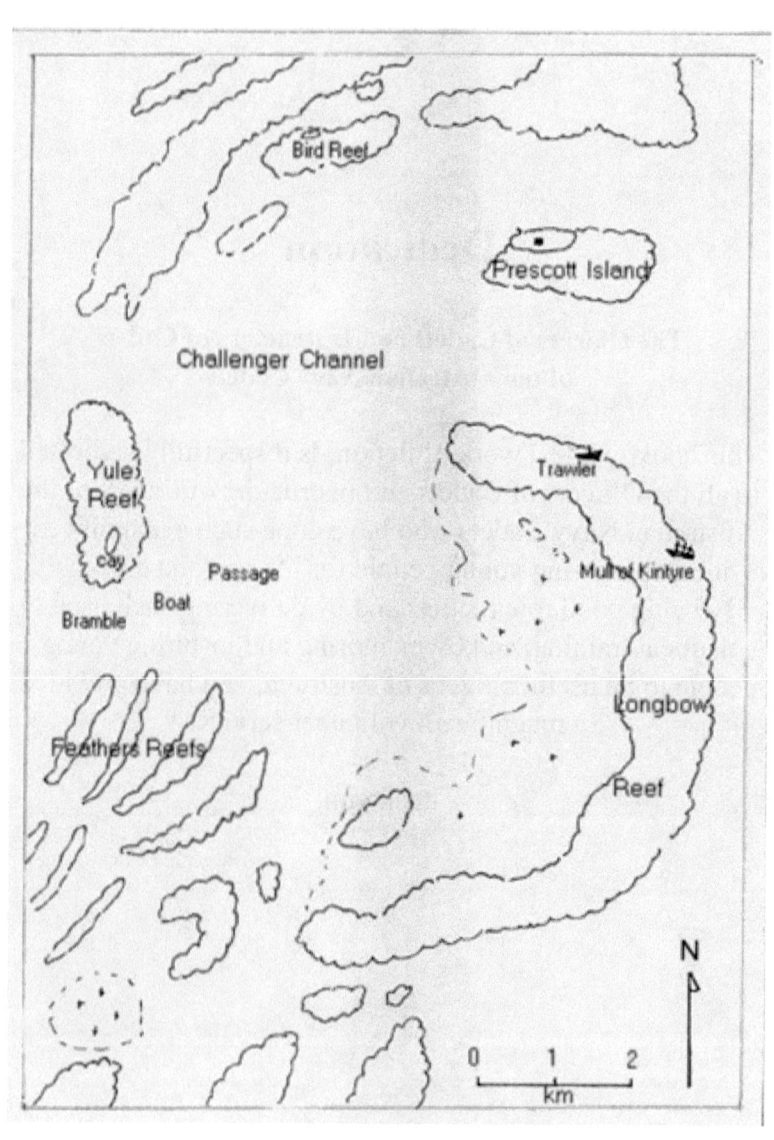

Bird Reef

Prescott Island

Challenger Channel

Yule
Reef

Cay

Passage

Boat

Bramble

Feathers Reefs

Trawler

Mull of Kintyre

Longbow

Reef

N

0   1   2
km

Chapter 1

RESEARCH PROJECT

April school holidays
The Great Barrier Reef
Between Cairns and Townsville, North Queensland
1030hrs. A bright, sunny day

Andrew Collins, sixteen, sat in the inflatable rubber boat and fidgeted with adjusting the straps of his Buoyancy Control Device or BCD. This is the inflatable vest that SCUBA divers wear to adjust their depth control and to which their compressed air tanks are secured. There were three other divers and a crewman in the boat and Andrew was hoping that they had not noticed how scared he was.

Particularly Carmen, Andrew thought glancing at his seventeen-year-old sister beside him.

It was her doing that had placed him in this predicament, but he was not going to let on that he was hating almost every minute of it. Carmen had been asked by her friend Ella if they would help her big brother Tristan with his university thesis in marine biology by taking part in a survey of marine organisms. Carmen, who obviously loved diving, had thought it was a wonderful idea and had agreed, then asked Andrew to make up the numbers.

So here I am, and I wish I was anywhere but here, Andrew thought as he looked around.

Not that he minded being in the boat. Andrew loved sailing and was a very accomplished and experienced small boat handler. It was below the water that his courage evaporated. Partly this was the way he had always felt but it was the traumatic experiences of being trapped underwater in the wreck of the *Merinda* with the skeleton of his grandfather that had really consolidated his fear.

That had been eighteen months ago and the only diving that Andrew had done since had been almost as traumatic. That had been three dives during their expedition to look for the wreck of a Dutch World War 2

Dornier flying boat the previous January. During that Andrew had been with Carmen when they had found a dead body in a wrecked launch after a cyclone.

And Andrew knew he only had himself to blame. *When Carmen asked if I would go I should have said no or told her the truth,* he mused. In fact, he suspected she knew the truth and had hinted that a dive trip might help him regain his nerve. *Like people who fall off a horse getting straight back on one,* he decided.

But it had still taken a real effort to hide his fear and to act normally. The first dive had been a real ordeal but since then familiarity had helped to ease the terror back to a nagging anxiety.

I hope there are no problems this trip, Andrew thought.

So far there hadn't been. It was the third day of the expedition and on the previous two days they had been diving four times each day. The first day had been spent travelling from Townsville out to the outer reef in the university research boat. This was a fifteen-metre dive boat that was at that moment anchored in the lee of the reef they were surveying. Andrew could just see its mast over the top of the tiny sand cay that showed among the breakers which fringed the reef.

The reef they were surveying was called Yule Reef and that pleased Andrew as he admired the work of Lieutenant Yule, Royal Navy, who as the captain of the British gunboat HMS *Bramble*, had done much of the detailed surveying of the Great Barrier Reef during the mid-nineteenth century. Yule Reef was only about half a kilometre long and perhaps two hundred wide and was completely submerged on the high tides.

At that moment Andrew and his friends were at the northern end. Separating Yule Reef from the next reef to the north, Challenger Reef, was a deep-water passage named the Challenger Channel. Andrew was glad it was behind them as it was half a kilometre wide and was so deep that the bottom was not visible. Instead the seabed just faded down through shades of blue to an inky blackness and was the sort of place that conjured up all of Andrew's worst fears about monsters of the deep. To make it worse a strong current was now scouring through it, running west with increasing force as the tide rose.

Andrew moved to look around. Off to his left rear, away to the northeast, he could just make out the tiny black square that was the old stone building on Prescott Island. That was their base camp and was five kilometres away with the main stretch of the Challenger Channel in between.

Directly to his left, to the east, was another set of distant reefs, the Longbow Reefs, so named because of their shape on the chart. They were also about five kilometres away and were marked by two dark lumps that Andrew knew were shipwrecks, one 19th century and the other a very recent 21st century wreck. Half a kilometre to the south of Yule Reef were a series of long parallel reefs called the Feathers Reefs. Between Yule Reef and the Feathers Reefs was a large area of shallow seabed and another deep-water channel, the Bramble Boat Passage. That was where they were swimming to on the next dive.

Carmen turned to Andrew and began checking his straps and the connections of his air tank. Then she took his alternate air source and tested it. Andrew managed to return her grin and then do the same safety checks with her equipment. Beside him the other two divers, nineteen-year-old Tristan Lyall and his seventeen-year-old sister Ella, were busy carrying out the same drills. Ella ruffled her curly fair hair and then zipped up her BCD and began doing up the buckles. In the process she squeezed her breasts together. Unlike the other three divers she wore only a brief bikini, preferring it to the neoprene wetsuits worn by the others.

Andrew tried not to look at those bulging bosoms but found it hard not to. He was at the age where he had become very interested in girls. But he did not want his sister to notice this, so he hastily looked away and pretended to check that his weight belt was securely buckled. It was a relief when Ella had the BCD done up as it covered her whole upper body. Now he could only see her very shapely hips and bare legs!

Another Uni student, Dan Powell, sat at the stern and was the safety boat crewman. The blue and white diver's flag fluttered on a short whip that doubled as a radio antenna. Dan had a small radio and now informed Mr Craig, the master of the launch, that the divers were ready.

Andrew spat in his facemask and leant over the side to swill seawater around in it. Then he pulled the facemask over his head so that it hung under his chin. As he did he heard a distinctive sound.

Aircraft, he thought, looking around.

The others heard it too and all stared at the sky. It was Duncan who saw the machine first. "There," he said, pointing south.

Andrew saw it then, a twin-engine machine that grew rapidly larger as it approached. The aircraft flew past about half a kilometre to the east and at only about a thousand feet altitude. It was painted a distinctive red and white pattern and Andrew knew what it was even before it was close enough to read the words painted on its fuselage.

"Coastwatch," he said.

Four times in the last four years the Coastwatch planes run by Customs had played an important part in his life so he was quite happy to see one flying by. They flew daily patrols to try to detect ships and boats involved in smuggling, illegal immigration and illegal fishing in Australia's Economic Zone.

Like that Taiwanese trawler over there on Longbow Reef, he remembered.

That had been fishing illegally in Australian waters but had suffered an engine failure during a storm the previous year and had been blown onto the reef.

As the aircraft flew past low overhead all five divers waved. Andrew knew that it would have been in radio contact with the dive launch and that the aircraft crew would know who they were. That was important as they were in a restricted zone where special permits were needed. As a university research activity they had these. The aircraft flew on and was soon lost to sight.

Tristan now looked at each in turn, a quizzical expression on his freckled, cheerful face. "All OK? Good, then let's get this done before the tide gets too strong."

With that he placed his regulator in his mouth, adjusted his facemask and rolled backwards into the sea. As Andrew watched Tristan's fins vanish into the water he felt his stomach churn.

Bloody hell! Here we go! he thought.

He would have dearly loved to stay in the boat, but he dutifully positioned his facemask, gave Carmen what he hoped looked like a cheerful grin and not a sickly smile, and then placed his regulator in his mouth. Carmen did likewise and then turned her head to check that she was not going to hit Ella with her fins as she went over backwards. Then she rolled away. Ella gave Andrew a grin and then put in her regulator and followed.

Andrew took a last quick look around at the clear blue sky and the sunlight sparkling on the blue sea then he also rolled over backwards.

It was something he hated doing and was a procedure he had never understood.

Why don't divers just lower themselves into the water? he wondered for the hundredth time.

But it was better than jumping with legs spread from the deck of a launch, so he just clenched his teeth and did it rather than excite comment.

The water closed over him, cold only on his head and hands to begin with. He heard the familiar rasping, sucking noises as he began breathing through the regulator and he allowed himself to sink and settle to a feet down position. The first thing Andrew did was look around to check on the position of the other divers and in particular his dive buddy, who for this dive was Ella. She was only a few metres away and was looking at him while she adjusted her buoyancy.

Andrew used the valve connecting his air tank to his BCD to adjust his own buoyancy so that he hung effortlessly and apparently weightless a few metres below the surface. Above him he could clearly see the outline of the rubber boat as it bobbed on what looked like a rippling silver ceiling. Then he took a quick look in all directions, this action motivated more by fear than anything else. It did not really reassure him when he saw nothing unusual.

But that doesn't mean they aren't there, he thought, 'they' being the sharks and other creatures of the deep that he feared.

What he saw was the wall of the reef only ten metres to his right. Ahead of him stretched the reef and a gently sloping sandy bottom. To his left the sandy bottom extended outwards, slowly getting deeper until it was lost in the blue. That was alright. He was on the right in the pair of divers so was the nearest to the reef. That meant considerably less danger of some giant shark suddenly rushing out of the darkness with jaws agape. But perversely it also meant it was the direction from which smaller but also worrying creatures like moray eels might suddenly lunge forth to snap and bite.

Now the dark abyss of the Challenger Channel was directly behind him and Andrew could not resist the urge to frequently glance back at that dark blue-black void of liquid fear. With an effort of willpower, he looked back towards Ella. She gave him a thumbs-up and he returned it, hoping his anxiety was not obvious.

Sharks rarely attack divers, he reminded himself. *Or only sharks like White Pointers and they are creatures of the cold Southern Ocean and are rare in tropical waters.* But the intellectual theory was small comfort to his worries.

Ella began swimming southwards with the reef ten metres to her right. Andrew set off parallel a few metres further in. He saw that Carmen and Tristan were already ten metres ahead and fifty metres out to his left front. They were going deeper and were doing a survey of the seagrass on the seabed. There wasn't much visible and Andrew did not think they would see much.

Not on the seaward side of the reef where the big waves work, he thought.

Checking the distribution and health of the seagrass was part of Tristan's thesis study and so far they had found little, only a few isolated pockets in the shallower, more sheltered water on the western side of the reefs. Andrew and Ella had the task of surveying the number and size of the brain corals on the edge of the reef. They also had the secondary task of helping Dan calculate the amount of seaweed that was growing on the actual reef. That was the topic he was researching as there was some evidence that the seaweed was encroaching on the coral. To do this Ella had an underwater camera and both had small plastic slates and crayon pens. At present the water was too shallow to swim safely across the top of the reef without risking injury to themselves or damage to the coral. They would do that from the boat during the high tide period.

Drawn on his plastic slate Andrew had an outline map of the reef overlain on a grid which showed every ten metres to scale. Using the pen, he began to mark on brain corals and seaweed as he saw them, using dots for brain coral and small squiggly strokes for the seaweed. The work at least took his mind partly off his fears. He swam just below and to the right of Ella so she could take photos every few metres. The distance swum they had to estimate.

All the usual small fish flitted among the coral, but Andrew had seen too many sunfish, clown fish and other colourful types to be really interested. Instead he kept glancing around to check that nothing large was eyeing him off as a potential meal. The day before a large shark had cruised by and just that one fleeting glimpse had reignited all of Andrew's fears.

The only really good thing was that the visibility was excellent.

Usually it was about fifty metres, but he estimated he could see clearly almost twice that.

Probably because we are so far from the mainland and there has been no strong wind for a week so the waves haven't stirred up the silt, he thought.

The sandy seabed was only about twenty metres below, with Andrew swimming at ten metres and Ella just above that. Carmen and Tristan appeared to be swimming along about five metres above the sand.

This isn't too bad, Andrew decided.

In an attempt to overcome his anxieties, he refocused on his job and made a point of trying to note all the different types of fish that he saw. Knowing that tourists paid big money to do exactly what he was now doing added a distinctive twist to his sense of the absurd.

After about two hundred metres Andrew noted that the wall of the reef was trending in to a sort of a bay. He had been expecting that because the air photos of the reef showed just such a shape. The increased current flowing into the 'bay' was also expected because they had found an obvious gap, like a miniature canyon, extending deep into the reef when they had surveyed the other side earlier in the morning. The old survey charts did not show any channel or gap but the air photos did and Andrew agreed with the suggestion that there was probably a narrow pass right through the reef.

So he swam into the narrowing gap behind Ella, noting that the current was increasing every second. The tide was now on the rise and was squeezing through all the gaps in the reef as the ocean level rose out to the east. *We need to be careful here,* he told himself. So he swam up beside Ella and got her attention. Using gestures, he shook his head and swept his hands across to indicate 'no'.

She looked at him quizzically, so he turned his slate over and printed the word 'current' and held it up for her to read. She looked, then nodded and gave a thumbs-up. By then they were right in the mouth of an obvious passage. It was about ten metres wide and the same deep with vertical sides and a sandy bottom.

Both now turned and began swimming back against the current. This turned out to be much harder than Andrew had expected and he quickly revised the current speed from three knots to five or six.

Anyway, enough to make this hard work, he thought as he finned

13

hard against the flow. The effort soon had him sucking in big lung-fulls of air and he knew that wasn't good.

Need to take it easy, he reminded himself.

As they swam back out into the wider 'bay' area the current eased and they were able to make more progress. Ella stopped to take another couple of photos and Andrew made more notes on his slate. Then they resumed swimming south along the outer edge of the reef. As they did Andrew looked around for Carman and saw her and Tristan in the distance. They were now on the limit of visibility and showed only as flickering shadows.

We had better catch up, Andrew thought.

He began powering after them and then flinched with fright when Ella touched his arm. He looked at her anxiously, but she just smiled and pointed to her pressure gauge. That made Andrew feel guilty as they had been down for fifteen minutes and he knew he should have remembered to check hers every ten. So he slowed while she looked at his gauge and then gave him the pressure reading by hand signals. 175psi she informed him. That was plenty for the twenty or thirty minutes they might still be down at such a shallow depth. Andrew checked hers and saw that it was 180psi and the thought that she was a more skilled diver irked him a little.

Both then resumed their survey, swimming slowly along the side of the reef. By then they were well away from the Challenger Channel and the inky blackness no longer threatened. Instead the visibility just shaded off through pale green to a dark greeny-yellow and then to a sort of shadowy darkness. The only larger creatures Andrew saw during the next five minutes were a couple of stingrays which kicked up sand as they moved or tried to hide. There was not even a large parrot fish or groper visible.

Then a flicker of movement up to his right front sent a shiver of fear though Andrew. He looked anxiously up and then breathed a sigh of relief. It was a large turtle. The creature had swum into view over the top of the reef and now dived across their front and swam rapidly off into the gloom. Andrew watched it with admiration. Turtles were reptiles that he really liked.

Green turtle or a Loggerhead? he wondered, staring hard to try to pick out the salient features as it swam almost directly away from him. *Green,* he decided.

Two minutes later, another flicker of movement out to his left resolved itself not into a friendly turtle but into what he had feared—a large shark! It had come from behind and was swimming slowly along in the same direction and he was sure it had seen them.

Andrew felt his heart skip a beat and he began to breathe rapidly. Reaching out he tapped Ella and pointed to draw her attention to the thing. It looked to be a bronze whaler and Andrew estimated it to be four metres long.

Big enough to chew me up anyway, he decided.

Ella looked and then nodded and even took a photo. Andrew watched with his stomach churning and his whole body cringing as the shark swam up level with them about twenty-five metres away. He tensed, ready to try to fend it off and then he fingered the handle of his sheath knife with his right hand. Then he realized that he was seeing dots and that his vision was going blurry.

I am hyperventilating, he told himself. With a conscious effort of willpower, he slowed his breathing.

For a moment the shark turned towards them and Andrew glimpsed the rows of vicious looking teeth and his blood ran cold.

It is going to attack! he thought. He gripped the knife, ready to draw it.

But it didn't. Instead the shark turned away and swam off to the left front out into deeper water. As it went Andrew sighed with relief and, despite his fear, was able to admire the sleek lines and absolute efficiency of its swimming style. Then it vanished into the gloom, leaving only Andrew's rapidly beating heart and the memory of those teeth and the unwinking eye. The memory of the creature stayed with Andrew, causing him to continually look around

Ten minutes later they reached the southern end of the reef. The location was obvious both by the trend of the reef, indicated by the compass on his dive computer, and by the increasing strength of the current pushing them. Also the shape and colour of the seabed began to change. As they rounded the curve to the southern end of the reef the bottom sloped gradually down on their left to a sandy valley which shaded into dark blue depths.

The Bramble Boat Passage, Andrew thought.

From studying the chart he was able to visualize the channel. He knew that the Boat Passage branched off from the main Challenger Channel near Prescott Island. It then ran Southwest gradually getting shallower. At its junction with the Challenger Channel the Boat Passage was one hundred and twenty-five fathoms deep, over two hundred and thirty metres, deep enough for the largest of ships, but by the time it reached the half-kilometre wide gap between Yule Reef and the Five Feathers Reefs to the south it was only five fathoms, nine metres. This was why it had never been suitable for ships to use, unlike the Challenger Channel which was still forty fathoms, over seventy-five metres deep at its shallowest.

The bottom is all sand and this end has a bathtub shape, Andrew remembered.

A careful look around seemed to confirm this as he could see the sandy slope rising from the deeper channel and then reaching an obvious crest off to his front. Beyond that the water became deeper again as it shelved away on the western side of the line of reefs.

Andrew noticed movement out to his left, well away from the reef. *What is that?* he wondered anxiously. Then he saw that it was Carmen and Tristan. They were right down near the bottom and were swimming directly away from the reef. *Where on earth are they going?* Andrew wondered. He could not remember any part of the plan about going south across the Boat Passage.

Quickly he checked his compass. *Yes, they are going across the Boat Passage.* That both puzzled and worried him. *If they aren't careful they could get caught by the current as the tide gets higher,* he thought. That could sweep them off to the west and give them a hard swim to get around behind Yule Reef to where the dive boat was anchored.

Andrew looked around and saw that Ella was also looking. She gave a shrug but Andrew shook his head, then moved to check her air pressure. '95,' he signalled. He looked at his own and it informed him that he only had 75psi left. That worried Andrew a bit as he knew he should keep about fifty in case of emergencies and they still had a few hundred metres to swim to get back to the dive boat.

But I have only been swimming at about five metres, he thought, *so I shouldn't have too much nitrogen to dissipate.*

As he worked this out Andrew watched Carmen and Tristan. They were now on the limit of visibility and that got Andrew even more anxious. Now undecided about what to do he looked up and noted that the inflatable was moving out across the Boat Passage as well, obviously following the trail of bubbles.

Where are they going? he wondered. Then he noted a dark bump on the seabed out on the crest line. *And what is that?*

Whatever it was Carmen and Tristan were obviously going to investigate it. *Probably just a rock or small outcrop of coral,* Andrew surmised. But even as he did this his eye noted a straight line half-hidden in the sand of the seabed. It came from down to his left and ran across the seabed towards the dark hump.

What the devil is that? Andrew wondered, pointing to it to bring it to Ella's attention.

It was clearly not natural, and Andrew guessed that it had attracted the attention of Carmen and Tristan. He had been about to swim on around the end of the reef and back to the dive boat but now he signalled to Ella that he was going to join the others. She shook her head, but Andrew was determined. Where Carmen was going he was going.

Quickly he printed on the back of his slate: We can always surface and go back in the boat.

Ella read this and gave a thumbs-up. Andrew at once began swimming, angling slowly down towards the straight line on the sand. To reach that he had to go down to fifteen metres but that did not bother him at all as he was qualified to go to thirty. As he went down Andrew noted that the current was moving him sideways to his right so he had to 'crab' to the left across it to reach the line.

As he got closer Andrew saw that it was not one line but a pair of steel wire ropes. Curious he swam right down and touched one to check. *Two steel wire ropes lying side by side, both new and in good condition,* he noted, grimacing with annoyance as the rope was coated in some sort of grease.

Looking to his left he saw that the ropes ran down into deeper water and then ended abruptly at what looked like a pulley block.

Curious to see if he was right Andrew swam that way, going another five metres deeper as he did. It was a pulley block. The block was shackled to a steel ring set in what looked like a large block of concrete. The concrete block was almost completely buried in the seabed.

What on earth is all this? he wondered.

Andrew looked around at Ella, who was close beside him. She met his eyes and shrugged. Andrew also shrugged, then checked both his depth and his remaining air. *Still got 65psi,* he thought.

Ella informed him she had 70psi. Andrew knew he was now moving into a potentially dangerous phase if he stayed down much longer but he reasoned that he would be going back slowly upwards if he followed the ropes.

They are going to that lump on the crest and it is only at five or six metres, he reasoned.

So he turned and swam back along the steel wire ropes, heading for where Carmen and Tristan could just be made out as tiny moving shapes at the dark mound.

What is it that they are looking at? Andrew wondered.

Chapter 2

STUNNED

As he swam quickly towards where Carmen and Tristan were Andrew puzzled over what it could be that they were looking at. From his study of the chart he did not remember any isolated rock or coral outcrop being marked in the middle of the Boat Passage.

And why has this steel wire rope and anchor point and pulley been put here? he wondered.

The whole group of reefs was in a restricted research conservation zone so there should not be anything artificial there. It wasn't even one of the anchor buoys that had been placed at selected places by the Great Barrier Reef Marine Park Authority. Andrew noted that the wire rope ran directly to the dark mound.

It only took a couple of minutes for Andrew and Ella to swim the hundred metres to where Carmen and Tristan were pulling at something on the dark lump. As they were swimming with the current they were able to skim along. The only thing they had to do was keep watching their depth so they did not come up too fast. Twice Ella caught Andrew's eye and tapped the dive computer on her wrist to remind him of both the depth and the time. He nodded and gave a thumbs-up.

Another quick check of remaining air showed that Ella had sixty-five and Andrew fifty. That was now becoming serious and he nodded to show he understood. But they were now only a short distance from where Carmen and Tristan were pulling at what looked like a net. So Andrew continued swimming, confident he could safely surface and reassured by the sight of the rubber boat bobbing only ten metres overhead.

But even as he looked up the rubber boat began moving, the propeller on its outboard motor becoming a sudden whirring blur and its engine noise very obvious. It sped away westwards.

Where is Dan going? Andrew wondered. *Must be back to the dive boat for something,* he decided as it was anchored in the direction the rubber boat was going.

Still curious about the net covered mound on the seabed Andrew switched his attention back to the dark mound which he now saw was the size of a large vehicle.

That is a net, he noted, seeing Carmen tug a section free. But how did it get there? *This whole group of reefs has been closed to all fishing for ten years or more,* Andrew thought. His first idea after that was that the net had come off an illegal fishing boat, Taiwanese or Indonesian perhaps.

But what is the net caught on? he wondered, seeing Tristan crouching right on the bottom at what looked like a piece of machinery. *Winches?* Andrew wondered, noting what looked like cable drums and several hand wheels. *Definitely man made anyway,* he decided.

Andrew was just about to swim down to look when his attention was distracted by cavitation and engine sounds and he looked back over his shoulder and saw the rubber boat returning from the west. Seeing it come to stop reassured Andrew. That was good as it meant he would not have to swim another half a kilometre if he had to surface.

A small anchor splashed into the water and fell to the seabed twenty-five metres away, the nylon rope slithering out behind it. The rubber boat came to a stop about fifty metres to the west, tugging at its anchor against the current.

That was a bit dangerous! Andrew thought irritably. *One of us might have been underneath that.*

Assuming that Dan had made sure they were safe before he threw the anchor, so Andrew turned his attention back to the net and the machinery it was tangled in.

Or is it? Those look like some sort of straps, he thought.

To add to the puzzle, he saw that a steel rod about three metres high was sticking up out of the seabed in the lee of the mound. Even more puzzling other sets of wires could be seen stretching off across the seabed, one directly under Andrew towards Yule Reef and another opposite it going south across Boat Passage.

What are these wires for? Andrew wondered.

He began swimming over to join Tristan and Carmen. This was hard to do as the current had carried him past the mound and he had to swim hard against it. He knew he had only a few more minutes of safe diving left before he must surface but he wanted to see for himself what this man-made object was.

Splashes back behind him made Andrew glance quickly over his shoulder. He saw it was two more divers entering the water but they did not interest him. *Dan and Mr Craig must be coming to have a look,* he surmised.

Andrew joined Carmen at the net and she held it up and he saw the query in her eyes. He reached out and felt it. It was nylon and both strong and new, the mesh about fifteen centimetres in size. *What on earth would they be trying to catch with a net with a mesh this big?* Andrew wondered.

Tristan waved his hand and then pointed down. Andrew turned to look, very aware that he must soon surface.

Whoosh! Bahwhoompf!

Andrew stared in uncomprehending shock as something struck the back of Tristan's head, resulting in a fizz and sudden eruption of bubbles.

Oh my God! His air tank has exploded! Andrew thought. And then he saw the steel rod and the dark streamers of blood.

It took a few more seconds before the impact of the horror he had just watched sank in. *A powerhead,* he thought in disbelieving amazement. Powerheads were special explosive tipped spears fired from a speargun. Usually the tip of the spear contained a large calibre rifle bullet: a .308, or a 7.62mm or even larger. They were used against sharks and other large and dangerous marine creatures. And it was obvious from the way Tristan's arms just flopped and his whole body sagged and began to drift back on the current that he was dead.

An accident? Andrew wondered as sickening emotion began to boil in him.

He knew there were a couple of old spearguns on the dive boat, but he had not seen any powerheads. Half-stunned with shock Andrew noted the look of horror on Carmen's face and then saw Carmen reach out and grab Tristan by the arm. Then she looked up to where the powerhead had come from and Andrew saw the whites of her eyes as they widened in terror.

Fear then overrode shock and Andrew swivelled to look back up as well. There were three divers there. Close to him was Ella, also staring up at the other two. Both of the other divers were about ten metres above and behind—and both held spearguns.

What the hell? Andrew thought.

His mind raced, trying to work out what Dan and Mr Craig might be up to. Then he realized that both of the other divers were fully clad in black and wore some sort of fully enclosed helmet. And they were not wearing the bright yellow BCDs of the university group. Nor did either have the build of Mr Craig.

What the? Who are these people? Andrew wondered.

Then he saw the closest of the two divers point his speargun at Carmen. As though in a dream Andrew noted that the speargun was of the compressed air type and that it had a double mount. One of the spears was gone but one remained—and it was a powerhead!

He's going to shoot Carmen! Andrew thought. He could not imagine why but a surge of sheer desperation set him moving rapidly. *I must save her,* he thought.

He whipped out his diving knife even as his fins began to bite at the water. All he could think to do was swim between Carmen and the man so that is what he tried to do.

Zzzut!

Andrew saw the bubbles spurt and the spear flashed down. It seemed to arrow straight towards him at an appalling speed but at the last moment his mind registered the fact that it would pass just in front of him. He made a desperate lunge with both arms and swept them downwards. The knife in his right hand just clipped the butt of the spear but his left hand actually struck it as it passed.

Did it get her? Andrew thought, anxiety pulsing through him along with the adrenalin.

He turned his head to look and to his intense relief he saw that the spear had just missed. A trail of bubbles led close past Carmen and down to the seabed. There was a distinct *whumpf* and a puff of bubbles and sand on the seabed to mark the spear's impact. For a moment his eyes locked with hers and he saw the shock, disbelief and horror he was experiencing being mirrored in hers.

Then anger surged as the shock took hold. *Bastard!* Andrew thought. *He has killed Tristan and tried to kill Carmen!*

And the man had fired both his spears. Andrew reacted, partly from the surging fury and partly from a coldly rational notion that he must fight to survive. He turned and began swimming towards the man, knife now held at the ready.

Thunk!

Andrew felt the blow and knew instantly that he had been hit. But there was no explosion and even as he turned to look he noted that the second diver had a speargun which used conventional spears.

I've been hit! Andrew thought, disbelief and terror both swamping his thoughts and emotions. Fear of death and rising panic at dying underwater, by drowning if not from being impaled, gripped him so strongly that for a few seconds he was quite paralysed.

As he regained thought and movement Andrew groped at his back and found the steel shaft. It had driven in just below his air tank and then angled downwards through his right buttock and across through his right leg to press against his left. Terrified of dying he found his heart racing and realized that he was gulping great lung fulls of air.

Slow down! You will run out of air, he told himself. But new fears were still swamping his consciousness and he had trouble acting on his own advice. *I must be bleeding*, he thought, groping to find the wounds.

But he could only feel where the spear went into his wetsuit and was unable to reach around to feel the exit. The whole time his eyes were on the man who had shot him, noting that there was a second spear still in the speargun and that it was aimed at him.

I am done for! he thought.

But he wasn't ready to just give up and ideas of making a last desperate lunge with his knife flashed through his mind. It was only then that he realized that he no longer had the knife. Stupidly he stared at his open right hand.

I must have dropped it, he thought.

Angrily he berated himself for not looping the thong on the knife's handle over his wrist to prevent that happening. Part of his mind told him not to be ridiculous as there had been no time, but the other part tried to come up with a plan.

Then Andrew noticed a third diver in black had appeared from the direction of the rubber boat. This diver also had a twin spear speargun.

We are all dead! Andrew thought bitterly. He turned to gesture to Carmen to swim. *Get away! Swim for your life!* his mind screamed.

To his dismay she had let go of Tristan's body and had swum over to grab hold of him. Frantic for her safety Andrew tried to push her away and then he gestured furiously for her to get going.

To his annoyance he saw that she was shaking her head and holding on to him. Groaning with defeat and despair Andrew saw that the third diver had arrived and was looking around and making furious signals with his left arm and hands.

No chance now, Andrew thought. He began to brace himself for death—regret and terror becoming the dominant emotions.

Then he saw that the third diver was making angry gestures and pointing towards the rubber boat. Both the other divers began indicating to them to start swimming that way.

Not yet then, Andrew decided.

But the dread was tight in his chest and he was still gulping air too fast. And now the pain was starting. Up till then the wound had felt numb, but streaks of agony began to shoot up his spine and down along his right leg. The steel shaft of the spear felt as though it was grinding against the back of his thigh bone.

But there was no doubt that the divers wanted them to go towards the rubber boat. Andrew made a few feeble strokes, but Carmen gripped him tight and looked close into his eyes, face mask to face mask. Andrew saw the mingled fear and concern in her eyes and then she began towing him, holding him close as she did.

Andrew found he could hardly move and at last managed to slow his breathing. As he was dragged along he saw that Ella was swimming beside them, her head moving from side to side and her eyes wide with terror. Behind them came the three divers, their weapons aimed at them. The diver who had killed Tristan was towing his body, gripping it by the gauges on his air tank. A swirl of blood still seeped from Tristan's head but was almost immediately dispersed in the water.

The sight of that blood got Andrew thinking. *I must be bleeding too,* he thought. But he could not turn his head enough to see. He found not knowing was worse. His imagination took over. *Blood attracts sharks,* he thought.

He remembered reading that even the tiniest amount, parts per million quantities, could be smelt by sharks at incredible distances. Another wave of gut squeezing terror engulfed him and he began looking around in an attempt to spot any attack before it struck him.

By then the combined effect of swimming and of the current had them close to the rubber boat. The third diver now pointed towards where the dive boat was anchored and made signals to the first diver. He dragged Tristan's body up to the rubber boat and then hauled both himself and it aboard. Andrew watched with fascinated horror as Tristan's legs and fins vanished up through the rippling silver ceiling that was the surface of the sea.

The third diver angrily gesticulated and pointed and the threat of his speargun got them moving again. Andrew tried to use his limbs but Carmen shook her head and held him so he stopped struggling and left it to her. As they swam they rose slowly and were now only five metres down.

I shouldn't drown now, Andrew thought, conscious that his air must be just about exhausted.

In the end his air did run out. He sucked and nothing came and a second suck just produced panic. Frantically he gestured to Carmen and pointed to his regulator. She at once unclipped her alternate air source and held it out for him. Andrew spat out his regulator and grabbed the alternate and placed it in his mouth. A quick blast cleared it and he thankfully gulped a breath of air.

Thank heavens for all that training, he thought, remembering how much they had been drilled by the instructor during his Open Water and Advanced Diving courses.

Carmen now angled upwards and a minute later they broke surface. Andrew sobbed with relief as his head broke through into the fresh air and sunlight. But he kept his regulator in his mouth as he knew from experience that if he did not he could easily swallow a mouthful of salt water as he tried to breathe and in his current state that could be disastrous. Once she was on the surface Carmen inflated her BCD to give them both buoyancy.

The rubber boat appeared near them and the man in it, his speargun reloaded, pointed behind Andrew. He screwed his neck around to see how far they were from the dive boat and immediately regretted it as a stabbing pain lanced through him again. The horrible thought that the spear had damaged his spine sent chills of apprehension through Andrew. But he had spotted the dive boat. It was about two hundred metres away.

Maybe Mr Craig can save us, Andrew thought. But it was a feeble hope as Mr Craig was just an unarmed, middle-aged man against three armed and fit younger men. *Who are they? And what are they doing?*

Andrew wondered. *And what will they do to us?* That was the real worry. *Will they kill us too?* he worried.

It took Carmen five minutes to swim the distance. Every minute added to the tension and apprehension building in Andrew. The rubber boat circled them continually and Andrew noted that Dan was not in it.

Where is he? he wondered. *Is he dead or is he a prisoner like us?* It was a terrifying mystery and it took all of Andrew's courage to face whatever might be ahead.

From time to time as his face mask dipped under Andrew got glimpses of the other divers. They were swimming towards the dive boat as well, shepherding Ella. To make things worse other fears continued to nag at Andrew. Chief among these was the worry about sharks and he kept glancing around as well as he could in the vain hope of spotting any that might be approaching.

They were in the lee of the reef by then and Andrew saw the exposed coral and the small sand cay off to his left as Carmen towed him on his back. The waves subsided to less than fifteen centimetres and the current also eased as it spread in the wider waters beyond the reef.

What is going on? Andrew wondered. *And how can we get away?*

That and dread over what injuries he might have suffered—and might be facing—kept him mentally occupied as Carmen struggled the last fifty metres. As she did Andrew saw that a large, modern fishing boat of the 'Game Fishing' type with three levels of superstructure on its gleaming white hull was tied on the far side of the dive boat. Seeing the other boat explained to Andrew where the three divers had come from but left him shivering with shock and filled with dread.

As they reached the dive boat, Carmen swung Andrew around to bring him in head first to the steel mesh dive platform which was hinged down at the stern so that it was just below water level. She reached it and hung on, gasping for breath and trembling from the exertion and obvious distress. Andrew felt relief tinged by anxiety about what was to happen next but he had the hope that the men had brought them back to question them.

They would have just killed us out there otherwise, he reasoned.

Lying on his back as he was Andrew was able to look up. Squinting against the glare of the sun he made out another strange man, bearded and dressed in black and armed with a submachine gun. The man with the SMG was standing at the stern of the dive launch and had the weapon aimed at Dan and Mr Craig.

At least they are alive, Andrew thought.

Three heads surfaced nearby and the third diver hauled himself up onto the dive platform. As the man hauled himself upright using the port ladder for support he unclipped his helmet and pulled it off. This revealed him to have a thin, hard face with high cheekbones. His hair was cut very short and as he turned to look down at Andrew the hard look in his dark eyes sent chills of apprehension through him. The man pointed the speargun at Andrew.

Staring up at the hard, angry face and the twin steel points of the spears Andrew experienced a rush of pure terror.

Is he going to kill me now? he wondered.

Chapter 3

TRAINING TELLS

S o severe was the panic attack that Andrew found he was gasping and shaking. Fear pulsed through him and he began to pray.

He is a cruel looking mongrel, he thought as he stared up into the third diver's hard face.

The third diver then looked at the other divers and snarled, "Get zem up! Get zem aboard!"

Andrew noted that the man had a distinct foreign accent, but his attention was diverted by several painful muscle spasms that wracked him, causing him to suck in his breath and to grit his teeth until they passed.

The third diver scrambled up the port side ladder onto the deck, pushed past the man with the SMG and then vanished aboard the game fishing boat. The second diver took his place on the dive platform. First, he placed his speargun flat on the deck over to port. Next, he took off his helmet and then dragged off his fins and tossed them up onto the deck. His weight belt followed. Then he scrambled up onto the stern of the launch and began taking off his BCD and air tank. The man with the SMG moved further forward to make room for him.

Then the first diver, the one in the rubber boat, called loudly, "Come on girl, get out!"

Andrew glanced and saw that the first diver had also taken off his helmet and his BCD and air tank and was aiming his reloaded speargun at Ella. To add ghoulish horror to the scene Tristan's lower legs and fins just showed above the inflatable sides and the sight sent a shiver of fear through Andrew.

It was obviously horror and shock that afflicted Ella as she could hardly haul herself up onto the dive platform. Then she just stood there, trembling violently and with the water dribbling and dripping off her and onto Andrew's face. The second diver, who had by now removed his BCD and air tank and picked up his speargun, shouted angrily at Dan, "Help her up you! Grab that air tank."

Dan, looking stunned and shaken, did as he was told. As he leaned down to grab hold of Ella's air tank Andrew noted that his face was bruised and bleeding. *He has been bashed,* he thought.

Ella was hauled up the starboard ladder onto the stern of the dive boat and Dan then helped her to take off her BCD and air tank. These were handed forward to a worried looking Mr Craig who stowed them on the racks that were set up on the centre line of the dive boat. Her weight belt was taken off and passed to Mr Craig as well. Ella then hunched and tried to cover herself with her arms. She looked blue with the cold and was shivering violently.

Andrew looked at her curvy body in the skimpy bikini and the thought crossed his mind that she might regret having not worn a wetsuit. *I hope those men aren't interested in her as a girl,* he thought. Ella moved to stand between Mr Craig and Dan on the starboard side of the deck.

The heat of the sun now began to fog up Andrew's face mask. Anxious to see as well as he could he reached up with his right hand and took out the regulator, then tugged at the face mask, pulling it down around his neck. As he did so he uttered a mental rebuke when he remembered what he had been taught on his diver's courses.

I should have pulled the mask up onto my forehead, he thought, the signal that the diver was in distress. Around the neck was the normal place for it to be. But it was done now and so he did not change it.

Carmen pulled her own face mask down around her neck and leaned over. "Are you alright Andrew?" she queried anxiously.

Andrew nodded and groaned a yes, still unsure of how serious his wound might be. The second diver interrupted, leaning over and gesturing to get up.

"Get up on deck!" he snarled.

Carmen kept a tight grip on Andrew while she hauled herself up onto the dive platform. In the process Andrew's head went lower and he felt water wash around his ears, but he managed to keep his face clear of it. Carmen then turned and reached down to lift Andrew. As she lifted him sharp darts of pain shot down his leg when the spear struck against the dive platform.

"Aargh! Ah!" he gasped. "The spear. Turn me over."

Carmen stopped lifting and looked to see what the problem was.

"Sorry," she said. "Dan, help me please."

Andrew was gently rolled over while most of his body was still in the water and he then tried to use his hands to help her. Dan scrambled down the starboard ladder and took hold of his air tank and BCD and helped to lift. After a short struggle Andrew got his knees up onto the dive platform but when he bent forward the spear sent more stabs of pain through him, causing him to groan and cry out. As always he was astonished at how heavy all the gear felt when it was out of the water.

For a few seconds Carmen stopped trying to lift but then the second diver snarled at her to get on with it and Andrew was hoisted to an upright position. Shaking and shocked Andrew stood there, gripping the starboard ladder. This put his eye just above deck level. Close in front of him were the bare feet of the second diver and beyond them the boots of the man with the SMG.

Ella and Mr Craig were ordered to help by the second diver and they moved to bend down and grab his arms and equipment. "Face down," Andrew managed to croak, fearing more pain from the spear. He knew it was stuck sideways somehow and did not want to suffer more agony. They heaved him up and lay him flat on the deck with his feet still sticking out over the stern. Andrew swivelled his head to the left to watch the men.

Carmen now climbed up, passing up her fins first and then her weight belt before clambering up over Andrew. She was helped to remove her BCD and air tank and it was placed in the rack by Mr Craig.

I wish someone would take off my air tank, Andrew thought as the weight off it on his back was pressing down on him, making it hard to breathe. But he could not seem to open his mouth except to suck in air. So he just lay there, gasping and groaning while something else went on down behind him on the dive platform.

The third diver now re-appeared, leaping athletically from one boat to the other. To Andrew's dismay he now also carried a submachine gun. It was a tiny thing and Andrew vaguely identified it as possibly a Czech Skorpion.

The third man now stood right at the stern facing the prisoners. But he spoke to the other men first and from his tone of voice Andrew had no doubt he was 'The Boss'. "Vich vone of you shoot zer man?" he demanded to know.

"Me, Mr Ivanoff," answered the first diver from just behind Andrew. "Vy?"

"He was undoing the net."

A look of fury crossed Mr Ivanoff's face and for a second Andrew thought he might be about to shoot Diver No. 1. "You blutty fool! Vot for ve need zer dead body to dispose off? You are zer idiot Barry."

"But the sub is due in an hour," Barry answered, truculence in his voice.

"Silence you idiot! Zey not need to know zat!" Mr Ivanoff snarled. "Now you giff us zer even bigger problem."

"Sorry Mr Ivanoff," replied Barry. This time his voice was tinged with anxiety.

Andrew's mind raced as it tried to grapple with the surprising information. *Sub?* he thought. *Does he mean a submarine?* He was sure the men were criminals and now he suspected they were smugglers.

Mr Ivanoff now faced the prisoners. "You are zer university research group yes?"

"Yes," Mr Craig answered. "Who are you?"

"Ve zer questions ask," Mr Ivanoff snarled. "Now, how you come to be diving here? Who tell you to come here?"

Mr Craig answered that. It took several minutes of questioning for the details of the research expedition to be described. During this Andrew lay on the deck enduring waves of throbbing pain and wondering if he should interrupt to ask for medical help. But fear held his tongue. *Might be better not to attract attention to myself,* he decided.

Mr Ivanoff listened and looked very thoughtful then said, "So you here come just to study zer seaveed?"

"Yes," Mr Craig answered.

"Ven are you due back?"

"Next Friday, five days' time," Mr Craig answered.

Mr Ivanoff tugged at his chin. "So who do you report to? How often zer radio reports?"

For a moment nobody answered and Mr Ivanoff's eyes narrowed. He aimed the small SMG at Dan. "You talk or zis vone he die."

"You are bluffing," Mr Craig retorted, "Now let us go and get off my boat."

Before Andrew could open his mouth to warn Mr Craig Mr Ivanoff moved. He jerked the SMG to the left and pulled the trigger.

Brrrrt!

There were gasps of fear and horror and Andrew twitched and jerked with fright. He swivelled his head just in time to see Mr Craig fold in the middle and go crashing to the deck, his hands clutching at his stomach. Blood began pouring onto the deck planks. Ella screamed and began to sob hysterically.

Mr Ivanoff shouted angrily, "Shut zer bitch up or I shut her up permanently."

Andrew was stunned and appalled at the brutality and unreality of it all. *This isn't true,* he tried to tell himself. *It can't be!*

Through what seemed like a fog of fear and pain he heard Dan speak to Ella and then heard a sharp slap. Carmen spoke loudly, "Be quiet Ella or you will be next."

Ella shut up as abruptly as a door being slammed. But she kept sniffling and sobbing. Mr Ivanoff hissed menacingly. "Now you know ve zer business mean. So, answer zer question. Vot is your radio skedule?"

Dan answered in a quavering voice. "Once a day, at thirteen hundred hours. It is all written in the radio log in the wheelhouse."

"Good! Now who is zer radio operator?"

Carmen spoke this time. "Andrew and I are, now that you have shot Mr Craig."

"Who is Andrew?"

"My brother," Carmen answered, indicating Andrew.

Andrew looked up and met Mr Ivanoff's eyes. The look he received in return sent chills of apprehension through him. Mr Ivanoff sneered. "So, if you can do it ve don't need him. Barry, get rid of him."

Carmen gasped and then screamed, "No! If you harm him I won't do anything for you."

Mr Ivanoff curled his lip. "If you not zen ve hurt zis girl here, and ve kill zis other vone."

At that the man with the beard and SMG gave an evil chuckle and said, "I will soon teach her to co-operate Mr Ivanoff. She's a real good looker. I reckon she will be a lot of fun to tame."

Andrew heard this with disgust and revulsion but that was overlain by his own rising terror as the import of Ivanoff's words sank in.

He is going to kill me! he thought.

But what to do? For a few seconds he contemplated making a desperate effort to attack the men but the searing memory of what had just happened to Mr Craig held him still.

They will just shoot me and I will never get up with all this weight on me, he reasoned.

Before he could react, Andrew was grabbed by the second diver. The man tried to turn him over. Mr Ivanoff snapped, "Vot are you doing Viktor?"

"Getting all this diving gear off him Mr Ivanoff. No need to waste that," Viktor replied.

"OK, make it quick," Mr Ivanoff agreed.

Once again Viktor tried to roll Andrew over. But the steel shaft of the spear dug into the deck and wrenched at Andrew's body. Pain lanced through him and he cried in agony. Viktor swore and dropped Andrew back on the deck, his face hitting hard enough to make his nose go numb. Andrew felt Viktor doing something on his back.

"What's the problem?" Barry asked from close behind Andrew.

"The spear," Viktor replied.

Mr Ivanoff spoke next. "Vot are you doing Viktor?"

"Taking off the air tank," Viktor replied.

There were several sharp tugs and Andrew was pushed to and fro as Viktor unscrewed his air hoses from the BCD. Then the air tank was lifted clear and he was able to suck in a breath. But Mr Ivanoff's next words choked off the tiny spurt of relief he felt.

"Leave zer veight belt on him Viktor. Zat vill help him stay down. But take out zat spear. If anyone find zer body ve don't vant zat sort of evidence."

Andrew was shocked and appalled. *I am going to be drowned!* his terrified mind screamed. But how to escape that fate? His mind raced with possible options but all he could think of was to stay still so that they did not knock him out. *If I can get the belt off once I am in the water I might be able to get back to the surface,* he thought. How to then survive the men with guns and boats was another problem.

A sudden stinging stab of pain made him gasp with shock and he actually did slump into semi-consciousness as the spear was pulled out. Part of Andrew's mind told him what had happened. The spear had been a standard fish spear with a folding barb on the tip. It could not be pulled back out the way it went in so Barry must have dragged it right through.

Luckily there was no line attached, he thought, shaking almost uncontrollably as the reaction hit him.

With Carmen's angry protests ringing in his ears Andrew felt himself being dragged backwards off the deck. For a split second he considered struggling but then he decided it was better tactics to make it easy for them. As he realized that he was about to fall onto the dive platform he tensed.

This is going to hurt, he thought.

Suddenly Andrew found he was flying through the air, terror swamping him and Carmen's scream sounding loud in his ears. To his own surprise he only just tipped the edge of the dive platform with his right hand. He had enough of his wits about him to see that the first diver—Barry—was standing on the platform and that the rubber boat was now tied to the starboard bracket of the platform.

Splash! Instantly the water enfolded Andrew and he began sinking. *Don't panic! Don't panic!* he told himself, but the fear was so overwhelming all he could do was squirm and try to release the weight belt.

Already the pressure was building but he was not worried about that because in a free dive it equalized. He opened his eyes to work out which way was up so that he could use his fins to try to stop himself going too deep.

I must get back up to the surface to breathe, he thought.

Suddenly something slid over his arm and he winced and his heart leapt and hammered. *What was that?* he thought notions of sharks and other sea creatures coming to his mind. Desperately he looked around. Then he felt the thing again and his eyes focussed as well as they could without a face mask.

It was a rope. *The shot line for controlled ascents,* Andrew realized.

Instantly he reached out and grabbed the rope. He came to a jerking standstill and looked frantically up. What he was looking for was the spare air tank that was attached at ten metres to the shot line. If a diver coming up from a deep dive needed more time to decompress his nitrogen, he had a reserve of air handy and avoid getting the bends.

And there it was, a dark blob against the rippling light of the surface. It looked a small thing and a long way above him but Andrew knew it was his only chance.

I must reach it or die, he told himself.

Already he was having trouble holding his breath and was running out of oxygen. Frantic to survive he began hauling himself up the line hand over hand.

Dark dots began to dance in his already blurred vision. Pain began to build in his chest and face and he could feel his lungs straining. The desperate need to breathe built up until he could only resist it from an equally strong determination to live. Having nearly been drowned several times Andrew knew he had only seconds left before he had to take that fatal gulp of water.

And there was the air tank. His hands grabbed at it and he began groping around it for the regulators. *There are two of the bloody things! Where is one?* his desperate mind cried. And now the urge to breathe was so strong he was starting to convulse while he resisted it. He knew that if he took even one gulp of water he was finished. If he did he would cough and choke and never be able to use the compressed air.

Then his fingers closed on a regulator and he whipped it up to his face, fumbled for a moment to turn it the right way, then shoved it into his mouth. Now the training told and he held one side valve and purged water through the other to clear the mouthpiece. For a heartbeat he wondered if it would work or not but he knew he had no choice. Either he tried it or he died.

I will never make it to the surface now, he thought. So he nerved himself and sucked.

Air! Andrew almost sighed with relief. Blessed air! He took another breath and then steadied himself, clinging to the rope as he did. For several more seconds he just hung there, gulping air and trying to get a grip on his thoughts and emotions. *I'm still alive!* he marvelled.

Andrew consciously tried to calm his breathing. *Think man, think! You are still alive but how are you going to get away from here?* he asked himself. That made him look up and he saw the dark shapes of the two boats lying side by side only ten metres above him. Then he noticed something else and his heart seemed to stop.

My bubbles are going straight up. If those mongrels see them they will be straight down to get me, he thought.

It occurred to Andrew that the crooks had not been aware of the shot line which had the spare air tanks. Such an arrangement was standard practice in both the marine research and diving industries but was probably not something groups of criminals might do.

I have to get away from here, he thought.

Then he realized he still had all the key elements he needed for safe diving: his BCD, his mask and his fins. *Even my weight belt will help,* he told himself, knowing it was hard to stay down without one.

Now all that unpleasant training that had caused him such anxiety suddenly made sense and paid off. Within half a minute he had pulled his face mask into position and then cleared it by blowing air through his nose while holding the top of the mask firm against his forehead.

Being able to see properly made a huge difference and Andrew again looked up, watching anxiously as the bubbles from his breathing rose in a steady stream towards the stern of the launch.

I have to get away from here, he thought. But could he somehow get the air tank off the shot line?

Once again training told. A few seconds of study and all his knowledge of knots from years of being a Navy Cadet told him it was easy. The air tank was secured by a simple loop of the slip type used in straining hitches and then passed through the shot line and around the gauges. Gripping the air tank with one hand he finned up the shot line until he was well above the knot, which then hung loose. Then he held the line tight between his feet, one foot under the other to tighten the rope between instep and the top of the other foot. That took all the strain off the knot and he was able to use both hands to ease the loop loose and then slip the air tank out. By a smooth tug he allowed the knot to slip out.

That will make them wonder if there was any air tank or not, Andrew thought with another anxious glance up.

But even as he looked up he saw a dark clad figure splash into the water beside the launch and his heart leapt into his mouth.

Oh bloody hell! Here they come! he thought.

Chapter 4

THE DEVIL AND THE DEEP BLUE SEA

Andrew felt a spasm of pure panic as he saw the diver splash into the water above him. Frantically he looked around to try to choose the best direction to escape. Where the boats were anchored was only about twenty metres deep with a clear sandy bottom. A downward glance showed Andrew there was nowhere to hide there. However, it did reveal a second air tank, the one placed at the eighteen-metre level. Andrew ignored it and began swimming to his left. He knew that the dive boat had been anchored about a hundred metres from the reef. The bottom sloped gently up to about five metres depth in that direction.

In the other direction it dropped away quickly into deep water—forty fathoms or more. This showed as a dark blue wall on what felt like three sides to Andrew. Even as Andrew glanced at it, the phrase 'Between the Devil and the deep blue sea' flitted across his mind.

As he swam Andrew glanced back at the diver, expecting to see more of the gang jumping in to pursue. But there was only that one diver and that person was not swimming after Andrew but seemed to be pushing themselves across the bottom of the dive boat and then the bottom of the game fishing boat. And the diver did not look right.

Andrew rolled on his back to get a better look, still clutching the air tank to his chest as he finned painfully away. Then he shook his head in puzzlement and slowed. The other diver had swum right under the game fishing boat and then risen to the surface near its bow.

Is he looking for me? Andrew wondered. And then he saw the blonde hair. *That is Carmen!* he realized.

Then it struck him what was odd about the diver's appearance. The person had no face mask, air tank or fins.

It is Carmen. She must have dived in—or been shot, Andrew thought.

Dread clutched at his chest and he stared hard to see if there was blood coming from wounds. By then he was nearly fifty metres from her and fifteen metres down. He could not see any obvious signs of injury.

She seems to be swimming alright, he decided.

Then he noted that she had surfaced right up under the bow of the game fishing boat. That gave him another clue. *She has dived overboard and is trying to hide,* he thought.

Admiration for his sister welled up along with a fierce desire to save her. He at once reversed course and began swimming back towards her, angling upwards as he did. That hurt! Stabs of pain from his wound pulsed through him with every movement of his right leg but he gritted his teeth and pushed himself to do it.

The advantage of being a Navy Cadet and familiar with boat construction, he thought. *She is hiding in under the flare and chine of the bow.*

Both Andrew and his sister had been in the Australian Navy Cadets for years—Carmen for over four and Andrew for more than three. Carmen was a Cadet Chief Petty Officer and Andrew held the rank of Cadet Leading Seaman.

It took an effort of deliberate courage to swim back as every second Andrew came closer to the killers. At any moment he expected to see divers armed with spearguns come plunging down to hunt them. But there was no way he was going to leave his sister without doing his utmost to save her. So he swam as fast as he could, disregarding the lancing pain. Carmen stayed where she was treading water and with her head just above the surface so she could breathe.

That gave Andrew a problem. As he got closer he began worrying about how to attract her attention so that she did not cry out in fright and inadvertently attract the killer's attention. Then while he was still about 20 metres away, he saw her put her face in the water and look around. From the way she twitched with fright Andrew was sure she had seen him.

To allay her fears, he slowed and waved one arm, holding the air bottle with the other. Then he gave a thumbs-up and beckoned her. By then he was in under the game fishing boat and reasonably confident that no-one on either boat could see him.

But they might see my bubbles, he thought.

So he stayed over to the port side of the game fishing boat so that the bubbles rose up its port side.

That puts the game fishing boat between us and the dive boat, he reasoned.

He was hoping that the killer's attention was still fixed on the dive launch. Carmen had gone over the starboard side of that and swum under both boats to escape.

For a few more seconds Carmen hesitated so Andrew finned slowly up towards her, still waving one hand. He could see she was looking but thought she probably did not recognize him. To make things quick he stopped waving and held out the alternate regulator on the air tank and squeezed it to expel some air.

Then he was up with her. She shrank away from him until he gave her another thumbs-up and held out the regulator towards her. Suddenly she nodded and pushed herself down. Andrew took out his regulator and grinned at her and to his enormous relief he saw her smile in return. Without a face mask she was obviously having trouble seeing properly but now he was sure she had recognized him.

She took the regulator, cleared it and began breathing through it. Andrew did not wait. *No time for explanations,* he thought. So he reached out to grab her arm with his free hand and she clung to him, the air tank held firmly between them.

We must get away from here fast, Andrew told himself.

Already they had begun to sink as he had stopped finning and he decided they needed to go right down deep to hide themselves as well as they could.

Otherwise the killers will spot us against the clear sand of the bottom, he reasoned.

To make sure that Carmen understood clearly what he intended he moved his right hand between their faces and pointed downwards. She nodded, then used her own right hand to grip her nose.

She is equalizing the pressure, Andrew thought, having just done the same thing automatically.

As they sank Andrew rolled over so that he could keep watching the boats. He also kept glancing at the depth gauge on the dive computer: 15, 16, 17, 18. Every metre down made the boats harder to see. Andrew's fins touched bottom at twenty-two metres. By then the boats were two dark blobs about fifty metres away.

Still much too close. We need to go deeper and further out, he thought.

That was not the direction he really wanted to go. That was north and then east back to the reef. Worse still he knew that the current was flowing west into the deeper water so it would be harder to swim back later.

But the killers will expect us to try to get ashore if we can, so we must take that risk, he reasoned.

So he allowed the current to push them west. That meant they kept sinking down the sandy slope into that terrifying blue depth. Andrew made no attempt to swim, only moving enough to keep himself upright and facing the boats.

Sixty metres away, seventy metres, he estimated. By then the boats were becoming indistinct. *And twenty-seven metres down. We can't go much deeper,* he thought anxiously.

Both were qualified to dive to thirty metres and had been a few metres deeper but his real concern was down time and the dissolved nitrogen he knew would now be accumulating under pressure in their bloodstreams.

We may not have enough air to decompress safely, he thought.

The air gauge showed 225psi so Andrew felt there was some margin for manoeuvre. But then his eyes detected movement at the stern of the launch and a stab of fear made him go tense. He quickly took out his regulator and put his mouth next to Carmen's ear.

"Don't move! Don't breathe!" he said, as clearly as he could.

Andrew focused on the tiny moving shape. *It is definitely a diver and he is leaning down from the dive platform to look,* Andrew thought. *He will expect to see my body on the bottom but he mustn't see any bubbles,* he added. So he just froze and held his breath. Carmen did the same. The whole time they slowly drifted away on the current.

The shape of the boats and diver became so indistinct that Andrew could not tell if the man was still there or not. But they had to breathe as the pressure was building up to agonizing levels in nose and eardrums. The pain was like a steel band squashing his skull. So Andrew nodded and began breathing and quickly equalized. Carmen did the same.

Holy mackerel, forty-five metres! Andrew thought as he studied the depth gauge. *Time we headed north and up.*

So he took the risk of being observed and began slowly finning. That hurt as his wound had tightened up and with every painful movement he felt apprehensive about what further damage he might be causing. But there was no help for it as he had the fins and the face mask, not Carmen. And much as he loved her he was not going to give up that face mask. It was one of his deepest fears and his most frequent nightmares. That dated back to when his supposed girlfriend had ripped his mask off and locked him in the strongroom of the wrecked *Merinda* along with his grandfather's bones.

I'm going to give up diving, Andrew promised himself. *In future I will have the courage to admit I am a coward when it comes to being underwater.*

The distinct sound of a small motor starting up made him look anxiously back up towards the boats. These were now at least a hundred metres away and were quite difficult to see.

That's the outboard on the rubber boat, Andrew thought. He experienced the sour taste of bile as terror welled up and he felt nauseous. *Here they come!*

But they didn't. Andrew was just able to make out the shape of the small rubber boat and he saw it move away from the launch and then slowly circle the game fishing boat. Then it went back around the other side of the dive boat before heading off east, towards the reef.

They are looking for Carmen alright but think I have drowned, Andrew decided.

So he kept on swimming. Now he used his compass and the visual clues of the sloping seabed and that horrible deep blue gloom to maintain direction. He stayed down close to the seabed but angled slowly up the slope so that the depth became shallower all the time. Within two minutes he had come up to thirty-five metres and swum at least another hundred metres.

By then the boats were no longer visible but Andrew could faintly make out the buzz of the outboard motor. *It did go over to the reef and now it is coming back out to the dive boat,* Andrew decided.

As he swam Andrew had to grit his teeth against the now throbbing pain in his side. But he knew there was no help for it.

I have to do this or we both die, he told himself.

So, clenching his teeth hard on the mouthpiece, he pushed himself to keep going. The whole time he kept looking at Carmen to check that she was coping. To his relief she kept looking back at him and nodding.

After another two minutes Andrew was sure he had swum another hundred metres northwards and the depth gauge now read thirty metres. He showed that to Carmen and then slowed and allowed them both to settle on the bottom. His plan was to allow five minutes for decompression and also allow himself a chance to recover his energy and breath as he was starting to gasp and feeling very weak. For a few seconds he studied their drift and decided that there was now almost no current.

Must be getting close to the top of the tide, he deduced.

While they rested Andrew gingerly felt his wounds with his right hand. He bent over to try to look but that hurt too much and all he could detect was a small rent in the wetsuit.

I can't see any blood seeping out, he told himself in an attempt at reassurance. But the thought of the blood and the predators it might be attracting kept him looking around for any sign of sharks. *Or even barracuda,* he added. They did not normally attack divers but would if conditions were right.

As they rested there Andrew heard the sound of the rubber boat's outboard getting definitely louder. He tensed and his eyes scanned the surface. *It is coming this way,* he thought.

His breathing rose with the mounting fear and he had to make a deliberate effort to stop himself hyperventilating. He saw Carmen's eyes go wider and she also looked towards the sound.

Then Andrew saw the silhouette of the rubber boat. It was between them and the reef and going northwards.

What are they doing? he thought. He was sure that at that distance any diver looking over the side would have trouble seeing him and his sister. *Maybe they are checking along the reef to see if we are there?* he wondered.

The boat went on northwards and Andrew and Carmen were left undetected. But that raised another problem. Andrew was close to the point where he had planned to turn east and swim to the reef. Now he began to worry that if he did the boat might come back and catch them in the shallower water before they reached it.

We can't wait here much longer, he thought, noting that the air pressure had dropped to 205psi.

By an effort of willpower Andrew stayed resting for another three minutes, making it seven since they had stopped. Then, just as he was thinking they must take a chance, he heard the rubber boat coming back.

This time they did not see it and he decided that it was over next to the edge of the reef. Two minutes went by before the sound faded to the south.

Sounds like it has gone back to the dive boat. Anyway, we must take the risk and go, Andrew thought.

The air pressure was now 195psi. After nudging Carmen to get her attention and then pointing they both gripped the air tank and Andrew began swimming.

The moment he did waves of pain swept through him that made him groan and pant. For a second of two he feared he was going to black out. Then it passed and he gritted his teeth and kept moving.

I have just stiffened up while we sat there, he told himself.

This time Andrew swam northeast, the compass and the slope both giving him guidance to help him to keep direction. The water grew quickly shallower and there did not seem to be much current. Twice Andrew spooked bottom fish into rapid flurries of movement and each time he flinched and gasped. Then he saw a large dark shadow off to the north and he went tense with fear. But it was not a shark. As it got closer he saw it was only a manta ray.

Breathing a sigh of relief Andrew continued on. All the while his attention kept returning to the depth gauge. When it reached twenty metres he considered stopping but decided to take the risk and continued up the slope until he found an outcrop of rocks and seaweed at seventeen metres.

There they did another five-minute decompression stop. The whole time Andrew was extremely anxious as he knew they were in great danger if the rubber boat came back. But balanced against that was the fear that if they swam too quickly and one or both developed the bends then they were finished.

Air down to 190psi. We must keep moving, he decided after four minutes.

So he signalled to Carmen and they resumed swimming. Knowing that they were crossing a possible danger zone and with vivid and terrifying images flitting through his thoughts of Tristan and Mr Craig being murdered Andrew swam as fast as he could. To his intense relief the dark shadow of the coral reef appeared ahead after only two minutes of swimming.

Now we have a chance! he thought.

Andrew swam right to the edge of the coral and then turned left and swam along the bottom until he found a small crevice that they could hide in if the rubber boat returned. A check of the dive computer showed they were at seven metres, so he signalled to Carmen and they settled to rest on the bottom.

Still 185psi. We are safe for a bit, Andrew thought. If need be they could just swim up to the surface which looked close overhead.

While he waited for another five minutes Andrew tried to consciously relax. He was very relieved that they were alive and that they had reached some sort of shelter and a hiding place. He was also very glad to be away from that awful dark blue where all the horrors of his imagination lurked. Where they were sheltering was a riot of staghorn coral and small clams and the hundreds of colourful fish were the sort that tourists drooled over, but Andrew barely noticed them. He was focused on dangers, not on the beauties of the tropical reef environment.

At the end of the five minutes, with the air on 180psi, Andrew pointed upwards and Carmen nodded. But he did not swim up. Instead he took out his regulator and used the second valve on his BCD to inflate it enough to give them positive buoyancy. The pair then floated slowly upwards, Andrew taking care to keep them away from the coral.

As they neared the surface Andrew tensed, knowing that breaking surface would be a moment of great danger. For that reason he made sure there was a large coral outcrop between them and where he believed the boats to be. A few seconds later he and Carmen broke surface. As the water poured off his head Andrew looked anxiously out at the sea. To his intense relief there was no sign of the boats.

But he could not see properly with the mask on and it quickly began to fog up so he reached up and pulled it down around his neck. *That habit saved me,* he thought.

Then he blinked and screwed his eyes up against the glare reflecting from the waves. Gripping a piece of brain coral—he was very aware some corals were poisonous or could inflict cuts which quickly became ulcers—he leaned out and peeked to the south.

There! he thought.

Closer than he had thought, perhaps only three hundred metres away were the two boats. The rubber boat was again tethered astern of the dive boat. That was good news as it meant the killers had at least temporarily given up.

Or they think we are both dead, he decided.

Carmen joined Andrew. "They are doing something on the game fishing boat," she whispered. She clung to him and to the air tank and Andrew realized she was trembling violently.

"Sorry to give you such a scare," Andrew replied.

Carmen shook her head. "You didn't really. I knew it had to be you. All the others were on the dive boat except that one called Igor who went back to the game fishing boat."

"I didn't see that," Andrew replied.

Carmen nodded. "He came out and said something to that horrible Mr Ivanoff. I think he said the word radio but I'm not sure. They spoke some foreign language."

"So why did you dive overboard?" Andrew asked.

Carmen looked down and bit her lip, then let out a couple of sobs. "Be... because they just shot Dan when he tried to save me."

Andrew was appalled. "Shot him? Dead?"

Carmen nodded. Tears sprang into her eyes and she trembled again. "That horrible Barry, the one who just flung you overboard, that made me so angry I kicked him in the face when he started climbing up the ladder."

"Good for you!" Andrew replied, squeezing her shoulders.

Carmen gave a sickly smile. "Thanks, but it was stupid really because it just made him mad and he scrambled up and punched me and began making disgusting threats about what he was going to do to me. Then Dan stepped in. Ivanoff started shooting and I just told myself now or never and I went over the rail backwards."

"But... but how did you think you could possibly get away?" Andrew asked, thinking of the divers and their spearguns and boats.

At that Carmen stared out to the west for a few seconds before answering. "I didn't think I would, but after I saw them throw you overboard and after hearing them say... say what disgusting things they would do to Ella and me if we didn't co-operate, I didn't care. I was determined not to give them any help and certainly no pleasure or satisfaction."

"You were ready to commit suicide!" Andrew gasped.

He knew his sister was very strong willed but that she was able to act on the death-before-dishonour thing was a revelation to him of just how tough she was.

Carmen shook her head. "Not really, but I was determined to die trying," she answered.

Then she shivered and Andrew hugged her. For a couple of minutes neither spoke. All Carmen could do was nod and sniff. Andrew turned and held her tight. While trying to soothe her Andrew's mind raced with the enormity of the situation. It all still seemed completely unbelievable and unreal but then the horrific images swirled across his mind and he knew it wasn't.

After a few seconds he said, "But you didn't even have your BCD on. Even if you escaped how could you survive?" he said, gesturing out to the rippling sea to the west. "The current would have taken you that way if you couldn't reach the reef."

Carmen nodded again. "I know. We are a hundred kilometres from the mainland and there are no islands in between. I heard one of the men say that. He said, 'Why worry Boss? She won't last long out here.' But that murderous mongrel Ivanoff ordered them to look for me and to shoot me if they saw me."

Just thinking about Carmen drifting for hours in the vast blue expanse while she slowly died from exposure brought back the terrifying memories of his own harrowing experiences of being left for dead far out to sea.

"Oh, you poor bugger!" he cried, hugging her tight again.

For a minute or so brother and sister clung to each, both trembling with shock and emotion. Then Carmen, who was still facing the boats, said, "They are on the move."

Andrew looked and saw that the game fishing boat had moved clear of the dive boat and was now turning towards them.

Bloody hell! I hope they haven't seen us, he thought, fear beginning to pulse anew through his veins.

Chapter 5

Andrew felt a spasm of pure terror slither through his stomach. For a moment he felt as though he was going to lose control of his bladder and bowels.

"Here they come. We must hide," he said.

Anxiously he looked around, seeking the best hiding place. Behind them was the main part of the reef. The tide was now well up over it, but many coral outcrops still showed above the surface. About a hundred metres away was the small sand cay that was exposed at low tide. This was about a hundred metres long and perhaps half that wide, but it was totally devoid of any cover.

We must get there later, Andrew thought.

But for a hideout their best immediate option looked like going back underwater into some coral crevice or cave. "We have to go under," Andrew said, pulling up his face mask and groping for his regulator.

Carmen did likewise. But then she stopped. "Look. It is turning away," she said.

Andrew pulled his facemask down again—it needed some spit anyway—and stared. To his enormous relief he saw that the game fishing boat was continuing to turn to port. It went on turning until it had passed astern of the dive boat. Then it went on south.

"I wonder where he is going?" he said.

"Out into the Boat Passage I reckon," Carmen suggested. "To where that net is."

"Yes, but why? What is the net for?" Andrew asked. He had a few ideas but was now very curious to know what was behind all the killing and sudden death.

What is so important that these men would just kill strangers on sight? he wondered.

Carmen shrugged but then said, "To RV with the submarine that Barry mentioned?"

Andrew nodded. "That's what I was thinking," he agreed. "But is it a submarine and whose is it and what is it doing here?"

"I don't know. Spies maybe?" Carmen suggested.

Andrew shook his head. "I don't think so. Smugglers more like. They don't look like professionals," he replied.

"Why do you say that?" Carmen asked.

"Because they have someone like Barry in their gang. He acted like a real loose cannon back there. I don't think his boss Mr Ivanoff was very pleased with what he had done. Besides, if they were a government group I think they would all be the same nationality."

Carmen nodded. "I suppose so. Killing Tristan wasn't part of their plan, that is for sure."

Andrew watched the game fishing boat turn to port again about half a kilometre away. "You are right. It is going into the Boat Passage. What language did Mr Ivanoff and the radio operator speak do you know?"

Carmen shook her head. "Not really but with a name like Ivanoff I guess he is a Russian. He called the radio man Igor and one of the crooks was named Viktor," she added.

"Russian. I agree. But not Russian Navy or Special Forces. These are gangsters. But a sub?" Andrew said.

"Might be like those little ones the Yanks have been catching in the Caribbean, you know the ones we saw on the TV news, the ones the drug smugglers use to get cocaine into the USA from South America," Carmen said.

"Could be, but it might just be an old Russian Navy one," Andrew answered. "I read that back when Russia was the centre of the Soviet Union they had about six hundred subs and when the Soviet Empire fell apart most of them were just junked or scrapped and that lots were just abandoned in disused bases. It might be one of them."

"Well, we will never know," Carmen answered.

The moment she said that an idea leapt into Andrew's mind and he was suddenly seized by a burning desire both to know and for vengeance.

"We might. I am going to have a look," he said.

Carmen was appalled. "Oh Andrew, don't be stupid!" she cried.

"Why not? Those men probably think I am dead. They won't be looking out for me—and I don't need to go close. It has to be near that net and you can just see that from the edge of the reef," Andrew replied. The plan had seemed to form in his mind as he spoke.

"No! Not only is it too dangerous but it is more important that we try to rescue Ella," Carmen answered, pointing to the anchored dive boat.

"Ella?" Andrew said. A spurt of guilt made him feel ashamed of himself. "Is she still alive?" he asked.

"I think so," Carmen answered.

"Why would they keep her alive?" Andrew asked. But even as he said the words the concept of her being kept for sexual gratification occurred to him and a wave of embarrassment made him wish he could bite his tongue off.

Carman made a wry face then said, "For the radio. I think the crooks need her to talk on the radio so that our family and friends think we are all safe and happy."

"But why? Why won't they just get their goods and clear off. They could just sink the dive boat to get rid of the evidence," Andrew said. By this time he could no longer see the game fishing boat. It had vanished behind the sand cay. He switched his attention back to the dive boat and tried to detect movement on it.

Carmen shrugged. "Because they have to stay here for at least five days or come back then," she answered. "I heard that Ivanoff creature say that to Barry when he asked. So they don't want this area crawling with search planes and boats looking for us while they do whatever it is they want to do."

"So we had better try to rescue Ella," Andrew said.

Carmen stared at the dive boat and frowned. "Yes, but it will be incredibly dangerous. I don't even know if she is still on the dive boat and we have no idea if any of the crooks are on it. They have machine guns remember."

Andrew did remember and he shuddered as horrific images of Mr Craig being shot down swamped his mind. Various concepts of swimming underwater to the dive boat flitted through his mind.

But the tricky bit is when you surface, he thought. *You have no idea if you have been detected and are blind for a few seconds.* The image of surfacing to find a gun aimed at his face caused him to shedder. *And then I have to get aboard undetected and find some sort of weapon,* he added. It did not appear possible and was very sobering stuff.

At that moment his eyes detected movement on the focsle of the dive boat. "There's somebody moving near the bow," he said.

"Winding up the anchor. They are getting under way," Carmen said.

Andrew experienced a mix of regret at not having rescued Ella, and relief that he would not now have to make such a dangerous attempt. "Too late!" he said.

"It is the thin man with the pony tail," Carmen commented. "I didn't hear his name."

Brother and sister watched as the man wound the anchor up. It was soon aweigh, and the dive boat began to drift astern, pushed westwards away from the reef by the wind and tide. The man obviously knew what he was doing because the anchor was lifted up and secured within a couple of minutes. The man then made his way to the wheelhouse. A few seconds later Andrew saw a puff of black smoke spurt out of the exhaust behind the mast.

"He's started the engine," he said.

Then the sound reached them. A few seconds later the dive boat began moving forward and swung its bows towards them. It then began travelling north just clear of the reef.

"Coming this way. We had better hide," Andrew said. Once again, he made preparations to dive. This time he spat in his face mask and rinsed it before pulling it on. Then he checked the regulator and put it in his mouth. By the time both were ready the dive boat was only a hundred metres away and approaching fast. Andrew knew it could do about 12 knots at full throttle and it looked to be doing that now.

Carmen took her regulator out and said, "I can only see that one man in the wheelhouse. There is no-one else on deck."

"You are right. I think this fellow is just moving it out of this area," Andrew agreed.

"You don't think he is looking for us?" Carmen asked.

Andrew shook his head. "No. He is going too fast. He might have a general brief to locate us if he can, but I think he is going somewhere. OK, we had better dive."

With that he replaced his regulator and let enough air out of his BCD to allow them to sink just below the surface. Carmen sank with him, again holding her nose and the air tank while Andrew held onto the coral and to her. He checked that they could move around into the shadows behind the coral outcrop and then rested to listen and watch.

I don't think we need to go any deeper, Andrew told himself. But his heart rate still went up as the dive boat got closer. Underwater the sound of its engine and the grind of its propeller shaft were very clear.

Then the boat came into view. Andrew tensed, ready to flee and he nudged Carmen to keep sliding around to keep the coral outcrop between them and any observers in the boat. From underwater the hull looked dark brown to Andrew, but he knew that close up it had a coating of marine growth and looked green. He could even see the whirring blur that was the rotating propeller.

The dive boat did not deviate from its course or slow down. Instead it just went on northwards. Andrew really wanted to take a peek to see if he could spot Ella but decided the risk was too great. To his own shame he thought that his survival and that of his sister were more important.

Only when the sound had receded and he was sure that the dive boat was at least two hundred metres away did he slowly surface, again making sure he was behind a coral outcrop. First, he stayed with only half the face mask above water until his eyes confirmed the location of the dive boat. Then he surfaced and took the regulator out of his mouth and pulled his mask down.

By then the dive boat was at least three hundred metres away and looked to be almost stern on. Andrew noted that it was towing the rubber boat and the sight of a dark lump in it made him feel ill.

That might be Tristan's body, he thought.

Carmen joined him and they both watched until the dive boat was half a kilometre away and rapidly dwindling into the distance. "Going north," Carmen said.

"Maybe to our camp on Prescott Island?" Andrew suggested.

"Possibly. If they know it is there. Now, let's get ashore. I am getting really cold," Carmen replied.

Andrew was too but had put his shivering down to shock. He looked around and could not see any sign of the game fishing boat. "We will still be careful," he said. "We will look silly if we just stagger ashore and those men are watching."

"Swim then. There is just enough water if we are careful," Carmen agreed.

"I am taking this air tank," Andrew said. "Lock it onto my BCD please."

Carmen shook her head. "Don't you think of doing anything silly," she said.

"I won't. Now hurry up," Andrew replied.

He turned his back to her and waited until Carmen had secured the air tank to the bracket on the BCD. Then he partially inflated his BCD by mouth. Satisfied it provided sufficient buoyancy he pulled on his face mask and began breast stroking, breathing through his snorkel. Carmen followed, keeping her head out of the water.

The tide was now sufficiently high to allow them to skim across the top of most of the coral so progress was relatively easy. Andrew thought this was good because a lot of the coral was branch or staghorn and was sharp and brittle. As much as possible he tried to follow the small gullies and dips to keep as much water under them as possible. He also kept a wary eye below them for possible hazards like the spiny sea urchins or creatures like moray eels and sting rays.

It only took the pair five minutes to cover most of the distance to the sand cay. For the last ten metres they had to stand and walk. Andrew slipped off his fins, slid his face mask down and then struggled to his feet, weighed down as he was with weight belt and air tank. A quick look around revealed that the dive boat was now a small dark blob two or three kilometres away on the far side of the Challenger Channel but west of the main reef.

Not going to Prescott Island then, he deduced.

There was no sign of the game fishing boat. Watching where he put his feet to avoid standing on sharp objects or brittle coral Andrew waded and sloshed his way to the sand. The sharp pains in his buttock and thigh he ignored.

As he reached the cay Andrew was able to look over the top. The sand was only a metre or so above the tide level and was quite bare and flat on top. The first thing he saw was the top of the game fishing boat's mast.

Carmen was right. It is in the Boat Passage, he thought.

But just the sight of it was enough to spark a panic attack and Andrew sank down behind the sand cay and signalled Carmen to keep low. As he looked back to check that she was doing that Andrew also looked northwards to check on the dive boat. By this time it was just a tiny dark spot on the horizon and he was sure they were not visible to people on it.

"The game fishing boat is there alright," he said.

Carmen nodded and sank gratefully onto the lovely warm sand.

"What will we do now?" she asked.

"You are going to dig a small hole here in the lee of the sand ridge so you can hide and stay out of the wind. Make sure you don't stick your head over the top and get seen," Andrew replied.

"And what are you going to do?" Carmen asked.

"I am going to have a look at this submarine," Andrew answered.

Carmen shook her head and looked very unhappy. "Oh Andrew, please don't. It is too dangerous. We have managed to get away with our lives, let's not risk them unnecessarily," she said.

But Andrew was determined. He pressed his lips together and then said, "But it is our duty. If there really is a submarine, then our navy will want to know. We have to have details to tell them when we report," he replied. That was true, but he did not add that not only was he now consumed by curiosity but as the shock wore off a burning desire to see the killers brought to justice was building.

Carmen shook her head but was still unhappy. "But if they see you they will kill you," she said.

Andrew really admired her for that because in his own mind he added the fact that if they found him they would come looking for her.

Her chances of escaping a second time will be nil, he thought. But it did not sway him.

"Sorry, but I am going. You stay safe here."

"But you have been wounded. You might not be up to it," Carmen said.

Andrew had been dimly aware of the throbbing ache but had actually forgotten. Now he bent to look, fingering the rent in his wetsuit. "Am I bleeding?" he asked.

Carmen leaned forward and examined the back of his thigh and both buttocks. "No, not really," she admitted.

"Then it can't be too serious," Andrew said. He was worried but equally was determined not to let his injuries prevent him finding out.

"But you could cause some permanent damage," Carmen said.

Seeing the distress in his sister's face caused Andrew to weaken for a moment but then he shook his head. "Too bad! I will worry about it when I get back."

"Oh Andrew, please don't!" Carmen pleaded.

"It will be alright, sis. I know what I am up against now. I will hide against the reef and just watch from a distance. Don't worry. I will be gone about an hour," he said.

"But it is unsafe. Divers should always dive with a buddy," Carmen said.

Andrew nodded. "I know, but in this case the risk must be run. Sorry, I am going, and you can't stop me," he said.

"If you must," Carmen answered. She bowed her head and let out a sigh, then clenched her teeth and looked directly at him. "You take care then," she said.

Andrew felt a rush of affection for her. "I will. You dig a hidey hole and relax. If you want something to do keep a lookout out to sea there for periscopes," he said.

"Periscopes?"

"Yes. That sub won't just navigate by sonar in amongst all these reefs. They will want some visual references too," Andrew explained. At the back of his mind was his own experience but also a comment he had heard about how hard it was to navigate safely through the outer reefs when the tide was up and there were no large breakers to mark the coral from the openings.

"OK," Carmen replied. "I guess those crooks will be in radio contact with it."

"Yes, but not much. They wouldn't want their transmissions to be picked up by the wrong people, like our navy or Coastwatch. Now stay down and rest. I will be back," Andrew said.

With that he set off crawling on hands and knees around the north side of the sand cay. As he did several sharp pains shot through his right leg and buttocks but he gritted his teeth and ignored it.

I will worry about that later, he thought.

As he reached the edge of the water again Andrew turned and looked back. He saw Carmen watching him and she gave a small wave but looked very drawn and anxious.

I should be worried too, Andrew thought. But to his own surprise he just felt determined. *I will make sure these murdering mongrels pay,* he vowed.

Pausing behind the last of the sand rise Andrew spat in his face mask and rinsed it then pulled it on. Then he checked his air. *165psi. That should last half an hour or so,* he thought.

Then he paused to study the sea out to the east. Even from right down at water level he was able to pick out the darker water of the Boat Passage and the distant wrecks on Longbow Reef. There was a light chop ruffling the ocean.

That will make it hard to spot a periscope, he thought.

Seeing none he placed his regulator in his mouth and slid forward into the water, crawling and pulling himself along using his hands until the water was deep enough to swim. Then he began to fin, taking care to avoid scraping or bumping the coral as much as he could. The shoals of brightly coloured fish that flitted away he barely noticed. Even a small octopus that he would normally have cringed away from Andrew just noted and ignored.

Not a blue ringed. It won't bother me, he told himself.

As he made his way east across the now flooded reef Andrew tried to use the remaining coral outcrops as cover to observe from. At each one he selected the next one he wanted to hide behind and then swam to it and carefully surfaced. Each time he remained as low as he could and with most of his head hidden behind the coral. And each time he noted the position of the game fishing boat.

It isn't moving. It must be anchored or moored to that net arrangement somehow, he decided. A check of his watch showed it was 1050. *Ten minutes to the top of the tide. If I was in a sub I'd want to use the slack water to get in and out,* he thought. That told him to get a move on as he had about five hundred metres to swim.

Andrew went under and finned fast east. He noted that there was now almost no current and that many more fish were in evidence. Ahead of him he saw the colour change and he knew he was reaching the seaward edge of the reef. Having swum along it only an hour before he knew what to expect he did not waste time but swam straight out over the edge and turned right. Then he went down to five metres to get out of the surface disturbance and began swimming as fast as he could.

I don't need to go any deeper, he told himself.

That would only give safety and decompression problems. As he swam he hugged the side of the reef. Every couple of strokes he looked in all directions. But now he was not thinking of sharks or gropers. In the front of his mind was that deadly powerhead striking the back of Tristan's skull. Fear made him very alert and very cautious.

The sand of the seabed was only about five more metres below him and out to his left, extending to the limit of visibility was the slowly shelving sand of the large triangular area between the Challenger Channel and the Boat Passage. That area was much too shallow for a submerged submarine to operate in and Andrew was pretty sure that the vessel would not surface in daylight.

Too much risk of being seen by one of our Coastwatch or surveillance planes if it did, he thought. *There would be no point in using a sub in that case. It will come in submerged along the Boat Passage.*

He also surmised that the sub would probably not even surface at night but would use a snorkel to recharge its air and batteries.

It must be an old diesel. No navy is going to lose even an old nuclear powered boat, he decided. His compass warned him when he began changing direction to southwest. *I am rounding the southeast corner of the reef. Almost there. I had better go slowly,* he told himself.

So he slowed down and began to hunch in crevices while he scanned the water ahead. Then he moved a few metres to the next one and repeated the process. His watch told him it was 1100—the top of the tide.

Can't be much further, he thought.

And it wasn't. As he peeked around the next coral outcrop Andrew saw dark shapes ahead and fear sent him close in against the seaweed and coral. At first he could not make out what he was seeing, but then the distinct shape of a diver showed against the lighter shade of the sand. That sight sent a stab of pure terror coursing through Andrew and he began to breathe fast and tensed, ready to flee.

But the diver was busy working and obviously had not seen him. The man was about fifty metres away and he appeared to have a long hose and was at the corner of a dark triangular object that was getting bigger and spreading on the sea floor. Then a large, dark spherical shape began to rise and as it did the hazy triangular thing went up with it. Then Andrew understood what he was looking at.

It is that net. They are using the winches to spread it out along those steel wires using the pulley blocks and now they are raising the corners of the net with air bags, he noted.

Then he saw a darker shape off to his right and saw that it was the back of the net. It was being winched up to where the game fishing boat was just visible as a dark shadow on the silver ripples.

They have lifted the whole of one half of the net by the boat and two air bags and have spread the other half of the net out across the sea floor and have lifted the two front corners by air bags, he thought. *How bloody ingenious!*

But he wasn't quiet sure why the murderers had done it or how it was to be used although he had a few suspicions.

Off to his left front a hundred metres away was the start of the bathtub shaped depression that led northeast as the deep part of the Boat Passage. Even as Andrew looked at it a dark shape began to materialize out of the blue background. The sight sent shivers of apprehension through Andrew because whatever it was it was big.

Is that the sub? Andrew wondered.

He thought it was and it was what he was expecting to see but he wasn't sure. But then his ears confirmed that the distant object was man made. The noise of a rotating propeller carried through the water to him. Fearful lest he be detected by some means he squeezed right in among the coral and tried to slow his breathing.

And then the shape was right there, close to the net and he was sure.

It is the sub! he told himself.

Chapter 6

CUNNING BASTARDS!

As the submarine crept into view Andrew stared in amazement. This was a real submarine, not some midget made by drug runners. It was at least seventy metres long and even in the gloom of the water he could make out details like torpedo tubes and openings for flooding the casing. The sub had a conning tower and the top of this was almost breaking the surface. It had its periscope up.

They will be using their periscope to keep a bearing on the fishing boat, he thought. *And they will be in radio communication with it.*

Over such a short distance he knew that there was very little risk of a low power VHF radio transmission carrying very far.

They might even have underwater radios so they can talk to those divers.

Andrew was no expert on submarines. Both he and Carmen had done surface tours of RAN submarines, but he had never been in one when it was dived. Nor did he want to be. Long ago he had acknowledged he was too much of a coward for that. One result of not being interested in them was that he had never bothered to study the different types. All he could decide now was that it looked longer and different from the RAN submarines.

It has a row of windows on the conning tower, he noted with amazement.

He could not tell if the windows were pressure resistant for people inside to look through when the submarine was dived but decided not to take the risk. He stayed huddled in against the coral.

The submarine came to a standstill. Several times spurts of bubbles erupted from holes along the lower side of the hull.

They must be blowing ballast to maintain depth, Andrew thought.

He knew that submarines could attain negative buoyancy in the same way as divers. He had also read that they could settle on the bottom if it was suitable. But he also suspected that a vessel that large would have difficulty keeping position if it did not have steerage way on.

The bow of the submarine was at least a hundred and fifty metres away and its stern stretched back to be almost invisible in the blue gloom. It was stationary over the last part of the deep section of the Boat Passage. Andrew watched intently, keeping an eye on the nearest diver who remained holding the corner of the net.

The net must be there to catch their cargo, Andrew thought. He did not think that the submarine would surface. *Too risky and if they were going to do that they would do it in deep water well out from the reefs,* he mused.

A minute later he was proved right. There was a humming noise and then a great puff of bubbles erupted from the lowest torpedo tube on his side of the submarine's bow. A short, stubby projectile shot into view and went spinning through the water. Andrew immediately noted that it was not a proper torpedo.

Too short and it doesn't appear to have a propeller or control fins, he told himself.

The object had a sphero-conoidal head on a short, cylindrical body. It obviously lacked its own motive power as its course followed a parabolic curve which ended in the net. There was a big puff of sand and silt and Andrew saw the net jerk and billow.

Very tricky! Andrew thought with grudging admiration.

There was another puff of air and a second container shot from another torpedo tube and lobbed into the net. A few seconds later a third and then a fourth followed. Andrew watched, fascinated.

I wonder what is in those projectiles? he thought.

In all six projectiles were spat out by the submarine. All landed in the net. Almost immediately the propeller noises of the submarine increased and Andrew saw it start to slide backwards.

That is it then. He is getting out of here, Andrew decided.

Gripped by the drama of the spectacle Andrew watched, quite forgetting that he was underwater. The submarine reversed for about a hundred metres until he could only just see it as a huge cigar shaped shadow out over the deeper section of the channel. Then the submarine's image began to change shape, even while still reversing.

Turning to port, Andrew decided.

Within another minute the submarine was side on across the channel. Then its engine note changed and it began to move forward, turning to starboard as it did. Andrew watched with appreciation at the skill involved in that manoeuvre.

I wouldn't like to try that on the surface with a vessel that large in such a restricted space, he thought.

But he did appreciate that the submarine was well clear of the reef and that if it touched bottom it would only hit sand and would be unlikely to damage itself.

Still, you would not want to be trying to a manoeuvre like that with any sort of current running. I can see why they do it at slack water on the top of the tide, he mused.

Before another minute had passed the submarine had vanished seawards in the gloom. Andrew was able to detect its propeller noises for a few minutes more and then they too were gone.

Well, fancy that! he told himself, amazed by what he had just seen.

Then he remembered to check his dive computer. To his relief he had 115psi of air remaining. *Plenty for me to get safely away,* he thought.

But he didn't go. Instead he remained in hiding and watched what the divers were doing. From his Navy Cadet experience he was both able to guess what would happen next and to concede that, as an exercise in seamanship, it was very skilfully done.

The divers swam in and attached a steel cable lowered from the game fishing boat to one of the projectiles. The projectile was then winched up. The whole operation took only a couple of minutes before the object vanished up through the surface.

The cunning bastards! Andrew thought, admitting grudging admiration for the men he both feared and hated.

A poem his English teacher had once taught him flitted through his brain. *The villain's aim was better than his cause and I was hit and hit again!* Andrew quoted. He found it deeply irritating and somehow offensive that evil men could also be very capable.

For the next ten minutes, Andrew remained watching. During that time three more of the projectiles were winched up to the game fishing boat. As the fifth was hooked on by the two divers visible Andrew remembered to look at his air pressure. With something of a shock he saw it had dropped to 95psi.

I had better start back, he thought. *I know how it is done now and Carmen will be getting worried.*

Andrew waited until both the divers that were visible appeared to be engrossed in their work and then he edged out of his crevice and began edging back around the outcrop behind him, hugging the coral as close as he could, eyes on the enemy. That way he made the next crevice and passed out of sight of the divers—but when he glanced at the coral beside him he got a real shock. Only centimetres from his right hand was the head of a large moray eel!

Bloody hell! Andrew thought, snatching his hand away and pushing himself off around the next outcrop.

He knew that moral eels were not poisonous like snakes, but they had vicious incising teeth and he had read that their bite was both painful and liable to become infected.

I don't need any more medical problems at the moment, he told himself, noting that his right buttock and thigh felt quite numb and painful.

Luckily the moray eel did not strike, and Andrew was able to relax and look around. For a few seconds he studied the coral and his surroundings. The first thing he noted was a subtle change in the pattern of the seaweed. Then his brain sorted it out.

The tide has changed. It is on the ebb and the current is now flowing the other way, he thought. That meant it was flowing east and washing across the reef. *I had better hurry back. I don't want to get washed away from the reef and have to battle with the current to get back to it,* he thought.

Another check of his air showed him he was down to 97psi. *Getting close to the safety minimum,* he thought. But he was not really worried about decompression. He had not been deeper than five metres the whole time and knew that he could just surface and swim back that way. *As long as those murderers aren't looking!*

Thinking about them sent stabs of anxiety through him and he wished he had waited to see what the crooks did next.

Will they stay there or head off straight away? he wondered. *If it was me I would get away from there as quickly as I could so as not to attract attention to my net.* He was sure that the net had been there for a while and that the crooks intended to use it again. *In five days' time possibly?* he mused.

For a moment he contemplated surfacing to see what the trawler was doing. But there did not seem to be any coral outcrops sticking out of the water where he was.

If I just stick my head out without cover they might spot me, he thought. That brought on a bout of shivering as horrific images of the murders and his own near-death experience swamped him.

After that Andrew found it hard to swim. His whole body seemed drained of energy and it took all his will power to keep finning north along the edge of the reef. Twice he stopped to listen, thinking he could hear the trawler but each time he wasn't sure. A glance at his watch showed him it was 1127.

They must have recovered all those projectiles by now, he decided. But how long would it take them to roll up and secure the net?

Andrew wasn't sure, but estimated fifteen minutes at least. *That means they won't leave until about 1145. So I had better stay very careful,* he warned himself.

He began to worry about his physical weakness and the fact that he was now having difficulty getting his right leg to move properly. It felt like it was stiffening up and he experienced several sudden but agonizing stabs of pain.

I had better get back to dry land while I still can, he told himself.

But that raised the question of when to turn left and swim across the top of the reef. It was a problem he had not thought about and when it occurred to him he cursed himself for being a fool.

I don't know when to turn, he thought angrily.

He did not want to turn too soon and end up on the murderer's side of the sand cay. Nor did he want to go past the sand cay and have to waste time and valuable energy swimming back to it. The only way was to risk a peek and hope that the murderers weren't looking.

I should be at least four or five hundred metres from them by now, Andrew reasoned. *If I am quick they might not see me or if they do they might think it was just a turtle or something.*

But it was still a real risk and the fear of the consequences of it going wrong was enough to get his heart hammering. Andrew found he was gulping air and that the pressure was down to 93psi.

Calm down! We might need some air, he told himself.

For a few seconds he forced himself to breathe slowly. He then made sure, using his compass and the visual cue of the reef edge, that he was orientated. He only wanted to break surface for a few seconds. Satisfied he was facing the right way and ready he forced himself to fin upwards.

His head broke the surface and then there were those few horrible moments of blindness until the water drained off his face mask. Then he could see. To his intense relief he saw that the sand cay was only a few hundred metres away and almost due west from him. Then he turned his head and caught a glimpse of the game fishing boat. It looked small and a long way off but it was still there.

The sight of it sent a chill of anxiety through Andrew and he at once allowed his head to slip back under. *They are still there*, he thought. *God, I hope they aren't going to stay.*

Using his compass to keep direction Andrew set off swimming Northwest. To his surprise he found that the water over the reef was at least two metres deep for most of the distance.

It must have come up a lot in that last half an hour, he thought.

He was swimming against the current now as the tide began to ebb, but it was slight and helped him keep direction. But there were very few coral outcrops for him to surface behind and he only came up once. To his relief he saw that he was on course and he slipped just below the surface and continued.

For the last fifty metres Andrew stopped using his regulator. The air was down to 85psi so he used his snorkel instead, reasoning that he was now so far away from the crooks that they would be unlikely to see such a small object.

And I'm in behind the sand cay too, he thought.

The next time he risked a peek he saw that this was so. He also noted a very relieved looking Carmen sitting in a small hollow she had scooped out of the southern end of the sand cay. She waved and he waved back and continued swimming. She had peeled off her wetsuit and only wore her dark green one-piece bathers.

As Andrew reached the shallows Carmen waded in to meet him and as he stood up she took the weight of his equipment.

"Thank God you're back," she said. "I was starting to get worried."

"Sorry, but it was worth it," Andrew replied. "Tell you when I have this stuff off me."

To his dismay he found he was so weak he could hardly stand and he was panting for breath. While he took off his BCD and air tank he recovered a bit. Then he removed his fins and his weight belt. That was a huge relief and he sloshed up onto the dry sand and just flopped down, feeling utterly drained. The dry sand was hot and felt wonderful to his chilled body and he just lay back and closed his eyes.

"Keep an eye out for that game fishing boat," he said. "I just need to get my breath back."

"You are shivering. You need to get out of that wetsuit," Carmen replied.

"Not yet. Not till those murdering mongrels have gone. We might have to swim for it again. You'd better put yours back on, just in case," Andrew answered.

Carmen nodded and picked up her wetsuit. "You are right. It just got so hot in the sun," she explained.

Andrew nodded and rolled onto his back. For the next few minutes he just lay there with his eyes closed against the sun, soaking in the warmth while his whole body trembled and shook. He felt nauseous but very relieved. Every muscle felt drained of energy and he ached all over. His buttocks and thigh had gone numb and he was afraid to even look at them.

But there can't be too much damaged or I would not have been able to do all that swimming, he reasoned.

After she zipped up the front of her wetsuit Carmen quizzed him about what he had seen. "So there really was a submarine?" she asked.

Andrew nodded. "Yes, a real live submarine, a full size one, not a midget."

"How big do you think?"

"Between sixty and seventy metres long," Andrew answered.

"Describe the conning tower," Carmen asked.

Andrew paused for thought and then tried to explain with his hands. "Sort of oval, but with a curved or rolled front where they con when on the surface. There was a row of windows just below that," he answered.

"Only one row of windows?" Carmen queried.

"Yes."

"Definitely a Russian then. Nobody else has windows on their subs. Did the conning tower have a sort of stepped down section at the rear?"

"No, but there was a drum shaped thing on top near the rear," Andrew answered.

"Sounds like a Kilo Class," Carmen replied. "They are old diesel electric subs built in large numbers in the nineteen sixties and seventies. The Russian built several hundred,"

Andrew nodded. He was often amazed at how much his sister knew about the world's navies and their vessels. *But then she is a Cadet Chief Petty Officer and has been a navy cadet for four years,* he thought. In fact, she was due to go on her course for promotion to Cadet Midshipman in the June School Holidays. *That is if we survive,* he added gloomily.

Carmen went on. "Of course it may not be Russian now. They sold quite a few to other navies, to places like Indonesia, India, China and so on."

"Or it could have just fallen into the wrong hands during the collapse of the Soviet Union," Andrew added. He knew enough history to understand what had happened to the huge Soviet empire when communism collapsed in the 1990s.

Suddenly Carmen sat up and pointed. "They are moving! The game boat is under way."

A spasm of pure terror galvanized Andrew. He rolled over and crouched to get a better look. The game fishing boat came into view.

Heading west, he noted. Then he flopped down and said, "Quick, grab all your gear and get into the water. Keep down! Crawl! And keep the island between it and us."

Carmen nodded and then reached out. "Give me your fins," she said.

Andrew let her take them as he rolled onto his back again and struggled to get the weight belt back around his middle. His fingers then seemed to be all thumbs and he fumbled and flustered while trying to do it up. But he was determined to keep the dive gear.

It may be what saves us again, he thought.

As soon as he had the belt done up he snatched up his mask and pulled the strap down around his neck. Then he crouched and grabbed the air tank and BCD and began dragging it down the sand.

Carmen had begun crawling away but she now stopped and pointed to the water. "Keep going and I will scuff out our tracks," she said.

Andrew looked and was appalled to see that the air tank was leaving a deep groove in the sand.

Bloody hell! I forgot that, he berated himself.

But he did as he was told and scurried on down to the water, angling around the slope to the right as he did. The sand cay was so low that he was afraid that they might be visible even when crawling.

It was with relief that he slid into the water. To his surprise the water felt quite cold and he found it pleasant. As soon as he was in waist deep water he knelt and pulled the BCD and attached air tank on and zipped and clipped it on. Then he raised himself until he could just see the tip of the fishing boat's mast over the cay. Carmen joined him and gave him a quizzical look.

Andrew ducked down again. "It has turned north. It is heading our way," he said.

"Oh my God!" Carmen cried, going pale and breaking into a trembling fit as she did.

"I don't think they have seen us," Andrew said to reassure her.

"I agree," Carmen replied. "I was just remembering what they did to Tristan and to Mr Craig and Dan. I…" She shook her head and broke into sobs.

Andrew experienced some gut-wrenching terror as the same images flooded his mind. But it was the callous way he had been tossed in to drown that really made the greatest impact and he shivered with what he knew was absolute fear.

These men will certainly kill us if they see us, he told himself.

So he moved deeper into the water and began moving to his left, edging around the northern end of the sand cay to its eastern side. From time to time he very cautiously raised himself on bent knees but only until he could see the tip of the trawler's mast. Satisfied that the game fishing boat was in fact heading north he lowered himself back into the water until only his head was sticking out.

"They are still heading north and are only a couple of hundred metres out," he explained.

"Do you think they will come and search the island?" Carmen asked.

Andrew shook his head. "No. I think they are heading off to meet the dive boat. Then they will take their booty ashore," he replied, although he was by no means sure and was gripped by a feeling of apprehension so strong he had trouble breathing.

For the next five minutes he and Carmen kept moving south, only their heads exposed. It was easy to do, just floating face down and pulling themselves along with their hands. Carmen slipped on the fins rather than carry them in her hands and risk dropping them. Both took turns at raising themselves up to check on the boat's progress. Andrew was always careful to make sure he saw no more than the tip of the boat's mast. He had no intention of risking being seen by any men on her deck or in her wheelhouse.

To his intense relief the game fishing boat maintained a steady course northward, slowly angling away from the reef. But Andrew still took no chances and he insisted that they keep moving southwards until they were at the southern side of the sand cay. By then the game fishing boat was at last half a kilometre away and almost stern on.

"We will wait till it is just a dot on the horizon," Andrew said. "We are not taking any chances."

Carmen nodded. "I agree. And then I can have a look at that wound of yours."

"And we can try to get ourselves rescued," Andrew added.

Chapter 7

DESERT ISLAND

For the next twenty minutes Andrew and Carmen remained lying in the shallows on the south side of the sand cay. Only when the game fishing boat was so small that it was hard to make out what type of vessel it was did Andrew crawl up out of the water and kneel on the dry sand while he took off his BCD and air tank. Placing those down he peeked over the low sand ridge to make a final check.

"We won't take any chances. We won't show ourselves or walk around until it is out of sight," he said.

"Suits me," Carmen agreed as she sat on the beach and rubbed her feet.

Andrew unbuckled his weight belt and took his mask and snorkel from around his neck. Then he lay back on the warm sand and broke into a fit of shivering.

"Are you sick?" Carmen queried anxiously.

"No, just worn out and feeling a bit battered," Andrew replied. In truth he felt very scared and totally exhausted. For the next few minutes neither spoke. It was only when he heard Carmen stand up that Andrew asked, "Can you still see them?"

"Yes, but they are just a speck on the horizon," Carmen answered.

Andrew nodded and sighed with relief. But he quickly found that the fear of the men had been replaced by a gnawing sense of apprehension.

Now we have to be rescued, he thought. In the back of his mind was the knowledge that he and Carmen were now in dire peril from the natural environment. *We are cast away,* he thought, *on a desert isle with no food or water.*

Carmen was obviously thinking the same thing as she said, "Well, this is the original desert isle. Not even a blade of grass, never mind the coconut tree they always draw in the cartoons."

Andrew could only agree. "Certainly bare," he said, his eyes squinting against the glare while he scanned the few metres of white sand.

"No shade," Carmen added, "Or water."

And it was the water that most worried Andrew. Already he had a real thirst. *If nobody comes along within a day or two we will die from thirst or heat stroke,* he thought gloomily.

Two years before, during the Cadet Annual Camp which had been held in Townsville, he and Carmen had done a two day Sea Survival training course on a rocky island in Halifax Bay and it was thirst and heat which had predominated, followed by exposure.

The heat stroke concept was reinforced now by his own bodily discomfort. Lying on the hot dry sand in his wetsuit was now making him sweat. With a groan Andrew rolled over and struggled to his knees.

"I need to get out of my wetsuit for a while," he said. "It is too hot."

Carmen agreed, and both stood and unzipped and peeled off their wetsuits. While he did that Andrew scanned the sea to the north and was surprised that he could still see the mast of the game fishing boat as a thin black line against the sky. The inconsequential thought crossed his mind that he had read somewhere that during the age of steam when British warships painted their upper masts black to hide the soot from the coal dust the French had painted their upper masts white to make them almost invisible against the sky.

Having pulled off his wetsuit Andrew laid it carefully beside his other diving gear. Then he twisted to look at his speargun wound. To his surprise it was just a small hole that was almost completely closed up. There was certainly no seepage of blood. Nor was the exit wound bleeding either. But it certainly hurt when he moved.

Carmen came and studied the wound, her fingers gentle as she dabbed around the puffy flesh. "I think being in the sea water so long has caused the flesh to swell and close up," she said.

"That should be good shouldn't it?" Andrew asked. They certainly had no bandages or First Aid stores.

"I think so. The salt will have certainly helped as an antiseptic," Carmen agreed.

"Well I am getting back in the water again for a minute. It is getting bloody hot," Andrew said. He glanced at his watch and saw that it was five to one. The sun was high overhead and blazing down with tropical intensity.

"I will join you, but only for a few minutes," Carmen agreed.

Both walked down into the shallow water and crouched to splash water over themselves. It was wonderfully cool for a few minutes but then Andrew began to shiver. Carmen lay face down and said, "Well, what exactly did you see?"

Andrew related all the detail he could remember, adding, "They are obviously smugglers."

"Smuggling what I wonder?" Carmen mused.

"Something very valuable. Something worth committing murder for," Andrew replied bitterly. Once again, he shuddered at the images of violent death that swirled in his mind.

"Drugs maybe?" Carmen suggested.

"Or guns or something like that," Andrew added.

"Why guns? Who would want guns in Australia," Carmen queried.

Andrew shrugged. "Illegal weapons, like handguns for bank robbers, or automatic rifles for gun nuts," he suggested. As he talked he felt his skin dry off and then begin to burn. He ducked into the water again and then stood up and limped back up to look around the horizon. Carmen joined him. There was no sign of the game fishing boat.

"Gone," Andrew said.

"What do you think they will do with the dive boat?" Carmen asked.

"Sink it in deep water to get rid of the evidence," Andrew replied grimly. Horrible images of the bodies of his friends being locked in the sinking vessel rose to cause him to shudder. Once again, he ran his tongue over lips that were starting to dry and crack, wishing he could have a drink. Then he gestured with his hands.

"I feel like we have been cheated. In all the cartoons the castaways on desert islands always have a single palm tree to sit under. We haven't even got a bush."

"No, you are right," Carmen agreed. "But we had better make some sort of shelter or we are going to get horribly sunburnt."

Andrew glanced at his already red skin and nodded. "Drinking water is more of a problem," he replied.

"I know, but talking about it won't help so let's try to get under our wetsuits," Carmen suggested.

So they sat on the damp sand rather than on the hotter dry sand and then covered their backs and heads with their wetsuits while trying to hold them up off their skin to provide shade but still allow a cooling breeze. It wasn't very successful but it was better than nothing. Every ten minutes or so they both stood up and looked in all directions then went and lay in the sea for a minute.

"Tide is going out," Andrew commented, indicating the numerous coral heads that were now exposed.

He then slowly scanned the whole horizon starting with the west. That showed nothing but a flat horizon line as they were so far from the coast not even the mountains were visible. And it was hard to look towards the west because the afternoon sun was now reflecting off the waves. Looking south across the Boat Passage showed no prospect of help. Beyond the water of the passage there were just the overlapping lines of coral that marked the Feathers Reefs. These extended off as far as he could see, surrounded by rock studded shallows.

No-one in their right mind would sail a ship through that unless he had to, he thought.

Andrew then looked to the east. First, he studied the deep water of the Boat Passage looking for any small spray of water that might indicate a submarine periscope, then for any large shadow under the water.

I'm being silly. They will be long gone, he thought. *They would want to be back out in the open ocean beyond the Barrier Reef before the tidal flow got too strong.*

His gaze then roved over the huge area of tidal shallows and exposed reefs inside the Longbow Reef. The dark bumps of the two wrecks on the northern end of it showed clearly and he even detected a few spurts of white as large waves broke on the outer reef. What he was really looking for was a ship on the horizon but there was none.

Andrew shook his head with anxiety and then looked at the tiny square of the stone building on distant Prescott Island.

Our base camp is there but I didn't see any water, he thought.

The camp had been set up to make a change from being on the dive boat. Looking further to the left his gaze followed around the long sweep of reefs that bordered the northern side of the Challenger Channel. Still nothing.

Carmen stood up and joined him as he stared out northwards. "See anything?" she asked.

Andrew shook his head and tried to keep the worry out of his voice and off his face.

"No. I was hoping some ship might pass through the Challenger Channel," he replied.

"Not much hope of that," Carmen answered. "All the commercial trade goes through further north."

Andrew knew that. The only big ships he was aware of that regularly passed eastwards through the Great Barrier Reef out into the Coral Sea were the bulk carriers that brought nickel ore from French New Caledonia to Townsville. They used the Flinders Passage as did most of the other ships like the coal carriers from Abbot Point.

"There might be a tourist launch," he said.

Carmen shook her head. "Not likely. Not only is this a restricted conservation zone but it is too far from any port where tourists might come from like Townsville or Bowen and any boats from the Whitsunday resorts will go to the reefs just near them," she said.

Andrew nodded. During their dive course they had gone out to Wheeler Reef from Townsville and it had taken nearly ten hours. He had been told that most tourists went to places like Cairns where the reefs were only one or two hours travel. As Cairns was his home town he was well aware of that and of the rivalry between Cairns and Townsville. But it was very disheartening to contemplate the unpleasant fact that there was a strong possibility that no vessel of any sort might pass near them for many days, even weeks.

We will be long dead by then, he thought grimly.

Carmen shielded her eyes against the glare and scanned the sea to the north and west. "There won't be any commercial fishermen in this area and probably no recreational fishers either," she said.

"No, so all we can hope for is another research vessel or some passing tourists," Andrew replied. It also came to him that their little island was in the wrong place.

It is over half a kilometre to the north edge of the reef near the Challenger Channel. A ship could pass through and not even see us, he thought.

That led to more unpleasant thoughts. To try to reach the north end of the reef would be a painful and difficult undertaking. With the reef exposed it would mean walking across the coral with all the risks of injury that entailed.

And if the tide is in and we have to swim the current will make things really hard and we will be very difficult to spot in the water, he thought gloomily. The thought of going back into that water chilled him as all his usual phobias about sharks resurfaced.

It was demoralising, but he did not want to voice his doubts. But what he was now painfully aware of was that he was not only very hot and thirsty but was getting badly sunburnt. A glance showed his arms, chest and shoulders to be bright red. His skin felt tight and tender and he shivered and knew it was from feeling sick, not from the breeze.

We are really in trouble, he thought. Dread clutched at his insides and he began to quietly pray.

To try to get some shade Carmen suggested they dig into the east side of the sand cay at the steepest part. They tried this but quickly gave it up as the sand was so dry that it kept crumbling into the hole almost as fast as they dug it. As Andrew pointed out the effort was making them sweat more than if they just sat quietly. By this time their arms were too tired to hold the wetsuits up as shade cover so instead they just sat with the suits draped over their head and back and faced away from the sun.

After a while Andrew walked around to the other side of the cay, cooling his feet in the puddles as he went. Once he was out of sight of his sister he relieved himself. To his concern he had very little urine and it was a bright yellow colour.

That is not good, he told himself. *It should be almost clear.*

The image of the colour chart they had been shown on the Sea Survival course rose to cause more chest-tightening apprehension.

Thinking about the possibility of dying of thirst sent little tremors of anxiety around Andrew's stomach.

Like rats scrabbling for food, he thought. And then his stomach grumbled as he had not had lunch. *It is a long time since breakfast,* he thought. But his rational mind told him that food was not critical. *People can go for thirty or forty days before they die of hunger. Thirst will kill us in a day or two.*

Once again, he scanned the horizon in all directions and found it empty. Then he became conscious again of the savageness of the tropical sun as it burned his skin. After splashing some water on it to cool it he walked back to re-join Carmen. She gave him a smile, but Andrew could see the worry in her eyes and knew she was scared as well.

No sooner had he sat down and pulled his wetsuit up over his shoulders that he heard an aircraft. He went tense and cupped his hand to his ear. *Yes, an aircraft!* he thought. He sprang up and began searching the sky. Then the sound came more distinctly above the whiffle of the gentle breeze and he scanned the sky to the northeast.

"There it is!" Andrew cried, pointing northwards at a tiny spec that was growing rapidly larger. His hopes went rocketing up and he sighed with relief and began to wave his arms. Carmen joined him and they both signalled frantically.

It was a Coastwatch aircraft—but it was at least five or six kilometres to the east. It appeared to fly directly over Prescott Island and then headed south across the Challenger Channel towards the wrecks on Longbow Reef.

"It isn't coming this way," Andrew commented, his hopes clashing with apprehension.

It was quickly obvious that the aircraft was not searching for them. It kept flying southwards in a direct line and was soon over Longbow Reef. Carmen let out a little sob of disappointment and then said, "We need a mirror to attract their attention."

"Mirror?" Andrew replied, his thoughts now in a jumble as fear began to overwhelm hope.

"Face mask!" Carmen cried.

They both dashed back to where the diving equipment lay. Carmen got there first and snatched up the facemask. Then she held it close to her with her right hand and extended her left hand to arm's length with a finger upright. She then aimed the finger at the aircraft and began moving the goggles of the facemask to try to get sunlight to reflect off them.

"Get the sunlight on your finger!" Andrew cried, remembering the instructor on the Sea Survival course. He reached towards the facemask, his fingers twitching with anxiety. An almost frantic urge to snatch the facemask from Carmen welled up and he had to consciously restrain himself.

She is a Chief Petty Officer. She has been trained at this stuff too,' he reminded himself.

"The angle's all wrong!" Carmen wailed.

Andrew understood the problem. The sun was coming from almost directly behind them and she was finding it very hard to get anything lined up where her own shadow did not block the sun's rays. Nor could she get any strong reflections and every second the aircraft flew further away southwards.

Within a minute the aircraft was just a speck in the southern sky. Andrew felt a sickening feeling of dread grip his stomach as his hopes came sliding down.

Carmen shook her head and muttered, "Sorry!"

"Not your fault, sis. We will be ready next time and know what to do," Andrew replied. But it was a terrible blow and they stood in silence and watched until the aircraft vanished. Then the sound of its engine died away. For something to say to try to lift his sister's spirits Andrew said, "I wish they'd flown over when that sub was here. They might have spotted it. They would certainly have seen the crook's boat and would have come to fly around it to investigate a fishing boat in a restricted zone."

"Yes, they would have," Carmen agreed.

Andrew thought of submarines and things he had read about them. He said, "I read somewhere that during the Second World War the Japanese never sent a submarine inside the Great Barrier Reef. I always used to wonder about that because they certainly sent them to sink ships off the coast of New South Wales and South Queensland."

"Yes, they sank that hospital ship, the *Centaur* out from Brisbane," Carmen agreed.

"Now that I think about it I can see why they didn't come inside the Great Barrier Reef. It isn't that the water inside the reef isn't deep enough. It is. Their problem was navigation. To try to find one of the gaps in the reef at night would be almost impossible, even by sonar and during the day they would have to be at periscope depth to try to spot the waves breaking on the reef and that would make them very visible to our anti-sub aircraft," he said.

Carmen nodded. "Even in daylight it would have been pretty tricky finding an opening," she said. "They would really need to be good navigators and pick the tides because there are some really strong currents through some of these channels."

An idea came to Andrew and he clicked his fingers and pointed. "You're right! They would've needed a visual reference. No GPS navigation in those days. That's why they've chosen this place."

"Why?" Carmen asked.

"Because there are some very good visual references. There is the stone building on Prescott Island and the two wrecks on Longbow Reef. They would give very good markers to get accurate approach bearings. They could then come into the Challenger Channel on the sonar and change course to come up the Boat Passage on the top of the tide using the smuggler's boat as a leading mark," Andrew explained.

"I think you might be right," Carmen agreed. "But the tide would need to suit."

"The Coastwatch aircraft would be their biggest worry," Andrew went on.

Carmen frowned. "Are you suggesting that they might have a spy inside the Coastwatch organization to tell them when the flights are due?" she suggested.

"Maybe, but they could also do it with less risk by having a couple of small boats with radios, one to the south and one to the north to give them warning," Andrew answered.

"Possibly. I wonder how big their organization is and where they base the sub for refuelling and repairs," Carmen said.

"One of the Pacific islands, in a failed state like the Solomons or Bougainville maybe," Andrew suggested.

"That's possible. It is about five hundred nautical miles across the Coral Sea. If they can do about twelve to fifteen knots they could cover the thousand miles there and back in about... er... um." she did a mental calculation. "In about thirty to forty hours one way."

"A couple of days to cross," Andrew added. "And you said that Ivanoff said something about five days. That figures. They could do that. They could be back in five days' time."

Carmen pressed her lips into a hard line then said, "They might be, but if we don't get rescued or don't find water we are not likely to be alive to see them."

Andrew swallowed as fear churned his stomach. "I know," he replied. "But I didn't want to frighten you by saying it."

"We need to face facts little brother," Carmen answered grimly. "Now, let's cool off in the water and then sit and try to stay calm and try not to sweat too much."

So they did. For the next few hours they sat with their backs to the afternoon sun. Neither talked much, trying to prevent their mouths from drying out. Andrew became more and more sunburnt and so did Carmen until both were lobster red. That caused shivering and a general feeling of sickness. Allied to that was the effect of shock and apprehension. Andrew was really scared and knew it.

The sun sank ever so slowly, burning at them with a horrible intensity. As much as possible they hunched under their wetsuits to gain a little shade. Time dragged. 1500 slowly changed to 1600. The tide ebbed further and further until all of the reef stood dry, a dark brown and black mass. The surrounding reefs also showed clearly.

This will be really dangerous to walk on if we have to,

Andrew thought, appreciating that he could not possibly walk on coral wearing his swim fins. The thought of trying to hurry over that jagged coral in bare feet made him shudder.

But there was no need. No vessel of any kind appeared. Andrew became thirstier and more uncomfortable and stopped sweating. His head ached and he felt nauseous. His tongue felt furry and seemed to fill his mouth and his eyes became sore. It took an effort of willpower not to rub at them as he knew that the dried salt in the corners would scratch the eyeballs. Blurred vision began to bother him and he knew he was entering serious heat stress.

Not heat exhaustion yet, he told himself, *But by this time tomorrow it will be heat stroke.*

Surreptitiously he studied Carmen to see how she was coping. She looked badly sunburnt and tired. Her face was drawn but it was the haggard look in her eyes that bothered him the most.

She is really hurting over Ella and Tristan, he decided.

That gave him a series of morbid flashbacks of death and rotting bodies. A crawly, sickening dread of dying crept within him until he felt he could not endure it any longer.

You've seen death before and you have faced death, he told himself. *So get a grip and face up to it like a man.*

That helped steady him and he settled to waiting and hoping. A glance at his watch told Andrew it was 1700.

Low tide, he told himself. *The tide will start to come in now.*

With that came the frightening thought that it would soon be dark— and that high tide was just before midnight. Andrew now wished he had studied the tide tables more carefully, but he was sure that the tide that night would be higher than the tide during the day.

The day tide was only about three metres, but I think tonight's is nearly four metres.

With that he looked around and tried to estimate how high the sand cay was above the level of the earlier tide. To his dismay he decided that the dry sand stood only about half a metre above that level.

Oh, bloody hell! This might be a challenge! he thought.

The fear tightened its grip on his chest and stomach and he licked his lips and looked anxiously around the horizon.

Chapter 8

WORST NIGHTMARE

Andrew stood up and looked around, his stomach churning with fear. Right around the horizon all he could see were the ripples of the waves and the flat, black stretches of reef. Nor did the sky offer any hope. There was not a cloud to be seen.

Our situation looks pretty hopeless, he thought, although he hated to admit it.

Once again, he walked to the far end of the cay to relieve himself and the sight of his urine depressed him even more. It was now a dark yellow, almost orange and there was very little of it.

We must have water soon or we are done for, he told himself.

His tongue felt swollen and seemed to fill his mouth and he had trouble making any saliva. To add to his discomfort his lips were now dry and starting to crack and his skin felt tight and sandy.

I am really burnt, he thought, then shivered and felt ill.

A dull, throbbing ache had begun behind his eyes and they felt sore and kept going out of focus. His stomach grumbled and he knew he was starting to feel a drop off in energy due to lack of food. The wound in his buttocks and thigh ached and throbbed.

Feeling more anxious that he could ever remember Andrew walked back to where Carmen sat. She looked up and said, "We had better start making preparations for the night."

"What can we do?" Andrew asked. He felt so tired and dispirited that he just wanted to lie down.

Carmen pointed to the air tank. "This diving gear to start with. You need to unclip the air tank and put the BCD on. It can act as a life vest," she said.

That made sense, but Andrew badly wanted to keep that air tank, just in case. "But what will we do with the air tank? If the tide gets too high it will just get washed away. We won't be able to hang onto it for hours."

Carmen stood up. "We will tie the lead weights from your weight belt to it and then bury the thing. That way it should be safe enough. I saw some nylon rope back near where we first came ashore," she said.

Andrew had noted several lengths of nylon rope among the human rubbish that littered the small beach. "That's a good idea," he said. "We can even use it as a sort of anchor if there is enough rope."

With that he set off walking around the beach looking for the rope. Carmen went the other way. Andrew quickly found two lengths of rope. One was blue and about a metre long and badly frayed but the other was about four metres in length and made of orange nylon. It had the remains of a polystyrene float attached to it. One end was partly unravelled.

Off a trawl net, he decided.

He picked up both and carried them back, noting a few other plastic objects and two rubber thongs among the rubbish.

Carmen came back with a two-metre length of yellow rope. Andrew picked up his weight belt and slid the heavy lead weights off and Carmen threaded the yellow rope through the eyelets and then tied the bundle securely around the gauges of the air tank. Andrew then tied the remains of the blue rope to the yellow one and hoped it would do.

For the next twenty minutes Andrew helped Carmen scoop a hole in the sand to bury the air tank. They managed to get it down about half a metre before the abrasive effect of the sand on their skin made their hands too sore to continue.

Carmen pointed to his swim fins. "What about them? They will be hard to hold."

Andrew shook his head vigorously. "I don't care. I will try wearing them. We might have to swim for it," he replied.

So they filled in the hole, leaving only the blue rope exposed to show its location. Andrew tied bowlines to make two loops in the blue rope. "To hang onto or to slip our ankles through," he explained.

Carmen nodded approval. They then collected their wetsuits and Andrew placed his swim fins next to his and slipped his facemask strap around his neck. He had a feeling that it might come in useful too.

Andrew stood up and brushed the sand off his hands. "You can tie this orange one around you and we can loop it through my weight belt," he suggested.

"Good idea. We don't want to get separated if a wave washes us into the sea," Carmen said.

That was the nightmare that was beginning to chill Andrew. By this time the sun was low on the western horizon and the tide had begun to make. Already the water had risen at least half a metre and some of the coral was submerged. The change of current was clear to see, the waves churning at the end of the reef where they swirled and eddied around into the shallower water.

What Andrew did not want to think about but found he could not stop doing was the tide rising so high they would be washed off by the current. Memories of those desperate eighteen hours of drifting while trying to keep Graham, crippled Ken and the badly injured float plane pilot afloat and in good spirits haunted him. It had been a terrifying experience, especially during the night. What had frightened him the most was constantly imagining sharks and other monsters of the deep suddenly grabbing his feet as they dangled down. Those thoughts had caused him to continually tense and want to pull his legs up and had been very wearing to both his spirit and his energy.

He remembered being so anxious about it that he reached a stage where he just wanted it all to end, where he had almost welcomed death rather than having to keep facing the continual, gnawing fear.

I must avoid getting into that frame of mind, he told himself. *Carmen will be depending on me.*

But as he watched the rim of the sun touch the sea his mind was also tormented by his other fears. One of his most common nightmares, recurring sometimes night after night, was being somewhere near the sea, then on a big vessel which unaccountably became a small boat which either sank or shrank to be a mere surfboard. Then he would be away from the land and in deeper water with the current dragging him out to sea. Then it would become dark and his fear would become almost unbearable when large dark 'things' began to flit around him under the water.

Only two nights before Andrew had had such a nightmare except that he and been wading on a nice beach and had suddenly found himself cut off on a small sandbar. Before he could wade back to the land the tide had come in so that the water was knee deep and the sand had vanished underwater. Then he had been swimming in deep water and big waves and the land looked to be many miles away, just a line of dark blue distant mountains!

At the time he had put that down to sleeping in a tent on Prescott Island with the sea all around but now he shivered and wondered if it had been a premonition.

This is not going to be any fun! he thought unhappily.

As the sun sank out of sight they sat with their backs to the breeze and watched the last of it dip below the horizon. As it went down Andrew shivered, noting only the tiny lines of jagged black ripples formed the waves on the horizon.

No sign of a ship, he thought anxiously. Apprehension rose into his gullet until it felt like he was choking, and he found he was almost hyperventilating with anxiety. *Calm down!* he told himself.

He glanced at Carmen, hoping she had not noticed his emotions. To his relief she seemed to be just sitting there thoughtfully, staring out across the sea. Then he realized that the sun was completely gone but that it did not seem much darker than before. To check he looked over his shoulder eastwards and the reason was immediately obvious. The moon was already well above the horizon and it was a full moon.

That's why we are getting such a high tide at about eleven, he thought.

He nudged Carmen and indicated the moon. By then the red glow of the sunset was fading so they turned to look the other way. Andrew was pleasantly surprised and for a while re-assured. The whole sea to the east looked either silver or black. Except for the dark patches of reef, the sea was shimmering and rippling as the moonlight reflected off the waves.

"That looks quite pretty," Andrew commented.

"It does, but it also shows the currents very clearly. Look how the wave patterns are different out in the Boat Passage and the Challenger Channel," Carmen replied.

Andrew looked and felt his complacency melt away. The streaky lines of ripples showed very fast tidal currents. Once again, he scanned the whole area. To his surprise he could still pick out the two wrecks on Longbow Reef as tiny black silhouettes but the stone house on Prescott Island, not being in line with the moon, was much harder to detect.

Carmen began arranging her wetsuit. "I am going to try to get some sleep," she said.

That idea instantly made Andrew realize how fatigued he was. But he was still worried. "Should one of us stay awake on guard?" he asked.

Carmen shook her head. "No. Even if the smugglers come back they aren't likely to spot us lying here," she said.

"What about...?" Andrew began, gesturing towards the sea. Even as he did he wished he hadn't started.

Carmen snorted. "Don't worry little brother. Sharks can't walk on land."

That stung! Andrew felt a flush of shame and retorted, "Crocs can."

"You don't normally find crocodiles on coral reefs," she replied.

"They swim in the sea though," Andrew answered.

"They do, but usually only going from one river to another. I've never heard of them being out at the reef. Stop thinking about things like that. You will scare yourself silly. Now relax," Carmen answered. She then brushed some sand off her wetsuit and lay down on it with her head towards the wind and rising moon.

Andrew felt both angry and foolish. *Carmen must have guessed I am scared,* he mused.

To hide this he followed her example, spreading his wetsuit and brushing off the larger bits of shell and grit. He clipped his facemask and snorkel to his BCD and placed them as a pillow. Then he stretched out beside her. As he did he felt the numbness of his speargun wound and then some sharp little pains.

I hope there is nothing serious wrong there, he fretted.

For a few minutes he lay with his eyes closed, aware that the salt had rubbed them raw and that they were very sore. But he could not make his tear ducts work so all he could do was lie there and try to relax. But that was hard to do. Hunger and thirst were starting to torment him by this time and the increasing crash and swash of the waves kept his anxiety level high.

Until he just slipped into an exhausted slumber.

The dream started well, walking near the seaside in bright sunshine, admiring the girls in their swimsuits. Then, for some reason, he had to try to cross a shallow creek. His subconscious tried to tell him to go back, to find a bridge, but he persisted.

It is only knee deep, he told himself.

But before he knew it the water had risen to nearly his waist and there were dark shapes flitting about in it—big, dark shapes. He turned and tried to wade back the way he had come but to his dismay he was much further out than he had realized. Suddenly he was in deep water and had to swim. He floundered and then struck out strongly for a small sand bar. Thankfully he made it and crawled up onto the dry sand. But then the water rose and the waves began to wash up over it and it began to get dark. A wave swept right over the sand bar, wetting his feet.

"Andrew! Andrew, wake up!"

Muzzily Andrew realized it was his sister calling, but not in the dream! And he was getting wet! Instantly he was awake and he scrambled to his feet, horrified to find water flowing around his ankles. Panic seized at his throat and he looked wildly around. Everywhere he looked all he could see were waves.

"The tide!" he gasped, his heart hammering rapidly and fear gripping his insides.

"Grab your wetsuit and put it on," Carmen yelled.

Andrew looked down and was appalled to see that a wave had washed right over the sand cay. Only the fact that he was standing on his wetsuit had stopped it from being washed away. As he looked down at it he felt something wrap around his right ankle and he jumped with fright and wondered what it was. Then he realized it was his weight belt. As that was important for his plans for their survival he quickly picked it up and looped it around his neck.

My BCD! he thought.

A spurt of panic had him down on his knees scrabbling in the foam until he found it. The BCD was already floating away and only the fact that the snorkel and facemask had snagged in the wetsuit had prevented that. Quickly he pulled the BCD on but left it unzipped. Hastily he stood up to look around.

And then he remembered his swim fins. But only one of the fins was still there, held by the swash against his left foot. Frantic not to lose it he bent and snatched it up, then grabbed at his wetsuit. The wave receded and in the moonlight Andrew saw his other swim fin five paces away. Tucking the other under his arm and dragging his wetsuit he hurried over and snatched the fin up just as another wave swilled up across the low rise.

This wave also washed ankle deep around Andrew's legs and he felt such a surge of terror that he cried out in dismay and could only stare wildly around. He noted that the wind had risen and that the waves were much larger. Nearby Carmen was struggling into her wetsuit, swearing in a most unladylike way about the sand which had got into it.

Carmen managed to get both her legs into her wetsuit and she called to him, "Andrew! Come back here and hold onto the rope so we don't lose our anchor."

Fear of that snapped Andrew back into motion. He hurried back to join Carmen then bent and felt for the rope. At first he could not find it and his anxiety level shot up but then the next wave washed it against his wrist and he snatched at it and clung on, bent double and desperately trying not to drop the wetsuit and swim fins tucked under his armpits.

Another wave sloshed around him as Carmen struggled to get her right arm into her wetsuit. Andrew watched, his heart hammering with fear as strong as any he had ever felt. In every direction there was nothing to see but rippling waves and spurts of spume. The entire cay had been submerged.

The tide is higher than we thought. We are done for! he thought.

Carmen managed to get her other arm into the suit and she then reached down and found the rope. She slid her right foot through one of the loops then shouted, "Pass me your BCD."

Andrew first unclipped his facemask and snorkel and pulled the rubber strap down around his neck. Then he slipped off the BCD and passed it to Carmen. "Inflate it," he yelled.

She nodded and quickly slid her arms through the BCD and did it up. Using the mouthpiece she partially inflated the BCD. Then she gestured to him.

"Now you give me your fins while you get your wetsuit on."

Andrew could only nod dumbly and pass them to her. She shoved one down inside the front of her wetsuit and gripped the other in her left hand. In the moonlight she looked very determined and Andrew suddenly felt ashamed of himself.

She might be my big sister, but I am stronger and I should be helping her, he thought.

He straightened up and checked that he still had his facemask and weight belt hung around his neck. Satisfied they were secure he picked up the wetsuit and moved to pull it on.

Carmen leaned across and shouted in his ear, "Wash the sand off if you can. If there is a lot of grit inside it will rub you raw."

That thought steadied Andrew. He had been driven by a desperate urge to get the suit on as quickly as he could, but he now realized that the waves had stopped for the moment. He looked around and noted that only odd groups of waves were washing over the sand cay. In places the sand was still exposed. So he said yes and walked slowly down the lee side until he was ankle deep in lapping surf. Here he bent to wash the wetsuit.

It was harder to do than he thought, and he wasn't sure if he was washing sand out or in. But he did realize he needed to have clean feet when he tried to pull the suit on.

If there is sand sticking to my feet it will end up inside the suit, he told himself.

So he stayed in knee deep water while he put his right leg into the suit. That worked and he was able to pull that leg on with only a couple of grains of sand scratching inside.

Now the other leg, he thought.

He balanced on his right leg and went to pull the suit onto the left. But at that moment a series of larger waves swept in. The first wave rose to almost his waist. Andrew felt the current scour the sand from under his foot and he hopped to try to keep his balance. But it was no good and he was dragged sideways. Suddenly he found himself lying on his side in the foam and being sucked into deeper water by the undertow. Salt water tasted in his mouth along with the bile of fear.

Bloody hell! My nightmare come true! he thought, panic again welling up to grip at his chest and throat. Desperately he rolled onto his front and floundered back into shallower water. As the next wave struck he scrambled to his feet.

More waves washed around him, a couple coming up almost waist deep. Each one tugged hard at the wetsuit and Andrew realized it was acting as a sea anchor and pulling him over.

I must get it on, he thought.

So he hobbled up to the edge of the surf and again stood on one leg. As soon as the next wave receded he shoved his left foot into the suit. He managed it but at the cost of falling backwards and ending up on his bum. Once again the backwash began to pull him into deeper water. But this time he was ready for it and lifted his buttocks and thrust so that he was able to get his left leg into the suit. Then he rolled over and clung to the seabed until the undertow ceased. Using the next incoming wave to help him he crawled back up onto the beach.

Standing up he groped at the wetsuit and got it all up out of the water. To his annoyance it had sand inside it, but he did not dare try to rinse it again so he pulled it on, right arm first and then the left. Having done that he again checked that he still had his weight belt. He knew his facemask was there because it was rubbing uncomfortably up under his chin.

Without waiting to zip the wetsuit up Andrew staggered back out of the swirling foam to re-join Carmen. She reached out and held his arm.

"Bloody hell little brother, I thought you were going to be washed away then," she said, the relief and anxiety very evident in her voice.

"So did I!" Andrew gasped. He grabbed hold of Carmen's arm and then realized he was shaking violently.

With an effort of will he eased his grip and slowed his breathing. But the shock had been too great and he kept breaking into shivering fits. The whole time, as he studied the surging waves the dread kept chewing at his stomach like tiny rats scuttling around.

Then his rational mind took in the fact that parts of the sand cay remained dry with each assault of the waves.

I thought we picked the highest point, he thought.

Then he decided that they probably had but that the combination of wind, waves and current was causing some parts of the cay to receive more attention than others. But it was plainly too late to move.

Carmen leaned over and said, "Put on your weight belt and I will tie this rope to it."

Andrew saw the sense in that. *We stand a better chance of surviving together,* he told himself.

So he took the belt from around his neck and buckled it around his waist. As he did he had to brace himself against another run of larger waves that swept knee deep over the cay.

I need to get a foot through one of the loops in our anchor rope, he thought.

But first he helped Carmen. She quickly tied a bowline around her waist and then passed the ends through his belt. Then she tied the ends together. Being a senior rating in the navy cadets she was able to do this with seemingly little effort. Despite this Andrew checked that the knots were correct and not likely to come undone. He knew this might annoy her, but he didn't care. He wanted her to be safe.

They are good knots. She can tie them blindfolded, he thought, having seen her do it many times.

Carmen then pulled one of the swim fins from inside her wetsuit and said, "Lean over. I will shove this down your back. It will be safer there."

Andrew did as he was told and then zipped up the wetsuit as far as he comfortably could, wincing at the sharp little pains from the trapped grains of sand and shell grit. That was a relief for a few minutes as the wind had become quite chilly but after that he began to feel hot, so he unzipped the suit to halfway down his chest.

I don't want to overheat or sweat, he thought.

"What time is it?" he asked, glancing up at the moon. It appeared to be almost overhead.

Carmen looked at her watch and then said, "Ten to ten. About an hour to the top of the tide."

That was bad news to Andrew. *The tide will keep rising for another hour! I wonder how deep it will get?* he thought anxiously.

Already he had noted that more waves were washing over the cay and they seemed to be getting wet feet with almost every one. That reminded him to secure his ankle to the loop in the buried rope, so he explained to Carmen and then bent and groped around till he found the spare loop. With her helping him to keep his balance he managed to slip his foot through.

But even that did little to allay his fears. If anything, they added the irrational thought that he might now be caught by the ankle and drowned if the tide got too high. To try to reassure himself he tried to remember the tide tables.

The average tide in this part of North Queensland is usually about three metres, he thought. *Only the spring tides and king tides go higher.*

But he could not remember if a full moon meant a spring tide, although he thought it did. Not knowing caused him a blush of shame. As a navy cadet he thought he should have such nautical knowledge.

For the next ten minutes he stood there, thinking hard and trying not to panic. Carmen took hold of his hand and he put his arm around her and held her close. She was shivering but he did not know if that was from being cold or from shock and exhaustion.

Probably both, he thought.

That was how he felt. And he felt very hungry and increasingly thirsty. He was also hot but he did not dare unzip the wetsuit further in case he had to swim in it.

For the next few minutes he studied the waves and weather, hoping that the change he had noted was not happening. But he decided it was.

The wind is getting stronger fast, he thought.

Biting his lip with anxiety he looked around. There was no doubt about it. The wind on his face had a cutting quality that made his sore eyes sting and chilled his face. He found it hard to look into it but made himself while he studied the waves.

Carmen turned to look as well. "The wind is getting stronger," she said matter-of-factly.

"And the waves are getting bigger," Andrew added.

There was no doubt about that. The next wave swilled over the cay thigh deep, nearly dragging both of them over. Only by bracing themselves did they manage to keep their feet.

If we hadn't had those loops we would have lost our footing and been washed away then, Andrew thought. His anxiety level shot up another notch as he noted that the waves were definitely increasing in both height and velocity.

To his further dismay he saw that the whole of the cay now seemed to be submerged in swirling water all of the time. There was no more dry land visible and as far as the eye could see there was nothing but a tossing waste of ocean. Andrew had the sickening feeling that his worst nightmare was coming true.

And then he realized he was having trouble seeing. At first he rubbed his eyes, an action he instantly regretted as the salt scratched and stung. Then, to his consternation, he saw that it was getting dark. With his heart pumping with worry he turned and looked around and saw that dark clouds were racing in from the ocean. A dark wall of them seemed to be drawing a vast veil of darkness towards him. To Andrew it gave the impression of some monstrous act of evil. To him it looked like doom sweeping in from the deep.

Oh my God! Half an hour to high tide and we are already nearly waist deep—and it is getting too dark to see, he thought. *How can we survive this?*

Chapter 9

ABSOLUTE FEAR

Andrew watched with growing apprehension the wall of darkness roll towards him. As it got closer he experienced a rush of absolute fear. As the dark shadows got closer his feeling of dread increased and he felt a strong urge to flee. But where to? All around was nothing but wildly tossing sea. Andrew cast a few nervous glances at where the cay was now covered in foam, hoping to see even a tiny patch of sand. But there was none.

Worse, the wind suddenly began to gust in fierce flurries. These whipped up the waves even more. Seeing that caused Andrew to swallow and he began to pray. Once again, he found himself gripping Carmen tightly to him.

Then they were engulfed by the storm. Foam flew up and waves that were waist high began to batter and pull at them. Grimly Andrew braced his legs and dug in his toes. With his right arm he clung to his sister. But he was afraid—more afraid than even when the men were shooting at him—or so he thought. Through his mind flitted the idea that this was nature itself they were battling. There could be no appeal to mercy or clever outwitting.

Through his mind flitted terrifying flashbacks of the cyclone on Cape Bowling Green that he and Carmen had survived a year and a half before.

That was like this, he thought, *except we were up on that little lighthouse and the wind and waves were much stronger.*

Andrew remembered how the gigantic waves had slammed in causing the lighthouse to shudder and sway as each wave broke. To his shame and dismay he was also flooded with frightening memories of his terror at that time. What really chilled his heart was the similarity to the scene as he looked around. In the darkness all he could see in any direction were tumbling, churning waves amid the driving rain. That cyclone had been the most awesome spectacle he had ever seen and he shivered as he remembered his fear and how the realization had struck him of just how puny he was when matched against the forces of nature.

I should get away from the sea altogether, he thought. But then she shook his head. *First, we have to survive this!*

The last of the moonlight was blotted out except for a rapidly receding glimmering off to the west. It became so dark Andrew had trouble making out any details. There were just the dark rolling clouds and the jagged waves topped with white foam. Salty spray kept hitting him and he hunched with his back to the waves and tried to keep the salt water out of his mouth. Twice he lost his footing and only Carmen's grip allowed him to regain his footing before he fell into the water. Then it was his turn to grip her as she was washed off her feet. With a mighty heave he hauled her back upright and she regained her balance.

Rain began to lash into his back. The sudden chill of the cold drops came as an unpleasant shock. Icy trickles began to run down inside his half-open wetsuit and Andrew swore, wondering if things could possibly get worse.

Then his brain clicked into gear. *Rain! Fresh water!* he thought. Suddenly the urge to drink made him face the rain and open his mouth.

"Rain!" he shouted. "Drink!"

But it was no good. Even with his mouth wide open only a few drops went in, not even enough to wash out the taste of the salt. And facing the oncoming waves was even worse. In the darkness they looked enormous and each one crashed in with sufficient force to make Andrew brace himself into a knee bent crouch against its shock. But the need to drink was too strong to worry about it. So he gripped Carmen tightly and stood there trying to catch a few drops.

Carmen suddenly began squirming beside him. "Wetsuit. Get your wetsuit off," she shouted. "I will untie myself first and get ready, then hold you while you do it," she added.

Andrew instantly understood. By holding the wetsuit as a rain catcher there was a chance of getting at least a trickle of fresh water. But he also understood that it would be difficult and risky to do.

If we aren't careful one of us could get washed away, and in this storm it will be very hard to swim back.

Carmen now took charge. The other swim fin was shoved down Andrew's back. She got Andrew to grip her tightly while she first undid her waist rope. This she looped around her neck. Next, she peeled off the BCD and gave it to him to hold. Next, she pulled off the top of her wetsuit and took the BCD back and put it on. Then she removed the bottom of her wetsuit, standing on one leg and jiggling. Andrew lost count to the times he had to hold her up against the surge of the waves.

Through his mind ran the refrain, 'Hurry up! Hurry up!' But despite his being anxious that the rain might stop before he could get a drink he had to use willpower not to say it. Instead he waited, holding her as steady as the surging surf allowed. Carmen at last pulled her foot out of the safety loop and then peeled the last leg of the wetsuit off.

She at once draped it over Andrew's shoulder saying, "Hang on while I get the rope back on."

Andrew nearly lost her wetsuit as the wind caught at it. Luckily it wrapped around his face and he was able to grab it and hold it with one hand while gripping Carmen with the other. She bent down, being totally submerged by the next wave. That knocked her to her knees, but she struggled up and then bent to slip her right foot through the loop. Straightening up she reached for her wetsuit.

"Your turn now. Give me your weight belt first," she shouted.

Desperate now to get a drink before the storm passed Andrew fumbled at the belt buckle. As soon as it was undone he passed it to Carmen. Then he pulled his swim fins from behind his back and passed them to her. She tucked them under her left arm. Andrew pulled his right arm out of his suit and then grabbed the rubber and hauled urgently at it to get the left free. As he did the next wave washed him off his feet. He found himself floundering on his hands and knees, fast running water and moving sand flowing from under and around him.

"Get up! Get up!" he told himself.

Carmen still gripped his arm and he was able to steady himself. The problem then was that water had gushed into the suit, ballooning it and dragging with such force that he was pulled out of Carmen's grasp. He ended up on his back with water pouring over him, even up his nose. For a terrifying second he thought he was going to be washed away into deep water but then he realized he was still held by his ankle.

Knowing that his life might depend on it he dug his hands into the sand and clawed frantically at it. But the sand kept washing away and moving under the force of the current. Until the wave passed Andrew did not have the strength to overcome the pressure. As soon as the strain came off Andrew squirmed onto his front and still clutching his wetsuit to his front pushed himself up onto his right hand and knees. Conscious that the next wave must be almost upon him he pushed himself upright, coughing and spluttering with his eyes, mouth and nose full of salt and sand. Carmen grabbed him and helped, and he was able to get his balance and brace himself just in time.

This time he held his suit up and was ready for the pull. Carmen cried out with relief and he held her tight. She sobbed, "I thought you were gone then."

Coughing and retching painfully Andrew nodded and croaked, "So did I. Your rope saved me. Quick, give me my belt and the fins."

Carmen handed him the belt. Andrew swung it around his middle and did it up, then pulled it tight. "Now the fins," he shouted. These were thrust through the belt. Carmen then took her wetsuit back Andrew immediately bent and peeled his wetsuit off his left leg. Then he picked his moment between waves and slid his right foot free. The next wave required him to cling to Carmen and brace himself but as soon as it was past he bent and peeled the wetsuit from his right foot.

He was just in time as the next wave struck as he was straightening up. Despite his efforts the water caught at his wetsuit and almost dragged it from his grasp. In fear of losing it he let go of Carmen so as to hold it with both hands. Then he tucked the wetsuit under his right armpit and held the legs with his left. To his dismay his feet began to move as the sand under them was scoured away by the wash of water. He tried to adjust his position, moving his left foot to keep his balance. Then another wave struck him unexpectedly. Down he went, sliding and floundering into deeper water. Despite that he clung to his wetsuit with one hand while he tried to dig the other into the shifting sand.

To Andrew's enormous relief the wave receded. He struggled desperately to his feet, fear of being washed right into deep water giving him strength. Before the next wave could strike he splashed back up to join Carmen. She reached out and grabbed him and Andrew let out a sob of relief.

Carmen shouted in his ear. "Wash your wetsuit in the rain. Get as much salt off it as you can. You must not drink salt."

Andrew knew that, and he nodded. Horrible stories he had read about the survivors of shipwrecks drinking sea water and going mad swirled in his mind.

The salt destroys the kidneys or liver or something, he thought, remembering a Sea Survival lesson. *The pain of it drives people mad.*

Acting on Carmen's instructions he quickly found the leg loop and slid his right foot back through it, then braced himself. The whole time his heart was pitter-pattering with anxiety lest the rain stop. Even as he stretched the back of the wetsuit out across his upraised arms he thought there had been a drop in the wind and a decrease in the intensity of the rain.

"Hurry! Hurry!" he told himself. Using one hand he rubbed and wiped at the rubber to try to get all the salt off it.

"What did you say?" Carmen asked. She now had her wetsuit held up across both her arms, a dip between them acting as a funnel to guide the rainwater to her mouth.

"Talking to myself," Andrew replied. He felt so scared, battered and worn that it all seemed just one long nightmare. Satisfied he had done the best he could he gripped the far side of the wetsuit with his hands and held his arms up so that the back of the wetsuit acted as a rain catcher. Like Carmen he allowed it to droop to channel the water to his mouth.

A steady trickle of water began to flow into his open mouth—cool, sweet fresh water. "Aaah!" he sighed as he stopped drinking to take a deep breath. Then he resumed drinking, bracing his body against the shock of each wave as he did. The water was pure bliss. He swallowed and drank and then even swilled his mouth out before drinking some more.

Suddenly his whole wounded buttocks and thigh tightened up in painful spasms. As the cramp wracked him Andrew did his best to ignore it. Fear of thirst overcame the pain and he kept on drinking, his whole body shuddering with the effort.

I can't go on much longer, he told himself, even as tears began to form in his eyes. He now rinsed them and was able to think more rationally as the cramps eased.

But now he was in no doubt that the rain was easing. The flow off the rubber became a tiny trickle but he kept holding the wetsuit up, even though his arm muscles were beginning to shake and protest at the exertion.

Keep drinking, he told himself. *You do not know when you will get some more.*

Finally, the muscles in his arms began to cramp and with a shudder he lowered them. By then the rain had eased to just a few tiny spits. Andrew hoped he had drunk enough to survive on but also feared it might not have been enough. Draping the wetsuit over his shoulder he looked around. Carmen did likewise.

"The moon," Andrew said, pointing to where a moonbeam had broken through the clouds to light a patch of wild sea to the east.

"The wind is dropping fast," Carmen added.

She was right. Andrew realized that the wind was now just a light breeze. The drizzle stopped completely, and Andrew began to shiver. He pulled the wetsuit around his front to shield his chest from the wind.

The fitful moonbeams vanished again as more dark clouds rolled overhead. Andrew hoped they were bringing more rain but they did not. He stood there on trembling legs, his whole back, right thigh and buttock one great throbbing ache and all he could do was hold onto Carmen to stay upright.

The wind died completely and with it the waves. They went down so fast that Andrew was astonished. In their place were the longer ocean swells that still sent mounds of water swilling across the sand cay thigh deep. Each one was so powerful that Andrew knew he would have been washed away if he had not had his right foot anchored and his arm linked through Carmen's.

"This is better," he said, then instantly wondered if it was as something big suddenly disturbed the surface twenty metres away.

Andrew's heart leapt into his mouth and he strained his eyes in the gloom to try to see what was causing the commotion. The foam subsided but not his heart rate and he kept looking in all directions. His imagination took over, pictures of sharks speeding in with jaws agape and rows of deadly teeth ready to rip his flesh.

The sea calmed and became almost flat, just moving up and down with each long swell. The current of each of these was strong enough to make Andrew and Carmen brace hard but it rarely reached their waists. Most waves were now only knee deep. But there was still no sign of any dry land. All that was visible was a sort of undulating dark grey sea under a thick, woolly blanket of dark grey and black cloud.

For Andrew the nightmare remained. His mind still conjured up fears of monsters of the deep and he found he was gulping air and almost hyperventilating.

Calm down! he told himself. *You don't want your sister to think you are a coward.*

With an effort of will he calmed his breathing and forced himself to relax. He sighed and let his heart rate slow down.

Then something slimy and large touched his leg and there was a flurry of water near him. He sprang up and let out a yelp in fear. But the loop in the rope brought him to a jerking halt that almost unbalanced him. He floundered as he tried to keep his balance while jumping up and down.

"What is it?" Carmen cried in alarm.

"Something in the water," Andrew replied. It was all he could do not to start sobbing in terror.

This is exactly like all my worst nightmares! he thought.

Suddenly a big fish jumped and landed with a splash about twenty metres behind him. It caused him such a fright he again winced and gibbered with fear for a few seconds.

Carmen held him. "It's alright Andrew. Calm down. It was only a fish."

"A big fish," Andrew replied, bitter with fear and shame. "And that means something even bigger is chasing it."

"We will be alright. It is past the top of the tide. The water is going down," Carmen said.

After checking his watch and finding it was almost midnight Andrew's rational mind told him that must be so. But it was small comfort as he stood there up to his thighs in the swirling, moving water.

But bit by bit things did get better. First the solid cloud cover slid away to the west leaving a mottled pattern of smaller cumulus clouds in its trail. The moon shone through the gaps with increasing brightness so that he could at least see more clearly. Then he noted that very few of the swells were reaching even thigh deep. Within half an hour they were rarely reaching his knees.

Once again, the wind picked up to a gentle breeze and that made him aware he was getting cold. He also had the urgent need to pee but did not want to offend his sister. After a while he began to shiver.

Should I put my wetsuit back on? he wondered.

He was still hoping for more rain but a study of the small clouds caused him to think there wasn't much chance.

Then something nibbled at his foot, sending him jumping with a cry of fright.

"What?" Carmen asked anxiously.

"Something just nibbled at my toes," Andrew answered as he danced noisily in the water.

Carmen snorted. "Huh! Just a little fish probably. And now it will be ill, poor thing!" she said.

"Very funny!" Andrew retorted. But a spurt of shame calmed him and he stopped moving.

Splashing attracts the predators, he reminded himself.

A few minutes later another swirl in the water about ten metres to his right caused his heart to jump in alarm. To his dismay the disturbance came again after a minute or so. Then it happened a third time before he noted the pattern. Suddenly the meaning clicked, and he let out a huge sigh of relief.

It is the tide going out, he thought.

"What now?" Carmen queried.

"The water level has dropped so that the sand is starting to show," Andrew replied. He pointed to where the ripples and small swirl of foam showed again. The knowledge that the worst was over was such a relief that a huge shudder went through him. Then he began to shiver.

"Are you cold?" Carmen asked.

"A bit."

"We could put our wetsuits back on," Carmen suggested.

Andrew shook his head. "No. It is better to shiver than to sweat. Besides, there might be more rain and I don't want to waste time getting the damn thing off again. It was hard enough last time."

"It was a bit of a drama!" Carmen replied with a chuckle.

Andrew noted that the water was now only ankle deep and that it was starting to swirl and drag at the sand all round where they stood.

Won't be long now, he thought. *That means about twelve hours reprieve before the next high tide. Maybe we will be rescued before then.* And with that the awful gnawing fear of having to endure another night like that rose up to choke at him. *The next tide is higher. We won't survive that,* he thought.

Ten minutes later he noted the first small patch of dry land. Twenty metres away a small area of sand was exposed and remained uncovered, even as each swell swilled up. Then more and more of the sand cay showed as the tide ebbed. Almost minute by minute the area of safety grew larger. For a few minutes water still washed over Andrew's feet and then he saw that he was standing on wet sand that the water was no longer reaching.

Safe! he thought. He realized he was shaking and his muscles cramping and it took an effort to bend and slip his foot clear of the loop in the rope.

"Just as well we had that anchor," he commented as he spread his wetsuit on the exposed sand.

"Yes. We would have been washed away for sure without it," Carmen agreed.

She copied his actions. Andrew tugged the swim fins from his belt and placed them down. With a groan of pain in response to his throbbing wound and cramping muscles, he lowered himself to a sitting position. Then he lay back, shivering and panting as though he had run a race.

For a few more minutes Andrew lay there, staring up at the small clouds drifting by in the moonlight. He noted that the sea had now receded so that almost the whole cay was exposed. Satisfied that no sea creature or rogue wave was going to get him he eased and massaged his cramped muscles and then closed his eyes to rest.

All too soon the gentle breeze began to chill him. He pulled the sleeves of the wetsuit over his body and chest, then swore as that put sand on his bare skin. A few minutes later both urgent need and modesty forced him to move. He struggled to his feet.

"Going to the toilet," he explained, in response to Carmen's query. Limping and groaning he took himself the fifty metres to the far end of the sand cay and there relieved himself.

While he did he studied the moon dappled ocean and wondered how they were going to survive. *If a plane or ship doesn't come along this is going to be pretty grim,* he thought.

Feeling more anxious than he cared to admit Andrew hobbled painfully back to re-join Carmen.

She watched him and said, "How is your wound?"

"Sore," Andrew admitted.

"I will look at it in daylight," she said. "Now let's try to get some sleep. We won't be able to once the sun comes up."

Andrew nodded. With a groan he lowered himself onto his wetsuit again. For a minute or so he massaged his aching thigh muscle and right buttock. As he did his eyes scanned the horizon for any sign of a vessel. In doing so he was just as anxious to detect any returning enemy as to spot possible rescue.

How will we know who is on any boat that does come along? he wondered.

With a horrible feeling of apprehension, he realized they would not know but would have to signal for help unless it was obviously the smuggler's launch.

Brooding on the events of the day before and on what the future might hold Andrew lay back and tried to relax. Once again he pulled the arms of the wetsuit over him. Then he closed his eyes and steadied his breathing.

Get some sleep while you can, he told himself.

And he did.

Chapter 10

DESPERATE DECISION

With difficulty Andrew opened gummy eyes and blinked in the sunlight. For a few seconds he lay there looking up, wondering where he was. Then the horrific events of the previous day and the terrors of the night flooded in to make him sit up with a jerk. Anxiously he looked in all directions to check that the murderers had not returned.

To his relief there was no sign of any vessels on the horizon—only the two tiny specks that were the wrecks on distant Longbow Reef. Andrew picked the dry sleep from his eye lids and began to rub at his eyes until he realized they were gritty and sore. Gingerly he eased the sore eyelids open and tried to make his eyes water. But no tears came and he bit his lip with anxiety. That reminded him that lack of drinking water was their number one problem.

Licking his lips with a tongue that felt puffy showed Andrew how dry and cracked they were and he realized he was already thirsty.

I thought I drank plenty last night, he told himself. But as he struggled to his feet he supposed that the wind and sun had both dried him out and that perhaps he hadn't drunk as much as he thought.

Carmen was lying beside him still asleep, her head pillowed on the partly inflated BCD. She looked drawn and pale and was making little snuffling noises and twitching.

Bad dreams probably, Andrew thought.

He vaguely understood that the horrific sights and events of the previous day could mentally scar and unbalance a person for life.

I hope she is going to be alright, he thought. Then it occurred to him that first she had to survive. *We must get out of this alive,* he thought. *Then we can worry about psychological trauma.*

Needing to relieve himself Andrew turned and started walking. Immediately he was assailed by sharp pains in his right thigh and buttocks and by aches in most of his muscles. For a minute or two he could only stand on shaky, trembling legs while he massaged and eased the sore muscles. Then he hobbled away to the other end of the cay.

Now the tide was right out. The Challenger Channel and reef stood out clearly and all of the reefs beyond it to Prescott Island. Noting the tiny square of the stone building Andrew shook his head.

We need to get there. It never goes under, even on the highest tide, and there are things there we can use, he thought. It was also the most likely place for searchers to start.

His watch told him it was already 0715. The sun had been up for an hour or so. As he limped back to where Carmen could now be seen sitting up Andrew studied the sky. He was hoping for more rain but there was hardly a cloud in the sky. Shaking his head with concern he tried to remember the weather forecast. But all he was sure of that there was going to be mostly good weather.

April is the end of the 'Wet Season' in North Queensland, he reminded himself. *But we need drinking water today or we are in real trouble.*

Carmen stretched and stood up. "Good morning little brother. How are you today?" she asked.

"Bit sore," Andrew admitted.

"Let me see that wound of yours," Carmen said.

Andrew blushed with embarrassment but then turned and allowed her to look. Carmen bent and placed her fingers near the exit wound in his right thigh.

"That looks a bit puffy and weepy," she said. "But it has closed up and isn't bleeding. Now let me see the entry wound."

"Aw, it is alright!" Andrew protested, embarrassed at the idea of his sister seeing his bare behind.

"Oh piffle! Pull your bathers down so I can look," Carmen said.

"But!"

"But nothing! How many times have I seen your bare bum?"

Andrew blushed and carefully tugged the back of his bathers down until Carmen could study the wound. She pressed and probed around it. "Does that hurt?" she asked.

"Not really. Just a bit of an ache inside," Andrew answered.

"Only a bit of puss. I think the salt water has saved you from infection. But we still need to be careful and to keep it clean," she said.

Andrew pulled his bathers back up, uncomfortably aware that the sun was again burning his dry skin. Already it felt too tight for his body and the surface had a slightly gritty feel from all the dried salt.

He said, "We need to get drinking water."

Carmen nodded. "I know. But if it doesn't rain we can't get any. And we don't have the stores to make a solar still or anything like that," she said.

"Do you think if we dug a well in the sand at low tide we might get some water?" he asked.

Carmen shook her head emphatically. "No chance! Any water in the sand will be brackish. It is vital we do not drink any salty water, or we may as well just drown ourselves now to save the agony."

Andrew pointed to the distant stone building. "Then I reckon we need to make our way to Prescott Island. There might be some water there. And even if there isn't there will be things among our stores that we can use to make a still or a solar still."

Carmen studied the distant island. "I agree. But it is a long swim. We will have to cross the Challenger Channel."

Andrew knew that and was terrified at the prospect. The notion embodied all his deepest fears of being in deep water where the monster sharks prowled. But he also knew they could not stay where they were. "I know," he answered. "But we can't stay here. There is no water. No-one is liable to come looking for us here. And the Coastwatch planes appear to track directly over Prescott Island so we have a better chance of attracting their attention. Also, any ship or boat coming in through the Challenger Channel is going to look at the stone house for sure."

Carmen looked thoughtful and nodded. "You are right. There is also the point that if we stay here we die when the tide comes in tonight. We will not survive a second night like that and tonight's tide is supposed to be something like twenty centimetres higher. That will just wash us away."

As flashbacks to the previous night crowded Andrew's brain he shuddered and could only agree. He then looked at the deep blue water of the Challenger Channel and the lines of distant reefs and tried to pick out the best route. He tried to visualize the chart to sort out distances and bearings.

"Prescott Island is about five kilometres away in a direct line," he commented.

The thought of cold-bloodedly trying to swim that distance in the open sea sent chills of fear through him. From experience he knew that swimming even a few hundred metres was tiring. His stomach churned just at the thought of being so far away from any sort of safety if a shark appeared.

Not that I will see it before it attacks, he thought gloomily. *It will just strike from under water with no warning, ripping off a leg or disembowelling me.*

His already heated imagination instantly conjured up memories of Max's torn and bleeding stump when he had helped rescue him the previous year. Grisly images of torn flesh, spurting blood, sinews and ligaments wrenched and cut all made the bile rise in his belly.

Carmen nodded. "Four or five. But we will have to swim around via the reefs. That will add a kilometre or so," she said.

"Why?" Andrew asked.

"Because low down in the water we will have trouble seeing that stone hut until we are only a couple of kilometres from it. We could get confused and waste time and energy going the wrong way. We will need to have a visual reference," Carmen explained.

Andrew understood that and was happy. Staying close to even that sort of 'dry land' was an attractive idea to him. "We can get out and stand on the reef to check where we are too," he suggested.

"Yes. But our other problem will be currents," Carmen added.

"Should we start now or wait for the tide to come in?" Andrew asked.

"I think we should start as soon as we can. Standing here is not going to help us. We will just dehydrate and sunburn and the longer we wait the weaker we get from lack of food," Carmen said.

"I can only agree with that." Andrew already felt weak and light headed, and from time to time his empty stomach growled and churned.

Carmen pointed north. "We can walk on the reef to the edge of the Challenger Channel. That will cut down the time we are in the water."

Andrew liked that idea. The Challenger Channel was about a kilometre wide and he was dreading the thought of swimming it. 'Shark Alley' one of the university people had called it.

Was that Tristan? Andrew wondered.

Then shocking images of Tristan's death and of his body sprawled in the rubber dinghy caused him to shudder and feel both nauseous and terrified.

It was nearly ten o'clock by then and Andrew was feeling the effects of the sun. It blazed down with tropical intensity. He could feel the heat burning his skin anew and it was making him sweat. Already his tongue felt swollen and rough and he was starting to resist the continual temptation to lick his cracked and split lips.

Andrew gestured to their diving gear. "We had better get dressed and get going then," he said.

Carmen agreed and they both picked up their wetsuits and carried them down to the shallows to rinse the sand off and to cool them down. Standing in the shallow water to wash sand off their feet they pulled the suits on. Even before he had his arms in the sleeves Andrew had begun to sweat. "This is going to be a bit unpleasant," he commented.

"We will lie in the water to cool down from time to time," Carmen replied. She began tying the orange rope around her waist.

"You wear the BCD and I will wear the swim fins," Andrew said.

Staying afloat is going to be our greatest problem, he thought. He buckled on his weight belt and bent to pick up the swim fins.

Carmen did not argue. She pulled on the partly inflated BCD but left it undone to allow the breeze to cool her upper body. "Got everything? OK, let's go," she said.

Andrew looked carefully at where they had been resting to ensure nothing was left behind. Then he cast a last long look around the horizon before following Carmen along the sand cay. She paddled in the shallows or walked on the damp sand. That made for easy walking, although Andrew found himself limping from his wound and sore muscles.

I hope I don't get a cramp in mid-channel, he worried.

For a few moments they stood at the northern end of the cay and studied the route. Being a very low tide, the whole reef was dry, standing half a metre or more out of the sea. Beyond the coral was the dark blue of the Challenger Channel and just looking at it made Andrew's stomach churn with apprehension. The swirl of a westward flowing current showed that the tide was strongly on the make. Seeing those tell-take swirls added to Andrew's anxiety.

If we aren't careful we could get washed away, he thought. The knowledge that there were no more reefs in that direction, just a hundred kilometres of open sea, made him swallow with fear. *When Graham and I were down in the sea we were only twenty kilometres from the coast and could even see the mountains,* he remembered. That had given them the hope they would eventually wash ashore and be safe—if they did not die from exposure first.

No chance of reaching land here, Andrew ruminated. *Even though the sea temperature is about twenty degrees we will be losing body heat all the time.* That made him grimace and remember stories he had read about men ending up in the sea during the great Atlantic convoy battles of World War 2. *Five minutes before the cold killed them on the convoys to Russia!* he thought.

Andrew and his sister scanned the horizon hopefully but there was still no sign of any rescue. Carmen shrugged and said, "Oh well, let's get it over with."

She walked forward, and almost at once came to a stop. "Ouch! Oh blast! This might be difficult," she said.

"Why?"

"I've already scratched my foot on the coral," Carmen replied.

That was bad news. Andrew tentatively touched the coral with his toe and immediately drew it back. He had forgotten just how hard and rough many corals were.

"We can't walk on that in bare feet," he said.

Lifting his gaze he studied the hundreds of metres of exposed coral between the cay and the deep water, searching for sandy shallows free of coral. To his dismay there were almost none. Worse still most of the coral was either large plate corals, which were hard, or the even sharper staghorn type. There were very few brain corals.

Carmen bit her lip then said, "I don't think we can safely do this. The coral will cut our feet to ribbons. That will lead to infection at least. And some corals are poisonous. We could end up in real trouble."

"There will be other poisonous sea creatures too," Andrew added. "Stonefish, sting rays, cone fish and others that could be the death of us."

"Even sea urchin spines will be enough to cripple us," Carmen added unhappily. Then she said something that sent Andrew's anxiety level shooting right up. "And I don't fancy swimming in the sea with bleeding feet. That could attract some unwelcome attention."

With images of sharks crowding his mind Andrew swallowed and nodded. "My oath!" he agreed.

Carmen made some sucking noises and shook her head. "I think we have to wait until the tide is in enough for us to swim out to the deeper water," she said.

Andrew nodded. "I agree," he answered, relieved that the ordeal was being postponed.

Maybe we will be rescued before we have to swim for it? he thought hopefully, again scanning the horizon.

So they sat on the sand, choosing the damp area just up from the wave level as cooler than the dry sand. That was now baking hot and unpleasant to walk on with bare feet. And it was not only the sand that was hot. So was the air. There was almost no breeze and the sun blazed down from a cloudless sky. Andrew and Carmen both took off their wetsuits again and draped them over themselves in an attempt to get some shade.

But Andrew knew he was sweating and dehydrating. His lips hurt, his sunburnt skin tingled and the glare of the sunlight reflecting off the sea hurt his eyes. Closing them gave some relief, but once again he did not seem to have enough moisture in his body to lubricate his eyelids, so his eyes quickly became scratchy and sore again. A glance at Carmen showed him that the whites of her eyes were bloodshot and red-rimmed.

I suppose I look the same, he brooded.

Once again, he licked his lips and tried to swallow. He was very thirsty and that scared him as he knew that was what would be the most likely to kill them. He got even more of a scare when he went to relieve himself. Not only did it sting to pee, but his urine was a dark yellow.

That is a very bad sign, he thought. It meant that his body was struggling to purge itself of toxic waste. *We must get a drink soon or we are in real trouble.*

But a look around the sky gave no hope. There was still no sign of any clouds. The only relief was a slight increase in the wind. A gentle breeze had sprung up from the Southeast.

As he limped back to re-join Carmen, Andrew noted that the tide was coming in. It had risen quite rapidly and was now lapping over the outer edge of the reef. When he sat down he pointed this out to Carmen.

She nodded and said, "I've been watching it. High tide is about midday and it's ten past eleven now. We need to get going as soon as the water is deep enough for us to dog paddle in."

Andrew croaked a reply and then looked around the horizon yet again. Still no sign of anything.

No sign of any aircraft either, he thought. He had been hoping to see or at least hear one of the Coastwatch planes but so far there had been nothing. *They don't fly the same route every day,* he reminded himself. Regular patrols would be too easy to note and avoid.

Fifteen minutes later almost the whole reef had a shallow covering of water. The larger outcrops of coral still remained exposed and Andrew remembered using them for cover the previous day when he had swum out to look for the submarine. He shifted his study to the sea. The current in the Challenger Channel was still obvious and still flowing to the west but not as strongly.

We need to get across there during slack water, Andrew thought.

The sea was almost flat calm, which was a good thing. *Swimming in waves is no fun,* he remembered.

Then he wished he hadn't, as a series of frightening flashbacks to previous incidents left him shivering and fervently hoping he would not have to enter that water.

If only a boat would come along! he thought.

Once again, he scanned the horizon. The only change he could detect were a few high-level clouds way out to the east and a slight increase in the breeze. There was no sign of rain clouds.

Carmen then sent his heart rate shooting up by saying, "Twenty to twelve. We had better suit up and get moving. I don't think the water will get much higher."

"It won't," Andrew commented bitterly.

The day tide was, he knew, nearly two metres lower than the night tide at that time of the month. Reluctantly he stood and began to pull on the wetsuit. As before they wet the suits to cool them and washed the sand off their feet before pulling the legs on. Within five minutes they were dressed.

Carmen held out the BCD. "You wear this."

Andrew shook his head. "No. You. I will have the swim fins. That is fair. You keep us afloat and I will propel us."

"Are you up to that?"

"For a while. We can always take turns and swap," Andrew replied.

Carmen held up the end of her yellow rope. "Once we are in the deep water at the edge of the reef I will tie us together. There is no way we are getting separated."

"I agree," Andrew replied. Through his mind ran the old adage: 'Reduce the danger of shark attack by 50%—swim with a friend'. That was followed by a flush of shame and he shook his head.

I would rather I got eaten and Carmen was safe, he told himself.

Then he stood and looked at that sparkling blue water. To him it was a place to avoid if at all possible and he really did not want to go there.

I am really scared, he admitted. But his rational mind told him that they had to cross that water to survive.

With a sigh he said, "Let's go. We had better get on with it."

Chapter 11

DEEPEST FEARS

A ndrew took a deep breath, clutched his swim fins tight, then stepped into the water. Within five paces he had to slow and then sit to pull on his fins.

If I try to put these on out in the deep water and drop one I will never get it back, he thought.

By the time he had done this Carmen was pulling herself slowly forward over the coral. The water was so shallow that her wetsuit kept scratching on it, but it was much easier and safer than trying to walk. Andrew took off his facemask, spat in it, rinsed it and pulled it on. Then he rolled over onto his front and set off after her. Before moving each time, he looked carefully and was very cautious about what he touched with his hands. The last thing he wanted was cut and bleeding hands. The ability to see clearly with the facemask made him glad he had it but he still disliked intensely the restricted vision, particularly when he lifted his head out of the water to look around.

Breathing was also easier for him as he had the snorkel attached to the strap of the facemask. The rasping, dribbly sounds it made when he sucked air in irritated him, but he knew it was better than getting a mouthful of salt water. He quickly discovered that his elbows, knees and fins were making the most contact, but the wetsuit protected them from scratches. Because he could see more clearly Andrew found he kept closing up on Carmen's feet.

Lifting his head and taking his snorkel out of his mouth Andrew called, "Car, I will go first. I can see better."

As he said this a small wave slapped into his face and he got some seawater in his mouth. It tasted incredibly salty and set him spluttering and coughing.

I must avoid that, he thought, anxious that there not be a salt build up in his body.

So he replaced the mouthpiece, put his head down and continued crawling and dragging himself across the reef.

From time to time Andrew lifted his head and looked back at the sand cay to keep direction. He was aiming for the closest deep water, which was on the eastern side near where he had entered the water when he went to look for the submarine. From there they would have to swim northwards along the edge of the reef but that was obviously an easier option.

For some of the distance they were able to swim but for most of the hundred metres the water was too shallow, so they had to very gingerly creep along. Both were very careful to avoid stepping or kneeling on coral that was obviously brittle or sharp and sometimes they dragged themselves. Luckily, they saw no dangerous sea creatures. Andrew kept a very good lookout for them, particularly as his hands and face were only a few centimetres from the coral most of the time. Stonefish and blue ringed octopi were his main worries, but he also kept an eye out for cone shells and the like. He saw many attractive little fish and lots of starfish of various species and sizes but had no interest in them. Even a small seahorse that would normally have fascinated him he just noted and then ignored. There were also dozens of clam shells, most quite small, but all with sharp edges that could cut so he carefully avoided them and warned Carmen.

Because they took it so slowly it took nearly twenty minutes to reach the edge of the reef. As they approached it Andrew noted that small waves were breaking on the coral and it was a bit tricky to cross the last ten metres and avoid being dumped by the surge or dragged on the coral by the undertow. In this they were not completely successful, and Andrew got a cut right hand and his wetsuit was torn over his right knee.

As he swam out over the edge of the reef into deeper water Andrew sighed with relief. *Thank God that's over!* he thought.

Then he made a wry face as he contemplated the fact that normally he hated getting into the deeper water. And he still did. The moment he thought about it his fears of sharks and other monsters came flooding in and he looked anxiously around.

But the water was clear of any fish at all. All that was visible was clean white sand ten or fifteen metres down, shading off into the distance and dotted here and there with odd clumps of coral or seaweed. Carmen swam out to join Andrew and they bobbed in the waves a few metres clear of the nearest coral.

Carmen held up her orange rope. "We must tie ourselves together," she said.

Andrew nodded and moved closer, finning to keep his head out of the water while she tried. But without a mask she could not see properly and several times she swallowed water.

"Let me," he said. Taking the end of the rope from her he put his head under and tied the rope through his weight belt, leaving about two metres of clearance between them.

We can both swim side by side then but can grab each other if we need to, he thought.

When he surfaced he took out his mouthpiece and said, "Ready?"

"Yes," Carmen spluttered.

Andrew saw that she looked quite sickly and pale and she kept coughing to clear the salt. She had the BCD fully inflated so she floated well up and Andrew could only hope it could support both of them if needed.

"I will tow you till I get tired," Andrew said.

He put the mouthpiece back in, and lifted his head well clear of the water to have a good look around to check his direction. That action gave him a real shock. Close to them he could see small patches of foam from the small waves that were breaking on the edge of the reef but he found it hard to spot the sand cay. But that was not all. To his dismay there was no sign at all of Prescott Island and its stone building.

Bloody hell, this might be trickier than I thought, he worried.

To try to spot the island he finned hard to propel himself further up. In this he was unsuccessful, but he did get a glimpse of white breakers which he assumed were on the other side of the Challenger Channel. As he came back down Andrew slid right under, as he knew he must. He took a deep breath before he went under and took the opportunity to look around underwater. But that didn't reassure him. All he saw was the dark blue abyss of the Challenger Channel and the sight sent his anxiety level shooting up.

As he bobbed back up Andrew got another shock. As far as he could see there were waves. *They look bigger than they were,* he thought. But with the facemask on it was hard to tell. It was even harder to judge the wind speed. *But at least the wind and the sun will help us keep direction,* he thought.

Now he was assailed by all his deep-rooted fears and it took real effort of willpower to make himself start swimming into the deep water.

Get it over with! he told himself. *The longer we hang around here the more likely we are for something to come along and even if it doesn't we will quickly run out of energy and get cold.*

So, with a reassuring thumbs-up to Carmen, Andrew began swimming. To begin with he used a breast stroke, but he quickly gave that up as his face seemed to slam into every wave. After about twenty-five metres he changed to a side stroke with his back to the wind and waves. That was easier and Carmen did likewise, swimming just in his lee.

Nearly a kilometre to swim, Andrew thought grimly.

The distance to the next reef was forbidding and he did not know if he had the energy to swim that far. Intellectually he knew it was no great distance.

People swim from England to France and that is about thirty kilometres, he told himself. *And there is a Townsville to Magnetic Island swim that is five or six. We should be able to do it.*

But theory was one thing and reality was another. After only a couple of minutes and what he estimated was perhaps a hundred metres, he had to stop and rest. For Carmen this was easy as she bobbed up and down supported by the BCD but Andrew had to keep finning or cling to his sister. He was very shy about such intimate contact but after another hundred metres of swimming brought him to a panting stop he had to grab her BCD.

Carmen had been slower and that had not helped. The waves tended to pull them both in different directions, dragging one or the other the wrong way. But there was no way Andrew would recommend untying that rope. Already he could see that if they got separated it would be very difficult to get back together.

However, with Andrew's weight added to the BCD, it pushed Carmen down until she was struggling to keep her head clear of the water. To take the weight off her Andrew had to keep finning to push upwards. Even then he was not entirely successful and Carmen several times got water in her mouth or nose. For Andrew it was easier as he kept breathing through the snorkel and the facemask kept his eyes clear of the salt spray. But the facemask did make it very hard to see.

Anxious that they were keeping direction Andrew tried again to fin up for a look. To his consternation he could not see any clear sign of surf on the other reef and when he looked back to where they had come from he had difficulty spotting the sand cay and the foam on the edge of Yule Reef. But there was nothing for it but to keep going as he knew that every second was draining him of energy. Fear took some of it, anxiety about the fact that his legs were dangling down as tempting morsels for passing sharks to bite off; and dread of dying from drowning or exposure. The rest was taken by the cold of the sea and the energy he had to use to swim.

We must get this over quickly, Andrew told himself.

He resumed swimming as strongly as he could. But every stroke was a mental hell. If he put his head into the water all he could see was black nothingness underneath him and that dredged up such phobias of monsters of the deep that his heart was in his mouth with anxiety. He found he was so frightened that he was gasping for air and whimpering.

Stop it you fool! he told himself. *Just focus on keeping direction and swimming. Stop imagining things that might not happen.*

After another couple of minutes, he came to an exhausted standstill and just tried to keep his head well up by treading water. Carmen took hold of his arm to help support him. "Are you alright Andrew?" she called.

Andrew took out his mouthpiece and nodded. "Just puffed. I need a rest," he said. While he panted and tried to allow his heart rate to settle he looked around. But what he saw sent his heart rate shooting up instead. As far as he could see in all directions was nothing but waves—and they looked bigger than before.

Where the hell is Challenger Reef? he wondered, craning his neck and pulling his facemask up to get a better look.

That was a mistake as the facemask almost slipped off and he quickly grabbed it and pulled the strap down around his neck. He knew that losing that facemask would be a major disaster. Blinking to clear his blurred vision of salt spray he looked in the direction he thought the reef should be.

Then a glimpse of white made him look to his left front. As he did he saw a sudden burst of white spray and then a flat black line amid a welter of white foam.

There it is, he thought. It looked a dismayingly long way off and the angle puzzled him. *It should be straight in front of us but it isn't,* he thought.

The reason burst in his brain like a breaker on rocks, again sending his heart rate shooting up. *We are being carried away by a current!*

When he mentioned this to Carmen she nodded. "I think we might have left our move a bit too late," she said.

Andrew looked at his watch and saw with a shock that it was ten to one. *We have been in the water nearly three quarters of an hour,* he noted. *We needed to be at the channel at the very top of the tide to cross during slack water.* But how long did that last? Andrew got the sickening suspicion that it might not have been very long at all. *The current must have reversed itself within minutes.*

"We're in trouble here, sis. We need to really swim," he said.

Carmen pointed to the distant line of foam where occasional strips of black were now showing. "If that is Challenger Reef we have a very long swim ahead of us now. We will never swim against this current to reach it. We must just swim across the current."

"The sooner the better," Andrew replied grimly. His mind had just calculated that the current through the Challenger Channel could vary from five knots to seven knots, depending on the tide and the wind.

Five knots is about ten kilometres per hour. We must not get carried that far down the channel, he thought.

Fear spurred him into action. He spat in his face mask, rinsed it and put it on then resumed swimming, aiming north across the current. As he did his mind dwelt on the shape of the reefs as shown on the chart and he knew that at best they would now be swimming into the large semi-circle of water formed by the reefs which led northeast to Prescott Island.

But once again he quickly tired. Worse still his wounded buttock and thigh began to ache and then to cramp. Andrew had to stop and ease the sore muscles and get his breath back. As he did Carmen took hold of him and held him up. Andrew shook his head with concern and looked around again. The sun seemed to be coming from the wrong direction and the wind was on his left cheek instead of his right ear.

Has the wind changed direction? he wondered.

Then he got another shock. As he rose on a wave he got a glimpse of a long reef off to his right and on top of it was a small cay of honey gold sand lit up by the sun.

What reef is that? he wondered. Then the truth struck him with sickening force. *That's Yule Reef!*

For a minute or so all Andrew could do was stare at the distant cay in disbelief. He shook his head and pointed to it. Carmen looked and then also shook her head. Her mouth set in a straight line.

She said, "Yule Reef. We are being pushed off course by currents."

"Some sort of back eddy," Andrew agreed. His mind tried to visualize what the currents might do in the triangle between the Challenger Channel and the Boat Passage. What was certain was that it would not flow in a straight line.

For a minute or so Andrew contemplated giving up and trying to swim back to Yule Reef. But he calculated that it was now at least two or three kilometres away and getting further away every minute.

We have no chance of swimming that distance against the current, he thought. Fear and a sort of sickening dread clutched at his insides and he found himself gasping for breath again.

He looked around and was even more concerned to note that they were entering an area of very broken water. The waves seemed to be coming from every direction and were short and sharp and breaking wildly. They were only small waves, a metre or so in height, but they were enough to make it seriously difficult to breathe.

Andrew was suddenly assailed by cramps and had to cling to Carmen. He found that he could barely keep his head out of the water.

I must not drag Carmen under, he thought as the agony of the cramps seared up his right leg and through his buttocks and lower back. *This is bloody serious,* he thought as he was pushed under by two waves clashing.

Several times Andrew's head went under as waves broke over them. The pattern was so confused and tumbling it was hard to predict which way to move and at times two waves collided, throwing up spray and spume that made it hard to breathe. Then two waves slopped together and then apart, and the force of their undertow broke Andrew's grip and he was torn away from Carmen. The waves sent him tumbling and all he could see were bubbles and dark water. Panic rose to grip his throat and as soon as his head broke surface again he looked wildly around. To his relief Carmen was close by and the sharp tugging at his belt told him the rope still held them.

As quickly as he could Andrew re-joined his sister and they clung together. This time Andrew had to stop finning as his legs were too cramped and tired. All he could do was hold on and gulp air when his head was out of water. Carmen did likewise, gasping and blinking as she tried to anticipate each dunking.

This went on for minutes at a time and all Andrew was aware of was being very scared and fearing they would be wrenched apart and that then he would get cramp and drown. Shaking his head to clear water from his ears he looked around but all he could see was more broken water. But then he noted that the light was different. Everything looked dull and gloomy and just before another wave pushed him under he noted that the sky had come over overcast.

When he came up, gasping and spluttering, Andrew tried to focus his eyes on the cloud. There was now a solid layer from horizon to horizon. This appeared to be moving quickly, rolling and boiling with the wind.

This is really bad news, he thought. *If there is no sun, it will be very hard to keep direction!* That added another layer of anxiety to his fear. *This is worse than my worst nightmare,* he thought. *My deepest fears come true!*

Part of him just wished it would all end and there was even a little corner of his brain that was beginning to suggest that it was hopeless, that he may as well just give up and get it over with. But that sparked awful images of his rotting body drifting in the water and being nibbled and torn apart by fish.

Driven by fear and by his instinct to survive Andrew forced himself to study the situation. First he looked carefully in all directions but there was no sign of any surf, reef, or island. He had no idea where he was in relation to either their start point or their objective and that knowledge chilled him to his core.

We are in trouble alright. I don't even know which way to swim, he thought grimly.

Then he noted that it was indeed completely overcast and that the sun was obscured. In the direction that he and Carmen seemed to be moving he noted darker banks of cloud low on the tumbling, jagged horizon. Even as his mind took this further bad news on board Andrew realized he was able to see a fair distance because he was up higher.

We are on a swell with small wind waves on it, he noted.

And that knowledge introduced another level of shock. A wave like that meant ocean swells.

We must be in the mouth of the channel, he thought. Even as he did

Andrew realized that he and Carmen were being carried along and swirled around by the eddying current. Suddenly a dark, solid object appeared in the edge of his vision. Instantly he focused on it—and got an even worse shock.

Andrew found he was looking at the deck and upper works of a vessel, a vessel that was lying over in the waves. But just as hope began to soar Andrew saw that the vessel was a wreck and that it was lying on its side on a reef.

That's the Taiwanese fishing trawler, he thought.

Catching Carmen's eye Andrew pointed to the trawler. She turned to look. As they rose on another swell Andrew got a clear glimpse of black coral, the edge of a reef. It looked to be only a hundred metres away and the wreck of the trawler not more than much than that. Then his eye caught sight of swirling water and foam marking an obvious current. To his dismay Andrew saw that the wreck was sliding sideways past him at a rapid rate.

That was when the full realization of their peril struck him and with it a surge of pure panic.

We are at the end of the Challenger Channel. That is Longbow Reef! We are being carried out to sea by the current!.

Chapter 12

DESPERATION

Andrew was aghast. A stab of pure panic set his heart hammering. He gulped and stared at the rapidly receding wreck.

We are being swept out into the open ocean! he thought in dismay.

Grabbing Carmen by the shoulder Andrew shook her and pointed. "That is the Taiwanese trawler on Longbow Reef. We are being swept out to sea. We have to get back before we get carried too far out or we are done for."

Carmen looked at the trawler and Andrew saw a look of horror cross her pale, drawn face. He also note that freckles stood out clearly against the paleness of her skin. Then he noted how rapidly they were approaching the trawler.

Bloody hell, this current is fast! We are almost out in the open sea, he thought.

He realized that once they were beyond the Barrier Reef and out in the open ocean they were as good as dead. Spurred by a stab of panic he yelled, "Come on, swim! Swim or we are finished."

Carmen nodded and as they rose on a wave pointed to the southeast. "Don't try to swim against the current. Remember what our instructors said about surviving in rips or flooded streams. Swim with the current diagonally."

Without another word they both began to swim. To start with Andrew used an overarm stroke but he very quickly tired and even more found it intolerable to have his head down in the water with nothing to see but eerie blackness. So he changed to sidestroke and tried to keep the wreck in focus. To his dismay he saw that he and Carmen were already abreast of it and that they were being carried past it at a rapid rate of knots.

Swim! Swim! he told himself.

Summoning up all the energy he could Andrew struck out hard for the edge of the reef. This was now only about fifty metres away, clear and black when not covered by surging foam. Andrew found it very hard to act on the advice not swim straight as the coral looked so close!

But he could not keep it up. The energy just seemed to drain out of him and he had to stop and try to get his breath back. He found he was gasping and spluttering and could hardly see for dancing dots and blurred vision amid the water droplets and condensation. He tried lying on his back and using his fins while he sucked in deep breaths. But his right leg would not work properly and began cramping.

And he was held back by Carmen. Without fins and held more upright by the fully inflated BCD she had been lagging behind, the rope dragging at Andrew. He gave her a hopeful grin to mask his sinking sense of despair and then resumed swimming.

To his horror the black line of coral seemed to be further away than before. *We aren't winning,* he thought. His mind worked out that the problem was not their swimming but the fact that the reef now ended and trended away from them. That thought sent more fear chilling through Andrew. *We have been washed out of the mouth of the channel into the open sea,* he thought.

That was a truly terrifying thought that made him redouble his efforts to swim. He kept it up until he was gasping for breath. Then a splash of water down his snorkel set him retching and coughing. He stopped swimming and trod water while he pulled the snorkel out of his mouth.

Carmen also stopped and looked at him with concern. "You alright?" she shouted.

"Yeah. Just puffed," Andrew spluttered and croaked back.

"I think we have missed it," Carmen added, indicating the reef.

"Let's hope there is a... cough... splutter... back eddy or this is going to be hard," he answered.

Bloody desperate! he thought grimly.

He again took the opportunity of another large wave to look around. His attempt to locate the sun failed, now hidden by solid overcast, but he clearly saw the wrecked trawler was well behind them. He also noted that the whole horizon out to the east was a line of dark rain and cloud.

That will give us a guide, he thought. *But we had better be ashore before that storm arrives or we will completely lose direction.*

As he finished speaking a wave broke over them and Andrew had to hold his breath and came up spluttering and coughing. Carmen also coughed and looked very pale and ill.

"Don't swallow any salt water," she cried.

Andrew could only nod and grab hold of her BCD as another large wave sent them sliding into a trough. The waves were now obviously bigger, at least two metres in height. Worse still the wind was increasing, whipping up the waves and skimming showers of spume off their crests. Then Andrew got another worrying glimpse of the trawler. It now looked to be several hundred metres away and he was looking at it from astern. Lines of surf marked where the bigger waves from the open sea were breaking on the outside edge of the reef.

Andrew now doubted if they would be able to swim if the waves got any bigger. He was also getting scared as he could feel his muscles tiring. It was all he could manage to just tread water to keep his head well up. So he replaced his snorkel mouthpiece and put his head down and began side stroking with his back to the wind. Carmen copied his actions and they resumed their struggle to survive.

Desperation now drove Andrew. *We will get only one shot at this,* he told himself. As he stroked in the rough water he was frequently half-submerged and all he glimpsed under water was blackness.

We are out over the really deep water now, he thought.

Through his mind flitted the facts. Inside the Great Barrier Reef the water was shallow and relatively calm. But almost immediately outside the line of reefs the water depth increased from a few hundred metres to thousands.

That's because the outer reef sits on the edge of the continental shelf, he told himself.

That was all well and good as intellectual knowledge, but the horrifying reality was that he and his sister were now being swept out into the Coral Sea.

We are done for if we can't get onto that reef, he thought.

Knowing that he was now floating over the abyss sent another spasm of terror coursing through Andrew but worry about sharks and so on was quickly pushed aside by the grim knowledge that it was actually drowning or exposure that were his real perils.

But it was both very hard to swim in the large waves and even harder to keep direction. The only guides were the approaching darkness and the lines of white spray. As he rose on each wave Andrew looked to check that he could still see the trawler and each time he was dismayed to note that it was further away.

At least half a kilometre now, he decided. *But we are only a few hundred metres from the edge of the reef.*

Knowing that he was dead if he did not reach that reef he used every ounce of energy to push himself through the water. But at almost every wave the rope tying him to Carmen pulled him back with a sharp jerk as they ended up on different sides of the crest. The rope also tended to pull them under and Andrew found it a struggle to keep his head clear to breathe. But there was no way he was going to undo that rope. In fact his real fear was that it might snap under the strain.

If the rope breaks now we will never get back together, he thought. His mind told him that it would have been much better to have a rope five metres long rather than only two. *That would give us a bit of slack to avoid these horrible jerks,* he thought as another painful tug wrenched at his waist.

But that was trivia compared to how tired his muscles felt. His arms now felt like they were made of lead and it took an effort of willpower to keep them moving. His legs were just numb or throbbing. Fear that another cramp might cripple him at the crucial moment gnawed at him, increasing his apprehension. So frightened did he become that he experienced a sort of panic attack and drove himself into a frenzy, dragging at the water until physical exhaustion brought him again to a gasping, sobbing halt.

For a couple of minutes Andrew clung to Carmen depending on her BCD to keep him afloat while he recovered his breath. As he floated there, chilled and battered by the elements his mind grappled with the ultimate realities of the situation. It quite terrified him to realize that he was in the grip of such powerful natural forces that he was almost powerless to do anything to save himself. *But not completely powerless,* he thought, gritting his teeth and summoning up his last reserves of willpower. With desperate determination he began to swim again.

Once again, the burst of energy only lasted for a minute. He and Carmen slowed to a panting stop. Andrew sucked in deep breaths and made an effort not to get any salt water in his mouth.

I think we made a bit of progress, he thought hopefully, blinking and wiping his facemask to try to see the reef more clearly. He sensed that if he once lost sight of that he was a dead man. *Maybe not today but certainly by tomorrow,* he thought grimly.

Rain and strong wind began to lash at them. Within seconds the visibility dropped dramatically and when he next looked for the trawler Andrew was appalled to note that it was almost invisible and looked to be a kilometre away. The waves rapidly began to mount in height, the only good fact being that the line of bursting surf along the reef edge was still clearly visible. That looked to be still about a hundred metres away.

We must make it! he sobbed.

But he was so worn out that it seemed to take all of his remaining energy just to stay afloat. Bobbing up and down on the waves and struggling to breathe without taking in salt water he felt utterly chilled both by the cold and by fear. Carmen floated with him, holding him to help him stay above water. Her devotion sent a tiny flicker of warm affection through him.

Then two things motivated him to make one more desperate effort. The first was the realization that they were not drifting further from the reef. The second was a glimpse of a black shape amid the bursting showers of foam.

We are out of the main current, he thought. *We have a chance.*

Squinting through the water droplets on the outside of his facemask and the condensation building on the inside Andrew focused on the black object. The moment he did his hopes shot up.

That is the other wreck. If we can reach that we still have a chance, he thought.

He had never seen the wreck close up but had been told that it was that of a 19th Century sailing ship. Having seen one on a reef at Endeavour Island he had some idea of what to expect. This one did not look anything like that. In fact, it did not look like a ship at all. Standing amid the bursting spray was a black shape which appeared to have a dome on top. More odd shapes were just visible beyond it.

To have lasted this long it must be made of iron, not wood, he thought.

As he rose on another wave Andrew stared back in the direction of the trawler. For a few seconds he glimpsed it as a rain squall passed. Then it was hidden from sight again. Swallowing with anxiety Andrew looked around and was appalled. For half the horizon out to the east all he could see was grey curtains of rain under rolling black clouds. The sea was now a maelstrom of churned up foam and racing waves.

Pointing to the black shape of the sailing ship wreck Andrew shouted. "There is the other wreck. It is our only hope. We must get to it."

Carmen looked and for a moment a slight smile lit up her face. Then she nodded and replied. "The *Mull of Kintyre*. You are right. Come on, let's try."

Andrew nodded, took a deep breath and began swimming, this time aiming for the wreck. For a few seconds all went well as he and Carmen slid down the face of an advancing wave. But then they went over the crest at different moments and once again Andrew suffered a painful wrenching at his waist as the rope held him back.

I have to swim slower, he thought. *Carmen can't keep up without flippers.*

But they had made progress. While he waited for Carmen they rose on the next wave and Andrew got a good look in the direction they were going. He saw the black shape of the wreck and at the same time observed a long line of boiling foam as a wave burst on the edge of the reef.

We are actually being moved towards the reef by the wind and the waves, he thought.

Even so he swam with the next wave and then again waited to check. This time, as he rose on the following wave, there was no doubt. Despite the backwash and undertow of each wave their overall movement was closer to the reef. *We might make it yet,* Andrew thought. But he did not voice it, not wanting to get Carmen's hopes up.

As he went up on the wave after that Andrew again studied the reef, now only about seventy-five metres away. This time he was somewhat shocked by the size of the bursting spray as a wave ahead of them crashed onto the coral.

Uh oh! This might be a bit tricky, he thought.

He noted that the waves were now even bigger, estimating their height at between two and three metres. They were certainly big enough to smash down on the coral with quite a vicious crash.

Now that he thought about it Andrew realized he could even hear the thunder of the surf above the shrieking of the wind. It also dawned on him that he and Carmen might not have any choice but be dashed onto the coral by the waves. The idea that they might be badly injured or killed in trying to reach safety occurred to him and he gave a wry smile at the cruel irony of the situation.

We are now at the mercy of the elements, he thought bitterly.

Through his mind flitted a passage from the Journal of Captain Cook. The *Endeavour* had been trying to find a passage through the outer reef but the wind had dropped. The ship had then been pushed inexorably towards the reef by the ocean swells. In the age before powered vessels there was almost nothing the crew could do. Towing with the ship's boats had only slowed the movement. Only a providential change in the tide and wind had saved the ship from being cast up on the reef and wrecked.

There won't be any change of wind or tide in time to stop us from being thrown onto the reef, Andrew thought unhappily.

Now he was thoroughly scared as he watched each succeeding wave crash down in a thunder of spume and gushing water. Images of being shredded and torn to ribbons of bleeding flesh by the sharp and jagged coral filled him with cringing horror.

How can we prevent that? he wondered.

A terrible feeling of helplessness engulfed him as the next wave pushed him forward. Gulping for air he struggled to keep his head clear. But seeing what was coming caused him to swallow with fear.

Andrew noted that they were now within fifty metres of the reef. The wreck was about a hundred to their right front, the current having moved them sideways even as the waves heaved them in. He took out his mouthpiece and turned to Carmen.

"This is going to be bloody dangerous Carmen," he shouted. "If we don't handle this right we could end up drowned or with broken limbs."

Carmen had obviously been thinking the same. She nodded and shouted back, "We need to pick our moment and then surf in. We need to get past the zone where the backwash and undertow are strongest or we will be scraped back across the coral and cut up."

"We need to do this together," Andrew answered grimly.

Even as he said it they rose on another wave and he eyed the boiling, surging water ahead. There appeared to be only two more waves ahead of them and he got a glimpse of a surging, sucking backwash that gushed back through gaps in the coral. The black edge of the reef was now only about twenty-five metres away.

Carmen tapped his arm. "If we untie the rope we will be able to swim better."

Andrew experienced a sudden warm flush of affection.

She means I will have a better chance because I have the swim fins, he thought.

But he shook his head. "No way! We must stay together. I think two more waves and we need to try it," he said.

"You are right. Not this wave. The next. I will say go," Carmen called back.

Andrew nodded and swallowed. Now the trial was upon him he tensed and felt the fear churning in his stomach. Feeling utterly exhausted he finned feebly, hoping desperately that he had enough energy and that he did not get a cramp at the critical moment.

This could really hurt! he thought as the next wave lifted them up and carried them forward.

Down the back of that wave they slid. As they went down Andrew's brain told him that now was the time to start swimming. *We must have speed to catch the front of the next wave,* he thought, anxious lest Carmen misjudge the moment. Fearful he glanced back and saw that wave starting to tower up.

At that moment Carmen began swimming. "Now! Swim!" she shouted.

Andrew did, finning for all he was worth and using every last ounce of energy to stroke with his arms, dragging the water back in a desperate attempt to get forward movement. Despite this they both slithered into the trough in a welter of spray so that all Andrew could see for a moment were towering waves and scudding grey clouds. Then the next wave was upon them.

This it is! he thought.

Chapter 13

BLOOD AND BARNACLES

Andrew swam with the strength of desperation. His whole being was absorbed by the frantic urge to survive. But within seconds the energy seemed to just drain out of him and he was conscious of rising panic, overwhelming tiredness and squirming terror. Then his mind noted that he and Carmen were actually up on the forward slope of the wave. That was good.

We are in the right place and seem to be moving as fast as the wave, he noted.

Survival instinct kicked in. He knew that now was the moment for maximum effort. Spurred by fear he forced his tired muscles back into motion, battling to stay on the front of the wave.

We need to ride it right in and then slide off the back just before it breaks. We don't want to be dumped by it, he told himself.

More spasms of fear made him internally cringe and he mentally braced himself for the shock and pain of being battered on the jagged coral.

Heart in mouth he felt himself get lifted and then he was swooping and rolling forward as the wave struck the edge of the reef and began to break. Another stab of fear shot through him as he realized he could not stop himself and that they were going to be dumped. Ahead of Andrew appeared to be nothing but boiling foam dotted with dark lumps. As he felt himself being rolled right over so that his feet were higher than his head Andrew made a maximum effort. But to his frustration and near despair he was held back at the critical moment by the rope around his waist.

Thump!

Suddenly Andrew was dumped onto the coral, his left buttock hitting something solid very hard. He was completely submerged in rushing, swirling water.

Keep swimming! Keep going! he told himself.

With a last effort he made his legs operate. His hands and arms struck the coral hard and then went numb. Next his elbows and knees made savage contact. The blows were so sudden and sharp that they sent darting pains shooting up his legs and he would have cried out if he had not been struggling to hold his breath as the water tumbled him over.

Then the pressure eased, and Andrew knew this was the next critical moment. The undertow was about to begin, and he did not want to be dragged back across the coral, with skin and wetsuit being scraped and torn off him. So he kept finning as hard as he could, until his right thigh suddenly seized up in a cramp so agonizing he did cry out. The pain caused tears to come to his eyes.

Bugger! he thought.

Panic surged as he tried to work out which way was up amid the bubbles and swirling water. Despite the searing pain he tried to keep moving and as the suction of the backwash pulled at him he felt the coral and knew he must grab it or die. Quickly he reached down and grabbed at the coral, hoping that he would not cut his hands too much. To his relief he found the edge of a large plate coral that felt rough but slimy. He was all too aware that some corals were hosts to deadly poisonous stingers, but no sudden burning sensations came so he thought he might be alright.

Hanging on worked. The water drained back but he and Carmen stayed there. Andrew glanced sideways, conscious of the rope tugging at his waist. Through the spray, drops on the outside of his mask and the condensation on the inside he glimpsed Carmen. She was coughing and spluttering and looked to be having trouble, but he managed to stop her being swept back.

Then the next wave arrived and water swirled around them, pushing them forward again. Andrew took the opportunity to kick off with his left leg. To his relief the cramp eased and he was able to gasp in several deep breaths after clearing his flooded snorkel. This time he was able to control their forward movement and he found himself touching bottom with his knees and fins. Glancing down he saw that the bottom was brain coral and seaweed, so he took the risk and lowered his fins to the sand.

Another wave washed by, pulling and pushing at them but they were just far enough past the surf zone for Andrew to be able to hold his position. He reached over and pulled Carmen to him and she lowered her feet and also got a grip.

Andrew was now gasping for air, so he pulled his snorkel from his mouth and gulped in a few lung fulls. Then he glanced back at the next massive boil of surf as it thundered onto the reef twenty metres back.

"We need to get a bit further away from the surf," he shouted.

Carmen nodded and as the forward flow reached them they both breast-stroked with it into calmer water. Twice the rope snagged but each time they were able to jerk it free or it came free as a wave lifted them. Andrew again found a safe footing and helped Carmen to stand. Then he looked around. Everywhere looked dark and dangerous and the rain was still lashing at them. With his face now fully exposed he realized just how strong the wind was.

And cold! he thought. Then he shivered and knew they could not stay were they were.

We must get out of the water and out of the wind, he told himself. But the only possible refuge was the wreck of the old sailing ship. *We must get to that wreck.* So he braced himself against the surge of the waves and looked around.

To his surprise the wreck towered up closer to him than he had realized. It looked to be only about fifty metres to his right. The thing looked all misshapen and black. It was also larger than he had thought and appeared to be half-smothered in foam and spray. For a few seconds Andrew studied the wreck, puzzling over what he was seeing. Once again, he noted the odd dome shape at what he took to be the stern. Then he saw that it really was the stern and that the shape was actually the edge of the quarter deck.

Or is it the poop deck? he wondered for a second.

The finer design details of 19th Century clippers and barques were not his particular area of nautical interest. He now saw that the entire stern had, at some time in the past, been driven upwards by storm waves so that the last quarter of the ship's length was almost vertical. Andrew realized that what he was looking at was actually the deck, which was now twisted sideways so that it stood straight up.

Or it would have been the deck if the decking was still there, he thought.

Noting that what he was actually looking at were the iron frames and girders to which the deck planks had once been attached.

Forward of that the whole hull was twisted and flattened so that the stern was almost severed from the remainder of the hull. The mid-section was still in place, but the sea had torn off or rusted most of the iron plates that had once formed the outer fabric of the hull. Andrew could see right through the many gaps. It appeared to be held together only by some cross-bracing and hull frames.

But it was the forward section that caught his attention and sent his hopes up. It was undoubtedly the bow. The curves and sheer all showed that. And there was even the stump of a bowsprit protruding from the very beak of the finely raked stem. The bow section looked to be mostly intact and offered some possibility of shelter. Now that he was focused the lines of the forward half of the old ship were obvious to Andrew and he saw it was a classic late 19th Century 'square rigger' design.

She must have sailed right onto the reef at high water to end up like that, Andrew thought.

Then another wave, larger than the others, almost washed him over. The water rose right up and he had to swim to keep his head out. Carmen floated well enough, but the receding wave dumped them hard on some rough coral. Andrew could just feel it through the soles of his rubber swim fins but grimace on Carmen's face suggested she had been hurt.

"You OK?" he asked.

"Just a bit sharp on my feet," Carmen answered. "Let's get to the wreck and see if we can get out of the weather."

"We need to swim or crawl," Andrew replied. He did not want to take his swim fins off and he did not want to lose them. He had a shrewd idea they had been a major factor in them reaching safety. When he saw Carmen nod in reply he at once began swimming, breast stroking and keeping his head clear of the water as much as he could.

Now they were swimming across the wave flow and each one lifted them and carried them to their left and then, as they slid down the back of it, they went to the right. But they were now just clear of the surf zone so breaking waves were not the main problem. Hitting bottom and scraping on the coral happened after every wave and Andrew kept trying to save the palms of his hands from getting cut and punctured. That cost him on the heels of the hands and on his elbows but mostly he managed it. There was also the problem of the rope continually catching on coral but there was no way Andrew would consider untying that, so he just swore and pulled it free each time.

Better still he could now measure their progress against a fixed object. With every stroke they got closer to the wreck. That provided encouragement to keep trying. Carmen stayed with him, puffing and splashing but keeping up. As he got closer to the wreck Andrew was able to note more details of its construction and he saw that it was indeed made of iron. The point he aimed for was the mid-section where gaping holes showed in the plating.

There should be a way in there, he thought. Getting aboard that wreck was now the most important single aim in his tired mind.

Two minutes later, Andrew and Carmen were within a few metres of the wreck. At that range Andrew noted that the iron was all badly rusted and corroded. Worse still large parts of the plating and exposed frames were encrusted with oysters and barnacles. Seaweed and coral also grew along the lower section that was obviously mostly covered by the tides.

Eyeing the clusters of barnacles and oysters Andrew hesitated. *They can just slice my hands open,* he thought.

He came to a standstill within arm's reach, his fins resting on the coral. Carmen joined him. As she reached out to grab a handhold Andrew shook his head and yelled, "Watch out you don't cut yourself."

Carmen pulled her hand back and then shook her head. "Thanks," she croaked. "I didn't think."

Andrew looked both ways and upwards. The rusty sides of the bow—dark brown, almost black—towered up and there was clearly no way to climb it.

We have to go in through one of those gaps, he decided.

That part of the rusted hull was on the edge of the surf and the large waves were almost sweeping them off their feet. *The quicker we do this the better,* Andrew thought.

After coiling most of the rope into his left hand he motioned to Carmen and began swimming along the side of the hull, keeping well clear so that a wave did not scrape them both back along the thick crust of barnacles.

Andrew reached a place where there was a gap that was large enough. It had rough, rusty edges and a beam or frame halfway across but by now he was getting very worried that he might collapse before he could get to safety.

Anxious to get inside he pointed to the hole and said, "You go first. I can swim better with my fins."

Carmen wanted to protest but a bursting wave showered them both with spray and almost swept them away. Andrew grabbed Carmen's arm and pushed her towards the hole.

"Hurry!" he croaked.

To his relief she grabbed the edges of the rusty plates, taking care to avoid the oysters and then she waited till the slack between waves before sticking her right leg in. Lifting herself with her arms she hung on as the next wave washed by. Then she gingerly lowered her foot into the flooded interior and felt around to get a safe and firm footing. Another wave came and nearly dragged her away. The wave was so large that Andrew was washed off his fins and swept sideways. The rope saved him, swinging him round to slam against the side of the hull, or against the barnacles which were thick at the main tide level. For a few seconds he felt the rubber suit splitting and then several sharp pains told him that he had been cut.

Bugger! he thought as he struggled to get a grip on the edge of the hole.

Carmen grabbed at him and held him till the wave had passed. Then she lifted herself and swung her other leg inside. Seeing that caused Andrew to almost sigh with relief.

At least she is safe! he thought.

Then he saw another big wave coming and looked for a safe place to grab the rusty plates. He was just in time before the water hit him. The wave was so big that he went right under. The rush of water was so strong that his fingers were wrenched off the rusty iron. Stinging sensations told Andrew that in the process several of them must have been cut.

The rope stopped him and the rush of water tumbled him against the rough sides of the wreck. He put out his hand to steady himself and felt another sharp sting. Then the pressure eased and he got his head out of water. The rope was now tight around his waist and he felt as though he was being pulled in two. He saw Carmen's anxious face at the hole and as he struggled to regain his balance he noted that she was straining to keep hold.

If this rope breaks or gets cut I could be washed away, he told himself.

Fear gave Andrew strength and he kicked and squirmed to stay upright and to regain his balance. As soon as he had his balance he reached up to the cross girder and lifted himself to get his legs inside. In doing this he forgot about his fins and they caught and stopped him. Worse still his right leg did not want to function and dragged. He had to lower himself back, hang on through another wave (luckily not as large) and then lift his left leg to get it in. Then he hoisted himself up to try to get his stiff and useless right leg inside.

The sight of another huge wave curling over and breaking motivated Andrew to move faster. With a heave he swung and dragged the injured leg inside. Carmen grabbed him and held him from falling flat on his back. He was just in time as spray deluged them and the water level inside the wreck rose to their chests. But the wave had no real force inside the hull and Andrew sighed with relief.

Made it! he thought.

An immediate impression of calm and relative peace swept through him. Just to be out of the wind and crashing waves! All he wanted to do was flop down. But the inside of the wreck was waist to chest deep in moving water and he groaned as he realized that more effort was required.

We need to find a place clear of the water, he thought.

Looking around he saw that the sensation of peace and calm was relative and illusory. Compared to outside the shattered hull it was but he now saw that there were so many holes in the hull that water poured in and swilled around with every wave. Worse still the wind blew almost straight in from astern and with it came showers of spray as each big wave slammed into the broken stern.

As his fins were now flat on the bottom inside the wreck and it felt rough but not too sharp Andrew took a firm grip on a rusty girder that did not have any barnacles on it. Then he looked around to study the possibilities.

His first impression was of darkness and size. He noted that the deck was completely gone and only the rusty cross beams remained. Many of these were buckled or broken. The internal decks and bulkheads were all gone.

Must have been made of wood, he surmised.

The bent-up stern towered over them, half-hidden in driving rain and spray. The flattened section of the hull with its rusty plates and twisted beams offered no sanctuary. Worse still it allowed the wind to howl directly in to where he and Carmen stood.

Nor did the mid-section they were in offer any shelter as most of the side plating was missing. However, the bow section looked to be mostly intact. But it was so dark it was hard to make out any details. To his considerable surprise Andrew saw that one of the masts lay in the hull, angling up to rest across the port side of the focsle. The diameter of the mast was at least half a metre, certainly bigger than Andrew could get his arms around. The reddish coating showing under the crusting of barnacles and weed indicated it was made of rolled iron.

"That way," Andrew said, pointing forward.

Carmen nodded but pointed to his right hand. "You've cut yourself."

Andrew knew that but now he looked and felt real stab of concern. Bright red blood was flowing freely over his hand and down his arm. He quickly rinsed the hand in the water and studied the wound more carefully at it. To his dismay he saw that the cut was about two centimetres long and looked to be quite deep.

I hope I haven't cut anything important, he worried, not wanting to be crippled if he lived and suspecting that he might need that hand functioning properly if he was to survive at all.

There is nothing we can do about it now, he thought. There were no bandages and he needed a dry place. *We need shelter, and fast,* he thought.

As he studied the hand he noted that the skin was very wrinkled from being in the water too long and even in the gloom the skin appeared to have a bluish hue.

Moving very slowly, both to keep his balance and to walk in the flippers, Andrew headed for the bow. Each step he took slowly, lifting the long swim fin forward before carefully testing the bottom to check that he wasn't going to step on a sharp object. Fear of stepping on a sea urchin spine or stonefish kept his movements very slow. There was also the problem of having to use one or both hands to lift his right leg by getting them behind the cramped up and aching thigh.

It took them nearly five minutes to move the twenty metres to the bow section. As they got closer the effect of the wind eased and it became darker as this section was mostly intact. Andrew was hoping to find some sort of compartment or even a section of deck but there was none.

If there was a bulkhead it was made of wood and has rotted, he thought.

Right up near the stem he climbed carefully around the rusting remains of uprights and cross beams that might once have been a bulkhead. Now he was in under what had been the focsle but a glance upwards showed nothing but the iron deck beams and the rain soaked sky. Just forward of the remains of the bulkhead was a jumble of coral encrusted and rusty machinery.

A winch or capstan, Andrew thought. *And that is an anchor chain.*

Coming in on his right through a hole in the upper hull plating was a very rusty chain. It hung down and ended in a large pile of chain that was heaped right in the bows.

This was the chain locker, he decided.

The heap of rusty chain was just above the level of the waves and a line of barnacles and oysters showed that the top of the pile was normally above the level of the tide. The links were each about thirty centimetres long and about five centimetres thick. The heap of chain was only a small 'dry' area but it looked to be all there was.

Bloody hell! This isn't much, Andrew thought unhappily. But he knew it would have to do temporarily. *We must get up out of the water and get warm,* he told himself.

Already he was shivering violently, and he knew that was the beginnings of hyperthermia as much as the result of overexertion. He tried to climb up but found he could not do it in his swim fins. Leaning on the rusty side plates he pulled off first one fin and then another. These were tossed up onto the pile of chain. Then Andrew began to gingerly crawl up onto the heap. This was difficult as the chain was so covered by barnacles and coral that he had to be very careful where he put his feet or hands and before he had climbed out of the water and above the tide level he had cut himself several more times in his feet, knees and hands.

On reaching the top of the pile, right against the large upright he guessed was the stem piece, Andrew turned to help Carmen. She climbed slowly up behind him and after a minute or so of careful work also got herself up out of the water. Thankfully Andrew helped her to the most sheltered corner.

"Thank God for that! Safe for the moment," he said. He looked around and began to lower himself to a corner where he hoped he would be both above the water level at high tide and out of most of the wind.

But Carmen reached across and stopped him. "Don't sit," she said.

"Get your wetsuit off and catch yourself a drink. This rain is easing up and we don't know when there might be more."

Oh bugger! thought Andrew. He felt so exhausted he did not think he could make the effort.

Chapter 14

MULL OF KINTYRE

Andrew groaned and leaned against the rusty iron plates to steady himself as a wave of shivering swept through him. All he wanted to do was lie down and sleep. But the thought of fresh water made him realize how thirsty he actually was. Soaked and cold as he was his mouth felt dry and rough. At the memory of how close they had come to heat stroke during the previous couple of days a spasm of anxiety caused Andrew to shudder. Fear then motivated him to keep standing and to act.

With an effort he jammed his swim fins into the rusty chains so they would not be lost. His belt he unbuckled and hung over a beam. Then he struggled to pull off the wetsuit. As he did he studied the sky and waves. The wind was still strong and low grey clouds were rolling past, but he thought they looked lighter. There was certainly less rain than he remembered from even a few minutes earlier. That knowledge spurred him to move faster. Once he had the top of the wetsuit off he struggled with the legs, handicapped by his numb and stiff right leg.

By then Carmen had unclipped the BCD and hung it on a rusty projection. She looped the rope through its straps then peeled her wetsuit off. By the time Andrew had his left leg free she was standing with hers draped across her arms to let the rain wash off any salt. She was trembling violently, and Andrew could hear her teeth chattering. He also noted that her hands and feet were all wrinkled and blue. And there were cuts which were seeping blood.

That reminded him of his own cut hand and he looked at it and saw that it was still bleeding quite freely, the blood thinning and smearing in the rain. Shaking his head at his inability to do anything about the bleeding and hoping it would stop he bent and tugged the leg of the wetsuit off his now cramping right leg.

For a minute at least, the agony of the cramp paralysed him and he shivered, clenched his fist and beat at the bunched muscle. The pain hurt so much he gritted his teeth and trembled. Carmen looked anxiously at him but began to try to channel a dribble of rainwater into her mouth.

Anxiety over thirst spurred Andrew to finally tug the rubber suit off his foot and to relax the cramp. Shuddering with the strain and afraid that the cramp would return he gingerly stood up. He found he was gasping from the effort and that he was shaking so much he had trouble keeping his balance. So as not to fall over he had to lean on the rusty sides while he placed his wetsuit over his arms and held it out to catch the obviously decreasing rain.

Carmen took a suck of water and turned to him. "Make sure you wash the salt off first. You must not drink salt," she cautioned.

Andrew nodded. He knew that but now he felt so thirsty it took an effort of willpower to just hold the suit in the drizzle and to rub it to wash off any salt. Only then did he spread it and hold it up to try to get a drink. But to his dismay the rain had eased up so that barely a trickle collected and he was reduced to licking at drops.

Oh no! What if that is the end of it? he thought.

But in his heart he knew. The grim spectre of death from dehydration caused his stomach to feel queasy. Once again, he experienced real, gut-wrenching fear.

This is all getting too much for me, he thought, his mind skipping back over the murders and attempted murders, the heat, sunburn and thirst on the cay then the terror of being swept away by the current and the desperate struggle to reach the reef.

But it had stopped raining and he had barely wet his lips. *I didn't even get a good mouthful,* he thought with dismay. He was now too weak to keep holding up the wetsuit and he lowered his trembling arms and looked at Carmen.

She was doing the same, leaning on the rusty stem piece and trembling. To add to Andrew's dismay, he saw that her whole body appeared to be goose bumps and he realized that the noise he could hear were her teeth chattering.

"Bloody hell! It is one thing after another," he muttered. "Now we are freezing to death!"

Carmen obviously realized the same thing as she took several deep breaths then looked up and said, "We must get warm. If we don't hyperthermia will set in and we will die of exposure. Run on the spot for a few minutes."

"Run!" Andrew croaked, licking at his suddenly dry lips.

But his own teeth were starting to click together and he realized he was shaking all over. With another effort of willpower, he summoned up the energy to copy Carmen. She carefully placed her wetsuit down and began waving her arms and moving her legs. It was much too dangerous and cramped to actually run. Besides Andrew could barely move his right leg but he tried.

A couple of minutes of this was as much as he could manage. His energy just drained away and he came to a panting standstill, still shivering but unable to do more. Part of his mind told him to get the wetsuit back on to shield him from the chill wind, but his thirst made him reluctant to do so.

It might start to rain again at any moment, he thought, eyeing the scudding low clouds. *I don't want to miss any water.*

But Carmen had made the same decision. She picked up her own wetsuit and began tugging it on. "Put your wetsuit on Andrew," she ordered.

"But it might rain," Andrew replied. His mind told him she was right but it all seemed to be too much effort.

"I don't care. Put it on or you will freeze to death. You are shivering like anything now and you've gone blue," she snapped.

Reluctantly Andrew picked up his wetsuit and began tugging it carefully onto his right leg. Trembling and little lancing pains kept him tensed in anticipation of another cramp, but none happened and he was able to get the leg on. The other leg and then the body and arms followed. Then he moved to the furthest corner against the stem piece where he felt the wind was least. Very gingerly he lowered himself to sitting position.

Even that took some doing as the chain links were uneven and dug into his buttocks painfully. At last he managed to find a relatively comfortable position. Carmen eased herself down beside him and pressed against him. "We need to share our body warmth," she said.

Andrew was now at an age where he was very sensitive to close contact with his sister but so exhausted and cold did he feel that he was able to push these inhibitions aside and put his arms around her to hold her tight. To his concern she was also shivering and her feet looked very wrinkled and blue.

We will be lucky to survive this, he thought grimly.

And the wind seemed to find them with chilling force. It froze his face and set his teeth chattering again. To try to avoid it he bowed his head and nestled against Carmen's neck. Then all he could do was tremble and wish it was all over.

Andrew lost track of time as several times he lapsed into a fitful, exhausted slumber. Both times he was woken by violent trembling in his legs and by cramps. His cries of agony roused Carmen and she knelt and pummelled and massaged his knotted thigh muscles until they eased. The pain was so intense it brought tears to Andrew's eyes. He became conscious of them when they trickled down his cheeks and chilled in the breeze.

They are good sign really, he told himself. *It means I have a bit of moisture in my body.* But not much, he decided as his lips felt wrinkled and cracked and his mouth had a dry, dog's breakfast feel to it.

But the wetsuit and the activity both worked. He stopped shivering from cold and was only aware of it on his exposed skin. He even did a pee in his wetsuit and that felt nice and warm for a minute or so. The action also deeply embarrassed him and he fervently hoped that Carmen could not smell it. Then he shrugged. He was just too exhausted to really care. Once again he drifted into a fitful slumber.

Only to be woken by a swill of icy water over his feet.

Andrew stared around in the darkness and his tired mind tried to work out what had woken him. Then his feet got wet again and he jerked awake. Peering around in the gloom he saw what had happened. He gave Carmen a shake and when she lifted her head and groaned a croaky, 'What?' he said, "Wake up! The tide is rising. We can't stay here."

Another wave slopped up, swilling right across the heap of chain. Andrew stared at the water washing up and down inside the hull and felt a distinct tightening of the stomach as a wave of fear washed through him. He was also embarrassed.

I am trying to be a nautical person and I can't even remember something as elementary as the tides, he castigated himself.

Then he saw one of his swim fins float by and that galvanized him into action. *My fins! They saved us,* he thought. He felt sure they would be needed again. *We aren't out of the woods yet,* he thought, then wished he was in the woods rather than marooned in the middle of the ocean.

He snatched up the fin and scanned urgently around for the other. He saw it still wedged in the chains and then remembered the BCD.

"Car, the BCD!" he cried, looking around.

Carmen reached across to the rusty projection she had hung it on and then looked at him in horror. "It's gone!" she gasped.

That thought sent another stab of fear through Andrew. He was also sure that without the BCD to keep them afloat they would have both drowned. Heart hammering with fear he struggled to his feet and looked at the churning water moving in the rusty hull. As he did he spotted it. It was bobbing on the waves and appeared to be about to be sucked out through a hole in the hull plates.

"There it is!" he cried.

"I see it," Carmen replied. Andrew went to move but as he did another cramp locked up his right buttocks and he could only stand in agony, clenching and unclenching his fists, and jaw. But Carmen kept moving, obviously unaware of his crippled state. She slid into the water and pushed herself forward. As she did the backwash sucked her off along the hull.

By then Andrew's cramp had started to ease but he was still unable to help. He could only stand and watch anxiously as Carmen swam among the twisted beams and rusty steel girders. To add to his anxiety was the fact that she was obviously having trouble keeping control in the moving water. This became worse when another large wave flooded in and came surging towards her. She was carried against a beam and Andrew heard her cry out. Her arms flailed at the water as she tried to swim clear.

Then the wave receded and Carmen went with it, breast stroking amid the wreckage. By then Andrew's heart was in his mouth with anxiety. To his enormous relief he saw her reach the bobbing BCD. She reached out and grabbed it just as it was about to be sucked out through the opening by the gushing water. Then she was dragged by the current against the rusty side plates. For a moment she struggled and then got a grip on a beam.

Andrew looked anxiously around and saw that she had to move fast. *She will be torn to shreds by the barnacles if she doesn't get out of there,* he thought. He saw her head turn and he met her eyes and pointed. "The mast! Climb up the mast! Quick!" he shouted.

Carmen nodded and as the next waves swilled and gushed in she pushed across to the great iron mast and straddled it. Andrew feared that the barnacles on the lower part of the mast would shred her thighs but she had thought of that and slid up onto it and came to rest on her feet and hands, balanced like a cat. Then, as that wave receded, she edged further up, the BCD gripped in her teeth. Before the next wave arrived, she was above the level of the water. That left her balanced precariously.

It was now Carmen's turn to point and shout. "Andrew, you can't stay there. Climb up," she called.

Andrew looked up and saw that he had no other choice. The only place where they might find a platform big enough to sit on was the remains of the focsle deck where the deck beams came together at the stem. The fallen mast rested on the focsle, bending and buckling the port side girders down. After studying the possible hand and footholds and bracing against another wave and making sure that the fins were firmly wedged in the back of his wetsuit he reached up.

As he hauled himself up Carmen called again. "Andrew, your weight belt," she said.

Andrew swore under his breath and berated himself for being a fool. Quickly he lowered himself back down. After getting a firm footing with his sore and tender feet on the rusty links he took the weight belt off the beam and buckled it on. He knew the belt was one of the reasons they had survived.

Without it we would have been separated and I would have drowned, he thought.

There was then the problem of putting his feet somewhere where they wouldn't get cut during the first two metres of the climb. That was the zone where the oysters and barnacles grew and every suitable surface appeared to be encrusted with them. Andrew was able to use his arms to lift himself up as high as he could but then he had to gingerly place his bare feet on a cross beam covered with barnacles. Very gently he eased his weight onto his feet, wincing as the sharp shells began to cut into the soft flesh. As quickly as he could he reached up to the next cross beam with his arms and hauled himself higher.

After that it was easier. He was able to put his feet on rusty iron which hurt a bit, but which did not have the same ability to slice open tender flesh. Straightening up he took the weight on his legs and stood for a moment, trembling while he rested. As he clung halfway up the side of the bow he noted that blood was still seeping out of his cut hand but mostly this was only when he released pressure in his grip.

I hope I am not slowly bleeding to death, he thought.

While Andrew slowly and carefully climbed up the rusty iron side Carmen straddled the mast and began to edge up it. She was also above the level where barnacles grew so this was safe. Her real danger was of losing her balance and toppling down among the tangle of twisted iron and rusty plates below.

But she made it safely to the focsle as Andrew hauled himself up between two beams. The last bit he found very difficult as he felt so weak and because his muscles were trembling almost uncontrollably. Puffing and gasping he heaved his legs up through the gap and was able to sit against the bow where the beams came together to form an almost solid seat. This was in beside the fallen mast and he squeezed himself in against it, both to make room for Carmen and to try to get out of the wind.

Carmen reached him and carefully transferred her weight onto the angled beams next to him. As she did Andrew saw that she had a nasty gash about 10cm long on the outside of her left hip and several smaller cuts and scratches on the insides of her legs.

"You've cut yourself," he commented.

She glanced down at them and grimaced. "I know. I don't think they are too bad," she replied.

Andrew wasn't so certain as blood was sheeting her upper thigh on the outside and trickling in thin smears from the insides of her legs. "You sure?" he queried.

Carmen handed him the BCD and then lowered herself carefully onto the rusty beams next to him, her back against the mast.

"No, but it isn't gushing so I think it will stop." She bent over to examine the gash on the outside of her thigh. "That was when the wave got me and slammed me against the wreck," she explained.

"I saw," Andrew replied. He took the BCD and clipped it around a beam so that it couldn't fall through. Just looking at the rip in her skin made him feel ill but after a careful examination he decided it was only a flesh wound and had not cut anything important. "You might be alright," he commented.

"I hope so. It is the cold I am more worried about," she answered.

Andrew could only agree. Now that they were up on the remains of the focsle they were almost completely in the open and the wind was able to get at them. Even hunched behind the fallen mast they had very little protection. He realized that his hands and feet were looking blue, even in the gloom. So did Carmen's face and lips.

This could be bad, he told himself.

"We need to keep moving," he said.

Carmen nodded. "And we must not go to sleep," she added.

Andrew glanced down at the water sloshing around on the rough and jagged beams below and could only agree. A fall would be very nasty, even if nothing was broken. Then he looked around at the jumble of waves and the seething froth of foam that now covered the reef. To him everything looked gloomy and dull.

"What time it is?" he asked.

Carmen looked at her watch. "Ten past six," she replied. "It will be dark soon."

That idea did nothing to cheer Andrew. It not only meant that the tide was on the way in but that they would have to endure another night before they got rescued. A close study of the sky offered little hope. Most of the clouds had cleared away, except to the west where they still blocked out the sun. Seeing the fading blue above him with the first stars twinkling in it depressed him.

I was hoping for more rain, he thought.

Now he was really thirsty and he wondered if he could endure much longer without water. Already his tongue felt dry and swollen and he found it hard to speak.

To cheer himself up, Andrew studied the wreck and the surrounding ocean. "At least we are better off than last night," he said. As he did terrifying flashbacks to standing waist deep in the swirling waves in the blackness caused him to shudder.

At least we should be well above the wave height here, he thought.

But the view was not very cheering. All he could see in the gathering dusk was the twisted black shape of the wreck and the spray and endless waves in all directions. The whole of Longbow Reef was now underwater and only bursts of foam showed where the higher outcrops were. Of the other reefs he could see nothing and only a dark hump indicated the location of the wrecked Taiwanese trawler.

For something to say he said, "This ship must have been driven onto the reef under sail."

"Why do you say that?" Carmen asked.

"Because the bows are so far onto the coral," Andrew replied. "The poor buggers probably didn't even see the reef until too late. And they couldn't have turned and stood away if the weather was bad and the wind was strong."

He had read many accounts of sailing ships and the ghastly image of the men seeing the reef and knowing the ship was doomed and probably themselves as well, chilled him.

No radios to call for help then, he thought. *No wonder they were so religious.*

Carmen studied the wreck and nodded. "I agree. If she had been trying to turn away she would probably have broached and been thrown up beam on. She must have hit the reef at high tide too."

Andrew had thought that and for a few seconds he tried to imagine what it must have been like: strong winds and possibly a storm, the sighting of the line of breakers and the awful knowledge that they were powerless to prevent the ship being dashed on the coral. Then the horrible crash and grinding as she struck and the hull was torn open by the coral.

There would have been a terrible crash as the masts and rigging came down too, he thought.

Just picturing all those massive iron tubes and timber spars and heavy blocks raining down amid a tangle of ropes and wires made him wince. He put this to Carmen and she agreed.

"I read that she lost all her masts at once," she said. "Three men were killed when they came down and three more were badly injured."

"What was her name again?" Andrew asked. He knew but he wanted to make conversation to take their minds off the gathering darkness and poor prospects.

"The *Mull of Kintyre*," Carmen answered. "She was an iron barque built at John Brown's on the Clyde in 1885. She ran aground here in 1893 on a voyage from Sydney to Calcutta."

Andrew tapped at the iron side plate. "I am surprised there is anything left at all after all this time," he said.

Carmen nodded. "Me too, but I read somewhere that there was a type of iron that they made which is very long lasting."

"I read that too, or someone told me," Andrew agreed. "Something to do with the type of iron ore or the amount of limestone and coke they added to the furnace or something."

"There is that wreck of a sailing ship on the reef at Cockle Bay in Townsville, the one we saw when we were sailing with that mob from T. S. *Coral Sea*. It had been all scrunched up by a cyclone but it was from the 1880s and was still in pretty good nick," Carmen said.

Andrew nodded. "She was. The *City of Adelaide* is her name. And there is the wreck on Endeavour Island. It was a lot like this one only in much better condition," he added.

"The *City of Perth* is her name wasn't it?" Carmen asked.

"Yes, and it had rolled iron lower masts too," Andrew agreed. "But you read up on this one didn't you? What is the story? What happened to the crew?"

"Apart from the ones killed in the wreck they all survived," Carmen replied. "They waited until the storm went down then launched the ship's longboat and sailed to Prescott Island. It took them four trips to ferry everyone there but then they dug a well and waited until another ship came along."

"Prescott Island. Yes, we must try to get there," Andrew said.

He then looked out into the gathering darkness to see if he could see the stone building but there was too much sea mist and spray.

If we don't get water soon I will be a goner! he thought.

Chapter 15

THE TOP OF THE TIDE

A ndrew felt his stomach turn over with apprehension and he licked his cracked and dry lips. Anxiety gnawed at him and he began to wonder how they might get out of the situation alive. A glance at his watch told him it was just coming up to 1900.

Top of the tide will be at about ten or a bit after, he thought. *We should be well above the level of that.*

But looking down at the water swilling up and down the hull did little to reassure him. It already looked to be halfway up to their level.

But it was thirst that began to worry him the most. He found he was having trouble swallowing. His tongue felt too big for his mouth and his throat was all swollen and constricted. His eyes were sore and felt scratchy and from time to time he had trouble seeing as his vision went blurry.

I can't even make myself weep a few tears to moisten my eyes, he thought.

To add to his concern Andrew noted that the stars had come out. Right across the sky from one horizon to the other there was now not a cloud to be seen.

No chance of rain from that sky, he told himself gloomily.

His mood matched the gathering night. The only relieving factor was the moonlight. The moon had come up and was a bright full moon that lit up the sea so that to the east it looked like a shimmering study in black and silver and to the west a constantly moving ripple effect without any depth. The moonlight also made it easier to study the waves and Andrew experienced the uneasy feeling that they were larger than they had been before.

As the tide rose higher each wave slammed into the stern of the wreck, sending a huge shower of spray into the air. This swept over Andrew and Carmen in a chilling shower that made them both shiver. The salt stung at Andrew's eyes and he considered putting on his facemask. He tried it but found it too claustrophobic and soon pulled the mask down again so that the strap hung around his neck. Worse still the waves all sent a tremor thought the wreck and the larger ones made the whole structure shudder.

Bloody hell! If the waves get any bigger they could batter this old heap of rust to bits, Andrew thought, fear knotting his stomach as he thought about being back in that unforgiving ocean again. *We won't survive another bout like the last one,* he told himself.

Beside him Carmen was squirming about and Andrew turned to see why. He saw that Carmen had buckled on the BCD and was now busy tying the orange rope around a deck beam.

"In case I go to sleep and slip off," she explained.

Andrew looked down just as a larger than normal wave burst over them and a mass of water gushed forward, swirling and churning among the twisted beams below. For a few seconds his imagination dwelt on what would happen to either of them if they were caught in that and the word 'maelstrom' flitted across his mind.

"We need to keep warm," he replied, making an effort to pretend all was well. He then forced his aching and tired legs and arms to windmill until he felt some warmth seeping into them.

Carmen copied him and added, "We must not fall asleep. We have to stay awake and keep moving. If we drop off to sleep we could fall into the water or just drift into hyperthermia."

"I know," Andrew agreed. But it was one thing to say it and quite another, in his exhausted state, to do. Within minutes he found his eyelids sliding closed and his head drooping. To keep sleep at bay he struggled painfully to his feet, clinging to the rusty remnants of the bulwarks for support. Standing there he worked his legs and arms and also scanned the sea and the sky hopefully.

"Can you see anything?" Carmen asked.

"No. Just the ocean," Andrew answered. He felt a sudden plunge in his spirits and had to admit that he had been hoping to see a light.

Some sign of other humans, he thought. But then he remembered the murderers and that sent shudders of emotion through him. *But not them!* he thought as the terror swirled up in his gut. He found he was swaying and panting for air and had to cling on to keep his balance. *Sit down before you fall down—or fall over the side!* he told himself.

A glance down into the waves breaking astern and alongside caused him another spurt of fear and he shook his head and lowered himself down beside Carmen again. As he did another big wave burst and the spray deluged them both in an icy shower.

Carmen huddled against Andrew. "Do you think the wind is getting stronger?" she asked.

Andrew nodded. "Yes, I do."

Once again, he looked down through the rusty beams and felt another stab of anxiety. The water now looked very close.

I hope this focsle does stay clear at high tide, he told himself.

His rational mind told him it probably did but his imagination made him wonder what happened during big storm waves. Once again, he found himself breathing fast and his heart hammering. He also knew he was very tired and lacking energy and dimly he was aware that he might not be thinking straight.

Another look around the horizon did nothing to reassure Andrew. There wasn't a light to be seen and he knew it was foolish to expect one.

There will be no ships trying to pass through the reef at night in this part of the world, he told himself.

And there was no doubt that the wind and waves had increased. Huge rollers were now bursting on the edge of the reef in a massive burst of spray several kilometres long. Each breaking wave filled the air with salt spray and made the whole reef and wreck shudder. The noise was almost deafening.

Like constant thunder, Andrew thought.

Andrew hunched down beside Carmen and tried to keep his limbs moving. With his left leg and both arms that was easy but memories of how painful the cramps had been made him very cautious about flexing any muscles in his right leg. He did wonder what was happening to the spear wound.

Probably festering by now, he thought gloomily.

His imagination dredged up images of tropical ulcers or gangrene. Then he inspected his cut hand but in the dark all he could determine was that the bleeding appeared to have stopped.

Time then seemed to drag. The moon climbed slowly up into the sky. The wind blew stronger until it was chilling their exposed wet skin and both were shivering despite their wetsuits. And the waves seemed to slam into the stern of the wreck with ever greater force, sending quivers through them as well as through the rusty frames and plates.

This is getting bloody grim, Andrew thought as he licked his dry lips for the hundredth time. Thirst was now beginning to torment him and he realised he was panting from anxiety.

Calm down! he rebuked himself. *You are safe and dry—well, almost dry,* he added as another shower of icy spray deluged him. Another check of his watch showed that it was only 2030hrs. *Another two hours to the top of the tide,* he thought. Then he did the sums and was even more depressed when he worked out that it was another eight hours to daylight. *How can I last that long?* he wondered.

His stomach gave a big grumble. It was so loud that Carmen stirred and nudged him. "Was that you?" she asked.

"Yes. I'm hungry," Andrew replied. He knew he was more than hungry; he was weak from lack of food.

"Could have been worse," Carmen commented.

"How? What do you mean?" Andrew queried.

Carmen chuckled. "You boys usually let out gas from the other end," she said.

"Oh poo to you! Bite your bum!" Andrew cried. "Anyway, you know why women don't fart much don't you?"

"No, why?" Carmen asked.

"Because they don't keep their mouths closed long enough to build up the necessary back pressure," Andrew answered.

Carmen gave him a playful hit on his arm. "Oh you sexist pig!" she said. But then she chuckled. "Do you have any other good jokes?"

So for the next hour they made a huge effort to tell each other jokes, even the saddest and corniest ones, to try to stay awake and to keep their spirits up. It was the increasing height of the water that brought this to an end. Andrew noted with concern that the largest waves were now swilling about only a metre or so below them and the crest of some waves were breaking on board amidships. This meant they were being soaked by cold salt spray every half-minute.

This is getting to be a bit of a worry, Andrew thought.

He could feel that Carmen was shivering almost uncontrollably. "Get up Car and let's do some dancing and jogging," he said.

To his relief Carmen nodded and with difficulty hauled herself to her feet. As she straightened up her stomach also made a series of gurgling noises that were so loud Andrew heard them above the noise of the surf.

"That was you!" he cried, nudging her playfully.

"It was too. God I could go a big steak now," Carmen replied. "Now forget food and start warming up."

Andrew tried. But he was afraid to jig about too much lest he slip or put his foot down between the narrow rusty beams. There was also anxiety about cramps. As he lifted each foot in turn he looked out and was appalled at the size and ferocity of the waves. All he could see was the half-submerged remains of the wreck and rippling, moving waves in all directions. The whole reef was now underwater and only the lines of surf indicated the edge of the coral.

This is getting really dangerous, he thought.

It sent a shiver of fear through him, to add to the trembling he was already experiencing from the cold. A huge wave crashed against the reef and hit the upright stern section. Spray deluged them with what felt like bucketfulls of cold water. Andrew spluttered and shook his head to clear it. With water streaming off his wet hair and face he had to blink to check that Carmen was still beside him.

She was but she was hanging on to the rusty bulwark. "That was bad," she commented. "I hope this water isn't going to get any higher."

"So do I!" Andrew replied grimly. He did some quick mental calculations and that added to his gloom.

The tide could rise four metres. That means we could get waves of nearly the same height above that. And this bow section is only about six or seven metres high. We could get swept right off.

That was really worrying, and he turned and anxiously watched the next few waves come smashing in against the stern. Then, to his horror, he noted that the surge of water inside the hull almost reached the beams they were standing on. After watching a few more waves he shrugged and decided there was nothing to do but pray and try to keep warm. So Andrew resumed his physical exercises. But that took an increasing effort of willpower as the strength quickly drained out of him. All too soon he felt too tired to lift his arms and his legs began to cramp again.

Puffing and still shivering he eased himself back to a sitting position with his back to the mast. Carmen did the same and then began untying the orange rope. Andrew watched her trembling fingers and shaking hands trying to undo the knots and asked: "What are you doing?"

"We are going to tie ourselves together and then tie ourselves to the wreck," Carmen replied. Then she swore as her fingers failed to get a proper grip.

"Let me," Andrew insisted.

But he found his own fingers were also stiff and hard to make function. He was amazed and appalled at how sore and cramped they felt. It took nearly ten minutes to undo the rope, thread it around his waist and through the straps of the BCD then around the deck beam between them.

As Andrew tried to tie a suitable knot another wave came crashing on board and this time it came gushing up through the beams they were sitting on. The whole wreck trembled and shook and he swallowed as a spasm of fear gripped his chest and throat.

I am glad we aren't on the sand cay tonight, he thought. *Carmen was right. We wouldn't have survived a second night with the higher tide.*

Once the knot was tied Carmen checked it. "That should do," she commented. "As long as we are secure up here we should be alright."

"What if the wreck disintegrates?" Andrew asked, spluttering to clear trickles of salty water from his lips.

Carmen shook her head. "I don't think it will. After all, it has been here more than a hundred years. I reckon it will take a real storm, a cyclone or something to really smash it up."

Andrew's mind had told him that but it was hard to push the irrational fears out when all he could see was line after line of huge waves rolling towards him. For a few minutes they discussed the possibility of a cyclone. Carmen shook her had and reminded him that April was after the official end of the cyclone season.

Both had survived a Category 5 cyclone on Cape Bowling Green at the start of the previous year. Andrew had found that a truly terrifying experience, one that he had hoped never to repeat, but which they had. That had been only three months earlier, in January when they had been through another Category 4 storm in Bathurst Bay. That time they had been on a ship and Andrew shuddered at the memories of the huge waves that had smashed the ship's wheelhouse windows.

I must be mad, he told himself. *I should take up hobbies that keep me safe at home and indoors.* But thinking like that just made him smile with a wry grin. The previous experiences also helped him to get a better perspective on his current situation. *These waves are nothing much. It is the cold that we have to worry about,* he told himself.

So he sat there thinking about those previous experiences. That led to memories of Letitia, busty, blonde and very nude clinging to the netting lashed to the small lighthouse on Cape Bowling Green. Letitia was his friend Martin's big sister and she lived in Townsville. She was two years older than him and he was not in love with her, but she had given him some very heated memories and even hotter fantasies. Some of those now helped to warm Andrew and to pass the time. Then a swirling flow of water from an extra big wave jerked his thoughts back to the present and he checked that the rope was still holding.

There was nothing else to do except to brace himself and cling to Carmen and endure the water as it swilled and washed around them, submerging them chest deep at times. Andrew knew real fear again and he became desperately anxious that either he or Carmen might die from exposure. He gripped her tight and tried to impart some body warmth, then silently cursed as each succeeding wave chilled them. The force of the waves began to push and tug at them so that he had to brace his feet against the beams and bulwarks to prevent them being dragged away.

I hope all this to-ing and fro-ing doesn't cut the rope, he thought.

There was also some sharp pains and throbbing aches in his leg muscles and buttocks as tired and overstrained muscles protested at being tightened every time he braced. Several small cramps stuck and Andrew tensed in fear of a real cramp. Anxiety about that occupied his mind for a while and he carefully felt the rope to check. It seemed a bit frayed, but his fingers were now so lacking in feeling he wasn't sure.

Then a wave washed aboard that reached right up to their necks and splashed them in the face. That sent a shudder of near despair through Andrew and, for the first time, he began to seriously contemplate death and the afterlife.

If there is one! he thought bitterly.

Through his mind went a series of images of his life and he felt several pangs of regret, some bitter and some sweet. The sweetest were images of his girlfriend Tina. She was his age and was a big busty girl who really loved him. Neither had spoken of it but in the back of his mind Andrew had decided that they would be married when they grew up. His real regret now was that he had not properly made love to her. In fact, he had never had real sex with any girl and that seemed to him a great pity.

I am going to die before I have really lived, he thought.

Then he thought about Tina again and experienced a series of mixed emotions: love, desire, regret, relief.

It is just as well I haven't done anything to her, he thought. *That is, after I am dead, she is still a virgin and will be able to give herself to some other lucky bugger when she marries.*

He knew it had to be after she married as he thought that was the sort of girl Tina was. He had never asked her for sexual favours although now that he thought about it he felt sure she would have long since given herself to him if he had asked.

Anyway, I love her and I will tell her so when I see her next—if I do. And I am glad she isn't here now, he thought.

Tina was on holidays with her parents visiting relatives in Brisbane. *She won't even guess I am in any danger,* he thought.

The notion that the first she would have any inkling that something had happened to him and Carmen would be in the news in few days' time when they did not return from the expedition and a search was mounted made him feel very sorry for her.

It will really devastate her, he thought.

Not for the first time he told himself he would give up diving. *I will take up some other activity that is safer,* he decided.

But he did not vow never to dive again. In the back of his mind was an idea and he also guessed there would be times when his duty might require it to help others.

His thoughts wandered back onto Tina. He knew he was glad they had never been lovers, but he still regretted not having done it.

Not with any girl, he thought.

At the back of his mind was that nagging worry about his manhood. He knew that his body was quite normal and worked alright but he had that deep insecurity about whether, when the great day arrived, he would be able to perform. He thought things would be alright when the time came because while he and Tina had never had actual intercourse there had been a lot of passionate petting and gentle pleasuring with their hands.

Images of Tina's splendid breasts helped cheer Andrew for a few minutes and he relished the memories. Then an icy wave poured right over his shoulders and head and left him shocked and gasping and drove all thoughts of girls from his head.

"Bloody hell! That was big," he cried. He twisted round to see if another wave of similar size was approaching.

Carmen twisted to look as well. "If there are any more like that we might have to stand up," she said.

Andrew tensed while the following wave broke but it was smaller and only washed around their lower body. Then he looked at his watch. "Ten past ten. It must be nearly the top of the tide," he said.

"I hope so because here comes a monster," Carmen cried.

Andrew looked and felt a stab of fear. The wave was a monster and it seemed to tower up and appeared to extend from horizon to horizon.

Holy Mackerel! This is going to hurt, he thought.

Chapter 16

STRUGGLE TO SURVIVE

A nd it did.

The wave smashed into the wreck with such force the whole rotten structure trembled and then the water hammered against Andrew and Carmen. The force of the water slammed them both against the rusty bulwarks and mast. Only the rope stopped them from being washed overboard. Andrew knew that because his own feeble grip on the beam he was sitting on was just ripped free as though he had not even tried.

Then the wave poured on over the sides and down through the gaps and holes. By the time the water had drained down both Andrew and Carmen were tumbled together and Andrew was on his head with his feet in the air and his arms tangled with Carmen's legs. Feeling shocked, battered and bruised he struggled to disentangle himself and then squirmed into a sitting position.

"You alright?" he asked.

Carmen nodded and then looked at her hand. It had been cut on the rusty iron and she frowned and sucked at it. Andrew realized his hand hurt as well and he saw that the cut was bleeding again. Anxiously he looked around to be ready in case of another large wave. To his relief the next few waves were much smaller and barely reached their level.

There were several larger waves which washed around them, buffeting and banging them against the iron plates and beams but none were as big. Andrew was able to retain some sort of control. In between each wave he checked that the rope had not been sawn through by the continual movement. It was now badly frayed but still held.

Another check showed that he still had both swim fins and his facemask. A few seconds after he checked this he wished he had the mask on when yet another extra-large wave deluged him. Blinking to clear the stinging salty water from eyes that felt raw he spat out the water that had made its way into his mouth. Then he swore.

Carmen nudged him. "No need for that brother," she said.

"Sorry sis," Andrew replied.

But he wasn't really. He was now too battered and exhausted to really care about her feelings. Survival was now his mental preoccupation. Satisfied that the waves were not getting any bigger he looked carefully in all directions.

Eleven o'clock, he noted. *We must be past the top of the tide.*

"God, I hate this!" Andrew cried. "I am never going to go near the sea again after this!"

Carmen nudged him. "What will you do?" she queried.

"I will join the Army Cadets," Andrew muttered.

At that Carmen broke into shrieks of laughter. "Army Cadets! Oh Andrew, that's a good one! That will be the day!"

Andrew was both peeved and then amused. "I will. I won't ever go near the sea again."

Carmen grinned at him, her teeth showing in the moonlight. "You will though little brother. You are a natural born sailor."

"Will not!" Andrew snapped, but inside he knew he probably would.

Carmen grinned again. "Tell me the one about the Army Cadets again. That was a good one and cheered me up a lot," she teased.

Andrew grumped but then had to laugh, thinking of his school friends who were Army Cadets. *They are tough and brave, but they would not have had the training to survive this,* he thought. He was deeply conscious that it was their Navy Cadet training and experience that had helped them survive so far.

The chattering of his teeth brought to his notice how cold he was. He realized that Carmen was shivering badly so he shook her arm. "Stand up and do some exercises. We need to warm up again," he called.

It took a few minutes to untie the rope. This was then re-tied around his waist. Trembling and fearful of another cramp Andrew heaved himself to his feet. As he did all his sore muscles protested and he groaned and had to grit his teeth to make the effort. His anxiety about having the rope untied was quickly dispelled. Glancing over the side he noted that the waves looked to be much lower.

And they look smaller too, he thought.

As he began pumping his tired arms he studied the sea and came to the firm conclusion that not only was the tide falling but that the waves were not as big. It came to him that the wind had dropped.

Over the next ten minutes this became obvious. The wind died away completely and with it the waves. Andrew was quite astonished at how quickly the sea calmed down. It seemed to be only a few minutes before the big waves had subsided completely. They were replaced by many small wavelets that were not much more than ripples, punctuated by long ocean swells that still surged and gurgled through the broken wreck below them.

Andrew realized he was actually perspiring so he stopped jogging on the spot and leaned on the rusty bulwark to get his breath back. Carmen did likewise. The water in the hull was now several metres below and even the big swells did not come close to them.

"We are safe for a bit," Andrew commented. But even as he did he realized how thirsty he was.

Bloody hell, I need a drink badly, he thought.

The moon was now right overhead, and the moonlight was so bright that Andrew was able to look carefully in all directions and was able to see a lot of detail. The most obvious things he could see were the long lines of surf that still thundered in on the edge of the reef as the swells rolled in, and the black shape of the Taiwanese trawler.

I wonder if there is any water on that other wreck? he thought.

Carmen must have been thinking along the same lines as she pointed to the wreck, a black, angular shape standing out on a shimmering field of silver. "We need to go to that other wreck. We can't stay here," she said.

Andrew tried to answer but his dry throat made his answer come out as a croak. With an effort he swallowed and answered. "I agree. There might be water there."

"And food," Carmen replied. "I am really hungry."

"Me too," Andrew replied. As though to underline this his stomach grumbled again. They both laughed and Andrew relaxed and felt they had a chance of surviving. "It is about a kilometre away I think," he added.

Carmen nodded. "About that, but I didn't take that much notice of the chart. I didn't think we would be visiting either when we set out."

That memory sent Andrew's mind churning over the horrific images of the last few days and he shuddered and was unable to speak for a minute. Then he said, "Do you think we should go now?"

He really did not want to do that. The idea of swimming in the sea in the dark was a bit more than his remaining courage was ready to face.

To his enormous relief Carmen shook her head. "No. Not in the dark. Low tide is about zero four hundred. We need a bit of water over the reef so we can swim. We can wait until daylight."

Andrew looked at his watch and saw that it was almost 1am. *About five hours then,* he told himself.

"I might try to get some sleep," he said.

"Good idea, but we will tie ourselves on again, just in case one of us falls off our perch in our sleep," Carmen agreed.

They did this and Andrew tried to get comfortable on the rusty beams. He eased his legs straight and rested his back and head against the mast. This allowed him to look out to the Northwest so that the wreck of the trawler was just visible. Sheltered from what little wind there was and no longer soaked by spray or waves he quickly began to warm up.

Perversely he soon felt hot and began wondering if he should take off the wetsuit. He decided not to, primarily because Carmen had fallen asleep with her head on his shoulder and he did not want to wake her. Instead he sat there and thought about how they might get out of their predicament. As he did he found thirst nagging at him. It soon came to dominate his thoughts and he found he could not swallow properly and that his throat felt all constricted. His tongue felt too big for his mouth and his skin felt hot and dry.

That got him studying the sky in the hopes of more rain clouds but to his disappointment and concern there was not a cloud to be seen. The wind dropped away altogether and Andrew became even hotter. What bothered him more was that he wasn't sweating.

I don't have enough fluid in my body to perspire, he thought.

Grim thoughts engendered by First Aid lessons started to build in his mind, scaring him more.

My body will start to shut down at the extremities, he thought.

That got him feeling his finger tips and toes. They felt warm and some of the immersion wrinkles had eased out of them, but he could not tell if they were colder than normal or not. Still thinking about his kidneys failing and his brain starting to boil he slid into a fitful slumber.

Sometime later, Andrew awoke with a start. He had been dreaming that he was diving and that he had slipped and put his foot into a giant clam that had snapped shut on it. For a few seconds he struggled to wake up. Then, with his mind still muzzy from sleep, he realized he could not move his left foot. Fear brought him to full consciousness instantly.

To his relief he saw that he was still high and dry on the old wreck but that it was much darker than he expected. As he rubbed his sore eyes to try to clear them he swore.

Don't rub! It will grind the salt on them, he told himself.

But he could not clear his eyes properly and he found that his vision was both blurry and full of dancing dots. That scared him as he knew it was one of the symptoms of serious heat illness. He found his heart hammering abnormally fast and tried to put it down to being scared but knew in his heart that it was from being dehydrated.

The body has less fluid to keep the heart pumping properly, so it must pump faster, he thought.

Once again stabs of fear about his heart, brain and kidneys bothered him. He tried to swallow and found it hard to move his limbs. The left foot still would not move and he reached along his leg and found that his foot was jammed through a gap in the rusty iron. That at least gave him some relief and he was able to free it and relax a bit.

Then he turned his attention to the darkness. *The moon was full and very bright only a couple of hours ago,* he thought.

He knew it should be somewhere off to his left front and at least halfway down the sky so he looked there.

He was rewarded by seeing a glimmer of gold amid swirling blackness. Then a shaft of moonlight struck down and played on the sea. The waves showed up as rippling black silhouettes.

Clouds! he thought. That got him even more alert and hopeful. So he squirmed to sit upright. In the process he disturbed Carmen and she began to groan and murmur as she was stirred to wakefulness.

Andrew did not care. He was panting now with anxiety and hope. *If I don't get water I will die today,* he thought.

To his great joy he saw that the whole sky seemed to be covered with clouds and only a few patches of silver sea still showed. The moon briefly shone through a gap and he tried to see the time on his watch. But he could not read the numbers. His vision was too blurred. That added enormously to his anxiety.

Carmen struggled to sit up. "Wh... wh... what is it?" she croaked.

Andrew tried to answer but his mouth was so dry and his tongue so swollen that he could not form words. At that moment a spot of rain hit his face. Immediately he twitched with anxiety.

I am still tied up, he thought.

Remembering how slow he had been to get his wetsuit off on the previous occasion he groped for the rope and pulled the knot to the front. With trembling fingers, he began to try to undo the knot.

Carmen understood and tried to help but two pairs of fumbling hands did not really achieve much. More spots of rain hit Andrew's face and he twisted his head around to look. A shower of rain was approaching, and he felt another spurt of anxiety. For a moment he contemplated sawing the rope against the edge of the rusty iron to try to cut it but then he shook his head.

We might need it again. It has saved my life a couple of times, he reasoned.

So he persevered and finally got the ends loose just as a real shower arrived. Almost panting with anxiety Andrew scrambled to his feet. Quickly he pulled the two swim fins from behind his shoulders. These were hastily laid on the rusty beams right in the bow. Then he began tugging at his wetsuit. The shower passed, making him worry that he had missed even that small chance, but a quick look around reassured him that there were other rain showers visible and that one was heading towards them.

As quickly as he could he peeled the wetsuit off, wincing at small cramps and stiff muscles. His wounds began to throb, but he ignored them. Rain drops began to strike his bare chest and arms and he raised his face, mouth open in a desperate attempt to get some moisture. As he did he shuffled the wetsuit around to get it draped across his arms. He was just in time as the next shower arrived.

Carmen had also peeled off her wetsuit and was holding it across her arms. "Don't drink until you have rinsed the salt off," she reminded him.

That took some willpower, but Andrew managed it. With cold rain running down his face and into his gaping, gasping mouth he used one hand to rub the wet rubber. Then the shower died away to a thin drizzle and he felt his fear level shoot up.

Have I missed it? he wondered.

His heart hammering with anxiety he looked around again and this time he gaped in puzzlement at what he saw. All around the wreck the sea was churning like soap suds being agitated in a washing machine.

What the devil? he wondered.

Then he understood. *It is low tide. The waves are churning up all this froth on the coral,* he told himself. It occurred to him that it would be impossible to swim in such conditions. *We will have to wait till the tide starts to come up again,* he thought.

After studying the frothing water for a few more seconds he looked around the horizon. *And here comes another rain shower,* he noted.

He held up the wetsuit as the first drops arrived. This time he held it high to channel the drops to his mouth. The rain was cold and quickly chilled his bare skin, but he hardly noticed. The first trickle was sweet bliss.

"Aaaah!" he sighed as he paused for breath.

Then he shifted his feet to brace himself and moved to drink again. Suddenly he slipped. His foot went through a gap between the rusty iron beams and down he went.

"Yaargh! Ow! Aaah! Help!" he cried.

Pain seared up his leg and with it came more fear. The dominant worry was that he might have injured himself so badly that it would place his survival in jeopardy.

Carmen turned in alarm and grabbed at him. "Andrew, are you alright?" she cried.

"Slipped. Aargh! Ouch!" Andrew replied.

Now he understood what had happened he was as much annoyed as hurt. *I need to get up and drink,* he told himself. *I need that water urgently.*

With an effort of willpower, he steadied himself. Ignoring the pain, he held the wetsuit up to Carmen. "Here, take this while I get my leg out," he said.

Carmen did as he asked and Andrew was able to brace his hands on two beams to take the weight off his leg. Having steadied himself he gingerly tested whether he could move the leg. To his initial dismay he could not. It was wedged hard, right down to the thigh.

"Help me," he asked as calmly as he could.

Carmen nodded and placed both wetsuits on the beams beside them. Then she knelt and peered into the darkness to see what had happened. Then she ran her hands down Andrew's leg until she found the problem.

After a minute or so she grunted and said, "Try moving your leg back. It is stuck in the narrow part."

Andrew nodded and had difficulty speaking as he was sucking in rapid breaths to try to counteract the waves of pain.

I hope nothing is broken, he thought.

Very cautiously he tried to move his leg backwards. As he did he was very aware of the cold rain running down, soaking his body but being wasted. He was able to suck in a few drops and trickles and even they were blessed relief, but he understood that he really needed to get a proper drink.

Driven by that need he felt around his thigh with his right hand and then asked Carmen to push his thigh back while he took the weight on his arms. She agreed and began firmly pushing while Andrew lifted himself as far as he could. That wasn't far and within seconds his arm muscles were shaking, and he had trouble keeping himself up. But it worked and to his immense relief the leg came free.

"I'm out. Give me a hand up," he cried.

Carmen did so, standing to lever Andrew upright so that his leg came straight up through the gap. A few seconds later Andrew had both feet firmly on two rusty beams. After making sure that he had a firm footing he looked down to study the damage. In the darkness he could see that smears of blood were trickling down both sides of his thigh.

"The knee hurts," he commented. Then he shook his head when Carmen knelt to look at the injury. "No time for that. We must drink. Give me the wetsuit," he said.

Carmen nodded and stood up. "They look like some bad scratches," she said. "Can you stand on it?"

Andrew placed weight on the injured leg and to his relief it took the strain. Trembling violently with shock and exposure he nodded and took the wetsuit Carmen held out to him. As quickly as he could he braced his left leg against the mast and spread the wetsuit to catch the rain. But even as he did this the rain shower began to ease off.

Bloody hell! I am too late! he thought.

Despair welled up but Andrew still tried. To his great joy he was able to channel a good trickle into his open mouth. Then he began to cough as his throat seemed to choke up.

My tongue must have swollen and be blocking it, he thought anxiously. But the water was good and some of it went down.

Then the rain stopped and fear returned. They stood there looking anxiously around in hope of another shower. Andrew knew he had only drunk about a cupful and also knew that his dehydrated body must lack many litres of essential fluid.

During this it had become even darker, the moon only showing briefly. There were other showers around and they even felt the edge of one for a few seconds, but it only delivered a mere drizzle that did not even wet the lips properly. Andrew began to tremble and had trouble standing but he was too desperate to relax.

There may not be any more rain for days, he thought. That got him trying to remember the details of the weather forecasts, but he could not recall much. *But there are usually rain showers in April,* he told himself to build up his spirits.

Carmen put down her wetsuit and knelt to examine his leg. By this time, it felt more numb than sore but there a few sharp stabs of pain as she probed and felt his knee and ankle.

"You are lucky," she said. "You have lost some skin but there are no deep cuts. Try to flex the leg," she instructed.

Andrew did but it took an effort to lift and bend the injured leg. Several times he wondered how much damage there was as pains shot through the limb and he had to brace his hands on the mast and the bulwarks. Then he leaned against the mast and began to gingerly massage the sore muscles.

Carmen glanced up as a moonbeam shone through, briefly lighting them up. The moon looked to be very low in the western sky and after she had checked her watch she said,

"Four o'clock. Should be the bottom of the tide."

Only an hour or so to daylight, Andrew thought.

That was a comforting thought but as he looked at the boiling sea that surrounded the wreck another thought came to chill him.

Then I will have to swim in the ocean again!

Chapter 17

TEST OF CHARACTER

Andrew hurt.

He seemed to hurt all over. His muscles ached. His right thigh and buttock throbbed. Every time he used his right hand the cut in the palm stung. Small niggling pains stabbed at him in unexpected places. And he had a throbbing, drum-beat headache.

I wish this was all over, he thought.

Then he studied the tumbling surf and jagged knobs of exposed coral and shivered. There was another real test coming up and he mentally shied away from it.

Must be nearly daylight, he decided. But his vision was too blurry to read his watch.

Carmen informed him it was almost five o'clock. "We will wait until seven," she added.

"I am happy with that," Andrew answered.

Carmen lowered herself down and held her wetsuit across her front. "I didn't get enough to drink," she said. "I still feel thirsty."

"Nor me. I hardly got any," Andrew added.

Despite his shaking legs he remained standing. Hopefully he scanned the darkness. Then he muttered a swear word and said, "If we survive this I am going to give up the sea. I will go and live in Central Australia, as far from the ocean as I can get."

Carmen made a noise that was a mixture of a chuckle and snort. "You will not, little brother. You are a born mariner."

"No, I'm not. I just took up sailing and diving because we joined the Navy Cadets," he answered.

"Piffle! You joined the Navy Cadets because your father and your grandfather were both seafarers," Carmen replied.

That was true, but Andrew then suffered images of his grandfather's skeleton amid the slush and mud of the wreck of the *Merinda's* strongroom. The memory sent shudders of ghoulish apprehension through him.

My bones won't even be found to give a decent burial to, he thought gloomily. *They will be scattered all over this reef after the fish have nibbled off my flesh.*

Thoughts of death came to oppress him. That sent him into a very dark mental pit and he began to pray. In the midst of that he began to brood on how upset their parents would be.

And Tina. Poor girl! She really loves me and will be devastated, he thought. *I am glad she didn't join us on this expedition.*

The thoughts of his girlfriend both stimulated and depressed Andrew. Lustful memories of her wonderful bosom and her cheerful, loving personality filled him with regret and he wished that they might have truly made love. Then he shook his head.

No, that is immoral. It would be wrong to leave her with a baby, a poor little nipper with no dad that she would have to bring up on her own.

But Oh! The idea of being in Tina's warm and loving embrace was an image that made staying alive worth doing. *I will make it,* he vowed. *And I will then tell her how much I love her.*

Suddenly Andrew jerked his face upwards. "Rain!" he croaked.

A big, cold drop had landed on his forehead. With trembling, fumbling hands he stretched out his wetsuit and held it up to catch the precious drops. Carmen scrambled up beside him. As he sucked the first few blissful drops Andrew noted that the light had changed to a sort of greyness. He realized he could see out to the horizon and that it was an approaching shower of rain that was obscuring his view to the east.

Real rain. Rain that poured down. It washed the torn wetsuit clean and then poured off it faster than he could drink. *I wish we had something to catch this in,* he thought as he stopped gulping to breathe.

The rain was cold and Andrew realized he was shivering violently but he did not care. Drinking was more important.

Water means life, he told himself.

In the end the shower lasted longer than he could drink. By the time it passed he felt bloated and was gasping and trembling.

Saved, at least for a while! he thought.

Then his eye caught the dark shape of the Taiwanese trawler and he felt the fear, just as icy, grip his throat and stomach. He stared at the seething, frothing foam covering the reef, at the sharp outcrops of coral.

I have to go into that soon, he thought. The notion made him tremble and feel ill. But he knew it had to be done. *We can't stay here. There might be food and other things we need for survival on that wreck,* he told himself.

When he said this to Carmen she nodded. "If nothing else it will give us shelter from the sun and the wind," she said. "There must be plenty of dry, protected spaces in a vessel that big. It will certainly be better than clinging to this rusty scaffolding."

Andrew could only agree. Ruefully he looked down at his scratched and bleeding left leg and at the numerous gaps between the rusty beams. Water still swilled and sloshed around in the hull below.

"Too dangerous to get down yet," he observed, wanting to postpone the swim as long as possible.

Worse still his skin was showing the effects of being wet for too long. Huge wrinkles had now formed in the soles of his feet and his fingers and palms were also deeply wrinkled and puffy. The cold kept making him shiver and he felt ill and weak.

We have to get dry, he thought.

He looked around the horizon and noted that the clouds were thinning but that it still looked dark and stormy out to the east.

There might be more rain, he thought.

But then he noted that Carmen was shivering almost uncontrollably. For a minute he weighed the chance of rain against the obvious effects of exposure and then shrugged.

The clouds often look threatening like that in the morning, but they usually just melt away with the rising sun, he told himself.

Then an almost uncontrollable fit of trembling wracked his body, leaving him feeling wrung out and exhausted.

We must get warm, he decided.

Andrew hugged Carmen tight for a few minutes and then said, "We must get back into our wetsuits to warm up. Come on, I will help you."

It took some doing as both were weak and their muscles stiff. But they managed it after about ten minutes of painful struggle. Andrew then carefully lifted the BCD over Carmen's head and buckled it firmly in place.

"Just in case," he said.

In reply she leaned close and gave him a kiss on the cheek. "You are wonderful little brother. You are a real hero."

Andrew shook his head and denied it but inside he felt good. *If only she knew how scared I am and what a weakling and coward I can be,* he thought.

To ease the situation, he picked up the orange rope and tied it around his belt, ready to secure to her when they began their swim. Then his stomach grumbled and churned from hunger and he felt giddy and had to lean on the bulwarks until the spots stopped dancing.

The thought of that swim was now gripping him with growing apprehension and he desperately did not want to do it. In an attempt to find some other option, he stood and studied the reef and the sea. The trawler was clearly visible now, no longer just a black shape in the gloom. He could even see some of the details and the rust streaks and weed growths on the exposed hull.

It isn't all that far, he tried to tell himself.

But between him and the trawler was all that reef and white water. The tide was so low that most of the coral was exposed and he could tell that any attempt to swim in those conditions would just lead to them being scratched and torn to bits.

Then he looked further out and realized he could see the stone building on Prescott Island. It stood out as a solid square of black on a haze of white and dark green.

If only we could get there, he thought, thinking of the base camp and the stores it held.

But he could also see the dark frothing waters of the Challenger Channel. *No chance of swimming that in our condition,* he told himself, remembering the last failed attempt and shuddering at how close they had come to being swept out to sea. The channel was at least two kilometres wide at that point and he was sure he did not have the strength to swim that.

Even if the current doesn't sweep us away.

Hoping to see a vessel of some sort he carefully scanned every point of the compass. It was fully light by then and the sky out to the east was tinged pink. The clouds were thinning and even a few rays of sunlight shone up as the sun began to peek over the horizon. Andrew turned and looked west to avoid the first blinding rays of sunlight as they lanced across the sea.

Off to the west Andrew saw the foam and surf that marked the Five

Feathers and Yule Reef. A few glimpses of flat, dark reef showed briefly, and he squinted in an attempt to see the sand cay they had spent the first night on. He thought he could see a tiny patch of yellow but wasn't sure. Finally, he shook his head.

"We aren't going to try to get back there anyway," he muttered.

Then his niggling idea surfaced and for a few minutes he brooded over the chances of making such a desperate plan work. Finally, he shrugged and returned to contemplating that swim. The very idea got him feeling anxious and ill and he realized he was gripping the rusty iron tightly and that he was breathing so fast that he felt giddy.

To calm himself he checked his cuts and bruises as well as he could, helped by Carmen. To his relief all of the bleeding had stopped but the wounds mostly looked all puffy and inflamed and there was lots of pink flesh that he suspected needed a stitch or two to help mend properly. Once again, he anxiously noted the wrinkled state of both their skins. Horrible thoughts of stories he had read about soldiers getting trench feet from standing in water too long added to his worries.

Then he sat down next to Carmen and tried not to think about the coming ordeal. But he found he could not stop glancing at his watch or at the steadily rising sun. As the sun rose the clouds to the east did melt away and that was bad news.

Probably no more rain today, he thought, suddenly feeling thirsty again.

Perversely he then had the urgent need to pee and had to beg his sister's pardon while he did so. She politely turned her back while he relieved himself.

Then he studied the sea, noting that there was less coral exposed and that the waves were not as big. *Not as much white water on the reef now,* he noted. *But still a heavy surf on the outer edge from the ocean swells.*

These were still sometimes big enough to shake the wreck and to drench them with spray. Once again, he gloomily stared at the distant trawler and wondered if there was any other choice, although he knew in his heart there was none.

I do not want to swim across the reef, he thought, the fear again rising as though to choke him.

Yet in the end it was his own nagging mind that got him up. *If we leave it too late the currents could wash us out to sea,* he thought. That was something he had been thinking hard about, without even really being conscious of it.

While the tide is coming in the currents flow west and we will be washed across the widest part of this reef. But if we leave it too late it will be like yesterday and we could be washed east out over the drop-off and into the really deep water beyond the reef. When he thought about that desperate swim to reach the wreck he shuddered. *I can't face that again,* he told himself.

So he looked at his watch, saw that it was ten to seven and nudged a dozing Carmen. "Time to go Sis," he said.

Carmen opened her eyes and blinked, then looked around. "OK," she muttered.

Andrew hauled himself carefully to his feet and then bent to pick up his swim fins. As he did a cramp seized his left thigh muscle and he cried out in pain. For a minute or so he was unable to straighten up, staying bent over and whimpering at the agony of it.

Carmen massaged and pummelled the solid lumps. Slowly the knotted muscle loosened, leaving Andrew sobbing and his leg trembling. As he sucked in a series of deep breaths Andrew looked out at the foaming water covering the reef and felt the fear tighten his gut.

Christ! If that happens to me while we are trying this we will be in real trouble, he thought.

That was very sobering, but he made an effort to hide his anxiety. *We have to do this so there is no point in scaring Carmen. It will be hard enough as it is,* he told himself. So he gave her what he hoped was a reassuring grin.

Carmen stood up and looked anxiously at him. "Will you be alright? Should we wait?" she asked.

Andrew shook his head. "No. We will both get weaker. The sooner we do this the better," he replied.

To forestall any discussion, he shuffled cautiously across the beams to a point where he could climb down into the hull. By then he noted that the water inside the wreck was much higher and was washing back and forth in quite large waves.

Sweating from exertion and anxiety Andrew slowly lowered himself between the beams and climbed carefully down into the hull. With every movement he tensed, anticipating another cramp. He found every movement hard. His muscles all felt stiff and as he went into the salt water and it worked its way into the wetsuit all his scratches and cuts began to sting and itch. Andrew tensed, expecting the water to be cold but it was only slightly cooler than his skin and he relaxed.

The water in the hull was nearly waist deep and the waves brought this to chest and even neck deep. The sheer force of it was enough to make it very hard to hang on and Andrew became very worried his feet might be slashed by the barnacles and oysters that he could not see. Gripping the rusty internal ribs of the ship he planned his next move while waiting for Carmen to join him.

To get out with the least risk of injury Andrew selected a large hole in the port side of the hull. Even though that was the side furthest from their objective it looked the biggest.

We should be able to swim out through that, he reasoned.

In his mind he had imagined them trying to climb out and getting rasped and cut on the rusty hull plates by the waves. He had also thought about when to put on his swim fins and decided it had to be inside the hull.

If I try to pull them on out in the open sea I might drop one and I will have to float and let myself go under as it needs both hands, he decided.

First, he spat in his facemask and rinsed it then pulled it on, knowing it was very necessary but hating the suddenly blinkered visibility that resulted. Then he set about pulling on the swim fins. Within seconds he was glad of the facemask as he had to bend to do so and the next wave washed over his bent form and the mask kept his eyes clear. But the force of the wave nearly pushed him right over and he had to cling on and struggle to keep his balance and not drop one of the fins.

So, with some difficulty, he pulled on both swim fins. By the time he had Carmen had climbed down and joined him. He pointed to the hole he had selected and explained his reasoning.

"We will tie ourselves together once we are out so that one of us doesn't get snagged and drag the other back onto the barnacles," he added.

Carmen nodded but looked so tired and anxious that Andrew experienced a moment of doubt. But the wreck of the trawler had now come to represent safety in his mind and he shook his head.

We have to do this, no matter what, he told himself.

So he slid forward and dog paddled across the hull, timing his move so that the backwash of one wave carried him aft past the fallen mast and the next wave washed him forward to the hole he was aiming at. The whole time he was trying not to touch any of the oyster encrusted iron. In this he was almost successful and only two small cuts in his left hand resulted.

Then he was at the jagged hole in the rusty side plates and the view outside made him falter. As far as he could see there appeared to be nothing but roiling foam and the surf of big waves breaking on the outer reef only metres to his left. Then he shook his head.

Don't hesitate. We have to reach somewhere dry, he told himself.

By a conscious effort of willpower Andrew pushed himself forward and swam through the hole, timing it to the very crest of a wave. He almost got it right, but the wave lifted him so high that his right shoulder and then his left buttock both jagged the irregular edge of the rusty plate. For a moment he hung up and then he felt sharp little pains and a sensation of ripping before sliding out into the sea.

Once he was outside Andrew felt a surge of real fear. The waves were bigger, the current was strong, and the sides of the rusty hull towered up like a scaly brown cliff. He had intended to wait there for Carmen but to his dismay he found that the current was sweeping him towards the bow of the wreck at a rapid rate. For a moment he tied to struggle against it and then his common sense kicked in.

Don't fight it! You will just wear yourself out, he told himself. *Just wait at the bow for Carmen.*

So he allowed the current to carry him towards the bow. When he got there, he picked a section of the rusty stem that was free of barnacles and grabbed it with both hands. Luckily the old builders had used huge rivets to fasten the stem pieces together and he has able to get a grip. But it was tenuous and he had to cling on grimly, allowing his feet to trail in the current while he looked back.

He was just in time to see Carmen appear. As she swam out into the waves she was almost at once engulfed in foam from a larger than normal wave that had broken on the reef. For a second Andrew feared Carmen was in trouble, but then her arms and head appeared amid the flurry of bubbles and she came stroking towards him. As she got closer she blinked to clear her eyes and then swam sideway over to join him.

"Grab me and tie us together," he shouted.

He had decided that he did not dare let got with either hand or they would be washed away and trying to tie knots while bobbing in the waves would be much harder. Carmen grabbed him and swung in beside him. Then she groped for the orange rope and quickly looped it through her BCD straps and secured it.

"Ready," she said.

Andrew swallowed and met her eyes. *I'm not!* he thought.

But all he did was smile and nod then let go. They were immediately swept away from the wreck by the current.

Here we go! I hope we haven't made another serious mistake, he thought.

Then he looked around to check the location of the Taiwanese trawler, blinking in the spray as he did.

Chapter 18

TIDAL CURRENTS

For a few seconds something close to panic surged through Andrew. Nowhere in the welter of foam and breaking waves could he see the wreck of the Taiwanese trawler. And the rusty old wreck of the sailing ship was fast receding, was obviously already beyond his reach.

There is no way we can swim back against this current, he thought.

A feeling of frantic desperation gripped his chest and sent his breathing right up. He blinked and shook his head to try to clear the water drops from the outside of the facemask, but condensation was now forming on the inside making it even harder to see.

I hope we haven't made a fatal mistake, he thought, knowing that they were now almost at the mercy of the tidal currents.

For a few moments he tried to salve his anticipatory guilt at having placed Carmen in such a situation of peril. But then he shook his head.

We had no choice, he told himself. *We could not survive another night on that wreck.*

Then a wave ducked him and he came up spluttering for air and retching at the effect of the salt he had swallowed. For a minute or so all he could do was fin hard to keep his head well up while he coughed and cleared his throat and eyes. Having restored his breathing and calmed himself he looked around again.

I will have to navigate by the sun, he decided.

Then he shook his head again and clenched his teeth tighter on his snorkel. *Not quite at the mercy of the currents,* he thought. *We can still swim and we can use our brains.*

That calmed him and got him remembering what he had already thought through earlier. *The tide is making and is flowing west. The main part of the reef is to the west. If we can travel diagonally with it by swimming we stand a chance of being carried back to near that trawler by the ebb.*

But the very thought of the dangers nearly made him give up hope. For a few moments he considered trying to swim back across the Boat

Channel to Yule Reef. His rational mind told him that was a futile hope. Images of being swept out to sea past the trawler the day before by the ebb tide caused him more spasms of fear. The whole situation felt so overwhelming that he experienced an intense desire to just give up and let what might occur happen.

Then a sharp tug on his waist made him look and he found himself looking into Carmen's eyes. She frowned and said, "Are you alright?"

"Just swallowed some water," he replied.

A spurt of guilt coursed through him. *Come on you selfish lubber! Your sister needs your help,* he berated himself. He again looked around, orientated himself and began swimming sidestroke through the choppy, turbulent water.

Every few seconds Andrew brushed against coral with his hands or legs and several times he was washed against coral outcrops that were just below the surface. Each time he was bumped or scratched, and he became afraid that he would get badly cut or stuck by some poisonous spine or shellfish.

Plenty of those on the reef, he thought.

The water was just deep enough to swim in but not deep enough to keep them clear of many outcrops. Worse still the water was very choppy and all churned up by foam making it hard to see any distance. Having the facemask on made it even more difficult but Andrew overcame the claustrophobic anxiety the limited vision engendered, knowing that it was saving his eyes and nose from the stinging effects of the salt water.

For perhaps five minutes he swam as strongly as he could until rapidly increasing exhaustion caused him to grab hold of Carmen. Panting and weak he clung to her. Once again, the BCD saved him but it meant that she was pushed lower and her head was quite often submerged by the waves. However, she kept a tight grip on him and gave him reassuring grins each time.

"It's alright," she told him. "You don't have a life jacket and you need to rest."

Thankfully, Andrew nodded and sucked in air. For a minute or so he rested. Then, out of the corner of his eye, he detected a large dark mass showing amid the foam only twenty metres away. A glance showed him it was a large brain coral.

We can rest on that and I can use it as a lookout, he thought.

As quickly as he considered this he acted. Pointing to it he gasped, "Swim!"

Carmen understood and swam. Both of them put all they could into the effort and they quickly got closer to the coral outcrop. As they approached it Andrew's mind calculated distances and speed and he decided the current would carry them past at least two metres clear, so he put his head down and struck out across the current, swimming overarm as hard as he could. Only when he had to lift his head for a gasp of air did he look to see if he was winning. To his intense relief he saw that they were and a few seconds later he and Carmen were swept against the huge lump of wrinkly coral.

The brain coral was slippery but had just enough wrinkles and crinkles in its surface for them to get a grip and they came to stop, feet trailing. For a few seconds they hung there and then Andrew hauled himself up onto it. The outcrop was almost awash and the bigger waves did wash right over it but much of the time it was exposed. He was able to get right up on the rock and Carmen followed. Once again, the rope tying brother and sister together played a vital part and Andrew knew that without it one of the other of them would have been swept away.

For several minutes they just clung there, gasping for breath and resting their swimming muscles. Only when the trembling had eased did Andrew try to crawl into a sitting position. With the swim fins on this was awkward but he knew they meant the difference between life and death, so he kept them on.

Andrew went to push his facemask up to get a better view and then hesitated. In his mind had been the concept that this was the signal for a diver in distress but he shook his head.

I am in trouble rather than distress and if a big wave hits me the facemask might get washed off. I need it, he thought.

So he pulled it down to hang under his chin instead. Then he wiped his eyes and looked around. What he saw gave him immediate relief and he was glad he had taken the opportunity to get up onto the coral outcrop. Off to his right front about half a kilometre away was the dark brown hulk of the wrecked sailing ship they had come from. Even more satisfying was the sight of the wrecked Taiwanese trawler. It was clearly visible and looked to be about the same distance to his left front.

Now, can we swim to it or will the current take us on westwards? he wondered. That worry got his mind working and he looked at his watch. To his surprise he saw that it was only 0930. *We have only been away from the wreck for about ten minutes!* he thought in astonishment. Now he did a quick calculation. *High water is at about 1000hrs. That means we are close to slack water. So we should wait another ten minutes or so,* he decided.

He explained this to Carmen and she agreed. But it was easier to decide than it was to do. The coral outcrop was being swept by waves several times every minute and it was rounded and slippery and they had trouble clinging on. And there were the problems of cold and cramps to add a strong strain of anxiety.

Then suddenly the problem resolved itself. A large wave struck and Andrew felt himself sliding. Frantically, he scrambled to get a grip on the ridges of coral but to no avail. The wash of water dragged him off into deeper water. He managed to close his eyes just in time and then felt the rope around his waist jerk taut. But any hope that Carmen might be able to drag him back up onto the outcrop was gone within a second as the line went slack. As he tumbled underwater, bumping and scraping at jutting stems of coral and trying to keep his eyes and mouth shut Andrew wondered if the rope had broken. But then it jerked again, painfully, and he knew it hadn't.

Car has been dragged in, he thought.

Feeling cold air on his face he opened his eyes and saw sunlight. Quickly he sucked in a breath and then started finning to stay up. A glance showed Carmen splashing nearby. The stark reality of the situation galvanized Andrew into action. Already the coral outcrop was twenty metres away and it was chillingly obvious that they had no hope of reaching it again. Nor was there another similar outcrop anywhere nearby.

Swim or die! Andrew thought grimly.

He glanced around to check his direction and was able to get some idea from the angle of the sun and the sweep of the waves and current. But he could not see the trawler and that bothered him enormously.

I need to get across to the north about half a kilometre so that when the tide turns and starts going out the current will take us down to the trawler, he reasoned.

So he pulled on his face mask and began swimming across the

current, trying to save his strength by not fighting the flow. As he swam Carmen tried to keep up with him but between the waves and the fact that he had fins and she did not there was a lot of bumping and jerking. Andrew was frequently pulled under and could only be thankful he had the facemask and snorkel. When he was submerged the view was mostly just froth and swirling bubbles but he did get occasional glimpses of coral stems or outcrops. As for the dangerous creatures that might lurk among the coral all he could do as shrug (or cringe) and try to block such thoughts out of his mind.

After a few minutes of swimming Andrew found that his arms and legs felt like they were made of lead and that he was gasping for breath. He stopped swimming and tried to float close to Carmen. This was also not very successful as the waves were building to short, choppy seas that frequently washed over his head. The snorkel went under each time and he had to snort it clear and then put up with the rasping, gurgling sounds that the remaining water caused.

To add to his panting concern Andrew saw that Carmen was looking very worried and pale. Worse still she looked to be gasping for air.

"Are you alright?" he queried.

Carmen nodded. "Just puffed," she replied.

"Me too," Andrew panted back.

He actually meant buggered and scared but he did not say so. But he was dismayed at how quickly his strength gave out. Once again he looked around, hoping for some visual clues as to how they were going. Memories of how he and Carmen had been swept out to sea past the trawler the previous day came to grip his insides with apprehension.

If we miss the wreck that will happen again, he thought. He doubted if he had the strength to swim back to the wreck of the sailing ship. *We will only get one go,* he thought grimly.

And there it was!

Amid the waves and spray Andrew suddenly glimpsed the trawler wreck. It looked to be several hundred metres away but judging by the position of the sun he estimated they were halfway across to it.

We have a chance, he decided.

Just having the wreck in sight was an enormous boost and he resumed swimming, this time angling slightly against the current so as not to lose too much more ground to the incoming tide.

It must be nearly the top of the tide now, he thought. With that idea came the realization that there was hardly any foam over the reef. *The water is so deep the waves are no longer breaking,* Andrew reasoned.

Placing his facemask underwater quickly confirmed this. There was now at least two metres of clear water between him and the bottom.

Mostly seagrass, he noted.

When he lifted his head and resumed swimming Andrew was filled with hope if not energy. After only a couple of minutes he found he was again gasping for breath. So weak did he feel that he experienced a stab of anxiety that he might not be able to keep his head above water. As he struggled to keep his legs moving Carmen closed with him and took his arm.

"Have a rest," she said.

Nodding his thanks Andrew did so although his weight added to hers was almost enough to drag them both under despite the BCD. But it was blessed relief and he slowed his breathing and allowed his overstrained muscles to relax.

I don't want a cramp at the vital moment if we really have to swim for it, he thought.

Then his eye again noted the trawler. For a few seconds his mind did not register what his eyes were seeing. Then the truth struck him with chilling force. *The tide has turned. We are closer to the wreck!* he thought.

Pointing to it he cried, "Car, we must really bust a gut. Now is the moment. The tide has turned."

Carmen nodded and began breast stroking. Andrew did likewise but quickly changed to a side stroke so he could swivel his head to alternately look at Carmen and at the wreck.

It is only a couple of hundred metres. Do I have the strength? he thought.

Then he clenched his teeth onto the mouthpiece of the snorkel. *I must have. If I don't get us there we die,* he told himself. Driven by that thought, and the notion that he had to do everything in his power to save his sister he began swimming as strongly as he could.

The concept was noble, and Andrew stuck manfully to the execution of it for as long as he could. But that was not very long. Within what seemed like only a minute or so he was gasping and floundering. The strength just seemed to drain out of him at every stroke until he was unable to move his arms except in feeble jerks. Worse still his right thigh muscles were seized by a series of agonizing cramps that caused him to double up in pain. Try as he might he could not summon the strength or the willpower to straighten up.

As he slipped under, writhing and whimpering in agony Andrew was sure he was finished. *Now I am going to die. I have let Carmen down,* he thought bitterly.

But even then he still tried to force his protesting and clenched muscles into action. And he was completely underwater and had to hold his breath.

Won't be long now, he thought. Dots began to dance across his vision and his focus went blurry. *Don't struggle! Lie still! Let your natural buoyancy take you back to the surface,* he told himself.

With an even bigger effort of willpower he made his limbs stop moving and he allowed himself to relax. *Only for a few more seconds,* he thought.

Anxiously he looked up, noting the rippling surface just above his head and the sand and seagrass only a metre or so below his dangling fins. But that old familiar sense of panic was rising, and his heart began to hammer and the desperate need—the frantic urge to breathe built up.

Suddenly the rope around his waist jerked taut and Andrew saw Carmen's legs kicking strongly beside him. He felt his hair grabbed and then he almost lost his mouthpiece as he let out an involuntary cry of pain. Carmen was pulling him up by his hair!

It hurt—but he reached the surface in time. As his head broke out into the air he let out a huge exhalation and then sucked in an equally big breathe in case he went under again. But he didn't. Carmen held him in a tight grip and held him up, his chest held hard against the BCD.

"What's the matter?" she croaked. She had swallowed some water and was coughing and her eyes were red and streaming.

"Cramp!" Andrew gasped.

He reached down to pummel the hard-knotted muscle. As he did the cramp released and he experienced a most amazing relief from pain. It was so sudden that he had difficulty accepting it and kept tensing in anticipation of the searing stabs of agony returning.

When they didn't he shook himself and looked around. *Where is the trawler?* he thought. To his enormous relief the trawler looked to be less than a hundred metres away. *We look like we are right in line with it,* he noted.

The wreck lay bows on to them and was canted over at about a forty-five-degree angle to starboard. Andrew saw that the only possible way of getting aboard was where the starboard rail was awash. The hull on the port side was almost completely exposed, showing the anti-fouling paint and battered hull plates showed through a matt of barnacles and marine growths.

But current was still a factor and as he finned to keep his head clear Andrew noted that they were slowly drifting towards the trawler.

Yes, the tide has definitely turned. We have an outgoing current, he thought.

But his satisfaction was short lived. As he drifted closer to the trawler Andrew realized that the current was growing markedly stronger. Worse still he noted that he could see the whole starboard side of the trawler.

The current is taking us away from the trawler! he thought.

Alarm coursed through him as he remembered the current sweeping them out to sea past the trawler the previous day. Twisting his head around Andrew noted that he and Carmen were now right on the edge of a distinct change in the water colour and the wave size.

The current is taking us out into the Challenger Channel again! he thought.

Fear galvanized Andrew into action. "Swim Carmen, swim!" he gasped. "The current is pulling us away from the wreck."

Suiting his actions to his words he began to swim as strongly as he could. Once again, he used side stoke so he could keep an eye on the trawler while checking on Carmen with minimum disruption to his stroke.

Swim! Swim! he told himself, even as he felt his breath starting to come in ragged, coughing rasps.

His limbs once again quickly lost power and with each tiring stroke Andrew's hopes went up and down. The trawler was closer with every stroke and he managed to get back into line with the hull.

Fifty metres, forty metres, thirty metres, he counted down, estimating to keep his own morale up.

Metre by metre brother and sister drew closer to the wreck. Details began to flick into focus, a rusty chain leading down into the water, broken windows on the front of the wheelhouse, dented hull plates, broken portholes, streaks of rust down the once white front of the superstructure, the twisted remains of the cranes used for casting and hauling the nets. A huge hole gaped in the deck and sides, but its edges were so straight that Andrew could only assume it was man-made.

As he swam Andrew kept glancing over his shoulder, terrified of being swept out into the deeper water of the main channel.

Close up the trawler looked quite large, larger than Andrew had anticipated. *But then it had to cross oceans to reach this area,* he thought.

By this time, he was sobbing with frustration and suppressed panic as he was still not close enough and the wreck was now only metres away. Suddenly, the current sped up and the swirl of an eddy sent Andrew twirling around. To his dismay this wrapped the rope around his body and legs and he had to consciously suppress the surge of panic that resulted.

That is just the effect of the current splitting around the wreck, he told himself.

The bow slid past, so close he could almost touch it. Then the sheer of the bow brought the gunwale down in a sweeping curve until it was awash. There, amid a flurry of foam were several steel uprights, stanchions that supported the boat deck.

Grab that stanchion! Andrew told himself.

Summoning every ounce of remaining energy, he struck out across the current and stretched out his right arm toward the steel post. His fingers tipped it but could not close, so he looked at the next and prepared to grab it.

But just as he reached for it another swirling eddy sucked him away from the wreck and his grasping fingers closed on thin air only centimetres from the next upright. Again, Andrew cast a panicky glance over his shoulder at the rippling blue waves of the Challenger Channel and a spasm of terror hit him like a blow.

We are going to be washed out into the open sea again! he thought.

Chapter 19

INTO THE FIRE!

Desperation sent Andrew into a last frantic effort.

We won't survive another night in the sea or on that old sailing ship, he thought. And there was salvation only a metre away. *It is the current eddying around the curve of the hull that is causing the problem,* he reasoned.

His mind raced to a solution and he knew he had to use that tiny back eddy or die. But he was having trouble swimming as the rope was entangled around his legs. Frantically he used his arms to breast stroke. Splashing beside him made him aware that Carmen was also swimming for all she was worth.

Then another eddy carried them both closer and Andrew twitched his whole body like a porpoise and was able to get some propulsion from his swim fins. Before he realized how successful the tactic was he had slammed hard into the steel side of the wreck. And there, right in front of his face, was a stanchion. Driven by the urge for self-preservation he lunged forward and grabbed it.

As his fingers closed on the rusty steel upright Andrew experienced such a surge of relief that he cried aloud. Then he wished he hadn't as a small wave broke and filled his mouth with salt water. Coughing and weeping but still galvanized by fear he clung on.

If I let go we are doomed, he thought.

Then he felt Carmen bumping against him and she also reached up and grabbed the gunwale. "Made it!" she gasped.

Andrew could only nod. He was so exhausted and coughing so much that speech was beyond him. And as he clung there the horrifying thought came to him that he might yet be swept to his death.

Christ, my fingers are weakening fast! he thought with dismay. The stanchion was an angle iron with a thin steel edge that dug into the fingers and which was difficult to grip.

So he tried to haul himself up out of the water and got another shock—he couldn't: he simply lacked the strength.

Bloody hell, to get so close and then to be too weak! he thought.

Carmen tapped him. "Get your arm around the stanchion and I will try to push you over the bulwark," she said.

Andrew knew what she meant. His knowledge of ships made the problem clear to him. The gunwale, the top of the steel bulwarks, was at the same level as he was and because the wreck was heeling over at forty-five degrees the space behind it was flooded.

If I can just lift myself a few centimetres I can slide over the top, he told himself.

By making what felt like a superhuman effort, Andrew managed to heave himself forward and get his left arm hooked around the stanchion. That hurt but brought his head over the gunwale and he whimpered with near despair as another cramp struck him. The pain was so agonizing that all he could do was cling on, trembling violently and feeling his strength ebbing away. And there was safety, right in front of him!

Carmen had washed against him and she also clung to the sides and tried to heave. The sight of her straining face gave Andrew the last ounce of determination he needed.

I can save her at least, he thought.

So he reached across and heaved with his right arm. Carmen struggled, flicked and squirmed and suddenly she was over the rail and splashing about in the shallow water between the bulwarks and the sloping deck.

Better still she was tied to him and as soon as she got her balance she turned, braced her feet against the side and pulled at his arm. Andrew tried to help but the cramp still had him in its agonizing power and then he got snagged on something. With a last failing effort, he wriggled and suddenly he was also over and floundering on his back in the waist deep water.

Carmen helped keep his head clear and then steadied him. To Andrew's relief the cramp eased, and he braced himself beside her.

Made it! he thought. *Safe!*

For several minutes brother and sister just lay in the triangular trough of water trapped in the heeled over bulwarks. Then Andrew began to shiver violently.

We need to get out of the water and get dry, he thought.

He looked towards the bows and saw that the deck sloped up to the break of the focsle. A short set of steel steps led up onto that. Aft the deck was mostly awash but got shallower as it led back past the superstructure to the working deck that took up the stern half of the vessel.

Close beside on their left was an open doorway, the steel door hanging ajar. Andrew pointed and said, "Let's get up to somewhere dry."

Carmen nodded and set to work to untie the rope. But her fingers were so wrinkled and swollen by the long immersion and she was shaking so much that she could not manage it. Nor could Andrew and after swearing to vent his frustration he shook his head and said, "Later. Let's get dry first."

So Carmen turned and groped her way along to the doorway and looked inside. Andrew tried to follow but then discovered that he could not walk in his swim fins. He paused to take them off and this resulted in Carmen pulling the rope taut. She looked back and then smiled. Andrew slipped the swim fins off and gripped them tightly. He was very aware that without them they would both probably be drifting somewhere out in the Coral Sea.

And dead, he mused. Besides, at the back of his mind was the notion that he might need them again. *If we are to somehow get across to Prescott Island,* he thought.

He glanced to his right and saw the distant square block of the stone house quite clearly. It looked tantalisingly close, but then the Challenger Channel sprang into focus and the notion receded. The whole expanse of it was a turbulent froth of white caps and streaks of foam as the outgoing tide clashed with the wind waves from the open sea. Suddenly a sense of despair swept through Andrew and he shook his head.

We could never swim that distance now, or only in the calmest sea with no current, he told himself.

He was suddenly very conscious of how weak he felt and he shivered and fought off a brief spasm of dizziness. Holding the swim fins tightly in his left hand he moved to follow Carmen, then slipped. In the process he stubbed his right toe on some metal projection and the pain brought tears to his eyes.

Carmen looked back again. "You alright, little brother?" she asked.

"Just stubbed my toe," Andrew replied, sucking in gulps of air to try to lessen the pain. Then he gritted his teeth and edged forward, determined to get out of the water. Carmen looked through the open doorway and then climbed inside. The angle of the deck was so steep she needed to use her hands to haul herself up the slope and Andrew had to do the same.

As soon as he stepped over the coaming and through the doorway the conditions changed. The first relief was that they were both somewhere dry and with a real hope that even a bad storm would not change this too much.

This wreck has been here a couple of years now so it has gone through two or three cyclone seasons, Andrew thought.

They were also out of the sun and the wind and that was a real relief as well. But the interior was gloomy and smelly. A sickly odour of rotting marine organisms mixed with the ship smells of diesel, paint and rust and that all made the air quite unpleasant to breathe. But it was better than being chilled and buffeted by every gust of wind, so Andrew ignored the odours.

The doorway opened into a flat that extend right across the superstructure. Five metres in was a companionway that ran at right angles along the centre line of the vessel. At the junction was a recess and in it was a set of steel steps going down to the next deck.

Engine room and so on, Andrew decided after a quick glance. Then he looked both ways along the central corridor. On either side were cabins, their doors ajar or broken off.

There were four cabins, two on either side, and a glance showed that the wreck had been comprehensively stripped. Even most of the furniture was gone, only a couple of bunk frames remaining bolted to the steel bulkheads. A rotting and mildewed rubber mattress hung off one of the bunks but there were no other fittings. Bare electrical wires showed where lights, fans and other equipment had been removed.

Seeing how bare the cabins were caused Andrew a stab of concern. He had been hoping to find food and water on the wreck but now doubt crept in.

If there is any food it will probably be rotten, he thought.

Carmen led the way forward and up a short flight of steps to the wheelhouse. As soon as he climbed up into it Andrew's worry increased. The whole space had been stripped bare. Not a single navigation instrument remained and even the captain's chair had been unbolted and removed. Only the dangling ends of wires showed where the radar set, radios and sonar might once have been.

Carmen looked around and then shook her head. "I was hoping there might be something here we could use, like a radio," she said.

"The vultures have scavenged everything," Andrew replied. The disappointment was so sharp that he had trouble keeping the quaver out of his voice and even in his dehydrated state tears prickled in the corners of his eyes.

He was not wrong. A detailed search of the trawler revealed that even the huge diesel engine had been removed, dragged out through a huge hole which had been cut in the deck and side of the hill. The empty engine room was awash with a sludge of oily water and dead marine creatures. The stench was so revolting that Andrew felt the urge to retch but his empty stomach produced nothing but a trickle of bile.

Out on the working deck Andrew pointed to what remained of the gantry for handling the nets. "They have even taken the booms and the winch."

"And unreeved the steel wire ropes," Carmen added, pointing where an empty bolt hole showed where a pulley block had once hung.

To hide the tears that prickled with his disappointment Andrew turned and looked over the starboard side. He saw that whoever had taken the engines and other large items had just hauled them across the coral to the deep water of the Challenger Channel. Deep channels had been gouged in the reef, leaving masses of dead coral pieces and grey powdery sand.

"Bloody vandals!" Andrew cried, his horror of the environmental destruction fuelling indignation.

Carmen looked and her mouth set in a firm line of disapproval. "I doubt if this was an authorized salvage operation," she commented.

"No, you are right. Just some parasites of the sea."

"Or the trawler owners," Carmen added.

"Let's see if we can find some food or water," Andrew replied, trying to hide his sinking hopes.

We might still be in real trouble, he thought.

They searched for an hour, groping along almost pitch-dark cabins and passageways. But there was nothing. The vessel had been completely stripped of everything valuable. There was no food or water. All they found were a couple of empty plastic bottles that had once contained spring water and some empty beer bottles.

Eyeing the litter of broken glass and beer bottles with distaste Carman stopped searching and leaned on the slimy bulkhead beside her.

"This is not good. We are sweating too much. We need to get out of these wetsuits and get ourselves dry and cool."

So they slowly made their way up to the wheelhouse. Andrew agreed with Carmen's choice. It was not only the natural one, but it was the highest dry area in the wreck, even with most of the windows broken. Here they untied the rope and stripped off the wetsuits and hung them on the rusty projections around the front. Andrew wedged the swim fins in a space where some electronic gadget had been housed. The rope was looped around another steel projection.

After peeling off the wetsuit Andrew looked down at his leg. To his dismay he saw that the hole left by the spear was now gaping and puffy, the surrounding skin all bluish and purple.

God, that looks bad! he thought. Fears of infection flashed through his mind. *Gangrene or septicaemia or what not,* he told himself.

Carmen was equally concerned. She knelt to examine the wound, gently pressing the flesh around it with her finger tips.

"Does that hurt? Are there any pains?" she asked.

Andrew shook his head. The leg felt more numb than sore. Carmen then looked him over and shook her head. "Heavens, you are wreck!" she said, indicating the bruises and scratches he had accumulated during the last few days. Andrew studied himself and was appalled at the number of red weals and small, festering cuts amid the blotched bruises.

"That's what comes from just lying around on the beach," he quipped, making a deliberate attempt at humour. But inside he was gripped by anxiety about his well-being.

Carmen gestured at him and said, "We need to dry out. Let's go up into the sun for a while."

Andrew made a wry face and nodded. He knew what she meant. Their skin was all wrinkled and blotchy from being too long in the water. So they made their way to the uphill side of the wheelhouse and then out through an open door to the boat deck aft. There was a low deckhouse and the sloping deck and the side bulkhead of this formed a V, which they were able to sit down in, resting with their backs against the deckhouse and their legs up the deck. This put them nicely in the sunlight but partly out of the wind.

For a few minutes all Andrew could do was shake and press his eyes shut as the relief took hold. Then, as he began to warm up and dry out he began to experience bouts of shivering. His eyes he kept closed most of the time, partly to shut out the fierce glare reflected off the water and partly to try to make them weep to ease the dry, scratchy feelings.

Perversely, after about twenty minutes, he began to feel hot and dry. His skin felt like dusty sandpaper and he looked himself over. "We will get sunburnt if we stay out here much longer," he said.

Carmen nodded. "You are right. We had better move into some shade," she agreed.

With a groan Andrew struggled to his feet. As he straightened up a wave of dizziness swept over him and he had to grab at the steel rail to stop himself falling. For a minute or so he just stood, trembling and feeling nauseous. Several cramps gripped his leg and arm muscles and he had to endure them for another couple of minutes. This time tears did come and that was some relief. Next to him stood Carmen, suffering similar attacks.

After several more moments of resting Andrew opened his eyes and looked out, squinting against the glare. As his eyes adjusted he noted that he was looking back across the length of Longbow Reef. In the distance he saw the black shape of the wrecked sailing ship. The sight caused him a wry smile.

Well, we seem to have escaped from the frying pan and into the fire, he thought.

Trembling in every muscle, reeling with light-headedness and with his stomach growling from hunger Andrew groped and staggered back to the wheelhouse, one foot on the deck and the other on the bulkhead. Once inside he looked for somewhere to sit with his back to the slope. The only place was the short section of panelling on the far side of the wheelhouse. This was the lower edge and was not easy to reach with so few handholds, but Carmen made her way to it and lowered herself to sit. Andrew joined her.

"This is not good, sis. I was hoping to find some water," he said.

Carmen nodded. "So was I," she replied, passing a puffy, whitish tongue over her cracked lips.

That's how I feel, Andrew thought, giving his own dry mouth and lips and probe with a tongue that now felt like old leather. Then his stomach grumbled again. The noise was so loud it startled him but Carmen laughed.

"We can eat that monster you are hiding in there," she said.

Andrew managed a smile in return but then a chilling thought came to him, product of reading many nautical books. Tales of shipwrecked people in lifeboats resorting to cannibalism to survive caused a spasm of revulsion and then doubt.

I would never eat my sister just so that I can live, he thought. But then fear of death began to darken his perception and doubts crept in. *Would I?* he wondered. With a resolute mental effort he swept such notions from his consciousness. *We are a long way from anything like that,* he thought. *Starvation takes forty or fifty days or so but we will die of thirst long before then.* He knew that in the tropical heat another day or so without water would be the end of them.

Once again, Andrew went to the port side and stared out across the rippling current of the Challenger Channel towards Prescott Island. Through his mind went all the calculations about tides and current speed, hoping he could find a way to reach the island. As he did he studied the water and the reef near him. The tide was now ebbing again and the area of gouged out and damaged coral between the trawler and the deep water of the channel was even more obvious.

At least we can easily reach the deep water without being mangled on coral, he thought.

But even as Andrew did, movement in the clear water almost directly below him attracted his attention. It was a sea snake, one of the black and white banded ones. The reptile swam lazily across the bottom and then vanished in under the hull.

Sea snakes are no real danger, Andrew told himself. He knew that they had very small mouths and short fangs and while they often approached divers out of curiosity they almost never bit one. *But their poison is even more deadly than most land snakes,* he remembered.

Pushing such thoughts from his mind he stared at the distant building on Prescott Island. There was possible salvation.

May be for only a few days before the supplies run out, he decided. But any hope was worth grasping for. *But how to get there?*

Chapter 20

FADING HOPE

A shiver of apprehension ran through Andrew.

If we don't get to safety soon we are done for. We will just dehydrate and die here, he thought. But still he clung to hope. For something to do he went on another tour of inspection, just in case they had missed something.

Carmen came with him but after they had peered into every compartment they could safely reach she shook her head.

"There's nothing here," she said. "I am going to lie down."

"I'll just go to the stern," Andrew replied.

"Why?"

Andrew blushed. "Oh, just to see a man about a dog," he replied.

Carmen nodded and made her way forward to the wheelhouse. Andrew carefully made his way aft along the sloping fish deck, clinging to the bulwarks for support. Once there he relieved himself, all the while scanning the sea and sky for any sign of rescue.

As he finished he looked around the deck.

What is that? he wondered, squinting against the glare to look up into what was left of one of the cranes used for net handling.

What had attracted his attention was the alignment of a small black box. It was only the size of a mobile phone or hand-held GPs and was secured by metal straps to the top of the old crane. The oddity was that the crane was leaning over, but the black box was not. Then Andrew saw that a small silver rod was protruding from the top of the black box.

Is that an aerial? he wondered.

He went to call Carmen but to his dismay his voice came out as a croaky whisper. So instead he made his way forward and climbed into the wheelhouse, then wished he hadn't. Carmen was there but she had pulled her swimsuit right down and was examining a mass of welts and bruise on her body. Andrew had seen his sister naked many times over the years but not in the last few. His mind noted that now she was a very shapely, fully developed women before embarrassment overcame him.

"Oh! Oh sorry!" he gasped, backing out.

"It's alright. You should check yourself too," Carmen called. "Especially that spear wound."

"I didn't mean to embarrass you," Andrew said. "But I've found something peculiar I want you to see."

He made his way aft again. A minute later Carmen followed, now dressed again. She joined him and studied the small object. "What do you think it is?" she asked.

"A radio beacon," Andrew replied.

Carmen nodded. "I think you're right. For the submarine to navigate by."

"Yes. They'd want a good fix to enter this channel under water," he answered, his mind now full of the problems of seeing the reef, even with a periscope. Then another thought came to him and the possible implications of it chilled him. "Those smugglers might come here to retrieve it."

Carmen blanched and looked around. "You are right. They won't leave it to be found by other people. We had better be on guard. If we see them in time we can hide in the wreck. They won't search it."

Andrew decided that was true but then another disturbing thought came to him. "If it was me I'd want a second radio beacon to get a cross-bearing from," he said.

"On the game fishing boat perhaps?" Carmen suggested.

Andrew shook his head. "Yes, they will have one on it for guiding the sub up the Boat Passage but I reckon they will have one over there on Prescott Island to help them determine when to turn out of the main channel."

They both turned and stared at the tiny black shape on Prescott Island and suddenly it did not feel like the safe refuge they had imagined. Andrew felt fear squirm in his bowels and he swallowed, or at least tried to, as his mouth was so dry and his tongue so swollen he had difficulty doing that.

Then he shrugged. "We still need to get there if we can. There's food and water there, and it's the most likely place searchers will come to."

For a few more minutes they discussed how they might do this, but Carmen agreed that swimming was no longer an option. "The current will just take us out to sea and we are now too weak," she said flatly.

"We need to keep watch now. We had better take turn and turnabout on watch," Andrew commented.

Carmen nodded. "You are right. We dare not let those murderers return and catch us napping. We will do two-hour shifts," she said. "You go and get those wet bathers off and dry out for a while. Then get some sleep." Glancing at her watch she added: "I will wake you at fourteen hundred."

Her comment caused Andrew to look at his own watch and he was astonished to see it was just after midday. Probing his dry and cracking lips with a puffy, foul tasting tongue he croaked his assent and began making his way slowly and carefully forward.

He went past the wheelhouse until he was out of sight of his sister and then he carefully shielded his eyes against the glare and hopefully scanned the horizon and then the sky. But there was nothing. Shrugging and trying to tell himself things would work out alright he checked that Carmen could not see him and then gingerly pulled off his bathers.

That hurt as several of the cuts were stuck to the cloth by scabs and he swore when he saw a trickle of blood start.

"Damn! I shouldn't have done that," he told himself.

Then he examined his body and got more shocks. There seemed to be bruises and welts everywhere and he counted a dozen small festering cuts. Then he studied his penis and knew he needed to get dry as it was all wrinkled and blue.

After carefully checking all his various wounds and injuries Andrew carefully placed his bathers on the deck and then lowered himself onto them.

I will just spend ten minutes in the sun to dry my skin and to give the wounds a bit of sunlight, he thought.

With a sigh he wedged himself on the sloping deck with his back to the wheelhouse side and closed his eyes against the glare.

* * * * *

"Wake up little brother! Wake up!"

Carmen's voice at last penetrated Andrew's sleep fuddled brain and he struggled to open eyelids that were gummed together. With an effort of conscious will he resisted the urge to rub the salt encrusted lids and then squinted at where his sister's head was poking around the corner of the superstructure.

"Get up little brother. You are going lobster red in that sun," Carmen said.

Andrew looked down and saw that she was right, and also saw that he was quite naked. Embarrassed he quickly covered himself with his hands. "Oh! Sorry sis! I was just drying out."

Carmen snorted. "Huh! Don't be silly! It's nothing I haven't seen before. Now get dressed and get into the shade," she said.

With that her head withdrew and Andrew was left to hastily stand and pull on his bathers. Shame added to his other emotions and he hoped he hadn't offended her. Since they had become teenagers, Andrew had become extremely sensitive to being seen by his sister and sex was a topic he avoided in her hearing. He was dimly aware that she was a normal young woman, and that at some stage in her life she might get married or at least have male lovers, but he was very protective of her and determined to see that it was the right man and in the right circumstances.

Which is how I feel about Tina, he thought as he climbed thankfully into the cooling shadows of the wheelhouse.

Once there he settled again, wedged on the upper slope by a steel frame that had once held a piece of navigational equipment. Then he tried to relax and sleep again. But sleep would not come. Instead the afflictions of his body grew in his mind till he felt he was itching or smarting all over. And the new pain from his sunburn added another dimension to it.

I'm a bloody fool! he told himself as he peeled down the top of his bathers to glance at the pink skin now showing.

Then he gingerly felt the blisters that had arisen on his sunburnt shoulders and back and on the tops of his feet. These hurt the most and Andrew was amazed at just how much pain there was.

So for half an hour he sat and battled with pain, sinking hopes and thirst. By now he was getting very anxious about the degree of dehydration they were both suffering and also by how weak he felt. This was really bought home when Carmen again appeared and told him it was 1400hrs.

"Your turn on watch little brother," she said.

As he hauled himself to his feet Andrew was dismayed at how weak his legs felt and how dry his tongue was. Then he got another shock when he nearly fell over as he tried to take a step. His whole sense of balance seemed to be gone and only by grabbing at a steel bar and clinging to it did he stop himself pitching headfirst down the sloping deck.

For a couple of minutes he stood there, legs quivering and his whole body in a sort of shiver before he was able to master his muscles sufficiently to make his way out onto the roof of the wheelhouse. Here he took over from Carmen who went down inside as quickly as she could. Within seconds Andrew understood her haste as the rays of the sun were like bars of heat from a griller and he knew his face and body were getting even more sunburnt.

To take his mind off his bodily discomfort Andrew braced himself against the steel railings and began to systematically study the surrounding sea and sky. First, he looked towards Prescott Island and then to the west, where he hoped to see a boat. Next, he swung round to look seawards. The sight of the black bulk of the *Mull of Kintyre* caused him an almost sentimental emotion.

Good old shipwreck! We were dead without you, he thought.

There was no sign of any ships or launches. And the sky was bare of clouds and empty of aircraft. It was all very depressing and Andrew again tried to swallow and to moisten his cracked and flaking lips.

Ten minutes dragged by, then twenty. Suddenly Andrew stiffened. *What is that I can hear?* he thought. *Is it a plane?*

It was. An aircraft came into sight to the south. It was heading directly towards them and Andrew began to croak and caper as hope soared.

"Carmen! Carmen! Plane!" he managed to yell.

Watching the aircraft fly directly towards him sent his hopes even higher and he waved his arms frantically and danced up and down until he lost his balance and had to grab at the railings. Then he shook his head.

I need a mirror! he thought.

By then the aircraft was almost overhead and appeared to be flying at an altitude of only a couple of thousand feet. It was a red and white painted Coastwatch aircraft. But it was not deviating from its course. A sharp stab of anxiety bit into Andrew.

It hasn't seen us, he thought. Again, he waved.

Carmen appeared, bleary eyed and muzzy. But she instantly grasped the situation. Andrew pointed and gasped: "A mirror! We need a mirror!"

Now in a state close to panic he ran into the wheelhouse and looked around. His eyes scanned the wheelhouse windows, most of which were broken. Seeing one which had several large pieces of glass still secured to the window frame he scuttled over to it, moving crabwise on the sloping deck.

But his haste was his undoing and his feet slipped from under him. A moment later he was slipping down the steel deck on his buttocks and back. He ended up crashing into the lower bulkhead. Only the fact that he was able to get his feet up to take the shock saved him from a nasty crash. As it was he was stunned and bruised, and he lay crumpled in the angle and knowing from the smarting of his skin that he had gravel-rashed his shoulders and shoulder blades.

Carmen had heard his cry and she came hurrying down to join him. "Are you alright?" she queried.

"Yes, just a bit scraped," Andrew replied. Ignoring the smarting pains, he squirmed onto his hands and knees and stood up. "Glass, we need some glass."

He reached for some of the glass pieces protruding in a jagged line from the nearest broken window and began to tug at one. Carmen grabbed at his arm. "Stop it Andrew! Stop! You'll cut yourself."

"I already have!" Andrew croaked in reply, holding up his now gashed finger to show her the blood seeping from the new wound. "Doesn't matter. We need a mirror." Turning to the broken window he resumed testing the jagged pieces.

Again, Carmen grabbed at his arm. "Stop Andrew, stop! It is too late. The plane is gone."

Hearing that Andrew suddenly slumped as despair replaced urgent hope. He leaned on the bulkhead and placed the bleeding index finger into his mouth. After sucking it he extracted it to study the cut. It wasn't a large cut but it stung and more blood seeped out.

Andrew sucked it again and he said, "Doesn't matter. It will be back, or another one. We need a mirror handy."

Carmen nodded. "Yes, but we mustn't risk cuts that might get infected. Let's see if one of those broken bottles is more suitable. I don't want to risk us getting another serious injury."

The pair groped their way back into the crew space where they had seen the broken bottles. Andrew crouched and picked up several pieces but they were small and made of thin, brown glass.

"These don't look much," he said.

Carmen picked up one of the 'stubby' beer bottles and agreed. Then she bent and picked up one of the clear plastic mineral water bottles. "I wonder if one of these will work?"

Andrew was doubtful if they could reflect enough sunlight off the curved surfaces but had to concede everything was worth a try so he picked up the second empty plastic bottle and they slowly made their way back out to the open air.

Bracing themselves with one foot on the sloping deck and one on the bulkhead they experimented with trying to send flashing light signals. Carmen held out her right arm and extended her forefinger then turned it upwards until it was vertical. Then she held a piece of glass in her left hand and tried to reflect the sunlight off it. "Remember to point your finger tip at the aircraft or ship," she said, "Otherwise you have no idea where the light is actually pointing."

Andrew knew that but found it very hard to do. He lined his fingertip up on the stone building and kept moving the plastic bottle until he at last saw a flicker of sunlight. Then, by patient experiment he managed to move the weak flickers along his arm and then up his finger.

"It isn't very strong," he commented.

"Better than nothing," Carmen replied as she aimed her piece of glass up at the sky.

"This is hopeless!" Andrew cried. "We are just getting sunburnt and dried out by the wind."

Irritated and disgusted he stepped to the doorway of the wheelhouse and tossed the plastic bottle down. The bottle bounced and fell through the doorway and clattered down across the empty space to the far side.

"You go back on duty while I try to find another mirror," Carmen said. She placed her plastic bottle and the piece of glass on the angle of the sloping deck and made her way back inside.

Andrew looked at his watch and saw that it was 1520.

That took up half an hour, he noted.

Without much hope he resumed his slow scanning of sky and sea. But as the minutes dragged by and he got more and more burnt and dry he continued to lose hope. His skin felt too tight and very sore and his head throbbed. Worse, his vision began to continually blur with black dots and squiggles flitting across his eyes.

I am drying out, he thought unhappily. *We won't last much longer like this.* And he felt very weak. With legs that had become shaky and tired he lowered himself to sit on the deckhouse.

Time dragged but at last 1600 came around. *Time for Carmen to come on watch,* he thought.

So he leaned into the wheelhouse and called, or tried to. To his dismay his voice came as a rasping croak. Unable to make himself heard he slowly climbed inside and made his way to the companionway.

He found her slumped on the floor of the first cabin. She was asleep, so he called and when she didn't stir he knelt and shook her. "Time to get up girl," he said.

There was no response and a moment of alarm bothered Andrew until he noted her steady breathing. *She is right out to it,* he thought. *I will let her sleep and do another hour.*

Slowly he made his way back outside. Finding a place that offered some shadow at the back of the wheelhouse he sat with his back to the bulkhead. From there he could see out to the east and the north. To look to the west he had to stand and look around the side of the wheelhouse. As there was no sign of anything he chose to do this only every ten minutes or so.

If it is a ship it will take an hour to get here, he told himself.

As he sat there, half-closing his eyes against the glare reflected from the waves, Andrew considered their situation. The prognosis was that it was desperate.

We are both too weak to swim across to Prescott Island and there is no way we can construct a raft or something on this wreck. So if we aren't rescued, we are dead, he told himself.

That got him brooding over what death and dying might be like. The concept of dissolution terrified him and he found he was trembling and almost whimpering. Images of people being killed and of dead bodies he had seen rose to haunt him and he started to sob and shake. He would have wept only he was too dry for tears.

To ease his sore and scratchy eyes he closed the lids and then began to pray. As he prayed he tried to moisten his lips and mouth but found that his tongue was swollen and seemed to be stuck to the roof of his mouth. The lips were rough and cracked and had angry little sores developing where the skin was split.

Lifting his head and opening red-rimmed and aching eyes Andrew scanned the empty sea and exposed reef. Half his mind noted that it was low tide and that the wind had dropped completely. So had the waves and the sea presented an oily swell, except where whorls and swirls revealed the tidal currents. The heat shimmered and seemed to envelop him. A sensation of being sucked dry added to his distress.

Watching the sun sinking to touch the western horizon in a ruddy ball added to his gloom. Andrew felt his hopes sinking with the rapidly vanishing daylight.

We won't last another day like that, he told himself.

Chapter 21

THIRD NIGHT

The sun sank until it was a shimmering red disk half-eaten by the sea. For a few moments the waves on the horizon showed as a jagged edge and then twilight began to soften the scene. Andrew scanned the entire horizon in an almost frantic hope that some sign of rescue might appear. But there was nothing. Groaning with pain and exhaustion he lowered himself to the deck and lay back, staring up at the slowly appearing stars as the sky faded from blue to purple to black.

It was very black. He was under water and struggling to work out which way was up. Dark, menacing creatures flitted around in the depths and he began to whimper and cringe and draw his legs up against his body.

I must reach the surface! his panicked mind cried.

But which way is that? And his muscles felt paralysed. Worse still the air in his tanks was running out and he could only suck and gasp at nothing. He groaned.

A noise penetrated his consciousness and he understood he was having a nightmare. The noise came again and he struggled to open his eyes. They felt stuck together and gritty and he had to rub at them. Then he remembered not to rub because of the salt and mucous. Too late! They were sore and he had to blink repeatedly to try to clear them. But still his vision stayed blurry.

If only I could get my eyes to water, he thought. Then realization burst on him. *We are dying from dehydration. We need water!* he told himself. Wakefulness came with awareness. *I have fallen asleep,* he thought, noting that it was quite dark. The only sound was the gentle lap of water against the hull of the trawler. *Salt water,* his now fevered mind told him.

A voice came to him: Carmen's. "Andrew, are you alright?"

Andrew hauled himself to a sitting position and tried to answer. But the reply came out as a groaning croak. *That is the sound that woke me!* he realized.

Then he managed to make words form. "Yes, just thirsty," he answered.

Carmen came into view, half-crawling, half-climbing. She looked so unsteady on her feet that Andrew feared she might stumble and fall. "Sit down Sis," he said.

Carmen slid down beside him and looked up at the stars. "You were supposed to wake me for watch," she chided.

"I thought I could last another hour or so," Andrew answered. "It was nearly dark and I don't think we need to try staying on watch at night."

Carmen looked around and nodded. "I agree. Nobody is going to try navigating these reefs in the dark, or nobody normal," she replied.

They sat in silence for a while. Andrew brooded over the chain of events that had led them to this and on their likely fate. "Sorry Sis. I don't think we will last another day. I wish you hadn't come on this trip," he said.

"Huh! It was me who persuaded you remember," Carmen replied. "Anyway, you have already saved my life. There is still a chance. While there's life there's hope remember."

In response Andrew grunted. He knew the old saying and it was nice to cling to hope but he was feeling very despondent. "I don't see what we can do to save ourselves," he muttered.

"Cheer up! Never say die!" Carman answered. Then she grinned, "Cheer me up," she said, "Tell me again how you are going to join the Army Cadets."

Andrew snorted and then chuckled. "I hope Graham and his mates are having a better time than we are," he said.[1]

"What are that lot doing these holidays?" Carmen queried.

"Doing some cadet parade at Herberton for the re-opening of the old steam railway and then going horse riding at a place called Wondecla," Andrew answered.

"Horse riding!" Carmen cried. "I can't see Graham and his friends being horsey people."

"His sister Kylie and her friend, Margaret, you know, Graham's little girlfriend in Year 9, are both very keen on horse riding apparently," Andrew explained.

---

[1] They weren't. Read *Kylie and the Kelly Gang* by C. R. Cummings.

"I wish we were horse riding," Carmen muttered. Then she dragged herself to her feet and looked around. "Gee it's dark. What is the tide?"

Andrew turned on his watch light to check the time then answered: "Out. Low. High tide is some time after midnight; one twenty or one forty."

"Is there a moon tonight?" Carmen asked.

Andrew nodded. "Yes. It should be a three-quarter moon coming up at about nineteen thirty," he replied. He suspected that Carmen knew perfectly well but was just trying to change the subject to something more positive.

I should be trying to cheer her up, he chided himself.

He hauled himself to his feet, but his legs were so weak and shaky he had to lean heavily on the wheelhouse. Scanning the horizon, he felt apprehension grip his chest. In every direction it was dark—no lights, no sign of any rescue.

Then he had to lower himself as his legs felt too weak to hold his weight and his muscles began to tremble. Lying back in the 'V' he stretched out and gingerly felt his blisters and wounds. His whole body seemed to tingle and itch. When he felt it his skin felt hot to the touch and was dry and powdered with salt. A headache throbbed, making it hard to think clearly and his throat was so constricted he found it hard to breath.

After touching his burning skin Andrew tested his pulse. It was rapid but very weak. *The body is withdrawing fluid from the extremities to try to keep cooling the brain,* he thought.

Fear of having heat stroke caused his stomach to churn and his heart to palpitate even more. *The poor old heart is working overtime trying to push what body fluid there is around the system,* he thought.

Then he gritted his teeth. "Let's rest," he said to Carmen. "In the, morning at slack water we must try to swim to Prescott Island. That will be our last chance before we become too weak."

He found he was croaking and panting for breath, so he lay back and closed his eyes. *If we aren't too weak already!* he thought glumly.

He fell into a restless slumber, forebodings of doom continually rising to the surface of his mind as it dug up knowledge about death he had gleaned from heat stroke lessons he had learned on Navy Cadet First Aid courses. Nightmares mingled with these to cause him to several times rouse himself to half-wakefulness.

His mind noted that it was lighter. *The moon has come up,* he noted through blurry eyes. *Waning. Be only a half-moon in a few days,* he told himself.

Then he slid back into a feverish and tortured slumber. Continually, or so it seemed, he kept changing his position to find a comfortable position. Throbbing aches and tingling itches added to his discomfort.

Hours later he woke to find he was shivering so badly that his teeth were clacking. With an effort he controlled his muscles until only spasm of trembling convulsed him.

Oh my God! That was an awful dream, he told himself. With what seemed like a massive effort he lifted his head to try and look around.

God it's dark! Where has the moon gone? he wondered. Then he became aware of a strong breeze and of a shuddering motion in the structure of the wreck. *What is going on?* he wondered.

Suddenly he was showered with water drops. They felt icy and shocked him into wakefulness. Then a strong gust of wind hit him and a moment later a patter of raindrops.

"Rain!" Andrew croaked, dragging himself upright.

As he did he saw that the whole sky was black and that to the east was just a rolling mass of grey and black. Then he heard the roar of heavy rain on the water and opened his mouth to cry again.

"Rain! Quick, get our wetsuits."

Carmen struggled to sit up and then sat there rubbing her eyes. By then the wind had really picked up and Andrew became almost frantic to catch some of the fresh water. *If we don't have a drink we die,* he told himself.

"Quick, Get up! Wetsuits," he yelled, grabbing at Carmen.

But she was in the way and in his haste to get his wetsuit from inside the wheelhouse he had no option but to scramble over her. In the process he stepped on her leg and accidentally kneed her.

Where did I leave it? he thought.

At the doorway he stopped and looked in, then lowered himself inside. As he did the whole wreck shuddered and lurched. *Big wave,* his mind told him. He knew it was a squall that was hitting them but he also knew that tropical squalls could be over very quickly.

The wetsuits were still hanging on the rusty projections along the front and Andrew lowered himself to them hand over hand, afraid that he might slip and suffer a nasty fall to the other side of the bridge. Grabbing the first one he turned and began hauling himself back up the slope.

Hurry! Hurry! he kept goading himself.

By then Carmen had appeared in the doorway and he handed the wetsuit to her. "Start drinking," he shouted, the blessed cooling drops loosening his dry lips and easing his tongue. By then the wind had risen to gale force and rain was deluging the wreck. Whorls of wind, rain and spray swirled into the wheelhouse, chilling Andrew but giving him hope.

Now mine, he thought.

Turning he began lowering himself down the front of the bridge towards the second wetsuit. As he did he realized that his arm muscles were feeling very weak and his legs were trembling. Grabbing the wetsuit, he turned and began to climb back up the five metres to the open doorway. To his dismay he could hardly haul himself up the slope and he came to a trembling stop.

"God, I am too weak to even drag myself up to save myself!" he cried. It was a terrifying revelation, and for a few seconds he could only cling on and shake. Then he shook his head. "No, by thunder! I'm not dead yet!"

Gritting his teeth and summoning up his last reserves of energy he managed to drag himself up to the open doorway.

Stepping out into the storm was a shock. The sheer strength of the wind hit him like a blow and almost wrenched the wetsuit from his grasp. Gripping it with the realization that grim death was no cliché in this situation he steadied himself behind Carmen and slowly handled the wetsuit to make a drain.

"Aaah!"

After that first big mouthful he stooped to draw breath. The water tasted the sweetest he had ever known. Once again, he drank. Then he continued to gulp, almost oblivious to the howling wind, shuddering movement in the wreck and the showers of icy water. Some of the drops were salt and tasted bitter and Andrew presumed they were from the big waves that were now hammering against the wreck.

The tide must be up, he thought. But it was almost too dark to see. Only the occasional flash of white showed spray. As it was he could hardly make out Carmen or the shape of the superstructure, even though both were within arm's reach.

As he drank more water Andrew's sense of panic receded. *We will last another day now,* he told himself. *There is a chance of rescue.* But then the worrying notion that there might not be any search for them for several more days came to him. *If those smugglers are using our radio to tell people all is well nobody will start to worry about us for a few more days. We need to be able to survive that.*

But how? Then an idea came to him. *Those plastic bottles we tried using for signalling. They will hold water.*

Grabbing Carmen to attract her attention, he shouted in her ear. "Keep drinking. I'm going to get those plastic water bottles for storage."

"Good idea," Carmen shouted back.

Driven by the fear that the rain might stop before he could achieve this Andrew again turned and made his way back into the wheelhouse. Once again, he was appalled at how weak and unsteady he felt. He was also worried by the lurching movement of the wreck. The motions were so violent he was almost thrown off balance a dozen times until he developed a sense of timing to anticipate the next hammering.

His wetsuit was hung on a projection and Andrew proceeded to lower himself hand over hand to the bottom of the canting deck. Twice his body weight was subjected to such sharp pressures from the movement of the wreck that his hands were almost wrenched from the sill they were gaining a tenuous grip on.

Careful boy! he told himself after slipping and nicking his fingers on broken glass sticking out of a window.

The next problem was to find the bottles. Having reached the 'bottom' of the wheelhouse he knelt and groped around in the darkness, blinking to clear his eyes from the mist and spray.

Where are the bloody things? he thought, cursing and scrabbling along in the V between deck and bulkhead.

To his dismay water was swilling around there and more was running down the deck and sides to add to it. Very quickly he found himself crawling in water that was almost knee deep. Then a floating bottle bumped against him. Andrew grabbed at it with the instinct of desperation and held it tightly.

There is another one somewhere, he thought.

But finding it in the darkness and the water sloshing back and forth proved more difficult. But now Andrew was determined.

We are going to survive this, he vowed.

Twice he was hurled off his feet by sudden lurches by the wreck. Each time he banged knees, elbows and hands. More skin came off and his eyes watered, a painful experience as they were still rimed with salt. But he ignored the pain and kept on groping in the sloshing water until he found the other bottle.

"Gotcha!" he cried.

Pleased at his small victory, he set to the arduous task of climbing back up the sloping deck. That led to more slips and skinned knees as he twice lost his grip and slid to a painful halt. Once again, he gritted his teeth and hauled himself slowly up to the open doorway at the top.

Carmen was waiting for him and reached in to help him through the doorway. "You hold the bottle. I'll hold the wetsuit," she said. She turned and held the wetsuit up but almost at once was thrown off balance and went slithering on to her bum. Swearing in a way her mother would never have approved of she struggled to her feet and braced herself then tried again.

Andrew found it very hard to position the small neck of the bottle under the end of the wetsuit as the wind kept flapping the neoprene and the motion of the wreck made it hard to hold the bottle still. But he kept on trying and after a time managed to get one bottle filled. That raised another problem: where to store it?

First, he tried leaning it against the deck but almost as soon as he took his hand away the bottle began to roll and then toppled over, spilling some of the water. Andrew snatched the bottle up again and refilled it. Then, for lack of any better idea, he shoved the bottle down the back of his bathers.

That worked, so when he had the second bottle full he slid it down the front of his bathers. *Now I have to be careful to stay upright,* he reasoned.

Tapping Carmen on the shoulder he called, "All done. We can get out of the wind now."

Carmen nodded and turned, gripping her wetsuit to her front. "I'm cold now," she replied.

Andrew nodded and agreed. While holding Carmen as she moved forward he looked around, noting that the sea all around the wreck was churning white like soapsuds in a washing machine. It was obvious there was no chance of swimming with any hope of survival. For a few moments he braced himself and squinted, searching the blackness for a sign of the other wreck. Then he edged back inside the wheelhouse. The relief was immediate. Only as he worked his way down to the companionway did Andrew realize just how cold he was. He seemed to be nothing but a mass of shivering goose bumps.

He and Carmen made their way into the first cabin, groping carefully along in the darkness. Then they seated themselves. Before he did, Andrew took out the two bottles and stood them in the corner. Satisfied they were as safe as he could make them, he lowered himself to the deck.

At that moment, an extra-large wave struck the wreck. The entire structure lurched to starboard and for a few seconds Andrew feared that it was going to roll right over. As the spasm of fear shot through him, he felt an urgent desire to be out in the open.

Maybe I shouldn't be planning to join the navy, he thought.

The suspicion that he might be claustrophobic came to bother him and he contemplated how he might endure being locked inside a warship at action stations. Then another huge waved slammed against the wreck. Spray even penetrated the cabin and Andrew heard water cascading into the wheelhouse and up the companionway from the engine room. Once again, he tensed with fear, but this time he remembered to grab at the precious bottles of water.

Swallowing with what he acknowledged as fear, he said, "Do you think we should move topside in case the wreck capsizes?"

Carmen shook her head. "No. We will chill too much. It isn't as bad as it feels. I think it's safe enough," she replied.

For a few seconds Andrew had a chilling flashback to that first night on the cay. "If there had been a storm like this on that first night we wouldn't have stood a chance," he commented.

"No, and I wouldn't like our chances if we were still on the *Mull of Kintyre*," Carmen replied.

Memories of the previous night's discomfort and anxiety caused Andrew to shudder. It made him even more determined to get to the safety of Prescott Island. For a few minutes he sat shivering in the darkness while his mind explored the possibilities and probable perils of such a swim.

It will be a desperate thing to try, he decided. *But we must do it.*

Chapter 22

LOWEST EBB

Andrew struggled into consciousness from a series of horrific nightmares. At the back of his sleeping mind had been the thought that he had to make sure they were awake at least half an hour before the bottom of the tide. Rubbing his eyes he rolled over and sat up. For a minute or so he wondered where he was. Then he noted daylight streaming in the shattered cabin window.

Sunlight. It must be daytime, he thought. Then the memory of his plan burst into his consciousness as a cascade of dawning horror. *Oh no! What's the time?*

A check of his watch showed him it was 0715. *Low tide was about 0620,* he thought.

A sickening sense of having failed made him feel bilious for a few seconds. Almost overcome by a sense of dread he struggled to his knees and crawled over and knelt at Carmen's feet.

"Car! Car! Wake up! We must move!" he cried.

Carmen groaned and rubbed her eyes. "What's going on? What's the rush?" she asked.

"We have overslept. We have missed the tide," Andrew replied. Gripped by a driving sense of urgency he stumbled towards the door. As he did he tripped and fell, banging his left knee and skinning the back of his left knuckles.

"Slow down Andrew," Carmen called as she sat up.

Andrew ignored her and hurried along the companionway and out onto the main deck on the starboard side. One glance confirmed his fears: the tide was well and truly out.

Oh no! he groaned.

His plan had been to enter the water about fifteen minutes before the turn of the tide. That way the current would have only carried them out to sea for that short period of time before slack water allowed them to make headway across the Challenger Channel. Then the incoming tide would have carried them in again and Andrew hoped by the time it became strong enough to really drag them along they would be across near Prescott Island. At the very worst he had thought it better to be carried into the waters inshore of the Barrier Reef rather than out into the open ocean.

Now he stared at the channel, his hopes sinking at the sight of the exposed coral and a very choppy, confused sea.

The tide has well and truly turned. It is coming in at a rate of knots, he thought.

Worse still the wind was very strong and was whipping up quite large waves. Some of these were so large they still broke onto the reef in massive churns of foam that shook the wreck when they struck it.

As he stared out across the churning waters of the Challenger Channel Andrew's hopes ebbed. His mind told him that there was no chance of swimming in such a sea.

It will be all we can do just to keep our heads out of the water, he thought. Despair began to seep in.

Carmen joined him, and Andrew explained the problem. "We need to go this morning, before we get any weaker," he said. As his emotions boiled he slammed his bunched fist against the steel bulwark. "Oh bugger! It is all my fault." he cried.

"Nonsense! I am the older. I should have made plans to cope with us being exhausted," Carmen replied. Then she bit her lip as she studied the turbulent ocean and currents and then the distant shape of the stone hut. "We still have to make the attempt," she added quietly.

Andrew shook his head. "We won't make it. The sea is too rough. We will be completely at the mercy of the currents." Even as he spoke he shuddered. That word 'mercy' had a chilling factor when applied to the sea.

The sea doesn't care, he thought. *It will just swallow us and we will vanish forever.*

An image of their rotting, corpses being shredded by the tugging teeth of fish caused him to shudder and the despair welled up again. He let out a sob.

Carmen moved to put her arm around him. "You are right little brother but don't give up hope yet. We can try it again at the top of the tide."

"If this wind drops," Andrew replied. He looked up and noted that

C.R. Cummings

there was a sullen grey overcast and suddenly the whole world seemed to take on a duller, leaden hue to him.

Carmen also studied the weather. "There might be more rain," she commented. "We might get some of those empty beer bottles up and have them ready to fill as well."

Andrew nodded and felt tears chill and prickle at the corners of his eyes. He shook his head at the cruel irony of the real world.

If we didn't have that storm last night we would probably be comatose or delirious from dehydration and heat exhaustion by now, he thought.

Perversely the mention of water made him feel thirsty and he ran his foul-tasting tongue around his cracked lips then winced. Then he became aware that he was chilled.

"We had better put our wetsuits on to stay warm," he said.

So they did. Andrew was shaking so much by then that he had great difficulty carrying out the task and he several times had to stop and lean on the bulkhead, panting as though he was an old man. But the relief was almost immediate except for having really cold hands and feet.

Another check outside showed that conditions had become worse. The waves were bigger and as the tide rose they began to cream onto the reef continually, battering and shaking the trawler. With nothing else to do the pair went on another slow search of the wreck to collect the empty beer bottles and anything else that might be useful.

They found five small beer bottles but nothing else of any use. Even the beer bottles seemed doubtful as seawater had gotten into them along with various marine organism and they now smelt badly. Even after rinsing in the sea they did not smell any good.

"These need washing in fresh water," Carmen commented as she held a bottle upside down to drain.

"Fat chance of that!" Andrew replied, looking out at the now racing clouds. The overcast had thinned and there was no sign of any dark clouds or rain squalls.

Once again, he scanned the horizon for any sign of rescue or the smugglers before stepping back inside out of the chilling wind. By mutual consent the pair made their way to the cabin behind the wheelhouse and settled themselves as comfortably as they could.

"No point in keeping watch," Carmen said. "Even if the crooks come they won't try to reach the wreck in this weather."

To emphasize her words the whole wreck suddenly shuddered as a larger than usual wave pounded against it.

Andrew picked up one of the plastic water bottles that were carefully wedged in the corner and sipped to swill his mouth of the salt and then had a good swig.

Carmen frowned. "Go easy on that little brother. It is all we have."

Andrew nodded. "I know, but I read somewhere that when you drink you shouldn't sip. That doesn't deliver enough liquid to flush the salts out of the liver, or kidneys, or both. You need at least two hundred millilitres in a flood to do that."

Carmen studied her bottl. "That sounds sensible. But we need to conserve it."

"If we need it now we must have it," Andrew replied. "We just have to hope we get more."

That was the rub! *If there isn't any more we are done for,* he thought. It was a depressing idea and his hopes ebbed lower.

Carmen also had a drink and the bottles were placed carefully in the corner again. They settled, hunched against each other to get warm. Andrew particularly felt the chill in his feet, but part from massaging them and moving his legs there was little he could do to warm them.

Another buffeting blow from a wave caused him to look up in time to see a spatter of spray on the window and he saw that it was now so salt encrusted that it was hard to see the sky.

I hope we don't miss any rain, he thought.

Worried by that he hauled himself to his feet and clawed his way to the wheelhouse to look out. But there was no sign of rain, just fast-moving grey clouds that roiled overhead. The wind now howled and eddied continually into the wreck, chilling him more so he retreated back to join Carmen.

Ten thirty. About two hours to High Water, he noted.

With nothing else to do he leaned back and closed his eyes, mentally preparing himself for the ordeal of trying to swim the channel.

Andrew fell into a fitful sleep, only to be woken by a warm sensation that jerked him awake. To his horror he discovered he had wet himself inside the wetsuit. A flush of shame caused him to glance at Carmen to see if she had noticed. To his relief she was asleep, so he very slowly eased himself out of body contact and then slowly got to his feet.

By then he could smell the urine and was experiencing a tingling, burning sensation in his penis. *That doesn't feel good!* he thought, his anxiety level spiking again.

Carefully he made his way out of the cabin, noting that it was 1130. *Half an hour to High Water. Will it be alright?* he wondered as he staggered along the passage way to the downhill side.

But, even before he stepped through the open doorway into the seawater swilling on the sloping main deck, he could tell it would not be. The waves looked enormous and were frothing and churning as a Southeast wind drove them straight in from the open ocean and along the channel.

We will never survive in that, he thought, his hopes sinking another notch. Dread clutched at his heart and he shook his head and muttered in dismay.

To his surprise the clouds were all gone but the wind seemed to be stronger than ever. And it was cold. So was the sea. When he stepped into it he flinched. It felt icy and as he unzipped the wetsuit and rolled it down to his knees to rinse the urine out he came out in goose bumps. Long before he had completed washing himself he was shivering violently.

As quickly as he could Andrew pulled the wetsuit back on and zipped it up. After another scan of the part of the horizon he could see he climbed back inside and hauled himself back up the slope. The effort required to even reach the companionway five metres in shocked him. He found himself clinging to the salt encrusted, rusty steel while panting, his whole body trembling.

It took him several minutes to limp and crawl back to the cabin. As he struggled through the doorway he saw that Carmen was waking up. She yawned, rubbed her eyes and then looked at him.

"Where have you been little brother?" she croaked.

"Just to do a pee," Andrew lied, blushing hotly at the shameful weakness he had experienced.

Carmen seemed not to notice. "Good Idea. I could do with one too. How is the weather?"

Andrew described it as he lowered himself next to her. She bit her lip and looked up at the window on the sloping wall opposite. "So you think it's too dangerous?"

Andrew nodded. "I do. I... Argh! Oooh! Bloody sore muscles!"

Carmen did not argue. "I will have a look while I go to the toilet," she commented. She got up and slowly made her way over him and then out of the cabin. Andrew licked dry lips and then eyed the waterbottle. It was only about three quarters full.

I should be strong, he told himself. But heavens he was thirsty! His throat felt like it was lined with sandpaper.

Finally, he gave in and had another drink, reducing the level in the bottle to about half. As he did Carmen came back in.

"Good idea," she agreed. "We both need a drink."

"What do you think our chances are?" Andrew queried, reluctantly placing the water bottle down.

"Of swimming across the channel to Prescott Island? About nil. The tide has begun to ebb but the wind is pushing big waves in against the outflow so there is a really choppy, confused sea building. We would never be able to swim in it and even if we did we couldn't hope to keep direction or even see where we were trying to get to."

Remembering his previous dismaying experiences Andrew could only agree but his hopes ebbed even more until he felt deeply scared and very dejected.

For the next three hours Andrew lay on the gritty wetsuit, alternately dozing and thinking. At times he was unsure if he was awake or asleep and began to fear that he was becoming delirious. But then he would jerk awake with his heart pounding and raw fear coursing through his veins.

During one of these periods of wakefulness he consciously relived every moment of the drama at the underwater nets and on the dive boat during the murders. To his dismay he found he had trouble picturing the faces of his friends. Even Ella's took an effort to call to mind. To his mild curiosity he noted that he had no trouble picturing the villains.

Especially that murderous mongrel Ivanoff! Andrew told himself.

He vividly remembered how the man had gunned Mr Craig down. The image was so powerful it left Andrew sweating and shuddering. After a few minutes he regained his composure and resumed his re-living. At the front of his mind was the notion that he needed to know everything possible about the men.

If I am to have any chance of beating them and of bringing them to justice. There were four on the game fishing boat, Andrew thought, *Ivanoff is the boss. And there were two other Russians: Viktor and Igor, and that mongrel Barry. He is an Australian low-life.* For several seconds at a time Andrew brought each man's image into sharp focus to try to find a weakness and to be sure. *That Barry mongrel is deadly and so is Ivanoff,* he thought. But what about the other two: Viktor and Igor? *I have to assume they are as well,* he decided.

During this Andrew dozed off again, to wake several hours later, shivering and with a throbbing headache. Groaning and feeling utterly drained he struggled to sit up. He saw that Carmen was lying nearby and that it was still daylight. Again he was conscious of a swollen tongue and a parched mouth.

I need a drink, he thought. For fully two minutes he eyed his drink bottle, torn by the urgent demands of thirst but held back by fear of dying of dehydration. In the end he shrugged. *I need it now or we won't be able to do anything. We will just have to hope there's more rain.*

So he took up the bottle and swilled a little water in his mouth to loosen the lips and tongue. Then he drank deeply. It tasted so good that he had to consciously resist the urge to gulp it all down. As it was he lowered the level to just below a quarter. Seeing how little was left bothered him and again the icy claws of dread clutched at his heart. Carefully he put the bottle down and shook his head.

What is the state of the wind and tide? he wondered.

His ears told him that the wind was still very strong and his hopes at once dropped. Then he was further dismayed to find that he was too weak to just stand up. It took a minute or so of conscious effort to squirm onto his hands and knees and then to lever himself up against the sloping bulkhead.

Through the window showed clear sky but little else. Slowly and painfully Andrew made his way out into the passageway and up to the bridge. The scene there did little to reassure him. The tide was running out, but the waves were still too big to safely swim in. Driven by fading hope he made his way up onto the top of the superstructure. Several times he had to stop as weakness and dizziness almost overcame him.

He was really hoping to see a vessel or even an aircraft to rescue them but after scanning in all direction he saw that there was no sign of any. The only dots on the horizon were the stone building on Prescott Island and the wreck of the sailing ship and a few exposed coral heads. Once again, his morale slumped.

Suddenly his stomach growled. The noise was so loud it startled Andrew and caused him to ruefully shake his head.

God I'm hungry! he thought.

As he did he noted several seagulls hovering in the breeze, maintaining their position with apparently effortless ease. The gulls were staring down into the water in the lee of the wreck, obviously eyeing fish and waiting their moment. Once again Andrew pondered how he might catch a fish but had to admit he could not think of any practical way using his bare hands.

Then one of the gulls landed a few metres away and cocked its left eye at him. Andrew eyed it hungrily back. Suddenly the concept of stuffing uncooked bird into his mouth had great appeal. "You bloody thing!" he muttered. "If only I could get my hands on you!"

Into his mind slid the old joke his friend Graham Kirk had told him about the two French Foreign legionnaires lost in the desert and starving.

They separated to look for food. After a few hours one of them noted vultures circling and then landing over in the direction his friend had gone, Andrew remembered. *Worried about his friend the legionnaire hurried that way, to discover his friend lying on his back in the middle of a claypan and surrounded by vultures that were edging closer. Fearing the worst, the legionnaire rushed forward and chased the birds away. At that his friend, far from being dead, sat up and yelled angrily: "Oh bugger you! I nearly had one then!".*

It was a good joke but, in the circumstances, cut too close to the bone. Andrew had a sudden mental image of himself lying there with the birds pecking the eye balls out of his rotting skull. The image was so powerful that he shuddered and began to sob as the self-pity and fear welled up.

It took him several minutes to calm down again and he sadly wondered if that was indeed to be his fate. *Even if we die inside the wreck the smell will attract things in,* he thought.

Again he shuddered, and he hugged himself and thought dark thoughts of death. His brain noted that it was late afternoon, the sun low in the west and his watch informed him it was 1730hrs. Staring gloomily at the churning mass of water that was the Challenger Channel, he thought, *Low water is at about 1830. We must go in the next half-hour if we are to have any chance.*

With that in mind he slid and crawled and stumbled his way back inside to where Carmen still lay. Seeing her in exactly the same position as he had left her sent Andrew's heart into his mouth. He hurried forward and knelt to check. To his intense relief he saw that her chest had a slight rise and fall.

She's alive! Thank God! he told himself.

Now driven by anxiety he shook his sister awake. She was so weak and befuddled that it took her a few minutes for her to wake up and regain her mental balance.

"What is Andrew?" she croaked.

"The tide. Time to go if we are going," he said.

Carmen cocked her ear to listen then said, "How is the wind?"

"Still strong. And the waves are big," Andrew answered.

Carmen bit her lip and began struggling to her feet. "We'd better look before we decide," she said.

So they slowly made their way downhill to the starboard side. It was now clear of water but from lower down the waves looked even more forbidding. It took only a few seconds for Carmen to make her mind up.

She shook her head. "We would have no chance in that; and it will be dark in an hour."

Andrew swallowed and nodded, his stomach and chest tight bundles of fear. *Carmen is right,* he thought. The idea of trying to swim and maintain direction to find a reef in those waves in the dark was obviously absurd.

By then the sun had sunk to the horizon and the whole western sky was a blaze of red. *Red sky at night, sailor's delight,* Andrew thought.

"Good weather tomorrow," he said.

"We will try in the morning. Let's get in out of this wind," Carmen replied.

Brother and sister made their way slowly back to the cabin and seated themselves. Carmen bent down and picked up her water bottle and had a drink, then looked at Andrew's.

"You don't have much left little brother," she commented.

A feeling of irrational guilt caused Andrew to flare up. "Nor do you! We must drink, or we die. There is no point in saving it and just slowly dehydrating. If we don't reach Prescott Island tomorrow, we will never make it."

With that he picked up his bottle and, ignoring his sister's objections, drank the remaining water. As he placed the bottle down Andrew gave her a defiant glare and then experienced a rush of regret at his outburst.

"Sorry, sis. But if it doesn't rain we are done for."

Carmen nodded and had another drink, leaving only one good swig in the bottom of her bottle. Then she re-arranged her wetsuit and lay down on it. The gloom of evening was setting in by then and with nothing else to do Andrew also lay down. For a while they discussed their plans but then conversation dried up. To Andrew it seemed they had said all they could and were just rehashing the same topics.

So he lay there in the gathering darkness and tried to pray. After a while he slipped into a doze from which he woke repeatedly, usually after another horrific nightmare that sent his heart rate hammering. Then he lay in the darkness and tried to fend off the ghoulish and terrifying thoughts about death and what it might be like.

During those hours both despair and hopelessness set in and Andrew began to resign himself to dying. His hopes reached their lowest ebb.

Even the wind is against me, he thought, listening to the howl of it around the superstructure.

Midnight came and went and again waves shook the wreck and caused him to stir from his fitful doze. On one occasion he woke up in a panic having dreamt that once again he and his sister had missed the tide. A bleary-eyed check of his watch showed him it was only 0315.

Hours to go yet, he thought. *But will we make it?*

Chapter 23

CRUEL DILEMMA

A ndrew struggled into wakefulness from another nightmare. At the back of his sleeping mind had been the thought that he had to make sure they were awake at least half an hour before the bottom of the tide. Rubbing his eyes and groaning he rolled over and sat up. Then he noted a beam of sunlight streaming in through the shattered cabin window.

Sunlight. The storm has gone, he thought. Then the memory of their plan burst into his consciousness. *Oh no! I hope we haven't overslept! What's the time?*

A quick check of his watch showed him it was 0715. *Low tide is about 0830,* he thought. A wave of relief coursed through him and he slumped back against the sloping bulkhead. *I had better not go back to sleep,* he told himself.

Then another worrying idea surfaced. *That sub might be back today. That means the crooks will arrive. We had better be on our guard.*

While sitting there, trying to work out what day it was and if it was the fourth day or the fifth day Andrew glanced at his sister. She was snuffling and shivering and every few seconds she would twitch and whimper.

Having a bad dream poor girl, he thought.

Then his eye noted the water bottle next to Carmen. In her sleep she had bumped it over, but the remaining water was still held by the shape of the bottle. For a few moments Andrew eyed that water and his thirst suddenly seemed to intensify. It occurred to him he could drink the water and then say she had bumped it over and it had all drained out.

It was a terrible temptation and Andrew even reached out towards the bottle before shame and self-loathing made him draw it quickly back.

"You bloody weakling!" he muttered. "She needs it."

Disgusted at his own selfish thoughts Andrew decided to remove temptation. So he shook his sister awake.

Carmen groaned and rubbed her eyes. "What's going on? What's the matter?" she asked.

"No problem. Just time to get up. We don't want to miss the tide," Andrew replied. Then he indicated the water bottle. "Drink your water. You will need it. I will just go to the toilet and check the state of the ocean."

Carmen nodded and made herself comfortable before picking the water bottle up. Andrew hauled himself to his feet, dismayed at how unsteady and weak he felt. Slowly he made his way outside.

It took him several minutes of painful movement to reach the starboard side but as he came out into the open he saw at once that his prophecy had been correct. The wind had dropped to a gentle breeze and the waves had subsided with it.

We have a chance, he thought.

Then he quickly scanned the sea and sky in the hope of seeing a rescue vessel but also out of fear that any vessel he might see could be the murderers.

But there was nothing. Nor did a careful scrutiny of the channel reveal any feather of white to indicate a periscope. *The sub will come in with the rising tide,* he decided, turning his attention to the distant stone building on Prescott Island. It looked a long way away and his heart sank as he contemplated just how weak he felt.

Remembering his plan to enter the water about fifteen minutes before the turn of the tide Andrew carefully studied the sea.

The current should carry us out to sea only for that short time before slack water allows us to swim across the Challenger Channel. Then the incoming tide should carry us in again, he thought. By then he hoped to be near Prescott Island. *Or at the very least we should be across the main part of the channel and be in the back eddy near Bird Cay or Long Reef.*

Now he stared at the channel and bit his lip. *I hope we have the strength,* he thought. *But at least it isn't too rough. Not like yesterday.*

Carmen joined him and Andrew explained the problem. "We need to go this morning, before we get any weaker," he said.

"You are right. No matter what we must make the attempt," Carmen replied.

"I know. We can't put it off," Andrew replied. "OK, let's get our wetsuits on and get ready as quickly as we can."

They both turned and groped their way back inside and along to the cabin. Once there Andrew snatched up his torn and tattered wetsuit and began to struggle into it. But in his haste he kept snagging his feet or arms and the neoprene seemed to cling and hold him back just when he was in a hurry.

Beside him Carmen did likewise. Five minutes later they were done, and both made their way to the wheelhouse to collect the BCD, fins, snorkels and facemasks. As Andrew collected these he kept glancing out through the broken window at the huge expanse of exposed coral stretching away to the Boat Passage. In the distance he got a glimpse of yellow and realized he was looking at the distant exposed sand of the cay on Yule Reef. It was such a tiny thing it brought home to him just what a speck in the ocean it was.

Once he had his wetsuit on he picked up the BCD and helped Carmen to buckle it on. Next he looped his face mask around his neck. Then he collected the ropes and his swim fins.

We don't stand a chance without them, he reasoned.

Then he shuddered and had to master a panic attack as the rising terror of cold-bloodedly swimming out into the deep water and allowing the current to possibly drag them out beyond the outer reef gripped him.

Shark Alley! he thought with a bit of a sob. But he knew it had to be faced so he took several deep breaths and made himself move.

As they began making their way back along the companionway, Carmen pointed into the cabin they had been sleeping in. "Should we take the water bottles with us if we can," she said.

"We can try," Andrew replied.

The pair made their way into the sloping cabin and picked up a bottle each. As Andrew tried to work out how to carry the empty bottle he licked his lips then realised that he was already sweating in the wetsuit and, perversely, that he felt an intense urge to do a pee.

That is good news, but I won't offend Carmen, he thought.

Deciding that they could not carry the plastic bottles Andrew shook his head and put his down. As he did beads of sweat began trickling down his face. The salt in them stung in his eyes. Then the need to urinate became urgent.

Pointing back topsides Andrew said, "I need to pump the bilges. I'll just go back up there."

Carmen smiled and blushed. "So do I. I will go out onto the starboard side.

Andrew placed the plastic bottle down, wishing he could have somehow carried it. But there was no way he could do this while swimming, so he shrugged and left it. Making his way back to the wheelhouse he crawled up to the port side. Once out in the open air he peeled down the top of the wetsuit and began to pee.

As he did he relished the cooling effect of the breeze on his sweating upper body. He was also worried as the urine stung and was a dark yellow.

I need to drink a lot more or my kidneys will be stuffed, he thought.

Then, as he pulled the wetsuit back on he looked around. From up there he got an even better view of the Challenger Channel and the sight of that two kilometres of deep blue water with its obvious tidal currents chilled him.

Bloody hell! This is going to be grim, he thought.

For a few seconds he stood there, nerving himself to face the swim. Then he looked around, partly to relish the pleasant breeze and sunshine and partly in vague hope that there might be some sign of rescue. But sea and sky remained empty and he felt a tightening in his stomach.

No good putting it off, he told himself.

So he made himself go below to re-join Carmen, first calling out to ensure she was dressed again. As he came out of the doorway onto the deck near the lowest side, Andrew saw that Carmen was already leaning over the bulwark preparatory to climbing over.

"Ready?" she said.

"Every minute we delay makes it harder," Andrew replied grimly. He felt both sick and terrified but tried not to show it. "Good luck, sis. Wait for me in the water so we can rope ourselves together," he said in a falsely cheerful voice.

Carmen nodded and climbed up onto the bulwark. Andrew reached forward to steady her as she turned and began to climb gingerly down the outside of the hull. It was about two metres to the water which looked to be about the same depth.

At that moment Andrew's gaze swept once more across the channel to the stone building that was their objective and then around what he could see of the horizon. Then he looked again and blinked. Squinting against the glare he gripped Carmen's upper arm.

"Wait, sis. What's that?' he asked.

Right out on the horizon, on the very limit of his arc of observation, his eye detected a tiny white speck. Whatever it was had just moved into view from behind the superstructure. Andrew frowned and stared, shielding his eyes in the traditional sailor manner.

Then he saw it again and his memory went into overdrive. *That isn't spray from a breaking wave. That is a sail,* he thought.

He had often read about the glimpses the old sailing ship men got of other ships in the distance but now he knew what they were talking about. The object was barely a pinhead in size and even as he looked it vanished. He stared hard at that part of the horizon and the speck reappeared.

"A sail!" Andrew cried, pointing. His voice almost cracked with hope.

Carmen paused and stood up, steadying herself on the superstructure. For a few moments she also stared and then she nodded. "I think 'Sail Ho!' is the traditional call," she replied.

Andrew could only grin. Now he was watching the object it had become definite; a real thing, not just a hopeful imagining, not just white horses on the open ocean. For a fleeting moment he saw sunlight reflect off the white sail and then he glimpsed a tiny black hairline against the sky.

That is their mast, he thought.

It was. For several more minutes brother and sister stood and stared at the almost microscopic white dot. Carmen climbed back down.

"Let's get up on top of the wheelhouse to get a better look," she said.

Andrew understood very clearly. *The higher the observer the further they can see around the curve of the earth,* he thought.

He turned and followed Carmen back inside and up through the wheelhouse to the highest point on the canted superstructure. From up there, there was no doubt. It was a sail.

"And it is coming this way," Carmen said.

"Do we try to swim or do we wait and hope they see us?" Andrew asked.

Carmen shook her head. "We wait. It will be here before we could swim across. They wouldn't see us in the water."

"What if it is the crooks coming back?" Andrew asked, the very idea sending little spasm of fear through him.

Again, Carmen shook her head. "No. Those smugglers wouldn't limit themselves like that. They will keep using their game fishing boat or our research launch. Besides they aren't due back until tomorrow," she said.

That made sense to Andrew, but he still felt anxious. Worry caused him to turn and look to the west to see if any vessels were visible in that direction. There were none. He turned back to study the distant sail and even as he watched he saw sunlight reflect off it again. A larger than usual wave lifted the craft and Andrew got a better look.

"It is a yacht," he said. "Ordinary triangular sails."

"You are right. It just changed course," Carmen answered.

Andrew nodded. "It is coming in fast," he commented.

"Got the wind behind it. Probably doing ten or twelve knots," Carmen agreed.

"We need to find some signalling mirrors so we can attract their attention," Andrew said.

"Yes. You try with your facemask and I will look for some pieces of broken glass," Carmen said.

"I'll just roll down this top of this wetsuit first. It's like being in a sauna now," Andrew commented. He was aware that sweat was now pooling and trickling inside the neoprene and even just unzipping the front was a relief.

Carmen agreed but she only unzipped her BCD and top. "We might have to swim for it and that yacht could arrive within the hour," she said. Then she made her way below to search.

Knowing exactly what they were looking for they did a better job this time. Andrew climbed to the top of the wheelhouse and began trying to signal using the sunlight reflected off his facemask and Carmen found a large shard of broken glass. She picked this up in the second cabin aft of the one they had spent the night in. The glass was from a broken window and was thick and large enough to fit into her hand.

Carmen made her way to the top of the wheelhouse to join him. As she climbed up she showed him the glass and Andrew grinned and nodded. That got him glancing at the sky. He was worried that clouds might come over and make signalling impossible, but he saw that there wasn't a cloud in the sky.

By then the yacht was significantly closer, at least halfway in from the horizon and details were becoming visible. "I hope we aren't putting some innocent people at risk by asking for help," Andrew said.

Carmen made a wry face. "You have to be alive to have a conscience little brother. We don't have a choice in this because we won't last another day without help. We have to get onto that yacht so keep signalling," she replied.

Andrew knew that she was right, but it also impaled him on the horns of a cruel dilemma. After a shrug to symbolically rid himself of such concerns he put up his left forefinger in line with the yacht and began trying to direct sunlight along his arm and onto his finger tip.

As he did this his mind was working overtime on what to do next. He had given this a lot of thought but felt sure that Carmen would strongly disagree. To settle the issue before any rescue he said, "Car, what do we ask these people to do?"

"What do you mean?"

"Well, do we ask them to take us to Townsville or wherever they are heading, or do we just ask for a lift across to Prescott Island?"

Carmen turned and looked at Andrew with astonishment on her face. "Prescott Island! Whatever for?"

"I've been calculating," Andrew explained. "If we go on this yacht it is probably a good ten hours to port. Then we have to convince the relevant authorities to act so they can be out here by dawn tomorrow," Andrew answered.

Carmen frowned. "What one earth are you thinking of? Have you got some wild idea about catching that submarine?" she asked.

Andrew shook his head. He did have but he wasn't going to admit that. His real priority was saving Ella. "No, I was thinking of Ella," he replied.

"Do you think she is still alive?" Carmen asked.

"Yes, I do. I reckon those smugglers are using her to do the talking on the radio to allay any concerns ashore about us," Andrew said.

"And you think they will be using our dive boat rather than their game fishing boat?"

Andrew nodded. "If it was me I would. The game fishing boat really sticks out for what it is, but the dive boat is registered as a research vessel so when the Coastwatch aircraft or patrol boat sees it, it will not attract any attention."

"You might be right, but you can't possibly hope to take on that murderous gang of thugs with any chance of winning," Carmen replied.

"I am going to try," Andrew replied grimly. He set his jaw, determined to argue his case.

"Andrew they will just kill you!" Carmen cried.

"They think I am already dead," Andrew replied grimly. "I will be like the Phantom, I will return and catch them unawares."

"This is crazy talk! Why not leave it to the proper authorities?"

"Because that sub could be back on tomorrow's high tide at about fourteen or fifteen hundred. I doubt that the police or navy could react that fast. They will only get the news tomorrow morning at the earliest, if these people will take it," Andrew answered.

Carmen looked troubled and bit her lip. She turned to him, "That is why you buried the scuba tank and kept all this diving gear." It was a statement.

"Yes. I want to save Ella, and I want to see justice done and I have a plan to do that."

"How?"

Andrew told her. Carmen frowned again and then chewed her lower lip. Andrew noted this and decided that she was weakening. "It is the best thing we can do."

"You could end up very dead," Carmen replied.

Andrew gave a sort laugh. "We have faced that ten times in the last few days. I believe it is possible and I am going to do it," he said.

"What if I forbid you?" Carmen asked.

"I will just defy you. You will have to physically subdue me and restrain me," Andrew answered with finality.

Carmen gave a big sigh. "I was afraid you'd say that," she replied. "OK, but you are not doing this on your own."

That raised another dilemma for Andrew. He did not want his sister placed at risk. "No. I want you safe," he replied.

This caused another argument to erupt as Carmen was adamant that she was part of the plan or it was no deal. Brother and sister both became hot and angry with each other, but Carmen was just as determined.

Then she looked around and gave a short, harsh laugh. "This might be all a bit academic little brother. If we can't attract the attention of the people on that yacht they will just sail by."

Andrew looked and saw that the yacht was now in the entrance to the Challenger Channel, was only about 3km away. Even as he watched it changed course slightly so that he was granted a beam profile. This showed clearly that it was just a standard six or seven metre sail yacht with a single mast. At that moment it was using only a mainsail and a jib.

"It looks like it is heading for Prescott Island," he said. A stab of alarm lanced through him.

If they don't see our signals then they might just sail right by.

Carmen thought the same thing. "Keep signalling," she commanded.

Andrew did, biting his lip with anxiety. Then another horrible thought came to him.

If it goes over to Prescott Island we still might have to try to swim across there!

Chapter 24

EMOTIONAL TURMOIL

His mouth dry from both dehydration and anxiety Andrew focused on getting the weak beam of sunlight reflecting from the facemask he held to shine on his left hand. By the time he managed it the yacht was only a couple of kilometres away and he saw that it was either heading straight up the centre of the channel or towards Prescott Island.

Several more minutes went by with continual attempts to get the sunlight to reflect off the glass. By then Andrew could make out people on the yacht. But the vessel held stubbornly to its course.

"Maybe they aren't looking?" he suggested to Carmen.

"Possibly not," Carmen replied, "But I can see at least four people. Surely one of them will look."

"You would think they would sail over here to look at this wreck, if only out of curiosity," Andrew said.

He was now feeling a tightening in the chest as anxiety became his dominant emotion. *They must see us!* he thought.

Apprehension at the consequences of not being rescued began to filter dark thoughts into his brain.Between attempts to flash sunlight Andrew stood high up and began waving his arms. This effort cost him a deal of pain from his spear wound and sore muscles but he kept it up. The apprehension grew as the yacht began to angle away.

"It is definitely heading for Prescott Island," he said.

In his growing despair he began to grind his teeth and several times he realized that he was involuntarily clenching his fists. After a few more minutes, the yacht was only a kilometre away and was almost beam on. By then the details of its rig and the number of people—four—were now plainly visible. Movement on board showed the people doing things on deck.

Suddenly the yacht swung round. At first Andrew thought it was turning towards them and his hopes soared but then he saw that it had turned the other way. It kept on swinging and then came to a standstill facing into the wind.

Carmen voiced Andrew's thoughts: "They are going to lower the sail."

"Yes," Andrew replied.

He clenched his teeth with frustration as it was obvious the people on the yacht were not looking. *They are focusing on the task in hand,* he told himself.

He said: "Four people: two adults and two kids."

"Yes. Might be a family. One looks like a girl," Carmen replied.

That made Andrew feel anxious again about involving innocent people in the situation. For a few seconds he considered not signalling. Then he shook his head and resumed waving his arms, hoping he was silhouetted against the sky.

He saw the mainsail come down and be furled. Then the jib slid down and the tiny figures clustered around it and Andrew watched helplessly as it was rolled and then secured to the forestay.

"Look this way! Look at me!" he muttered, waving his arms even harder.

In desperation he began to shout. "Ahoy! Help! Ahoy!"

But that did no good. The sound seemed to be snatched away by the breeze or muffled and lost in the splashing of the waves. After several minutes, during which the tide carried the yacht on past the wreck, a small puff of blue smoke appeared above the cabin of the yacht and a feather of white spray appeared at its bow.

"They have switched on their engine," Carmen commented.

Real fear gripped Andrew now and he began shouting again and waving his arms frantically while Carmen used her piece of broken glass to flicker the sunlight.

Then, to Andrew's dismay, the yacht turned away from them and began powering towards Prescott Island. *Oh no! They haven't seen us,* he thought.

A sick feeling of dread began to settle in his stomach and he redoubled his efforts, unaware that he was gasping and muttering.

Suddenly, the yacht swung up into the wind again. *What is it doing now?* he wondered.

He held his breath as he watched the yacht's bows swing further and further around. Only when it was plainly pointing directly at them did he dare to hope.

Carmen stopped signalling and grinned at him. "I think they have seen us," she said.

"I hope so! Keep signalling. We will look silly if they just sail away," Andrew answered. His heart was now hammering and he felt suddenly weak and dizzy. With an effort of willpower, he mastered the sensations and resumed waving his arms.

After another two more minutes there was no doubt; the yacht was sailing directly towards them. *We are saved!* he thought, the elation swamping his emotions and making him gasp and grin.

Several times he experienced severe doubts, fearing that the people on the yacht might be the murderous smugglers. *Oh, I hope not!* he thought. Thinking back over the ordeals of the last four days he doubted if he had the strength to survive another.

But as the yacht got closer his anxiety eased. He saw that the yacht's crew were indeed two adults and two children: a small boy and a girl of about ten or twelve. The man looked to be in his late thirties or early forties and the woman a bit younger, a slim blonde with her hair in a pony tail.

The yacht swung bows on to the tidal current when still about fifty metres from the edge of the reef and it then used its engine to stem the flow. Andrew saw the four people staring at them and he waved again. This time they waved back.

A small red ensign fluttered at the yacht's stern and that cheered Andrew even more. Carmen noted it as well and said, "Kiwis."

The man holding the wheel of the yacht shouted, "Hello! Are you in trouble?"

That seemed a silly question to Andrew, but he nodded and Carmen yelled back, "Yes. We have been marooned. Please help us."

"Certainly. Can we get in there?"

Carmen emphatically shook her head. "No. Too shallow. We will swim out," she called back.

Andrew knew that was a sensible thing to do but the thought of yet again swimming in that current caused him little stabs of fear. Fleeting images of sharks and other groping monsters of the deep caused him to wish he had less imagination.

The man called back, "We will get our dinghy ready just in case."

"Thank you," Carmen called. She waved and then turned and said to Andrew, "OK little brother, back down to the starboard side and we will kit up again."

Feeling immensely relieved but still anxious about yet another swim, Andrew followed her down through the wreck. Brother and sister came out on the main deck again and began preparing to swim. As they did Andrew noted the people on the yacht inflating a small rubber dinghy. This had an outboard motor added to it and it was then lowered over the side. The man climbed in and the woman took over the yacht's wheel from the girl.

"They seem to know what they are doing," Andrew commented as he placed his face mask over his head.

"They should if they live on a yacht," Carmen answered. "Now make sure we haven't left anything behind. We don't want these crooks to find anything and guess we are still alive."

That was a chilling thought that had not occurred to Andrew and he shuddered and experienced a series of vivid flashbacks to Tristan being shot with the powerhead and of Mr Craig being gunned down. Clenching his teeth to hide his fear, Andrew nodded and did a mental inventory of the gear.

Satisfied they had everything he looked out to see if the rescuers were ready. They were. The rubber dinghy was now moving towards them, its motor purring nicely. The yacht remained in position, stemming the tide.

Carmen nudged him. "Ok Andrew, you go first."

Torn between fear and hope Andrew nodded and climbed up onto the bulwark. Turning to face the wreck he pulled on his fins and facemask then lowered himself and let go. He landed with a splash in water that shocked him by its chill. It was so shallow he touched bottom briefly but then he bobbed to the surface and side stroked out away from the wreck.

Carmen followed. By the time she was in the water Andrew was already at the edge of the reef. His instinct was to get this over as quickly as possible. As he stroked out into the deeper water he found the dinghy just upstream of him.

The man smiled and called, "I will keep near you but only come closer if you need help. Swimmers and revolving propellers don't go well together."

Andrew could only agree with that so after a glance back to check that Carmen was alright he set out for the yacht. It was only fifty metres but before he had done even half that he found he was weakening and gasping for breath. Several small waves broke on his face, making him glad he had his facemask on. Some made its way into his mouth and he felt like retching and began to cough.

To make it easier he stopped and put in his snorkel and then continued swimming. The dinghy circled nearby, weaving back and forth between him and Carmen. Because she had the BCD she was higher in the water but that also made it harder to get an efficient swimming stroke and Andrew saw she was also gasping in great gulps of air.

The man noted this and within seconds he was beside her and she reached across and grasped the rope looped around the circumference of the inflatable. Seeing this reassured Andrew so he also resumed swimming.

The yacht seemed to grow slowly in size but after a glance back to check that Carmen was safe he found it towering close overhead. Three welcoming but anxious faces lined the yacht's rail and hands reached down where a short Jacob's ladder had been placed over the side.

With a heaving sigh of relief Andrew swam the last few strokes and grabbed the rope ladder. Pushing up his facemask he blinked and sucked in air. For a minute or so he just clung there, too exhausted to do anything else. Then Carmen joined him. She was also puffing and looked worn out.

Summoning up some energy Andrew bent down and removed his swim fins and passed them up. The little boy took them and then the woman reached down. "Give me your hand," she instructed.

But Andrew preferred to do the climb himself. He shook his head and said, "Grab me when I get up a bit." Even as he did he experienced a fleeting stab of anxiety at the thought that these people might be part of the smuggling gang. Then he shook his head.

No choice now, he told himself.

With an effort that left him gasping Andrew heaved himself up and the woman grabbed his belt and a moment later he was lying on his back on the deck. Carmen joined him a few moments later and then the man scrambled aboard and led a painter aft to tow the dinghy.

"We will get that aboard later," he said. Then he sat on the deckhouse and the other family members sat beside him. All were smiling but plainly very curious. As Carmen sat up he held out his hand, and said, "Hi! I'm Bernie Warren and this is my wife Kiri. And these two scamps are Tammy and Simon."

"Carmen, and this is my little brother Andrew," Carmen replied, shaking his hand.

Bernie raised his eyebrows and said, "Well, what happened? Shipwrecked eh?"

"No," Carmen replied. "Marooned, or left for dead anyway. I will tell you about it later. I don't think I should say in front of the children."

"Oh piffle!" Bernie snorted. "There are no secrets with our children."

"It might be a good idea if there was, for their sakes," Carmen replied seriously.

Bernie and his wife exchanged worried glances and both children looked anxious. "What do you mean?" he asked.

Carmen shook her head. "Sorry. This is life and death stuff, and if they know too much it might be their lives at risk."

"What do you mean? What are you saying? Are you threatening us?" Bernie cried angrily.

"No," Carmen answered. "Please give us a chance to explain, but not in front of the kids."

"Oh alright! Righto Tammy and Simon, go below," Bernie ordered.

As they did Andrew heaved himself to a sitting position, letting out an involuntary groan as he did. Then a sharp pain lanced down his side and he rubbed at his spear wound.

The woman saw this and said, "Are you hurt?"

Andrew nodded. "Yes. I was shot by a speargun."

"Speargun! Let me see. Bernie, get the First Aid kit and a towel," the woman ordered.

Andrew was moved so that they could work on him. Suddenly he just felt exhausted and began to shake. Little spasms of uncontrollable trembling swept through him.

Safe, he thought.

Then he heard the man coming back up from below and experienced another stab of fright. The man was holding a handgun!

Chapter 25

EXPLAIN!

Andrew stared at the tiny black muzzle of the pistol and nearly wet himself with fear.

Oh no! They must be with the smugglers, he thought.

Bernie aimed the pistol at him. "Explain, and it had better be good or you go back into the sea," he grated.

Carmen at once reacted. Her hands shot up and she shook her head. "Please, we are victims here. We need help," she said.

"So what's going on? Who are you and why are saying this is life and death stuff?" Bernie demanded.

"I can explain. Please don't point that gun at us," Carmen replied.

Bernie shook his head and called his wife to move over beside him. Carmen quickly outlined their story. As each incident was mentioned the look of disbelief on both the listener's faces grew until Bernie cut her off by snapping, "This is fantastic. You are making this up."

That so annoyed Andrew that he sat up. "No we aren't! I was... aargh! I really was speared. Look!" He rolled over to point to the holes in his wetsuit. As he did the pain wrenched a groan from him.

That seemed to convince them as a look of anxious horror grew on the woman's face. Bernie frowned and said, "Let me see the wound."

Carmen moved to help and with difficulty Andrew unbuckled his weight belt. He was then helped to sit up so that he could peel off the wetsuit.

When she saw the entry and exit wounds the woman let out a gasp of concern and knelt to study them. "These look nasty. When did they happen?"

"Three days ago, or was it four?" Andrew replied. He twisted to look and was appalled at the puffy red holes in his flesh.

"Four days ago! And you survived here on this wreck?" the woman cried.

Carmen shook her head and pointed westwards. "No. We managed to reach Yule Reef and spent a night there."

Bernie now looked very doubtful but lowered the pistol. "You are claiming that these foreigners turned up and murdered your friends and hijacked your boat and then left you for dead?"

"No," Carmen answered. "They threw Andrew into the sea to drown and then I dived overboard to try to escape. Luckily Andrew had retrieved the emergency air tank on the shot line and was able to save me as well."

Bernie frowned. "But why didn't these people then hunt you down?" he queried.

"Because they thought we were both dead," Carmen answered. She then explained how they had stayed under water and then swum to the reef to hide.

"Unbelievable! Amazing!" Bernie said. Then he put the gun down and moved to study Andrew's spear wounds. "Sorry, but you can't be too careful. So why do you think the story might put us at risk?"

"Because they are obviously part of a dangerous gang and if they hear you have heard about them they might try to silence you as well," Carmen replied.

Andrew nodded. "Or they might come after you out of revenge."

"And they have a real submarine?"

Andrew nodded. "An old Russian one. I saw it. And it is due back tomorrow."

"So we need to get out of here and tell the authorities," Bernie commented.

"Yes," Andrew Answered, "But we also have a plan."

Bernie raised an eyebrow. "Don't you just want to go straight to the nearest town to report this to the police?" he asked.

Andrew glanced at Carmen and then emphatically shook his head. "We want you to do that. We will write a letter to give them, but we want you to take us to Prescott Island."

Bernie and his wife both looked over their shoulder at the distant cay. "Prescott Island? We were going there anyway, but why?"

"Our base camp is there and there are some things we need," Andrew answered.

Even now he had only the glimmerings of a plan and did not want to reveal it to anyone in case they let it slip or were forced to talk.

Bernie shrugged. "OK, so we go there. Can the kids come up now?"

"Yes," Carmen agreed.

The two children were called up and they both looked at Andrew and Carmen with very curious, half-fearful eyes. Bernie said to them, "These two are in a bit of trouble. Some bad men are after them and you are not to tell anyone you have seen them, got that?"

"Yes dad," both chorused.

Bernie's wife now increased the engine revolutions and spun the wheel to port. The yacht at once sheered off away from the reef and proceeded northwards across the channel. As it did Andrew looked back at the wreck of the trawler and then at the now distant black lump that marked the wreck of the *Mull of Kintyre* and he silently gave thanks for them being there.

Otherwise Carmen and I would be dead, he thought.

Bernie and Carmen now set to work doctoring Andrew's wounds properly. This required him to lie on his side and a pillow was placed under his head by young Tammy who was obviously just itching to ask what the story was. Old long-sleeved shirts were handed to both Andrew and Carmen and he sat up to pull it on then lay down again, his head reeling from the effort.

Lying in the sun and out of the breeze Andrew began to sweat. That reminded him of how thirsty he was and he croaked a request for a drink of water. Young Simon hurried below and a minute later bobbed up with a cupful. Andrew drank this greedily then sighed and lay back to allow the doctoring to go on.

There wasn't much that could be done but after the wounds and worst scratches were washed out with warm water (bliss!) antiseptic was applied. Bandaids or Elastoplast coverings were then applied. By then Andrew had begun to relax and he would have gone to sleep except that his stomach gave a loud grumble and he realized how hungry he was.

The two children giggled at the sound and Carmen said, "We haven't eaten for four days. Could we have something to eat please?"

"After we anchor," the woman replied.

By this time they were halfway across the Challenger Channel and the stone building on Prescott Island was clearly visible, along with a few other details.

Bernie gestured to the building. "You are very lucky. We only came this way out of idle curiosity. We were on course from Wellington to Townsville and would have gone through the Great Barrier Reef via the

Flinders Channel, but Tammy noted that hut on the chart and the wording intrigued her."

Tammy nodded. "It said: 'Historic ruin'. I really want to see it," she explained.

Bernie took up the tale again. "So we detoured a bit. I take it you have been there?"

"Yes," Carmen answered. "Our expedition base camp is in the lee of that little clump of trees to the west of the building."

"So what's its story? What happened here?" Bernie asked.

"You tell it Andrew," Carmen replied. "You are better at it than me."

Andrew just wanted a feed and a sleep but despite sore eyes and a throbbing headache he complied.

"Prescott Island was discovered in the 1850s by Captain Prescott of the schooner *Flying Scud*. Prescott by all accounts was a bit of a rogue and later became a notorious 'Blackbirder.'

"A what?" Young Simon asked.

"A Blackbirder. They were men who went to the islands to the South Pacific and kidnapped or cajoled natives to bring them to Queensland in the 1880s to work as indentured labourers in the sugar plantations," Andrew explained.

Tammy frowned. "Like slaves?" she enquired.

"Sort of," Andrew answered. "Indentured means they had signed a binding contract but in reality they could not read or write so did not understand what they were signing."

Kiri made a face. "So they were tricked?"

Andrew nodded. "Mostly. And some were just taken by force or purchased from their chief who used it as a good opportunity to get rid of his rivals and enemies. When they got to Queensland their contracts were sold to plantation owners."

"So it was slavery?" Kiri commented.

"Not legally," Andrew replied. "Slavery was abolished in the British Empire way back in 1803 or something and this part of the world was part of the British Empire then."

"But a long way from London," Bernie commented with a wry smile.

Carmen nodded. "Yes, and a long way from Brisbane, which was the colonial capital."

"So there would have been a lot of abuses," Kiri added.

Andrew again nodded. "Possibly. But there was some law enforcement and it can't have been too bad for most of the Kanakas stayed on after their five or seven years contracts were up."

"But what's that got to do with Prescott Island?" Bernie asked, nodding towards the reef they were rapidly approaching.

Carmen pointed to port. "Go around to the west of the island and come in in the lee. There's a sort of harbour there in sheltered water. It was made by Captain Prescott by blasting and dredging the coral."

Tammy was horrified and so was Kiri, but Bernie chuckled. "Not very environmentally friendly, the early pioneers, were they?"

Carmen shook her head and turned to Andrew. "Go on Andrew."

Andrew studied the island, which was now less than a kilometre away. "The island is a coral cay but over thousands of years it has also been a bird nesting site and their droppings had built up."

"Guano," commented Bernie with a knowing nod.

Andrew nodded in reply. "Yes, guano."

Tammy put her hand up like she was in school. "Please, what's guano?"

Bernie answered that. "Bird poo Tam. It makes very good fertilizer. It is some sort of chemical."

"Phosphate," Andrew said. "So there was a thick layer of guano and Captain Prescott realized it was worth a lot of money as the sugar farmers needed lots to fertilize their fields."

Tammy wrinkled her nose in distaste and Simon giggled. Tammy said, "But how does it work?"

Andrew shrugged. "I not a chemist but from what I have read I understand that tropical soils quickly degrade and lose fertility unless the farmers use crop rotation and leave some fields fallow to recover. Fertilizer puts some of the goodness back in so that plants grow better."

Kiri pouted. "Yes, it does, but it also causes environmental problems for coral reefs with things like algal blooms and build-up of unnatural chemicals."

"It does," agreed Andrew. "Anyway, Captain Prescott organized a gang of Kanakas and some white overseers."

"What's kanakas?" Simon interrupted.

Carmen answered that. "Black men from the South Pacific islands.

In French New Caledonia and the surrounding islands, the locals call themselves Kanaks. The word comes from that."

Simon nodded and said, "I see."

Andrew picked up the tale. "Well, Captain Prescott organized a schooner load of Kanakas and four white overseers and took them to the island. He then set them to work. First they built that stone building." He pointed to it.

"Why?" Tammy asked.

"To store the guano when it was mined and bagged, to keep it out of the weather," Andrew replied.

They all nodded so he went on. "Prescott went back and forth between the island and the mainland ferrying out food and supplies and carrying back the phosphate. He had the men lay small narrow-gauge railways so that the guano could be moved more easily to the shed and then to his loading point."

"Railways?" queried Simon, his interest aroused.

Andrew nodded. "Yes. Or maybe they should be called tramways. They are two-foot gauge, the same as most of the sugar mills use in North Queensland to move the cut cane from the farms to the mills."

"Were there steam engines and all?" Simon asked.

Andrew shook his head. "No. There were only small skips like they used in the mines to move ore to the surface. The men had to push them by hand."

Simon looked disappointed. "Is there anything left of these railways?"

"Only a few rusting rails near the quay and a couple of old rusty skips," he replied.

Bernie raised an eyebrow. "Quay?"

Carmen answered him. "Only a small one, made of blocks of coral stone. You won't be able to get your yacht alongside. It is only big enough for rowing boats."

"Did they dig big holes?" Simon asked.

Andrew shook his head. "Not really. The guano was in a layer on the top and they sort of shaved it off. There are a few rough areas where they dug right down to the old coral reef the island is built on but a lot of that has since been filled in by drifting sand."

Kiri frowned. "We've been to Nauru and it was mined for phosphate.

It is a real environmental disaster. It looks like the surface of the moon in most places, all jagged limestone."

Andrew shrugged. "This place probably would to except they never completely mined it."

"Why not?" Bernie asked. "Wasn't it economic?"

Andrew shook his head. "No, there was a massacre, and nobody ever restarted the mine," he explained.

"Massacre?" Kiri queried.

"Yes. The schooner arrived one day in 1889 and anchored in the lagoon, just there off the western side of the island where we are going now," Andrew, said, pointing just ahead.

By this time they were close to the western tip of the island and the motion was easing as they moved out of the main current and wind waves. When he was satisfied Bernie knew where to con the yacht, Andrew continued.

"Anyhow, during the first night the Kanakas rebelled and began killing the overseers and then swam out and seized the schooner. They hacked Captain Prescott to bits with cane knives and killed the mate, who was the only other European on the schooner and then chopped up any of the native crew who wouldn't join them. Then they sailed away."

"Where to?" asked Tammy.

Andrew shrugged. "No idea. They were never seen again and nor was the schooner. They might have got back to their own islands safely as they were all good seafarers."

"They are that," Bernie agreed. "Pacific Islanders would have no trouble navigating across the Coral Sea."

Young Simon frowned. "So how do we know what happened?"

"Because one of the white overseers survived," Andrew replied. "He pretended to be dead and waited till the schooner had sailed away. Then he just lived on the island for four months before somebody came to see why Captain Prescott hadn't returned to Townsville."

"You know this story well," Kiri commented.

Carmen grinned and nodded. "It is a skeleton from the family cupboard of local history," she explained. "The survivor was our great grandfather's brother."

"Lenny was his name," Andrew added. "He died seventy years ago but there is a photo of him at home. He looks horrible."

"Oh, why?" Bernie asked.

Andrew grinned ruefully and shook his head. "Because when the Kanakas attacked he was working in the cookhouse and one of them struck him in the face with a tomahawk. It hit him so hard it split the bone of his skull and stuck in. The cut was up on his left forehead."

He placed his hand up to show where and both Tammy and Young Simon looked horrified. Amused by their reaction Andrew again placed his hand to represent the tomahawk blade. "It broke the bridge of his nose and cut open his right cheek and knocked out a couple of teeth."

"Urgh!" cried Tammy with a shudder.

Andrew went on. "Old Uncle Lenny was stunned and fell down. As he did he hit his head and went unconscious. When he came to he found the axe still embedded in his face, blood all over him and the Kanakas all gone; or so he said."

Carmen nodded and added. "According to family legend he thinks that is why he survived. The other white men had all been hacked to death. He believed that the Kanakas thought he was dead and just left him lying there while they looted the food store."

"But how did he survive the wound?" Kiri asked.

Andrew chuckled and remembered the old family tale. "He said that he tried to pull the tomahawk out of his face, but the movement caused such an intense pain that he blacked out. When he woke up he very carefully tried again but claimed that he heard the bones of his skull grating against each other."

"Errk! That's horrible!" Tammy cried.

Andrew suddenly shuddered as horrific flashbacks of the massacre on the dive boat came to him. Then he shrugged and went on. "His story was that he was too scared to pull the axe head out in case it opened up his skull, so he packed around the wound with cotton wool and then bandaged the blade tightly to his head. Then he burnt off the wooden handle."

Young Simon looked puzzled. "But why?"

Andrew used his hands to demonstrate as he explained. "He was scared that the handle might catch against something and act like a lever and prize his skull open and kill him."

Once again, the children cried in horror and looked disgusted. Then Tammy asked, "How did he burn it off?"

"By setting fire to it."

"But... but wouldn't he get burnt?"

Andrew nodded. "He did. He forgot about his beard and it caught fire and so did the bandages and he had to run into the sea to put the flames out. He got badly burnt up the left side of his face and that added to the scars that made him look horrible."

"Errk! How awful!" Tammy cried.

Young Simon frowned. "But how did they get the tomahawk out?"

"Apparently the wound became infected and Uncle Lenny soused it with rum as an antiseptic. But that stung so much that he drank some rum to deaden the pain. Then he drank some more and became really drunk and while he was sozzled he fell over and at some stage the blade worked itself free and fell out. That was two weeks after the attack."

"Two weeks!" gasped Tammy.

Andrew nodded. "It was four months before a ship arrived to investigate why the schooner hadn't returned. By then the wound had healed and he was left horribly scarred."

"What happened to the people and the schooner?" Tammy asked. She was obviously fascinated by the tale.

Andrew shrugged. "Uncle Lenny said that when he came to after the attack the Kanakas and the schooner were gone. They were never seen again, or not seen by any white man who could identify them."

"Did they just go home?" Tammy asked.

"They might have, in which case they probably burnt or sank the schooner," Andrew answered.

Bernie turned to look at Prescott Island which was now only a few hundred metres on their starboard beam. "Four months of sitting and waiting in the hope that someone would arrive. It would send me barmy."

Kiri grinned. "I thought you already were!" she quipped.

Bernie snorted. "Huh! But you've go to admit this place is the original desert isle. It is not the place I would choose to play Robinson Crusoe!"

Carmen gave a wry smile and shook her head. "I don't think you get to choose where you will be Robinson Crusoe," she commented.

They all smiled or chuckled at that. Then Tammy frowned. "But what did he eat for four months? There are no coconut trees or fruit trees or anything."

Andrew glanced at Prescott Island and studied the straggle of bent cottonwood trees that grew on the Southwest side of the island near the stone house.

I hope our base camp hasn't been looted, he thought.

Then he answered. "He ate fish, birds eggs, birds and the food left in the store room."

"Didn't the Kanakas take it?" queried Young Simon.

"Only some of it. There was enough for fifty people for three months," Andrew explained.

"What sort of food?" Tammy asked.

"Salt beef, salt pork, dried peas, biscuit, flour, that sort of thing," Andrew answered.

Young Simon wrinkled his nose and went "Errk!"

Kiri shook her head. "Four months! On salt beef and not knowing if you'd be rescued. It would drive me mad," she said.

At that Andrew shuddered. He thought: *Carmen and I haven't even survived four days and it seems like four months.*

Chapter 26

PRESCOTT ISLAND

Bernie looked at Prescott Island and shook his head. "This island certainly has a terrible past," he said.

At that Andrew experienced another series of vivid flashbacks to the murder of Tristan and the massacre on the dive boat and he shuddered and broke into a sweat.

Now I have to survive a few more days, he thought.

As the yacht began rounding into the sheltered lee of the island Tammy frowned again. "But what did those people, those Kankys or whatever, drink?" she asked.

Carmen pointed to the stone building, now looming much larger than it had earlier appeared. "Kanakas they were called. There is a cistern built into the stone building," she explained. "It collects rainwater. When it was new, the water would've been alright. But not now."

"So what did you people on the expedition drink?" Kiri asked.

"We brought our own water on our dive boat," Carmen answered.

Just thinking about drinking caused Andrew to feel a raging thirst so he lifted the cup and gulped the remaining down then asked for more. The next cupful followed nearly as fast. Carmen also drank some more.

They were right in the shelter of the island by this and Bernie conned the yacht slowly around to where an obvious ending of the brown colour of the submerged coral showed the yacht now had a sandy sea bed under it. Here the waves were mere ripples and the water crystal clear.

Andrew pointed ahead. "See that little gap in the coral? That is the boat harbour."

The artificial gap stood out very clearly. It was about ten metres wide and fifty long and extended all the way from the edge of the fringing reef to the sand of the beach. Near the shore rocks that were awash indicated where a small quay had once been constructed.

At Carmen's guidance the yacht was hove to and preparations made to drop the anchor. Then the rubber boat was hauled alongside. While this was done Andrew studied the island. He had been there twice before but was still struck by how much larger it looked close up than it did from a distance. The actual sand cay was almost half a kilometre long and several hundred metres wide. It stood at least five metres above sea level in the central part and he knew that only the highest storm waves and cyclonic storm surges were able to wash over it.

Directly in line with the boat harbour was the stone building, now revealed to be constructed of massive blocks of coral rock and even granite. It had one door and a number of small windows high up and some tumbled rocks on the roof reminded Andrew that there was even a set of stone steps leading to the flat roof.

During the last few minutes the family had all been scampering about the yacht and Andrew saw that they were preparing to anchor. All was done with barely a word of command and was obviously a practised drill. With a spin of the wheel Bernie brought the yacht's head to the wind and the anchor was hove over. Within minutes the sails were down and brailed and the vessel was secure.

Kiri stood up and said, "Morning tea."

Andrew thought that a wonderful idea and his stomach grumbled again just at the thought of food. Cake, biscuits and cordial were quickly provided and they sat and ate in the shade of an awning the children had rigged across the boom. The sweet cordial tasted heavenly to him and he wolfed down the cake and biscuits, hardly noticing their taste.

"Sorry," he apologized. "We are a bit hungry."

To emphasize this Andrew's stomach grumbled again and the children laughed. Kiri smiled and replied, "It looks it. Have some more cake."

So they did. For twenty minutes they just sat and relaxed and consumed more food and drink. Andrew was sure he could feel the energy flowing back into his body but he still felt very weak and drained.

The dinghy was then hauled around and Bernie climbed down into it. He then invited Carmen and Andrew to join him. This took a bit of an effort as Andrew felt so weak that he shook and felt dizzy as he lowered himself slowly into the tiny rubber boat. Carmen was obviously feeling the same as she stopped halfway and clung on for a moment while she shook her head and trembled. Andrew reached up and steadied her until she was seated. They then pushed off. In what seemed like no time at all they had reached the shore.

Both Andrew and Carmen climbed slowly out. As he stood on the sandy bottom Andrew experienced a rush or relief and felt tears prickle in his eyes. But when he tried to stand up he found he was so dizzy he had to cling to the dinghy for a few seconds. Then the dizziness passed and he turned and waded ashore, but was troubled to find that he could hardly keep his balance. He felt so weak he was worried he might just fall down. Carmen joined him, holding her head and muttering.

Bernie gestured back to the yacht. "I'll just get Kiri and the kids," he said before pushing off again.

As Andrew watched the dinghy moving away the notion crossed his mind that Bernie might not come back. *He might just leave us,* he thought, the stab of fear at being again marooned leaving him shaking and feeling ill. Then he saw the mother and children climbing down into the dingy and he felt bad at having such negative thoughts.

While the dinghy headed back for the shore Andrew stood waiting, his thoughts and desires in turmoil. Having been rescued he was almost overwhelmed by the urge to get away, to get to normality and safety.

We could just ask them to take us to Townsville, he thought, images of hot showers, warm beds and good food flitting through his thoughts to tempt him. But that warred with his deep urge to exact justice on the murderers.

The dinghy ran onto the beach and the family climbed out. Tammy at once went running towards the stone house. Her little brother followed. Kiri called for them to wait and Carmen had to call out as well. "It is not safe children. You are not allowed in," she explained.

Even so the two children hurried to the door and looked at it, then quickly ran around the outside of the building. Andrew and Bernie followed more slowly once the dingy had been safely beached above high tide level.

At the stone hut Andrew pointed to the warning notice forbidding people from entering the old structure. A steel door with a heavy padlock made it difficult to do that in any case.

Young Simon returned from scampering around the outside. "It looks as strong as anything," he grumbled.

"It does," Carmen agreed. Andrew could only nod. It did. The blocks of coral stone were quite massive, over half a metre square, and looked to be hardly weathered at all.

"It is the roof. The supports are starting to crumble," Andrew explained.

So they contented themselves with walking around the building and discussing how it was built. As they did Andrew again marvelled at how hard working the early European pioneers had been.

As he walked along the south side and into the stronger winds Andrew looked to his right across the Challenger Channel and saw the two tiny black lumps that were the ship wrecks and he could only shake his head and offer a silent prayer of thanks. For days he had been yearning to reach the relative safety of Prescott Island.

And here we are, he thought thankfully.

For a few moments he stood and shielded his eyes against the glare while he scanned the rippling waves and dark flat sections of distant reef for the sand cay on Yule Reef.

There it is, he told himself as he glimpsed the tiny strip of pale yellow sand in the distance.

Suddenly, searing memories of murder and desperate survival swamped him and he shuddered and broke into a trembling sweat. The urge to be gone, to hurry away from this place to safety, gripped him and he had to battle with this.

Don't be a coward, he told himself. *You can ensure justice.* Then more worrying thoughts sobered him. *If we don't bring these crooks to justice, they might hunt us to silence inconvenient witnesses.*

The notion of having to live in fear, of constantly looking over his shoulder wondering when a murderer might strike chilled him and added to his resolve.

So he steeled himself and vowed to see the thing through. Turning away from the others he walked with slow and stumbling steps the hundred paces to the small tangle of cottonwood trees on the sheltered NW side of the island to check if their camp had been discovered.

Carmen followed with the two children scampering behind. The parents strolled around the stone building and stood talking. Andrew glanced back and noticed this and the thought crossed his mind that they were probably discussing what to do about him and Carmen.

On reaching the cottonwoods Andrew detoured to their northern side and went around to the leeward end. There, tucked in below the rise of sand but well above high tide level, was the camp. It was just two tarpaulins stretched between overhanging branches. Under each were several stretchers and a pile of plastic storage boxes and personal gear in bags or packs. Several of the plastic storage boxes were sturdy affairs with carrying handles and it was to these that he directed his attentions.

Andrew walked in under the first tarpaulin and at once sighed with the relief of being in deep shadow and out of the direct rays of the sun. Memory then guided him to the box he sought and he was able to locate the items he wanted fairly quickly. While he looked Carmen explained the camp to the children and they proceeded to test the stretchers.

Tammy lay on one and then sat up. "But why have a camp when you had a boat you could sleep on?" she queried.

Carmen smiled. "Because you get tired of bobbing around all the time. It makes a nice change to sleep in camp on a beach."

"Where did you cook?" Tammy asked.

Carmen pointed. "Here, on a gas cooker."

Young Simon joined them. "Can we have something to eat now?"

Carmen laughed and said she would ask their parents. But that made Andrew very conscious of how hungry and weak he was. He found he was panting from the exertion of lifting boxes and walking and a sudden bout of dizziness made him sit on a stretcher.

"Is that your stretcher?" Tammy asked.

Andrew shook his head. "No. That is mine," he said, pointing to the next shelter.

He was about to say 'This is Ella's' when horrific images of the murderers flooded his mind and he found he was clenching his fists and panting hard.

Ella! he thought. *Is she alive, or dead?*

That thought fired him with more determination so that when Bernie and Kiri joined them and said they thought they should just all sail to Townsville he was able to shake his head and defy them.

"No! There is unfinished business here," Andrew replied. "You must go quickly and carry the letter to the authorities."

"But we can't just leave you," Kiri protested.

"You can. And you can leave us your dinghy," Andrew replied.

"And some food and water," Carmen added.

Bernie shook his head. "We can just radio the authorities." he said.

Andrew was appalled, and Carmen looked it. She answered at once, gesturing vehemently while she spoke. "No! You mustn't use the radio. The crooks might be listening. If they know their secret is out they will just vanish and they will never be caught."

"Or be brought to justice," Andrew added.

Carmen nodded. "If you use the radio the story will be in the news within the hour and the crooks will know we are still alive. Then they might come back to get us, or hunt us down later out of revenge."

"Or you," Andrew added grimly, searing images of the murders adding conviction to his tone.

Bernie looked both worried and baffled. "But you don't need to stay."

"We do," Andrew insisted. "If I don't carry out my plan the killers might get away Scott free."

"And what is your plan?" Bernie asked.

Andrew shook his head. "I'd rather not say. Then you can't let it slip by accident."

Or be forced to reveal it, he thought, but did not say.

Bernie looked hard at him and then shrugged. "How do we know we can trust you with our dinghy? Do you have any experience with small boats?"

Both Andrew and Carmen nodded. "Lots," Andrew replied. "We own our own sailboats and we are both navy cadets who have been trained to handle small craft."

Bernie nodded but still looked doubtful. "It is worth a fair bit."

Carmen answered. "We will give you our parent's phone numbers and address. They both run businesses, so they will be able to repay you."

Bernie looked at Kiri and she made a face and nodded. Andrew then pushed his luck by asking, "Could I have your gun please?"

Bernie at once shook his head. "No. I am not going to be responsible for giving a child a gun."

That annoyed Andrew. "I am a Quartermaster Gunner in the Navy Cadets. I have been trained to use all sorts of guns. I know how to use the pistol."

Bernie looked doubtful but again shook his head. "No. Sorry. I do not want to be legally responsible for anything that... that... er... that might go wrong if you use that weapon."

Andrew bit his lip and nodded. It was the reaction he had been expecting but it was still a sharp disappointment. He began casting around in his mind for what other weapons he might be able to find or use.

Bernie shook his head. "I still think you should be coming with us."

Andrew bit his lip. "You should get going as soon as you can."

Kiri and Bernie both looked surprised. Kiri said, "But why? We planned to stay overnight."

"Because those murderers are due back tomorrow and they might turn up early. If they find you with us your yacht will be sunk and you and your family will mysteriously disappear at sea."

That shocked them and both children looked frightened. Andrew then increased the pressure by saying, "And then the crooks won't be brought to justice because the authorities won't know."

Bernie nodded. "OK. I see your point. So write this letter while we have a look around and then we will get going."

"Thanks," Andrew answered.

Young Simon now spoke up. "Andrew, where is this railway you talked about?"

Andrew stood up. "I will show you. Car. You write the letter while I show them around."

Carmen nodded and went to open her bag which was under the next bunk. Andrew led the way outside, his stomach growling loudly as he did. Then he had to grab an overhanging branch as a wave of dizziness swept through him.

Kiri saw this and at once moved to hold him up. "You aren't well. You should be coming with us to get a doctor to see to that spear wound."

Andrew shook his head and waited for the waves of dizziness to pass. "No. I will be alright. I just need a good feed and a sleep," he replied.

"But some of those cuts and scratches are looking very inflamed. They could get infected and turn into ulcers," Kiri replied.

"I am not going. You will have to force us. I have to do this!" Andrew cried.

"Oh, you silly boy!" Kiri retorted. She looked to a very worried Bernie and then shook her head. She went on: "Then you sit there while we organize food. The children can find the railway on their own."

Andrew nodded and moved back to slump onto Ella's stretcher. Carmen looked up in alarm. "Are you alright Andrew?" she queried.

"Yes. I just need a rest and a feed," Andrew answered.

"Maybe we should go back with them?" Carmen suggested.

"No! We must bring these mongrels to justice!" Andrew croaked heatedly.

Kiri and Bernie both hovered looking anxious. Kiri gestured towards the yacht. "I will go and cook you a proper meal," she said. She and Bernie turned and walked away. Andrew sighed and lay back, dots dancing before his eyes and waves of blankness sweeping over him. Carmen came and studied his wounds and felt his temperature and pulse and then bit her lip.

That annoyed Andrew even more. "Just write the letter Car. Address it to Commander Hazard. I will be fine. Just let me rest for a bit." With that he relaxed and closed his eyes, and promptly went to sleep.

He was shaken awake an hour later. It was Carmen. "Wake up Andrew and sit up. Here is some food."

Kiri was there with a pot of hot soup and a warm drink, Milo. Andrew struggled into a sitting position, letting out several involuntary cries of pain as he did. All his muscles felt tight and painful and his wound and scratches all itched. A headache threatened to split his skull in two.

For a minute or so he just sat, feeling both groggy and nauseous. His stomach churned and he did not think he could eat; he felt more like being sick. But then the aroma of the soup made him salivate and he nodded and took the offered bowl and spoon. Carmen was already eating but giving him anxious glances. When he lifted a spoonful of soup to his lips and sipped it she nodded and smiled.

It was good soup, thick and so full of chunks of meat and vegetables it was almost a stew. Andrew almost slurped it down as his body rushed to replenish its depleted energy supplies. Within a couple of minutes, he was finished.

"More?" Kiri asked.

"Yes please."

"Drink the Milo first," Kiri said.

Andrew did and it went down in one gulp.

Kiri smiled and shook her head. "That was quick! I will get you another. Here is more soup and you can have a corned beef sandwich."

Andrew took the soup bowl and thanked her. "How do you make fresh bread on a yacht?" he queried.

"We don't. We keep it in the freezer and thaw it when we want some," Kiri explained.

So the meal went on. The children returned from exploring and sat to watch. Andrew and Carmen ate three bowls of the thick soup. Then they managed some biscuits before Andrew felt too full and nauseous. Sighing with satisfaction he put the bowl down and thanked Kiri.

She smiled her appreciation and then said, "How are you off for food. Is there some here?"

That was something Andrew couldn't answer. Nor could Carmen. She did a quick check and found a box full of tinned food and condensed milk but there wasn't much variety.

Kiri studied the items and shook her head. "We will give you some."

"It is only for a day or two," Andrew protested.

Again, Kiri shook her head. "You never know. Something might go wrong. We will make sure you have enough for a week."

Carmen then held out the letter. "Here is the information. There are addresses and phone numbers there," she explained.

Bernie reluctantly took the letter. "I still think you should be coming with us. I feel very bad about leaving two children marooned on an island and knowing there are killers coming. It is wrong."

Carmen met his eyes. "Maybe, but you can't force us to come so just do as we ask and get that to the authorities as quickly as possible and protect your own family. Keep them out of it."

Reluctantly Bernie nodded. "Against my better judgement. Alright, we had better get going. There are a few hours of daylight left and we can get through the reef before dark."

Andrew sat up and was astonished to see that it was mid-afternoon. "You have checked your course?"

Bernie nodded. "Yes. That is what I have been doing while Kiri got the food ready."

"And your dinghy?"

"Yes, you can have it. So take us out to the yacht and we will get going," Bernie replied.

Andrew felt simultaneously relieved and apprehensive. He stood up and the rested, still feeling dizzy. Limping on his injured leg he made his way out into the blazing sunlight. The sun was so fierce that he immediately felt it burning into his bare skin and he wished he had more on than just the shirt and his bathers. But he was also driven and wanted them gone so he shrugged and kept on hobbling.

It took half an hour to ferry the family out to the yacht and for Kiri to pass down some food and their diving gear. As she did she made a last appeal for them to come with the yacht.

Andrew, holding onto the gunwale of the yacht with his right hand, shook his head. "No. We will see this through. Anyway, the navy or the police should arrive tomorrow if you are quick."

Bernie shook his head and let his face show his disapproval but then he said, "On your head be it! I hope I don't have to face your parents if anything happens to you. Well, good luck. Let's have that anchor up Tammy. Simon, stand by the jib."

Andrew let go of the yacht and the rubber boat drifted clear as the family began preparations to get underway. Inside he was churning with anxiety and knew he was very scared. It took him quite an effort of willpower to keep his face calm. He was helped in this by Carmen's cheerful demeanour as she wished the family bon voyage.

Within a few minutes the yacht was under way. Its engine rumbled to life and the jib was smartly hauled up, pushing the bow around to port. The yacht at once gathered way and proceeded back the way it had come to get clear of the fringing coral reef.

As he watched the yacht receded into the distance Andrew waved while inside he was gripped by apprehension.

Oh, I hope we haven't made a terrible mistake staying, he thought.

Chapter 27

PLANS AND PREPARATIONS

Carmen turned to Andrew and the smile slipped from her face. "Well, that is that. Let's hope we can manage whatever it is you have planned," she said.

To that Andrew returned a non-committal grunt. Carmen noted this and raised an eyebrow. "You do have a plan?" she queried.

"Of a sort," Andrew replied with a shrug. In truth he had only part of a plan and that was fairly sketchy.

"So what is it?" Carmen demanded to know.

Again, Andrew shrugged. He didn't really want to discuss it until he had thought it through in detail but now he had to answer.

"You are going to take me over to Yule Reef in the dinghy and then come back here and hide. I am going to swim out and stick a radio transmitter on the submarine and then swim back to the cay and wait until the crooks are gone. Then you will come and pick me up," he said.

Carmen looked horrified. "Radio transmitter? Do you mean one of these little transponders, the GPS trackers we attach to the turtles and so on?"

Andrew nodded. "Yes," he replied. "I was going to glue it on like the sub was just a big marine creature so the navy can track it."

Carmen shook her head. "It's a good idea as far as it goes, but it is far too risky. We will just hide and report."

"Not good enough. The sub will escape," Andrew replied. "Those little radios can be tracked by satellite whenever the sub surfaces and that way it will be discovered."

"If you aren't discovered first and bumped off!" Carmen retorted angrily. "How were you going to attach the radio?"

"I was going to use that air tank we buried on Yule Cay to swim out underwater when the sub arrives and glue two radios on, one on its periscope and one somewhere on the hull where it won't be noticed."

Carmen looked appalled and shook her head, "And what if they see you, those divers I mean?"

"Then I swim for it and try to hide," Andrew replied. Just thinking about that made him feel sick but he could see no other way. "There has to be a degree of risk," he added.

"Degree of risk! You are mad!" Carmen cried angrily.

"Well you think of a better plan!" Andrew cried. He was so overwrought he began to sob and slumped down on the stretcher.

"Calm down little brother. It is a good idea but we need to make it more workable. The first change to it is that I hide on Yule Cay."

"How will you do that? That dinghy will be really visible," Andrew answered.

Carmen shook her head. "It is an inflatable. You pump it up with that little foot pump. Once we are there I will deflate it and bury it or sink it in the shallows. The outboard will just look like a lump of coral and we hide the same way we did last time, behind the sand rise or among any exposed coral. Then we wait."

Andrew nodded. "That sounds OK," he replied. In truth it sounded even better to him as it meant that possible help and rescue were close at hand, although it placed Carmen at much greater risk and he wasn't happy about that.

Carmen then said, "What if we can't find the air tank? It might have been washed away during that storm."

Andrew had not wanted to think about that possibility but now he shrugged and replied, "Then the plan isn't viable and we just hide and hope."

"Then let's see if we have the stuff we need," Carmen said.

Andrew hauled himself to his feet, steadied himself against a wave of dizziness and then limped over to help her search the storage boxes. The radio transponders weren't hard to find as they had used several during the days before the drama began. Carmen checked that each was fitted with a battery. She switched one on.

"It seems to be working," she commented. But without a radio receiver on the correct frequency they had no way of knowing.

"I hope so," Andrew answered.

The notion that he might risk both their lives for a radio that wasn't working made him feel distinctly uneasy. He dug through the stores in the box and found the tube of epoxy glue that was used. It was special waterproof, quick-dry glue they used in a 'catch and release' situation.

There were several signal flares there as well and Andrew placed six of them to one side.

They might come in useful, he mused.

Andrew dug out a copy of the Tide Tables and checked the tide times for the next day. He was pleased to note that he had been almost right.

High water is 1510hrs, he noted.

Other items were checked and placed ready before Carmen suggested a break for refreshments. "The crooks aren't due until tomorrow," she commented.

"No, but they might come early, and we need to be ready," Andrew replied.

They had a big drink of the bottled water left for them and then nibbled at biscuits. Andrew found he was still ravenously hungry but perversely felt nauseous and unable to eat when he had food. It took him an effort to eat and several times he retched. Washing his mouth and drinking more fluid helped. So did a drink of warm Milo with condensed milk and sugar. Carmen prepared this on the small spirit stove in the emergency supplies.

Andrew went on searching the boxes for anything that might be useful. He lamented the fact that all the scuba tanks had been on the dive boat and could only hope he could find the air tank he had buried. One of the things he looked for was a knife but to his regret all he could come up with was a butter knife from among the food supplies.

Not much use against that lot of murderous thugs! he thought wryly.

By then both felt exhausted. Carmen looked at Andrew and shook her head. "You look a wreck little brother. Your eyes are all bloodshot and you look very drawn. Let's have a lie down for a while."

"Should one of us stay on watch in case the crooks arrive?" Andrew asked.

Carmen shook her head. "No. We need to rest and the odds are they wouldn't come here anyway."

"Where do we go if they do arrive here?"

Carmen pointed down. "We get on our bellies below the sand rise. Same as before-we just crawl around to stay on the side of the island opposite where they are."

"And try to wipe out our tracks," Andrew added.

Then he lowered himself onto the stretcher, suddenly aware he felt dizzy again and that all his muscles seemed to be trembling. With a sigh he lay back and tried to relax.

For a time sleep would not come as waves of horrifying memories swirled through his mind in a series of graphic images that caused him to shudder and tremble. With them came a weakening of resolve as fear grew but then the gentle lap of the waves on the beach and the caress of the pleasant breeze on his bare skin lulled him into a deep sleep.

He woke from this to find it was dark. With a start Andrew went to sit up but sharp pains in his buttocks and thigh stopped him. Lifting his head he looked around, his heart beating wildly.

Where am I? What is going on? he thought.

For a moment the blackness above him bothered him until he remembered it was the tarpaulin.

Oh! That's why you can't see the stars silly! he told himself.

Very gingerly he eased his legs over the side, wincing at the sharp little pains and muscle spasms until he was seated upright. For a minute or so he sat and looked around, his eyes probing the night to try to determine if there was any danger.

But all seemed quiet and normal. The weather remained mild so the waves were just gentle slaps of swash on the nearby shore and the breeze had dropped to almost nothing. Andrew found he was perspiring. Then he heard Carmen's gentle breathing and he felt better. Feeling the urge to pee he slid off the stretcher, taking care to stop it creaking lest he wake his sister. Then he took a step and had to bite his lip to stop himself crying aloud in pain. Sharp, stabbing pains shot through his right side and he had to grab at an overhanging branch. He hung there while the pain passed. What worried him was that he thought he had felt some sort of tearing in his wound.

For fully two minutes he stood there, trembling and anxious while he gingerly explored the wound dressings with his fingertips.

Maybe it was just a scab pulling off? he thought hopefully. The dressings felt dry and the pain eased.

The urge to relieve himself was now insistent but he was not going to do it there in case his sister woke up so, summoning up his courage he carefully took a step. There was soreness but not the same pain. Another step and he had to let go of the branch. Then he limped out onto the open beach and was pleasantly surprised at how cold the sand felt on his bare feet.

For a minute he stood and looked in all directions. There was a half-moon low to the east and it and the starlight lit up the waves sufficiently for him to be able to see that there was no vessel anywhere on his side of the island. Nor was there any sign of anyone on the island itself. But to make sure he hobbled off around the clump of cottonwoods to the highest point of the low sand rise and carefully scanned in every direction.

Nothing. Not a light or even a dark shape that might be a boat. It was all quiet. *Not a cloud in the sky,* he thought, marvelling at the brilliant display overhead.

While he relieved himself, Andrew tried to make out the shapes of the wrecked trawler and the *Mull of Kintyre* but they weren't visible over that distance in such poor light. Once again he experienced some vivid flashbacks and he wondered if he should not just abandon his plan.

It just places Carmen at terrible risk, he thought. There was also the worrying thought that he might not be physically up to the task. *If my wound lets me down it will put both of us at risk,* he thought.

Slowly he limped back to the shelter and found a water bottle. Carefully he lowered himself onto the stretcher and then he sat and drank while thinking deeply. He began to calculate when the yacht should reach Townsville. But he was unsure of its speed.

They left under power but then put up their sail. They wouldn't use both. So, a good yacht can do ten to twelve knots under sail in a good wind, he thought. *But it hasn't been a good wind, so did they use their motor more? Do they have enough fuel to do that?*

Andrew had to give up. He simply did not have enough information. Even guessing at the yacht's speed under power was not much help.

Five to seven knots possibly? he decided.

All he could do was some gross maximum time calculations. At five knots he calculated the yacht must reach port in a maximum of thirty hours.

Thirty hours! They left at about 1500hrs yesterday so that would be... er... er... 1500hrs tomorrow is twenty-four hours plus six more is... er... is 2100hrs tomorrow night, he thought with some dismay. *And then they have to try to contact someone in authority and get them to act at that time of night!*

It was a depressing prospect and left Andrew feeling quite dejected. Even hopefully recalculating to ten knots did not reassure him much. *That means fifteen hours, so they might reach port by dawn tomorrow, or is that already today?*

A check of his watch showed him it was indeed tomorrow. *Zero one thirty. Another two hours yet,* he thought, his gut tightening with fear.

But it would be the problem of convincing people in the customs or police to act that might take more time. *And they have to have the resources available,* Andrew thought.

Still clinging to that dawn-off-Townsville timing, Andrew eased himself back into a prone position and stretched out, gently massaging sore muscles as he did. Then he nodded.

Even if they got to Townsville earlier they wouldn't try to enter in the dark, he decided.

Knowing what the port was like at night he realized it would be much safer and simpler to anchor in Cleveland Bay and then enter in daylight.

They have to do all those arrival in foreign port things too, he mused. *Customs and health and so on.*

That got him worrying that Bernie or his wife might use the radio but then decided they were sufficiently frightened not to take that risk.

I hope they get there quickly and can make things happen, Andrew thought. He presumed that on arrival in Townsville they would immediately ask the Harbour Master to contact the police.

Andrew then lay and dozed, drifting in and out of sleep and frequently tormented by nightmares which relived the horrors of the last few days. But he had trouble sleeping as he was too worried about not moving on time. The plan was to sail across to Yule Reef while it was still dark. Andrew did not think the crooks would arrive until just before high water because of the risk of being seen by a Coastwatch aircraft or Customs launch but he did not want to take the risk.

Better to be sure than sorry, he thought, picturing them being caught halfway across the Challenger Channel in broad daylight.

At 0330 he sat up and woke Carmen. They had a hot drink and another feed then carefully checked their stores and equipment and carried them down to the dinghy. To Andrew's relief the weather was very mild, with gentle breezes and almost no waves.

Bad weather would have wrecked our plan, he thought.

The rubber dinghy was so small he did not relish the idea of crossing rough water in it, particularly with the load of gear and food and water.

Next, they changed into their wetsuits in case they had to swim. Carmen strapped on the BCD and Andrew made sure they had ropes and his swim fins and masks. Just pulling on the wetsuit set his heart thumping with anticipation and anxiety but the night air was cool enough by then for him to be glad of it.

Loading the dinghy and pushing it into deeper water sent his emotions into a higher pitch. His heart hammered and his whole body tingled with a mixture of fear and excitement.

Now it is our turn! he thought, the desire to strike back to exact revenge—if not justice—burning hotly in him. The chill of the water only added to this mix of emotions as it gave a sharp little reminder of reality.

They set off at 0430. It was still quite dark but there was enough moonlight to pick out the shape of the island and the stone house. Not having a compass, they would have to navigate by the moon and stars but neither felt any concern about that. The moon was now clearly in the west and Orion was also low down in that direction. The Southern Cross was also clearly visible, and both knew how to use it to find south. They did not have a chart, but Andrew had the layout of the reefs and currents clearly in his head, so he sat in the bows while Carmen acted as cox'n.

The outboard motor started at the first pull and it had a soft purr that meant that the sound would not carry far in those conditions. As the dingy nosed out from the lee of Prescott Island Andrew looked around and then experienced a savage burst of emotion which was only slightly tinged with fear.

Now we will show the mongrels! he thought.

Carmen took the dinghy around the western end of the island and then held a westerly course for ten minutes to be sure they were well clear of the fringing reef before she turned south. The plan was to go south to the centre of the Challenger Channel and to go west through the gap between Yule Reef and Long Reef; then turn south again so to that they were on the western side of Yule Reef.

But within minutes Andrew realized it was not going to be as simple as that. Even with a cloudless sky and a half-moon to guide them he found he could not make out any real landmarks. With the moon going down to the west the stone building on Prescott Island was quickly lost to sight, as was the island itself. Bothered by this more than he wanted to admit Andrew turned to look to port in the hope of spotting one of the wrecks on Longbow Reef but they were invisible as well.

Shielding eyes that felt raw and which were blurring as the cool wind brought tears to them he looked in all directions. For a minute or so he stared at the sea and sky. All he could see ahead were small waves rippling in a path of moonlight. Astern and on both sides it was more of the same but much less obvious in the starlight. There was no sign of any landmark or reef.

A small stab of panic lanced through Andrew as the sheer immensity of the ocean was made apparent to him. His anxiety level shot up and he thought, *What if we can't find the channel or any of the reefs?*

It occurred to him that the sand cay on Yule Reef was possibly under water as it was the top of the tide so even that would be hard to find. Silently he berated himself for not noting the tide heights when he had checked the tide times.

You bloody fool! he thought.

Then the horrible thought came to him that they could miss the reef in the darkness and end up out of fuel and drifting on the current. Or they could run onto a reef and have the jagged coral rip the rubber boat open so it sank!

Maybe crossing in the dark wasn't such a good idea, he thought as he anxiously scanned the waves.

Chapter 28

ANXIETY

It took Andrew an effort of willpower to calm his growing anxiety. Swallowing and breathing deeply he did another careful scan of the ocean. Still nothing. Now deeply concerned that they might have made another serious mistake he turned to Carmen.

"Car, we are going to have trouble finding Yule Cay in the dark. I think we had better come at it from the east to try to get it silhouetted against the moon," he said.

Carmen looked around and nodded. "I agree. I just hope it is well above water. I don't want to run onto a coral reef in a rubber boat."

That concept sent Andrew's anxiety up another notch. Mental images of sharp coral ripping the rubber and of the boat sinking in the dark sea caused him to shudder.

"No fear!" he replied, and turned to study the waves again.

Southwest we want to go, he thought.

But how strong were the currents and how far off course might they pull the boat? The memory of being on the bridge of the Kirk's landing barge *Wewak* on a voyage down the west coast of Cape York Peninsula in January came to him. It had been night time and the sea had appeared calm, but the GPS navigation system had informed them that they were moving sideways as well as going ahead. In the end they were ten nautical miles off course and Captain Kirk had commented that without the GPS they would never have known and if he had chosen a course closer to the shore they would have run aground.

After studying the Southern Cross and doing the calculation of extending the long axis with an imaginary line four and a half times its length, and then dropping a perpendicular to the horizon to determine south, Andrew pointed to where he thought southwest was.

"That way Car," he instructed.

Carmen nodded and obviously trusted his calculations as she turned the dinghy onto that course without argument. They began quartering the small waves and that felt right to Andrew.

The wind and waves are coming at slightly different angles, he thought. *The wind will be from the southeast, but the waves are coming in from the open sea along the channel so from the east.*

Andrew knew he did not know the actual wind direction but was working on the average for that part of the world at that time of the year.

All I can feel is the Apparent Wind, he thought, that wind generated by their own movement.

Andrew also did not know the speed of the rubber dinghy, but guessed at five to seven knots in calm water.

So possibly five, and it is two nautical miles from Prescott Island to Yule Reef. That meant only half an hour to cross and he decided they had started too soon. *We should have left just before First Light,* he mused.

A look to the east showed no sign of any greying where the sky met the sea. In fact, it was all just a dark gloom and he could not even detect a horizon.

This could turn out to be tricky, he thought.

Now he began watching the minutes on his watch and after fifteen with no sign of any reef or cay he began to get even more anxious. Finding their way back to Prescott Island before the fuel ran out might not be possible!

"Slow down Car and we will wait till we get some daylight. We don't want to hit the reef at full speed," he called.

Carmen nodded and complied. The engine note dropped and the dinghy slowed until it was barely making way in the moving water.

Now we really are at the mercy of the tide, Andrew thought. *It will be on the ebb by now so at worst we will be carried back east.*

The notion that they might end up marooned again on the trawler wreck caused him a spasm of anxiety and a wry smile. But he did not say anything to Carmen. Instead, he kept scanning the sea and acting as though everything was under control. This went on for another ten minutes until Andrew noted a distinct lightening in the sky to the east. The horizon appeared as a sharp grey line and then he let out a sigh of relief. Clearly silhouetted against the eastern sky was a dark lump.

That is either the wrecked trawler or the sailing ship, he told himself.

As he raised his arm to point he spotted a second dark lump to the right of the first. "There are the wrecks," he said, masking his relief as well as he could.

Carmen gave a nod and then replied, "We will just hold our position until it gets a bit lighter. The cay should be visible then."

It was. A few minutes later, as the first tinge of pink showed to the east a tiny bulge showed in the moonlight to the west. Carmen saw it first and pointed. "There it is," she said as she turned the boat towards it and opened the throttle.

Andrew let out a sigh and only then remembered that he was trying to hide his anxiety from his sister. "I was a bit worried," he admitted.

"I was bloody scared!" Carmen replied. "I didn't fancy bobbing about the ocean in this little rubber boat for the next few days."

"Better than swimming," Andrew answered cheerfully then shuddered at the flashbacks.

To cheer himself up he recounted the tale to Carmen of what he had read in one or the Emergency Rations during a flight in an RAAF Hercules.

"The story was set during World War Two," he explained. "This pilot had crash landed in the sea while on anti-submarine patrol near the Bahamas. The story claimed that he survived for something like three hundred days before he was rescued."

Carmen smiled. "I hope we don't have to spend that long in a tiny rubber boat," she replied.

Andrew laughed at the image and then went on, "Apparently this bloke's dinghy was carried north on the Gulf Stream into the North Atlantic but then it got carried right across to near Europe and then circled back on that huge circular current that goes across from Africa to the West Indies. He was picked up back over near there, so he'd done a full circle in a year."

"What did he drink?" Carmen asked.

"I think the dinghy had a little solar still and he must have collected rain water," Andrew asked.

"And I suppose he caught fish and seabirds for food," Carmen added. Then she chuckled.

"What's so funny?" Andrew queried.

"Remember that silly old comedy movie we saw on TV a few months ago? Where the pilot ejected and landed in the sea and then climbed into his little rubber boat and then saw bubbles coming from under one side, so he stuck his hand into the water to stop the bubbles."

Andrew had, and he now laughed at the memory. "The movie was called 'Lieutenant Robinson Crusoe' or something like that. Yes, and then a shark fin appeared, and he had to pull his hand in."

The image of the shark circling the tiny dinghy and of the pilot putting his hand into the water to stop the leak as soon as the shark was past and then pulling it in again as it came around again caused Andrew to convulse with laughter. Carmen joined in and both laughed until tears trickled down their faces.

The chill of the tears on his skin and then the worrying thought that there might be big sharks in the area stopped Andrew smiling. He wiped his face and then studied the waves, but said nothing to Carmen. Instead he concentrated on looking for the coral as they drew closer to Yule Reef.

Because the dinghy was pushing against the outgoing tide their actual progress 'over the ground' was very slow and it seemed to Andrew that they weren't making any headway at all. The light grew until the first rays of sunlight struck them. They also lit up the exposed sand on the cay tinging it pink. The visibility was very good, and Andrew stopped worrying about hitting the coral and instead became anxious about the crooks arriving. He began to scan the horizon in all directions.

To his relief there was no sign of any vessel. The dinghy was making headway and quite abruptly they crossed into almost still water with coral close underneath.

"We are over the reef," Andrew called.

He now concentrated on watching for coral heads that might snag the bottom of the dinghy. But they had timed it right and reached the sand of the cay with at least half a metre of water under the dinghy. Andrew eased himself over the side and waded ashore, hauling the dinghy behind him. Carmen stopped the motor and climbed out to help him. They carried the small rubber boat well above the tide line and then stopped to have a drink.

Andrew then walked slowly and painfully up to the highest point of the sand cay, his eyes scanning the sand. He was looking for the rope he had tied to the air tank.

If we can't find that we need to start back for Prescott Island immediately, he thought.

Rubbing thoughtfully at the teenage stubble on his chin Andrew looked around anxiously. But his worries were groundless. The end of the yellow rope was just near his feet, lying half-hidden in the sand. He bent and picked the rope up and pulled, just to check it was the one.

Whatever it is on the other end is well anchored, he decided.

Hoping it was the air tank he fell to his knees and began to dig with his hands. Carmen joined him and within two minutes they had dug down to expose rounded steel.

"The air tank," Andrew said with satisfaction.

As quickly as he could he scooped the sand away, wincing as the rough grains cut into his flesh. Then he dragged the air tank free and banged it to shake the damp sand off. A squint at the gauge showed there was still pressure in it and he grunted with satisfaction. This was tempered by reading the numbers and noting that it only contained 75psi.

Maybe half an hour if I am careful, Andrew mused.

The lead weights off his weight belt were still tied to the air tank so Andrew untied them and threaded them back onto the belt. Then with a grunt he stood up and picked the air tank up with one hand. To his dismay it felt so heavy he had trouble picking it up.

Christ, I am weak! he thought.

Worrying about whether he might be unable to carry out his plan he lugged the air tank to the east side of the cay. Carmen kicked sand back into the hole and smoothed it over then followed.

"What do we do now?" she asked.

Having his big sister defer to his plan was a big boost to Andrew. He looked around the cay and the rapidly drying reef and then the horizon before answering.

"We hide the dinghy and set up a hide of our own and then wait," he replied.

These took half an hour. First wetsuits were stripped off and shirts pulled on in their place. Then the dinghy was deflated and secured at the edge of the coral so that the outboard motor was clear of the water and it was just an indistinguishable black lump among other black lumps. A large hole was scooped out with sticks they had brought with them and into this they placed their wetsuits and diving gear, all wrapped in plastic tarpaulin to protect them from the sand. Then another tarp was used to set up a sun shelter over the hollow. The upper end was secured by pegs and the lower end held up by the sticks so that brother and sister could sit side by side in the shade.

"That's better," Andrew said as he relaxed in the hidey hole.

The morning sun was shining directly into and he gingerly felt the peeling skin on his sunburnt face. Then he shrugged.

It won't be for long, he consoled himself.

As the sun rose the plastic tarp would provide good shade. "Now for some breakfast," he suggested.

They had brought tins of food and bottles of water from the stores on Prescott Island but no stove, so they ate the food cold. There were biscuits and muesli bars as well and Andrew was content.

After eating and packing away the empty cans and wrappers Andrew stood and looked in all directions then sat in the shade again. At the front of his mind was the time, 0645.

"The yacht should be entering Townsville about now," he commented.

"If nothing went wrong, yes," Carmen agreed.

For ten minutes they discussed how long it might take Bernie to convince the authorities and then for them to mobilize the resources needed to act.

Hours for sure, he thought.

Part of him wanted the authorities—he had to call them that because he did not know if it was a navy problem or one for the Federal Police or Customs—to get there as quickly as possible but deep down he still wanted to try to bring the murderers to justice.

"We had better stand a watch," he said.

Carmen nodded and they quickly worked out an hour-on-hour-off roster until 1500hrs. Andrew was first up so Carmen went off to go to the toilet and he sat and watched the other way until she returned.

As Carmen sat down Andrew knitted his brows. "What day is it Car? What is the date?"

So much had happened that the days and nights all seemed to blur into a long ordeal. Carmen did some calculating and then said, "Saturday the sixth of April. Today is the fifth day since the sub arrived."

"We are supposed to be going home today. Mum and Dad will start asking questions if we don't," Andrew replied.

Carmen shook her head. "No. That is why the crooks took Ella. They will force her to radio some story to explain that we aren't coming back until tomorrow."

"You think she is still alive?" Andrew queried.

Carmen nodded but looked grim. "Yes, but I suspect she has had a truly horrible time and that they will kill her when they have finished."

The notion of what that 'truly terrible time' might involve made Andrew feel ill. He nodded. "They won't want any witnesses, that is for sure," he agreed. It all made him even more determined to try to bring the killers to justice.

"Sunday tomorrow," Carmen added.

Andrew shook his head. The first week of the school holidays already gone!

And we are supposed to be going on a family holiday to the gem fields near Forsayth for the second week, he thought. And Tina was part of this plan. *Poor Tina! I hope she is safe, and I hope I get back safely to love her,* he thought.

For a few minutes his mind dwelt on the pleasures of loving Tina and of what a wonderful and brave girl she was. Then he began to brood again.

It was Good Friday when we started this trip. I hope we don't get crucified! he told himself grimly.

And only a few weeks to Anzac Day, he thought.

As a navy cadet Anzac Day, April the 25th, Australia's national day of remembrance for her war dead, figured large on his mental calendar for that time of year. He pictured himself and Carmen in their best white ceremonial uniforms taking part in school ceremonies and providing cenotaph guards at the smaller towns around and then taking part in the main street march. Memories of previous parades where he had been extremely self-conscious about doing good drill in front of his school friends who were in the army cadets or air cadets now made him smile.

If I am still alive it won't bother me much now, he thought.

Carmen lay back and closed her eyes. Andrew stood and scanned the horizon, mostly studying the arc to the west but from time to time staring at the rippling waters of the Boat Passage for any sign of a periscope. He knew that was just irrational anxiety. *The sub won't come in on a falling tide,* he thought.

Just before he went to wake Carmen at 0750 the sound of aero engines reached Andrew's ears.

An aircraft! Have the authorities begun to act? he wondered.

He shook Carmen awake and scrambled up to the highest point to look. The sound was coming from the southeast and after a few minutes he spotted the plane. It was well out to sea and heading north.

"Not coming here at all," Carmen commented as the aircraft flew past to the east of the two wrecks.

"No. Should we try to signal with our face masks?" Andrew said.

"No. If they know about us we are safe and it might spoil some plan to catch the crooks. Anyway, they're past us now."

Andrew watched the aircraft fly on northwards on the seaward side of Prescott Island. *God, I hope that Bernie has reached Townsville and not run into trouble,* he thought anxiously.

Carmen gestured to the shelter. "Your turn to rest," she said.

Andrew nodded but then blushed. For the last half-hour his body had been telling him things were returning to normality. "I need a crap first," he explained.

"Go for it brother. I went earlier," Carmen replied with a grin.

She went into the shelter and Andrew took himself off to the southern end of the cay and relieved himself in the shallows. While he washed himself afterwards he anxiously scanned the horizon.

Still no sign of the crooks, but the tide is well on the way out, he noted. By this time large areas of coral were exposed and the whole pattern of reefs was clear.

Andrew now lay down in the shade and tried to rest. But he only dozed as anxiety kept his stomach churning and bad memoires plagued his thoughts. Time began to drag. He found it almost a relief to be called out by Carmen to take over the watch at 0900.

The next hour went by slowly with almost no change. The tide dropped further; the sun rose higher and the wind stayed gentle. No vessels appeared on the horizon and the only objects visible in the sky were the gulls, dozens of which swooped and strutted around the cay, giving the pair a wide berth but eyeing them continually.

Carmen did the 1000 to 1100 watch and again the time dragged, and Andrew only dozed fitfully. He began to sweat and kept drinking more water. They had four bottles each and he reasoned that there was no point in saving any.

If I am still alive this evening we can go and get more from Prescott Island, he told himself.

It was the worry about what might happened when the crooks arrived that got him all anxious again and he kept rehearsing in his mind how they would prepare and what he might do.

At 1100 Andrew took over again. The tide was on the way in by then and he studied the ripples which indicated currents and also plotted his route to the edge of the reef. He drank some more; licked his cracked lips continually and applied some lip salve then tried to ease the itching and irritation of the dry salt and clothing rubbing on his sunburnt skin.

They had another cold meal of canned meat and biscuits washed down with another bottle of water at 1200hrs. Neither spoke much but Andrew could tell by her expression that Carmen was having the same fears and doubts that he was. By now he was regretting staying.

It places Carmen at too much risk, he told himself.

But regrets were no use. *Not unless we just hide here and don't try to mark the sub,* he decided. The option of just hiding now had great appeal but he kept the idea to himself. *I wish it was just me at risk,* he fretted.

Then he worried about the footprints they had made all over the cay. He toyed with trying to wipe them out and then shrugged.

The cay is so small the crooks will find us instantly if they come ashore, he thought.

The only safe hiding place was in the water and even that was no good at high tide as all the coral heads would be submerged. It was all food for more anxious thoughts.

Carmen did the next watch and again Andrew dozed. He also went to do a pee and was pleased to note that his urine was a golden colour and not the dark orange of the day before.

I hope my kidneys haven't been permanently damaged, he thought. Anxiety about his health then dominated his thoughts for a while.

The day seemed to drag really slowly and the tension slowly built as the tide came up and covered the reef.

Won't be long now, Andrew thought, wishing he didn't feel so sick in the stomach with what he knew was plain fear.

Then he dropped into a deep sleep. But even his dreams were anxious ones, the usual nightmares of ending up in deep water and of being dragged out to sea by the current and of dark flitting shapes under the water and then of men with guns and faces like grinning skull masks chasing them in a speedboat while their own boat just sank.

"Andrew! Andrew!" Carmen's excited voice penetrated.

"What?" he croaked, opening gummed up eyes and squinting at her.

"A boat. Heading this way," Carmen replied.

Andrew scrambled out of the shelter and stood up. Carmen pointed the Northwest and he saw it at once. It was a launch of some sort and still too far away to make out any detail, just a dark speck on the horizon.

"It is coming straight towards us," Carmen said.

It must be the crooks, Andrew thought, his anxiety level shooting right up so that his heart began to hammer and his palms became instantly sweaty.

Oh God! This is it!

Chapter 29

DEEP BREATHS

Andrew sucked in a deep breath and felt his heart rate shoot up. He focused on the tiny shape of the approaching launch and then ducked down. "We had better get out of sight in case they are using binoculars," he said.

Carmen crouched beside him. "Right little brother. Now let's get ready. Dress first."

They had discussed the sequence of actions and now quickly began to prepare. Standing in the scooped-out hole they quickly pulled on their wetsuits and then Andrew buckled on his weight belt and looped his face mask around his neck. The air tank and BCD were lugged down to the water's edge and his small carry bag and swim fins placed nearby. The shelter was quickly dropped, and their shirts tossed in to join the food and water bottles and other items already there. The tarp was then rolled up.

As they did this Andrew kept bobbing up to peek over the crest of the cay. To his dismay the launch looked to be much closer than was safe and he began to sweat and feel even more anxious. Scooping sand with both hands he began to cover the bundle.

Carmen knelt beside him to help but then reached across and held his arm. "Slow down little brother. They will be half an hour yet. Take a few deep breaths. You are hyperventilating."

"I'm scared," Andrew admitted.

"That's good. It might stop you doing anything too risky," Carmen replied.

Andrew could only nod and give her a sickly grin. Now that the reality was upon them he felt so frightened he had trouble speaking and had to struggle to master the rising sense of panic.

"Let's get into the water," he said.

His concern now wasn't the fast approaching launch which was still at least two nautical miles away but the submarine. It could be approaching along the Boat Passage behind them.

We will look like a pair of real geese if we are seen by it, he thought.

Andrew looked over his shoulder and scanned the Boat Passage, but the water appeared calm and unruffled with barely a swirl to indicate any currents. There was no sign of any periscope, but he was sure the two vessels would be working to a timetable, if not actually talking to each other by low-powered radio.

He and Carmen finished hiding their gear with the sand and then crawled down the twenty metres of gentle slope to the edge of the water. Luckily the tide was not as high as it had been the night they had been marooned so there were still a few coral heads poking out to give some cover and the cay had a rise of a couple of metres to shield them.

A glance at his watch reassured Andrew that the situation would not change much. *1455, nearly the top of the tide now,* he thought. He wished there were a few small waves to hide his bubbles when he swam out.

They lay in the shallow water with the partly deflated rubber dinghy, the water surprisingly cold on feet and hands. The transponders were switched on and placed back in the carry bag. Andrew sat up and heaved on the BCD and air tank, helped by Carmen.

"I wish you would give this idea up," she said. "We could just hide and watch."

"We could," Andrew replied. "But I am going. You just have that dinghy ready to inflate so you can run for it if things go wrong."

To avoid her eyes and to hide his fear Andrew stood up and looked over the top of the sand. The launch was now only a mile or so away and he could make out some details. It had turned slightly to starboard, so he was able to see it clearly.

"It is our dive boat," he hissed, his chest tightening with spasms of fear as the ghastly memories crowded in.

Carmen stood to look and then bobbed down again. "It is," she agreed. "Now get ready. You only have about a quarter of an hour and you need to be out at the edge of the reef by then."

Andrew lowered himself and sat in the shallows while he pulled on his swim fins. Carmen knelt behind him and turned on his air and Andrew tested the purge valve and alternate then rinsed his face mask. Suddenly he found he was gasping for air and his whole body trembled.

Carmen knelt and held him. "You OK little brother?" she asked.

"Just scared," he replied truthfully. "I'll be alright." In his heart he knew he could not back out now.

If I do it will haunt me for the rest of my life and I will despise myself for being a coward and a weakling, he thought.

Knowing that he might be going to his death he steeled himself, took a couple of deep breaths and then slid forward into the shallow water.

Lying on his front with the weight of the air tank pressing on him he managed a grin for Carmen then he spat in his face mask, rinsed it and pulled it on. Placing his snorkel in his mouth he lowered his head into the water.

Once he was satisfied that he could see clearly and that there were no leaks in the mask Andrew took a couple of deep breaths and then pushed himself forward into deeper water.

This is it! No backing out now! he told himself.

To his surprise his fear seemed to subside and he focused on swimming, amazed at his own determination to see the thing through. The water was just deep enough for him to submerge completely and that removed the uncomfortable weight of the air tank. As he finned forward he adjusted his buoyancy so that it was almost negative. Then he swam out across the last of the clear sand and above the coral.

The coral was a bit of a challenge. The tide was just high enough for him to stay underwater most of the time, but he had to break surface a couple of times to get over a few large outcrops. He also had to detour around several large outcrops which were sticking out of the water. The usual marine life he just ignored. The only things he was careful to avoid were spiky looking corals and anything that looked jagged.

Two minutes later Andrew saw the edge of the reef where it dropped off into deeper water. Here he paused to look around and then swam sideways to come to the surface behind a coral outcrop. It wasn't very big, barely larger than his head but he decided that it was enough to hide him from all but the most careful observer.

This will do, he thought.

He knelt on a large brain coral and peeked around the coral outcrop. There was no sign of the dive boat yet, but he saw Carmen lying in the shallows and gave her a thumbs-up. She waved and then lay flat with just her head exposed.

Andrew replaced his face mask and peered out into the deeper water, hoping to get a sight of the submarine.

I hope it comes in, he thought. He understood that the sub and the launch did not have to arrive at the same time. *The crooks could leave the net set up and go away and come back later after the sub had fired its projectiles into the net,* he thought. But last time they had not done that and he did not think they would this time. *It would be risky leaving that net set up for any length of time. Somebody could spot it,* he decided.

A check of his watch showed 1507. *A few minutes to the top of the tide,* he thought. *If I was the sub captain I would want to ease in and then stem the tide while I unloaded.*

And there was the dive boat! It came churning into view around the southern end of the cay. Andrew crouched and watched, intently studying the vessel to try to determine how many men were on it. He could only see one standing on the focsle but was sure there would be others in the wheelhouse and on the dive deck aft.

The dive boat came to a standstill and Andrew detected movement at the stern.

More of them. One, two, three. Good! he thought.

With his heart beating faster from excitement he watched as two divers in black wetsuits jumped overboard. Then a rubber boat similar to their own was lowered in and a third diver climbed down into it. The rubber boat had a small outboard motor and this was started. While this was going on one of the divers swam to the front of the launch and took a rope passed down to him by the man on the focsle. The diver then vanished.

Securing the launch to the net or to an anchor? Andrew wondered.

When the dive boat began to drift and turn end on to him Andrew suspected this was the case. He saw the man at the bows pull in and belay the rope. Then he picked up another thin black line and lowered it to the second diver. The second diver went under and Andrew could only speculate that this was the rubber air hose to inflate the lifts to raise the net.

Time I was ready, he thought, his gut clenching with fear. He turned and scanned the Boat Passage, sure that the sub would come in with its periscope up.

And there it was!

About half a mile out Andrew detected a tiny feather of spray. He got several fleeting glimpses of a thin black object and was sure.

Out I go, he told himself.

After again spitting in his facemask and rinsing it he put it firmly on then put his regulator in his mouth and tested it. The compressed air tasted slightly oily, but he ignored this and nerved himself to make the attempt.

But as he faced out towards the deep water his mind was suddenly crowded by searing flashbacks of all the horrible diving incidents he had experienced. For a few seconds he was literally paralysed by fear and clung to the coral, trembling and gasping. Then he shook his head.

I have to do this, no matter what! he told himself.

Forcing himself to be calm he took several deep breaths he pushed himself forward and began swimming.

A moment later, he was out over the edge of the reef and his chest tightened up again as all his fears of the deep and its monsters momentarily gripped him. Then he angrily shook his head to clear it and used willpower to focus on the task.

Holding up his dive computer and compass Andrew checked his course and began to swim due east. His plan was to stay well clear of the divers at the net and to circle around to come in behind the submarine.

Provided I can see the bloody thing! he thought. But there it was, a dim shadowy shape in the distance. *So, no excuses. Get going!* Andrew told himself.

As he swam, Andrew kept looking to his right to check if any of the divers were visible. *To be seen will mean disaster,* he thought grimly. To maximise his chances of not being seen Andrew now selected to swim at fifteen metres. *That is about the same depth they will be working at so I will be against a dark, murky background,* he reasoned.

Any higher and he might be silhouetted against the light from above and any lower and he might show up against the clear paleness of the sandy bottom.

The whole time he was swimming Andrew kept the submarine just in sight as a distant grey shape.

Like a bloody great whale, he thought.

The swimming was easy, almost no current he could detect and the water clear and empty of fish. He had been worrying about that, thinking that startled shoals of fish might attract enemy eyes towards him.

Just once he caught a fleeting glimpse of one of the divers. The man was doing something on the seabed about 200 metres away and Andrew assumed he was setting up the net. Then he was out of sight, so Andrew changed direction and began angling towards the submarine.

He saw that he was coming in at almost right angles to the stern of the sub and that got him anxiously looking to his right to check that the divers weren't visible.

If I can see them they can see me and they will be looking towards the sub, he reasoned. So he turned left and swam away from the net for another fifty metres. Then a glance at his air told him he needed to move faster. *Down to 55psi. Getting towards the danger level,* he thought.

After another check that no divers were in sight Andrew turned right and swam across until he was directly astern of the submarine. Then he turned right again and began to fin towards it. As he did he kept staring ahead for any hint of the other divers. To his relief he saw no sign of them and he noted that even the bow of the submarine was hard to see.

But it did seem to be hard work and he realized that the tide must have turned. *The sub is stemming the tide and I am also swimming against it,* he decided.

He realized he also had to take the propeller wash into account and that sent him up a few meters to get clear of that stream of turbulence.

It was hard work, and by the time he had reached the stern of the sub his air was down to 45psi and he was panting as though he had run a race. As he got closer he eyed the two propellers that were spinning fast down below the stern hydroplanes.

Just as well it isn't a modern sub with one big prop at the back, he thought. His plan would not have been possible then!

But he was acutely aware that once he was forward of the propellers they presented enormous risk. *If the sub increases revolutions I could be sucked down into them,* he thought.

Chilled, but also spurred on by this, he pushed himself to reach the hull. The sub was painted a dirty grey colour and the whole area below the waterline was a green and brown mat of weed growths. Andrew reached the hull and grabbed a hole in the casing.

This is what I want, he thought.

The sub's pressure hull had an outer hull for ballast tanks and a casing over the top to house winches, mooring ropes, anchors and similar items. A visit to a museum sub, the ex-HMAS *Onslow,* at Darling Harbour in Sydney gave Andrew that knowledge.

First he used one hand to try to clean any slime or growths of the inside if the casing so that the glue might stick to steel. Then he reached into his small carry bag he pulled out one of the radio transmitters but then found that it was going to be harder than he had thought. The current was so strong that he needed one hand to cling on with!

Taking care not to drop the radio transmitter he wedged it in the front of his BCD and then groped in the bag with his right hand to extract the glue tube.

Bloody hell! This is a bit tricky! he thought in dismay.

It took him a real struggle to hang on while placing glue on the transmitter. Then he had put the tube back in the bag and kneel to place the transponder inside the hole in the casing. He had to press it up against the steel and hold it for a full minute to allow the glue time to adhere. He knew he should have scraped and cleaned the steel surface but apart from another quick rub with his fingers he had neither the time nor the tools to do this.

I hope it doesn't just wash off, he worried.

A sharp 'Thump!' caused Andrew to twitch in terror. He looked forward towards where the noise had come from and saw a cloud of bubbles rising. These were swept back to envelop him as they dispersed.

They are firing the torpedoes! I had better get a wriggle on, he thought.

His plan was to place one of the transponders on top of the periscope standard, reasoning that it could transmit every time the sub put its periscope up. To get there he had to swim forward half the length of the sub. He set out to do this, his head swinging from side to side as he scanned for the divers.

And there they were!

Both divers suddenly swam into view down on the sea bed to starboard and Andrew's heart froze in fright and then hammered rapidly. He took several very deep breaths as he gulped in fright and then got control of himself. The men were just visible and looked to be at least a hundred metres away.

They are collecting one of the torpedo things which has rolled down the slope, he noted.

But where was the third diver in the rubber boat?

There was no sign of him and no sound of the boat's propeller so

Andrew steeled himself and kept on swimming, sliding down to port to put the hull of the sub between him and the two divers.

Within a minute he had reached the conning tower. *Or do they call it a fin?* he wondered as he studied the doors, hatches and hand and foot steps and weld seams in the structure. Rust was very evident. *They don't look after this tub very well,* he thought as he swam slowly up.

There he was presented with a dilemma. The periscope was extended and stuck up four or five metres above the top of the tower.

They might see me when I go up there, he worried.

To check he looked for the divers. They were just visible off to his right front but their whole focus seemed to be the object on the seabed.

At that moment the sub fired another torpedo. Andrew clung in fright to the coaming of the tower as bubbles swirled past him. Looking down he could see into the conning tower area with its windows and controls. The hatch, which led down into the interior, was just there. The notion that it was a good sheltered place to prepare the next transponder with its glue caused him to slide over into it. Crouching, he pulled out a transponder and squeezed glue onto the base.

For a moment had had the irrational thought that a diver might emerge from the hatch under his feet and find him.

I will look a bloody goose if this thing surfaces! he thought.

Then he shook his head and carefully squeezed more glue onto the radio. After screwing the cap back on he placed the glue tube back in his bag and looked up at where the periscope stuck up out of the water. Then he flinched as the sub fired another torpedo.

Come on boy, get it over with! he told himself.

So, after another glance at the divers, he pushed upwards, one arm around the steel tube to keep him in place. A moment later his head broke surface and he got three almost simultaneous shocks. Firstly, the top of the periscope was at least a metre above the water. Second the dive boat was only a hundred metres away and there were people on it. And third the rubber boat was alongside the dive boat and there were more people there.

Andrew slid back under and found his heart beating so fast that he had trouble breathing. *Calm down! Think! OK, put the radio on top and then slide under quickly,* he told himself. A quick glance showed the two divers still working and still about a hundred metres away.

Once again, the sub fired a torpedo and bubbles swept back. *Now!* Andrew thought.

After taking two deep breaths he finned upwards and then gripped the arrangements at the top. It all looked bigger and more complicated than he had expected but he was able to get a firm hold. Hoisting himself up with his left arm he was able to slap the radio onto the very top. For the count of ten he held it.

As he did the notion came to him that he could have made a fatal mistake if he had put his fingers over the lens of the periscope! A check showed he hadn't. Satisfied that the radio was in place he slid back down underwater.

As he slipped under Andrew saw movement at the dive boat that clicked something in his brain. He noted that the dive boat had its stern to him.

Swung to face the current, he told himself as he went under.

Despite being all a quiver from anxiety he risked poking half his head out for another look.

I was right! That is Ella! he told himself.

Ella, bare breasted and wearing only a cloth wrap, was standing on the aft deck of the dive boat. Near her was another man but he was helping a person down into the rubber boat. Andrew now focused on the rubber boat.

There is a diver in it and two other people. What are they going to do? he wondered.

The fearful notion that they might be going to search the cay caused him a spasm of anxiety.

To check if this was in fact the smuggler's plan Andrew risked another peek. To his dismay he saw the rubber dinghy with the three people in it sheer off from beside the dive boat and swing around towards the cay.

At that moment there was a huge hiss of air and bubbles began to erupt right along the hull and all around him. For a moment Andrew just clung there, too terrified to move.

What's happening? his frightened mind cried.

Then it came to him like a thunderclap.

The submarine was surfacing!

Chapter 30

SURFACE!

As the bubbles swirled around Andrew he was convulsed by a dither of indecision. He knew he had to get off, but in which direction? He really wanted to go back to the cay but that meant swimming across past the two divers.

And that rubber boat is heading that way too, he thought.

Andrew's first idea was to retreat the way he had come but then he shook his head. *If I go back I might get sucked into the props,* he thought.

So the only other choice was going to port, away from Carmen. But there was no time left to hesitate. Andrew looked down and saw the conning tower rising towards him. Just in time he kicked away, his ankles whacked by the steel coaming as it rose. He went tumbling off and had trouble getting his bearings. For a few seconds he was completely disoriented as he swam among all the bubbles.

I must get clear! he thought. *If I don't get out of the way the hull will whack me and I might get sucked back into the props.*

So he finned for all he was worth, instinctively taking direction from the lighter water which had become visible. Just knowing which way was up and sensing the looming dark shape of the submarine allowed him to determine direction.

And he was just in time. The slimy grey and brown bulk of the hull slid up past him, almost hitting his fins as it did. Then fear of being seen by the two divers became paramount.

They are probably watching the sub. I need to get well away from them, he thought.

That meant swimming south, even further away from Carmen. But not having a realistic alternative made Andrew do just that.

Swimming for all he was worth he finned away from the sub as it rose to the surface in a welter of bubbles and foam. A glance back showed him that much. As he swam Andrew kept looking back, searching for any sign of the divers. To his relief there was none but he suspected that when the agitated water settled down he might still be visible to them.

But where do I go now? he puzzled.

For a moment he contemplated swimming across to the Feathers Reefs and trying to hide there. That was the direction he was heading in, or should have been until he realized that the outgoing tidal current was now pushing him sideways off course.

I could let the tide carry me down away from the sub, Andrew thought. *Then I could swim back the way I came.*

That seemed the best plan but his ears then detected the cavitation of the propeller on the rubber boat's outboard engine and he got a glimpse of it passing towards the other side of the submarine. It appeared to be going that way.

I had better keep clear till I am sure, he decided.

There was also, to his shame, a numbing fear of being swept out to sea along the channel by the outgoing tide. Having suffered that terrifying experience once he was loath to risk it again.

I don't have the strength to go through all that again, he thought.

So he decided to go the other way. To adjust his course, he turned to his right and began swimming against the tide. As he did, Andrew again glanced to his right, to check if the divers were visible. To his horror they were. So was the rubber boat. He could just make out the churned-up water from its propeller and he realized it wasn't heading for the cay but for the submarine.

At that moment he sucked a breath of air, and nothing came!

Surprised Andrew sucked again. Still nothing. The regulator made no noise and only pumped out his exhaled air. For a few seconds Andrew was puzzled and then realization of the probable cause sent his heart racing in anxiety. A check of his dive computer showed him the appalling truth: he was out of air!

For another couple of seconds Andrew was paralysed as terrifying images of being trapped in the strongroom of the *Merinda* without his regulator and then of waiting to die in the darkness when his air ran out swirled in his mind.

Then he shook his head and the will to live asserted itself. Looking up he saw what he knew from the computer depth gauge; the surface was just up there, only about five metres away.

But if I surface the men in the rubber dinghy or on the dive boat might see me—will see me! he thought.

Desperation and panic welled up in him but there was no choice. *I either surface and take the risk or I drown,* he told himself. By then he was already finning up, his survival instincts well ahead of his rational mind.

His head broke surface and he spat his regulator out and gasped a deep breath of air. Fear kept him moving and he went to dive again when his gaze caught the dive boat. To his surprise it looked to be only about fifty metres away.

But he had other, more pressing problems than the men. *My weight belt is dragging me down!* he thought as he struggled to stay up near the surface.

He was very reluctant to drop the belt but when it seemed to use all his strength to fin up for another gulp of air he knew he had to. In fact, it was a poor gulp, and included some salt water that set him coughing and spluttering and made it hard to hold his breath.

Get rid of the belt! Get rid of it! his panicking mind told him. He grabbed at the buckle and struggled with it while trying to swim. *I need air in my BCD,* he thought as he felt his legs weakening and sharp little pains stabbing through his wounds.

But to get air for the BCD Andrew knew he had to get to the surface and looking up and seeing a stream of bubbles rising to the rippling surface told him he was deeper than before. Now he had to battle with rising panic as well as the catch on the belt buckle. Then it came undone and he gripped the web belt with its festoon of heavy lead weights, still not wanting to drop it.

But it had to go and very reluctantly he opened his hands and let it fall. As he watched it spiralling down towards the sandy bottom he shook his head.

It saved our lives. I hope I don't need it again, he thought.

But air was the higher priority, so he again finned up, breaking surface and gulping a deep breath. Struggling to try to keep his head above water he grabbed for the mouth tube to manually inflate his BCD. As he blew, then sucked another deep breath Andrew looked around. He noted the submarine was now on the surface about one hundred metres to his right rear. The rubber boat was edging in against its starboard side and men were appearing on the submarine's deck.

They don't seem to have noticed me yet, he thought, puffing again and swimming with his legs to keep his head out against the weight of the air tank.

Now Andrew scanned around, noting the cay as a white glare from the sun reflected off the coral sand. There was no sign of Carmen. Twisting around even further Andrew located the dive boat. It was still about forty metres to his right front and as he looked he saw movement on the dive deck. It was Ella and she was looking at him.

Ella! She is alive! Andrew thought. Even as he thought this the crazy notion of somehow rescuing her came to him. *There is still a man on board the dive boat,* he thought. But how to deal with him?

Andrew began to swim towards the dive boat, driven by desperation and knowing he was weakening fast. He had only managed a couple of puffs into his BCD and it was barely supporting him. For a few seconds he considered ditching the BCD to get rid of the weight of the air tank, but he rejected that, knowing he needed the buoyancy as he was too weak to keep afloat.

I will drown if I don't get it inflated, he thought, knowing he was rapidly tiring and that the pain in his wound was quickly spreading and becoming a cramping ache.

Then he put his facemask under water and got another shock: one of the divers appeared to be swimming in his direction.

And he's got a spear gun! Andrew noted, fear again stabbing through him.

There seemed to be nothing for it but to swim away from the diver and that meant upstream against the current, and towards the dive boat. Going across to the Feathers Reef he realized was beyond his strength.

And if they have seen me they will just follow and catch me, he thought.

The whole situation just seemed to be going from bad to worse and the only option Andrew felt he had left was to try to fight back.

The dive boat then, he told himself, although he had no practical plan for when he got there.

Another look under water told him that his first impression was correct: one of the two divers was swimming straight towards him. The other was still working on the torpedo at the bottom of the net.

Andrew surfaced and began breast stroking, gulping air as he swam. His heart was now hammering so hard he began to hyperventilate, and his vision blurred. Several times he sucked in salt spray along with the air and the wracking bouts of coughing almost defeated him. Drowning was now a real possibility and the dive boat at least represented possible safety.

Another glance behind showed him that people from the rubber boat were climbing up onto the casing of the submarine, helped by some of its crew who were dressed in dark blue clothes.

And some of them are looking in my direction! Andrew noted with alarm. Then an arm came up to point and there was no doubt. *They have seen me!* he thought, the panic spurring him to dredge up every last ounce of energy.

Knowing that he was doomed if the rubber boat came in pursuit before he reached the dive boat he began to sob and wheeze as he swam.

The fear was all but overpowering but also boosted him with a surge of adrenaline. Swimming as fast as he could Andrew made for the dive boat. It was only twenty-five to thirty metres away but the current and the small waves both made it hard going, as did his rapidly growing weariness.

And there was Ella, arms folded across her chest and watching him with a puzzled look. *If she can help me out I can at least go down fighting,* Andrew told himself. He was now in desperation mode and a sort of blind rage was controlling his mind.

Thunk! Phuut!

Suddenly Andrew felt his right leg twitch and pull and then he had trouble bringing it back for the next stroke. He glanced down and gaped in shock.

There was spear through his right swim fin! It was right next to his foot!

Bloody hell! Not again! he thought, another wave of terror washing over him.

Through a face mask misted by condensation he saw the diver who had fired it. He was still about twenty-five metres behind but the speargun had a second spear.

He will get me with the next shot, Andrew thought.

But he couldn't swim with the spear through his fin, so he curled up and wrenched the fin off, casting it away and then straightening out, all in one second.

There was a moment of regret and anxiety at getting rid of the swim fin, but with the diver in close pursuit there was no time for emotions. Andrew began to thrash forward on the surface, now using arms as well as his unbalanced leg pressure to propel himself.

He glanced up, gasping and sobbing and saw that the stern of the dive boat was only ten metres away. Ella was still there, staring wide eyed but puzzled. Then the boat was only seven metres… five metres.

Then what Andrew had been fearing happened: the smuggler on the dive boat appeared. Andrew saw him walk to the stern and push Ella aside as he looked down. By then Andrew had reached the small dive platform at the stern and even as he struggled onto it an idea formed in his mind and he acted on it.

The man looked puzzled and it occurred to Andrew that he had not realized that Andrew was not one of the gang.

He thinks I am one of his divers in trouble, he thought.

He acted on that. Scrabbling to get his left knee and right foot onto the dive platform Andrew reached up, even as he struggled to hoist himself with all the weight of the air tank up out of the water. The man bent down and reached for his hand. As their hands met Andrew let go of the rail with his left hand and grabbed the man's shirt with it. Then he flung himself backwards, hauling with all his might.

Knowing that he would end up back in the water with the diver and his speargun fast approaching acted as a stimulant to Andrew. To his satisfaction, and amazement, his plan worked. The man was caught completely off guard and went cart-wheeling off the boat and as Andrew rolled downwards into the water the man went over Andrew's upraised feet and fell heavily on his back in the sea.

Not pausing to delay for a second Andrew wriggled and floundered around to face the boat again and grabbed at the dive platform. With his whole body cringing in anticipation of a spear strike or of the man grabbing him Andrew dragged himself back up out of the water. His mind told him this was it, do or die! In another second he had reefed off his other swim fin and tossed it onto the boat.

I can't climb a ladder or run with flippers on, he told himself.

Using what seemed like the last of his fast waning strength he stood up and grabbed the railings of the ladder leading up to the dive deck and heaved himself upwards, water cascading of him as he did. As he climbed he gasped and groaned and had to grit his teeth because the weight of his body and equipment seemed to be too much for his tired arms. It was only six steps, the height of a man, but it took all his strength to even lift himself one step. But driven by desperation he somehow managed it, falling forward heavily onto the dive deck.

There, right in front of his eyes, were Ella's bare feet. Andrew looked up to see alarm and fear flooding through her face. She backed away, cringing and keeping her arms across her bosom. But he had no time for her.

The diver! he thought.

Frantically he pulled his facemask down and then rolled on his back and clawed at the buckles of his BCD.

I must get this off, he thought.

With it on he had no chance of any nimbleness. Luckily, the two snap catches came undone easily and Andrew grabbed the zip and hauled it down. The vest came undone and he gasped and struggled to worm his arms out of it. But he found that the strap of his carry bag was caught across his chest and was blocking it. Desperately he grabbed at the strap and tried to get it over his head. And as always with wet things and when in a fluster it seemed to do nothing but to catch and snag!

And there was the diver!

And the man I pulled overboard!

Both were trying to climb onto the dive platform just below Andrew.

The man came first. Whimpering with fear Andrew rolled onto his front and dragged the strap of the carry bag over his head and off. Casting it aside he swung the air tank to get the BCD vest off. But there was the man, almost up the ladder! He was within arm's reach. Without a weapon Andrew reacted instinctively. He continued to swing the BCD and air tank and flung them at the man as hard as he could.

The bundle slammed into the man. He tried to fend it off with one hand, but the blow made him lose his grip. Mouth open muttering a curse the man fell heavily onto the dive platform. From there he rolled into the water again. For a fleeting instant Andrew experienced a surge of almost euphoric glee at having downed one of his enemies, until his eyes saw the diver aiming the speargun at him!

Andrew tried to jump aside but his feet tangled in the strap of the carry bag and he stumbled. Unable to stop himself he fell heavily on his knees. Even as searing pain shot up both legs and through him he heard a sharp 'Whang!'

The spear came so close it almost parted his hair. In agony Andrew rolled on his side, crying out in pain and clutching at his knees. As he did his eyes noted the spear which was now embedded in the sun roof over the dive deck. A wave of chill swept through him as he realized just how close he had come to death.

The diver! he thought.

No time for pain! Ignoring the agony and gasping for breath Andrew rolled onto his smarting knees and sprang to his feet. He was just in time. The diver was now climbing onto the dive platform and as he straightened up he hurled the speargun at Andrew.

Andrew flung is arm up, but it still struck him a savage and numbing blow on his left forearm. Luckily the throw was off line and the butt end of the speargun struck an upright and the weapon spun away to fall over the side.

But that did not deter the diver. Through a mist of tears as more pain engulfed him, Andrew saw that the man was now unsheathing his diver's knife.

The sight of that shining blade caused Andrew's to blanch and he felt his stomach churning with terror. "Oh help!" he whimpered, looking frantically around for a weapon.

And there was one, a boat hook! Snatching it up Andrew lunged at the diver. The man twisted aside and tried to grab the boathook. Just in time Andrew pulled it back. He raised it ready for another lunge.

But the diver slid back into the water and grabbed at the man who was now trying to haul himself out again. The man was spluttering and cursing and looked very angry. Pointing the diver shouted, "Both sides at once!" He then pushed the man to the port side.

Andrew knew exactly what the diver intended. The dive boat not only had a ladder at the stern but had one on each side halfway along the hull at the front of the dive deck.

They are going to rush me from both sides at once, he thought.

He knew he could probably block one of them but would not have time to run around to the other side because a platform crowded with air tanks, BDCs, and other equipment took up the centre of the dive deck for ten metres of its length.

Who is the more dangerous? Andrew wondered as the two smugglers began to put their plan into operation. *The man,* Andrew decided. *The diver still has his fins and his air tank on. He will move slower.*

Then movement on the sea astern caught Andrew's eye and his stomach churned with even more fear. The rubber dinghy had left the submarine and was heading back towards the dive boat!

Oh, bloody hell! They can come at us from three directions at once now, he thought.

Chapter 31

ELLA

For a couple of seconds Andrew dithered in near panic, his breath coming in rasping gasps.

Three directions at once! I will never beat them off, he thought.

Then he turned to check if the diver was swimming along the starboard side. And there was Ella. She was standing a few paces along the starboard walkway, wide-eyed with fear and with her arms across her front.

Instantly ideas flooded Andrew's racing brain. "Ella, stop that diver getting aboard!" he shouted while pointing forward.

"Diver?" Ella croaked, shaking her head.

As she did Andrew noted that her whole body seemed to be a mass of brown and blue bruises including on her breasts and that she was badly sunburnt. For an instant Andrew felt ill at the thought of what she might have been subjected to. She shook her head in bewilderment.

That sparked real anger in Andrew. "Stop that diver getting aboard!" he yelled, pushing her with his left hand and turning her to face forward.

As he did a noise behind him made him look over his shoulder. It was the man! *Igor!* Andrew remembered.

Igor had not swum along the port side at all but was heaving himself up onto the dive platform again, water streaming from his wet clothes. He looked very angry, and in his teeth was a knife!

Andrew spun round, trying to manoeuvre the boathook in the confined space. As he did Igor sprang onto the platform. Sobbing with fear Andrew lunged at the man with the boathook. But Andrew was off balance and as he moved his right thigh muscles cramped. The strike missed and before Andrew could withdraw the boathook Igor knocked it aside and grabbed it. Then he pulled, hard. The sudden change of direction nearly succeeded in making Andrew lose his balance.

Igor wrenched and the boathook was torn from Andrew's grasp. Dismay at his own weakness momentarily disarmed Andrew. The boathook went clattering down over the stern and into the water. As it did the man leapt at the ladder and began to climb. Andrew ran forward to kick at the man but the man paused, took the knife from his mouth and slashed at Andrew's ankles with it. The knife was thin and looked razor sharp.

Fish filleting knife? Andrew thought as he sprang back in fright.

Then Igor was up on the top tread and Andrew knew he had to act. With a sob of fear, knowing instinctively that this was life or death, he forced himself to jump forward. The knife flashed and cut up his forearm, but somehow he avoided it slicing open his stomach and he managed to grab the man's right arm. For an instant they both were locked together as their muscles snapped taut and Andrew was nearly sick from the fear. His eyes met those of the man and Andrew recoiled mentally from the evil, fish-like stare in them. Worse still he could smell the man, and feel him; feel his wet, sweating flesh, flesh that was moving and full of muscular strength. And he was slippery.

If he gets that hand free he will fillet me, Andrew thought grimly. He had no doubt that the man meant to kill him.

To his dismay Andrew found that he needed both of his hands to grip Igor's arm that allowed the man to claw his way fully on board and then to start punching at him with his left.

Bowel watering terror now surged through Andrew. The knife was only centimetres from his face and that close up it looked wicked.

Hang on! Hang on or you are dead man! he told himself.

He tried to step back but his heel caught on his carry bag and he stumbled. But even as he fell Andrew did not let go. Both he and Igor fell heavily on the deck, Andrew on his back and the swearing, sweating, cursing man half on top of him. For several seconds they wrestled violently as Andrew tried to wriggle out from under. In this he failed but he did manage to hold the knife away after being nicked in the neck. Andrew saw blood, his blood, on the knife point and he shuddered with terror and hung grimly on, trying with all his strength to hold the point away from him.

And there was more blood. Andrew noted it dripping from where it had trickled around his left forearm from the slash in it. The smell and then the taste of it added another whole new dimension of terrifying reality to the fight. And at the back of his mind Andrew was conscious of what would happen when the diver climbed aboard.

I have to get free before then, he thought.

But how?

Igor stopped punching Andrew and suddenly moved his left hand to grab Andrew's throat and with his right he tried to turn the knife blade down. Andrew had been aware that the man had been holding the knife correctly for a knife fight, as his own father had taught him, thumb on the blade and ready to strike upwards. But that at least put the blade at the wrong angle for a downward stroke.

To Andrew's horror he realized that he was simply not strong enough to hold the man. The point of the blade began moving closer with every second of gasping breath and quivering, tensed muscles.

I am done for! Andrew thought, gritting his teeth and straining with every ounce of energy he still had to hold the man.

Then movement beside him caught Andrew's eye and he flicked a glance to see what it was, fearing it was the diver. To his relief he saw that it was Ella. She was still standing there gasping and with one hand to her mouth in dismay. That was too much for Andrew.

I came to rescue you, you silly bitch! he thought resentfully.

Twisting to free his throat for a moment Andrew croaked, "Ella! Ella, do something! Ellaaargh!"

Igor tightened his grip and Andrew's already laboured breathing was cut off. He began to feel dizziness and dots began to dance across his vision. This now narrowed down to the knife point which was only centimetres from his right eye. Still gripping the man's arm and wrist with both of his hands Andrew strained with all his might to keep that point away from his face. But then he began to choke and black out and a sickening sensation of defeat began to seep in.

Whack! Thud!

Andrew felt the man's grip suddenly loosen and then his body slumped heavily on Andrew's chest. For a few seconds he could not work out what had happened and then he realized he was still holding the man's arm, but the knife had fallen from nerveless fingers. He saw that the man was lying heavily on him, apparently unconscious.

Then Andrew saw Ella standing over them, her face a mask of fury. She was holding an air tank which she had obviously snatched from the nearby rack and then used to hit the man. Their eyes met and she stared in wide-eyed horror.

"I hit him," she croaked. "I hit him on the head."

"Thanks. Good work," Andrew croaked in return, while freeing his throat from the unconscious man's grasp.

And not before time! he thought.

Then a splatting noise caught his attention and he twisted his head to look sideways along the deck. He saw that a wet swim fin had just landed on the deck at the starboard entry port. As he watched a second followed.

The diver! Andrew thought, another spasm of fear coursing through him.

Pointing and trying to push the unconscious man off him at the same time Andrew cried, "Ella! Stop the diver!"

Ella turned and looked, then went racing along the deck, the air tank swinging in her hands. Andrew shoved the unconscious man off him and rolled onto his front, dimly aware that he was dripping blood and that it was now smeared all over his face and clothes. He struggled to get to his hands and knees, driven by a desperate urge to get to the entry port to stop the diver.

But once again his feet tangled with his carry bag strap and he stumbled and fell to his knees. An agony of apprehension surged through him as he watched, fearing that Ella might not be able to stop the diver. He saw two hands appear on either side of the entry port as the diver moved to haul himself inboard. Then Ella swung the air tank, swung it very hard, so that it slammed into the man's face.

There was a sickening thud and the two hands vanished. A large splash indicated that the diver had fallen back into the sea and Andrew sighed with relief. He saw Ella stop and stare down at the water, her breasts heaving with emotion and exertion and the air tank poised ready to use again. Then she shook her head and dropped the air tank and slumped down.

Andrew wanted to move to help her but first he untangled his feet. Then the sound of an outboard motor drew his focus to the stern again and he saw that the rubber dinghy had arrived. It was surging in to the dive platform. In the stern was a big man in a wetsuit and he looked both angry and annoyed.

The Boss! Andrew thought, clambering to his feet and kicking to free the strap from around his right ankle.

As he did he looked to see if the man had a gun and was relieved to see that he did not appear to be armed. One hand was holding the outboard motor and the other was shielding his eyes from the sun.

"But I need a weapon," Andrew muttered.

He looked around, decided that an air tank could be thrown at the man and stepped forward to grab one, only to nearly trip again because the bag strap was still caught around his ankle.

"Bloody bag!' he shouted as fear welled up in him.

Then he shook his head as an idea came to him. The bag was not done up and some of the contents had spilled out on the deck. Among these were some flares.

Yes! Just the thing! Andrew thought.

Instantly he bent and snatched one up and then thanked his lucky stars for those training sessions at Navy Cadets and in small boats on how to use the things.

By that time the rubber boat was at the stern. As the Boss reached across to grasp a rope hanging down Andrew ignited a hand-held flare. It began to spew brilliant red and white flames and a dense cloud of orange smoke. Without hesitation Andrew tossed it down into the rubber boat. Then he snatched up the nearest air tank and lifted it above his head.

The man in the boat—Ivanoff?—who cares, saw this and even as he bent forward to try to grab the blazing flare to toss it into the sea he lifted his other arm to shield himself. Driven by both a savage desire to hit back and desperation Andrew threw the heavy air tank. The man just managed to deflect it from his head, but it struck him a hard blow on his left arm and shoulder. The force of the blow knocked the man sideways and he took several seconds to struggle upright.

By then Andrew had snatched up another flare, a rocket flare this time. To arm it he had to peel off a safety sticker and then shift the cap from the top to the base. As he did this Andrew held the flare up in front of him. The man's eyes widened with alarm and he stopped trying to grab at the spluttering flare in the bottom of the rubber boat and instead pushed his boat clear of the dive boat. The man then reached for the throttle and began to power out of range.

Andrew changed his grip to aim the flare and then struck the base to fire it. But because it was a flare designed to be fired up into the sky it was awkward to hold at that angle and when Andrew struck the base to fire it the tube jerked sharply. The rocket shot out leaving a trail of smoke, but the aim was poor and it went shooting past the man to strike the sea fifty metres beyond. It sizzled on the surface for a few seconds then spluttered out and sank.

Andrew bent and picked up another flare. This was a hand held but he hesitated. The rubber boat was now out of range and the Boss was trying to pluck the still blazing flare from out of it. A huge cloud of orange smoke was billowed out and streamed away on the breeze. The rubber boat had circled southwards and was now about a hundred metres to starboard. While Andrew watched the Boss finally picked up the flare and tossed it into the sea. The smoke cloud died away and the last of it blew away on the breeze.

Andrew's gaze then moved to the submarine. It was still on the surface a hundred metres astern, a cluster or heads showing above the coaming of the conning tower.

They must be wondering what is going on, Andrew decided. Then he had another anxious thought. *What if they come with guns?* For a few seconds he stood there, wondering what to do next. *There is another diver down there too,* he remembered, turning to look towards where he had last seen the diver.

And there he was!

A head had just popped out of the water fifty metres away over in the direction of the cay. Movement there also caught Andrew's eye.

Carmen! he thought. He had forgotten his sister. *She needs to join us. We must get out of here,* he thought.

To attract her attention, he ignited the flare then leaned out and waved to her. Then the noise of the outboard attracted Andrew's attention and he looked at the rubber boat. The Boss had opened the throttle and turned the rubber boat towards the submarine.

He is going to get more men—and guns! Andrew thought, another spasm of fear surging in his already churning guts. *I need a gun too.*

Knowing there must be guns on board Andrew tossed the still burning flare into the water and turned to limp forward towards Ella, finally kicking his ankle free of the strap as he did. "Ella, what is that diver doing?" he called.

In response Ella just sat on the long bench on the platform and stared down through the entry port. Andrew called again and she continued to stare. He grabbed her arm and shook her.

"Ella, where is that diver? What happened?"

Ella looked up at him, her face a stricken mask and her eyes bleak. "He just sank," she whispered.

"What?"

"I hit him and he just sank," she repeated.

Andrew stepped across and looked down at the water and felt his emotions churn again. There was no sign of the first diver, only rippling waves and the vast blue sea. Not really wanting to think about the man's fate Andrew turned back to Ella and gently patted her shoulder.

"You did the right thing. You saved us," he said.

"The bastard... He..." Ella cried, a note of hysteria in her voice. "He... It was... It was..." She broke down and began to weep.

Then he deserved what he got, Andrew thought, knowing what she couldn't say.

In an attempt to console her he patted her again. But she did not look up, just curled up and sobbed. Anxiety now made Andrew look aft and he saw that the rubber boat was still heading for the submarine. But the rubber boat looked odd. For a second or two Andrew stared at it puzzled. Then it came to him. Not only was it lower in the water but it looked all crumpled.

The flare has burnt a hole in it! he decided.

Even as he thought this the rubber boat suddenly stopped and the outboard motor coughed and vanished under the water. The Boss grabbed at the rumpled remains but they sank beneath him and then he was floundering in the water, still a hundred metres from the submarine.

There were men on the sub waving their arms and shouting and that got Andrew going again. A quick glance showed the second diver was now swimming towards the dive boat and the Boss was swimming towards the sub.

I still need a gun, Andrew told himself. He turned back to Ella. "Ella, where are their guns? Ella!"

Ella did not look up. She just remained curled into a ball, sobbing and shaking. Andrew was almost overwhelmed by the urge to comfort her but the fear of his own predicament overrode his finer feelings. Noting with dispassion that a badly bruised right breast was showing under Ella's uplifted arm he gently shook her. "Ella, watch this other diver. Don't let him get aboard," he cried.

Then he left her and dashed into the passenger saloon just forward of the entry port. There was a litter of gear and food scraps there but no guns so he hurried forward and into the small wheelhouse.

Ah! There is one, Andrew noted. *An AK47.* He grabbed the weapon and for the first time smiled. *Now we have a chance,* he thought.

After checking that the magazine was full he cocked the weapon and then hurried back to the starboard entry port. He was just in time. The diver was now close to the side. As Andrew arrived breathless at the entry port the diver looked up. Through his face mask his eyes met Andrew's and Andrew held the rifle up for him to see.

The man shook his head and then looked around while treading water. Then he started swimming towards the dive boat again. *Oh no! What will I do?* Andrew thought.

In his heart he did not think he could shoot the man. In an attempt to scare him off Andrew aimed the AK downwards. The man stopped swimming and stared up at him.

He thinks I am bluffing, Andrew thought. In desperation he aimed near the diver and pulled the trigger. The bullet struck the water and the man flicked his arms up and went under. A stream of bubbles rose.

For a moment Andrew was horrified. *I didn't aim at him. Surely I didn't hit him,* he thought. Leaning out he watched and then felt relief when he saw a burst of bubbles nearby. *He is swimming underwater,* he decided. But where to? And to do what?'

Anxiously Andrew watched as the bubbles reached the side of the dive boat. *He is under the boat. He could come up anywhere,* Andrew thought.

That reminded him of his other perils and he looked around. The submarine was still there and the Boss was closer to it and swimming.

When he gets to the sub he will get more men with guns and come and get us, he thought. *We need to get this boat under way!*

Chapter 32

SHOCKS AND SUPRISES

For a few seconds anxiety almost paralysed Andrew. There was the submarine, a huge grey monster just a hundred metres astern. And somewhere under the dive boat was the second diver.

And he could come up suddenly at any of three places, no four. He can climb up onto the bow as well, Andrew thought.

Mental images of the black clad diver hoisting himself up the anchor chain and then grabbing a gun from the wheelhouse caused Andrew to almost dance with fear.

I can't watch it all! he fretted.

That problem got him to turn and face Ella. "Ella, I need help. Get up and watch that the other diver doesn't climb on board here," he said.

But Ella didn't respond, just stared at him, her face a tear-streaked mask of abject misery.

"Ella! For Christ's sake! We aren't safe yet! Help me!" Andrew cried. He was tempted to slap her but even in this extremity couldn't bring himself to do it. "Oooh bloody hell!" he shouted, gnashing his teeth and looking frantically around.

Then another idea came to him. "Ella, is the boat anchored or moored?" he asked.

This time she responded. "Moored," she whispered.

Andrew didn't wait. Clutching the AK he pushed his way into the saloon and ran through it to the front door. This opened onto the focsle beside the wheelhouse. There was no sign of the man but Andrew knew he must act fast.

While I am up the front he could be climbing on at the stern, he worried.

His idea was to move the dive boat. *The current will carry us and then we can get the engine going,* he thought.

Hurrying out onto the focsle Andrew scanned the mooring arrangements. Once again, his Navy Cadet training and seagoing experience paid off as he knew exactly what he was looking at. Placing the rifle down he bent to where a rope was secured to a cleat after coming in through the port bow fairlead. With rapid movements he undid it and let it slip. Then he hurried to where the other end was wrapped around the anchor capstan.

As he grabbed the rope to pull it in he detected movement out of the corner of his eye. Turning quickly to see what it was Andrew looked out to starboard. The sight of a moving dark object on the sea caused his heart to skip with alarm until he focused his eyes and he saw it was Carmen in their rubber dinghy.

Carmen! If she can get here we have a chance, he thought. Then a second idea came to him and he smacked his forehead. *You drongo! You've forgotten her and have let the boat loose.*

And the dive boat was adrift. Already the bow was turning as the outgoing tide took control. Looking helplessly towards Carmen Andrew could only shrug.

She will just have to catch us up, he thought. He felt sure that the powered dinghy could do that. Now he returned his focus to the diver. *And that bloody sub! We are drifting towards it now,* he thought.

Grabbing the AK he hurried back through the wheelhouse and out to the aft deck. As he came out there he half-expected to meet the diver but there was no sign of the man.

Nor was there any sign of the submarine. For a moment Andrew stared in bewilderment and then realized he was looking in the wrong direction. The sub was there but the dive boat had spun almost completely round on the current so it was now on the port bow.

And close, only about fifty metres away.

"Bloody hell!" Andrew muttered, grinding his teeth. He hobbled quickly around to the port side and peered out. There was no sign of the second diver or of the Boss.

Then he gaped. Water was swirling around the sub and it was moving away from him. *What is it doing?* he wondered.

This quickly became apparent. The submarine was moving astern under power and at the same time turning to port. Suddenly the whole dive boat jerked and listed. The motion was so unexpected and so hard that Andrew nearly lost his balance. Then the dive boat slewed sharply around. The submarine seemed to slide across Andrew's line of vision as the dive boat rotated rapidly so that it was stern first to the current.

Rushing water began piling up against the transom and swirling along the side, clearly indicating that the dive boat had come to a stop and was somehow anchored.

"What the hell?" Andrew cried.

He hurried aft to check what the problem was. Stepping over the unconscious smuggler who was still sprawled on the deck Andrew looked down. The reason was at once clear. Projecting from the stern was a small triangular derrick which was used to hoist dinghies and heavier items. It was swung out and locked and a block and tackle hung from it. Four ropes, vibrating from strain, vanished down into the disturbed water from the block showing that it was in use.

The smugglers are using it to hoist their torpedoes up, Andrew thought. *And it is caught on the net or something. I must cut it!*

That caused Andrew to look down. *That man had a knife now where is it?*

To his relief it was there lying in the scuppers and it took Andrew only a moment to lay down the AK and pick up the knife. After a quick glance to check that the second diver was not climbing aboard he turned to the ropes and began to slice at the one tied to the block.

Then noise of an outboard motor caused him to pause and lean across the port rail. It was Carmen and she was angling the rubber boat in to come alongside. A spurt of alarm went through Andrew and he waved and yelled, "Carmen, watch out! There is a diver down under us somewhere. Get aboard quick!"

Carmen nodded and waved then eased the rubber boat alongside the port entry port. Then she switched off the motor, grabbed the painter and scrambled up the ladder. A moment later she was aboard and busy tying the rope to an upright.

"Andrew, what's happening?" she called.

"We are caught on the net. I'm trying to cut us free. Watch out. There is a diver down there who is trying to climb aboard. Ella is over on the starboard side. Can you watch the port side and bow?"

Carmen nodded and turned to look down and forward. Andrew resumed cutting. The knife was sharp but the rope was high quality and made of woven nylon so took some cutting.

As he sawed at the rope Andrew glimpsed the submarine again. It was crossing their bow heading from starboard to port and was moving ahead at increasing speed. As it came into view he saw that there were no heads visible on the conning tower. When bubbles began spewing from the casing and the hull began to dip he nodded.

Diving, he told himself.

Carmen called to him. "Andrew, that sub is diving!"

"I know. I hope that means it is clearing out. If they attack us with guns we are done for," he yelled back.

"Running for it I reckon," Carmen replied. "They won't want to be caught on the surface or in one of the channels in daylight by an aircraft."

She was right. The white foam round the hull increased and in less than half a minute the submarine had dived. Andrew noted that the periscope was still showing, trailing a feather of foam as the sub made its way down the Boat Passage. At the sight of the periscope Andrew smiled.

I hope that radio transponder is working, he thought.

Turning to Carmen he said, "I suppose the blokes in the sub must have wondered what was going on."

"They probably thought they had sailed into a trap. It certainly looked dramatic when you started firing those flares and throwing people overboard," she replied.

Andrew glowed at the exaggeration even as he shuddered at the memory of those terrifying minutes. "If it was me I would want to get out of here fast," he agreed.

Suddenly Carmen screamed. "Andrew! Here he is!"

"Don't let him on board Car!" Andrew yelled. He sliced through a few more strands, hoping to sever the rope. But it still held, although now three quarters cut through. Dropping the knife, he bent and scooped up the AK. Jumping over the unconscious smuggler he hurried forward to join Carmen.

But by the time he had painfully hobbled the distance the diver was gone. Carmen pointed down and then said, "He just slid under."

"Keep watch. He might try the other side now," Andrew replied as he aimed the rifle down at the water and the rubber dinghy bobbing alongside. He then realized that Carmen was staring at him in horror.

"Andrew!" she cried. "What happened to you?"

Realizing she was staring at the blood on his face and clothes, he shrugged. "Knife fight. It's nothing," he said. Then he turned and limped aft again to finish cutting the ropes.

Carmen called after him. "Nothing be blowed! You are dripping a trail of blood."

"We will fix it in a minute," he called back as he stepped over the unconscious man yet again. Once again, he placed the rifle on the deck and picked up the knife. Then he looked over the stern, and his heart skipped with fright.

The diver was there, gripping the ropes and starting to hoist himself onto the dive platform!

Andrew didn't dither this time. He grabbed the rope he had almost cut through and attacked it with a frenzy of sawing. Two good slices were enough. The rope suddenly parted and the end whipped down out of sight, the pressure of the current forcing the rope to unreeve through the blocks.

The diver was thrown off balance as he had been gripping only one of the ropes. He fell sideways and then clawed at the dive platform of hang on. Andrew stared down and shook his head with a mixture of satisfaction and fear.

If he had been gripping all four ropes that wouldn't have happened, he thought, knowing that if that had been the case, the man's grip would have caused the pulling in both directions to be cancelled out.

The diver looked up and then began to crawl onto the dive platform. But hampered by his swim fins and his scuba gear he was obviously finding it awkward. Andrew dropped the knife and snatched up the AK again. Trembling with fear and the apprehension that he might have to shoot the man he aimed it.

"Back off or I shoot!" he yelled.

The diver stopped climbing and looked up. Andrew met his eyes and stared back. *He is Barry, the man who shot Tristan,* he recognized. That caused his finger to momentarily tighten on the trigger. But he still refrained from pulling it. *He thinks I'm not game,* he thought.

To convince the man Andrew shouted, "You murdered my friend, you mongrel! If you try to climb up you are dead. Now take all that gear off and sit there."

At that moment the last of the ropes unreeved and the dive boat was free again. Caught by the tide it lurched and began to spin bows on to the current. Barry suddenly rolled off the dive platform and vanished in a flurry of spray kicked up by his swim fins.

Carmen came hurrying aft. "Where is he?" she asked.

"Gone under again," Andrew replied.

Carmen pointed across the channel towards the cay. "Who is that?" she asked.

Andrew saw a tiny head visible among the small waves. It was a person swimming slowly against the current towards the cay. For a moment Andrew was flummoxed as to who it could be and wondered if it was the first diver. Then he shook his head and said, "I think it is their boss, Ivan or whatever his name is."

Carmen shielded her eyes and stared at the man who was now a good two hundred metres away. "Could be. He is the man who was swimming towards the submarine."

Andrew glanced at her in surprise. "You sure? That was their boss. He was in the rubber boat I threw the flare into."

"That's him then."

"But didn't the sub pick him up?" Andrew asked.

Carmen shook her head. "No. They just reversed and left him. I saw it," she explained.

Andrew was both shocked and appalled at the ruthlessness of the smugglers. "They are certainly murderous bastards," he commented.

"Where is the other diver?" Carmen asked.

"Ella smacked him in the face with an air tank and he went overboard," Andrew replied, gesturing to where Ella still sat hunched in a quivering ball on the bench.

Carmen looked and then let out a gasp. Shaking her head, she pointed down. "And this guy here, what happened to him? Where is all that blood from?"

Andrew shook his head in reply. "Me. He was trying to knife me," he replied.

"What happened to him?"

"Ella whacked him on the head with the same air tank. He is just unconscious," Andrew answered.

"Poor Ella!" Carmen muttered. She turned and hurried forward.

"She's had a really bad time," Andrew said as he limped after her.

As they reached her Carmen looked at Andrew. "You find a first aid kit and I will get a bandage on that arm; and put that safety catch on."

The realization that he was carrying a loaded weapon in an

unsafe condition caused Andrew to burn with shame. As a Navy Cadet Quartermaster Gunner he prided himself on being a good weapon handler. Not really wanting to be with the girls when Ella told her story to Carmen he clicked the safety catch on and pushed his way past and into the saloon to where he knew there was a first aid kit.

After pulling the case from its bracket on the bulkhead near the wheelhouse door Andrew limped back towards Carmen and Ella. As he hobbled painfully along between the rows of seats and tables he looked around and noted that the dive boat was drifting on the current and that the cay on Yule Reef now looked to be half a kilometre away.

He emerged from the saloon to where Ella was sobbing in Carmen's arms and immediately found he had yet another gut-wrenching crisis to solve: the man on the stern was no longer unconscious. He was standing up and holding the knife!

The man glared at them and hefted the knife into a fighting hold then took a step forward. Andrew felt his blood freeze and his stomach clenched in fear as dread of another hand to hand struggle swamped him. But he was now even more determined. Pushing past Carmen and Ella Andrew held the rifle across his front so that the man could see it.

As he did his mind raced. *I must shoot to incapacitate this bloke,* Andrew told himself. Raising the butt to his shoulder he clicked off the safety catch and aimed the weapon at the man's legs.

"Drop the knife!" he croaked, fear making him hoarse.

A look of fear crossed the man's face as he stared at the rifle. For a fleeting moment his eyes met Andrew's and then the man turned and jumped behind the stacks of air tanks and diving equipment.

Damn! Andrew thought.

"Surrender! Drop the knife or I shoot," he shouted.

Shaking in what seemed like every muscle Andrew began advancing slowly along the deck, weapon at the ready and finger on the trigger.

A scuffling noise to his right caused Andrew to glance that way and to swing the barrel to point in that direction. Through the gaps between the rows of hanging BCDs and wetsuits he glimpsed the man scuttling forward along the port side.

He is heading for the saloon, he thought.

"Carmen! Watch out! Watch the saloon to make sure he doesn't come that way," he yelled.

Then he dashed to the stern and around to the port side, ignoring the pain in his right thigh and buttocks. As he jumped around the corner to face along the port side he had the rifle ready at the hip.

He was just in time to see the man vanishing over the side through the port entry port. *The rubber dinghy! He is getting away!* Andrew thought.

He ran forward and came to a halt at the entry port. The man was there, down in the rubber dinghy. He had untied the painter and pushed the dinghy clear so that it was already five metres from the dive boat.

Andrew raised the rifle and aimed it. "Hands up or I shoot!"

But the man ignored him and turned to the outboard motor and began pulling at the starter cord. Andrew's stomach went all queasy with anxiety. He swallowed and tried to slow his breathing. To further distract him he found he had dots dancing in his eyes and his vision was blurred. Worse still the rifle sights seemed to be jumping and shivering. Anxiety swamped Andrew.

He is getting away! his mind cried, but he could not bring himself to tighten his finger on the trigger.

The outboard spluttered into life and the man sat down and opened the throttle, then looked at Andrew. Carmen arrived via the saloon, a heavy wrench in her hands. She stopped beside Andrew and watched but said nothing.

The rubber dinghy began to power away. Andrew followed it with his rifle sights. For a few seconds he was tempted to shoot holes in the inflatable but couldn't even bring himself to do that.

I might hit the man, he worried.

When the rubber boat was about twenty-five metres away Andrew lowered the rifle and turned to Carmen.

"Sorry sis, I just can't shoot," he said.

Carmen gripped his right arm. "That's alright. It doesn't matter. We are safe. The police can pick him up," she replied.

"Yes, the police, where are they I wonder?" Andrew said.

Both he and Carmen leaned out to scan the sky and then the horizon. Andrew found that the dive boat had rotated again on the current so that it was travelling stern first. He found himself looking at the white-water ringing Longbow Reef and then saw the two wrecks sticking up almost directly astern.

The man in the rubber dinghy kept looking at them and then around the horizon as he changed course and headed west. Within a minute he had passed out of sight across the bows of the dive boat.

Going to pick up his boss on Yule Cay? Andrew thought.

He was about to go forward to keep an eye on the man when a small black object a hundred metres to port caught his eye. Pointing he said, "There is one of the divers," he said.

"He has his mask on his head and his BCD inflated," Carmen said.

"We just need to watch the bastard. We won't want him back aboard," Andrew replied. He then remembered to click on the safety catch before he pushed his way through into the saloon. Crossing to the wheelhouse he looked out to the west.

The first thing he saw was the rubber dinghy, now several hundred metres away and still heading away from them. Next Andrew looked towards Yule Reef which was almost directly beyond the rubber dinghy, perhaps a kilometre away, and saw the tiny figure of The Boss standing on it.

But he was puzzled. Something didn't look right. *Where is the man in the dinghy going?* he wondered.

For a few seconds he studied the course the rubber dinghy was taking. "He's not heading for Yule Reef. Is he heading for Prescott Island do you think?" he suggested.

Carmen looked and shrugged. "Might be. That's where I'd go I suppose," she replied.

"I thought he might go and pick his boss up," Andrew replied as he scanned Prescott Island and then the horizon to the west. He was hoping to see a navy patrol boat or a police launch but had also just remembered that the smugglers had arrived in a game fishing boat the first time.

There might be more of them, he worried.

Carmen looked around then said, "OK little brother, let's get things sorted. I will look after Ella and then get on the radio, if it works. You get the engine started and get this thing under control so that we don't get washed onto the reef and wrecked. I've had enough of shipwrecks for a while."

"Aye aye Ma'am," Andrew replied, using the formal navy jargon in an attempt to hold his emotions at bay. Now he just felt completely drained and the urge to flop down and sleep seemed overwhelming.

Not yet boy! We aren't out of the woods yet, he told himself as Carmen turned and walked away.

Andrew put the rifle on the shelf above the control panel in the wheelhouse and then leaned on the shelf, mostly because his legs were shaking so much he was afraid he might fall down. Then he studied the controls. He had never started the engine but he had watched it done several times and his gaze went straight to the ignition key, or where it should have been.

It's not there! he thought, surprise and a sense of dismay giving him an unpleasant shock. The keyhole was there with the label IGNITION taped underneath it. A quick look around showed no sign of the key. Andrew began to worry and anxiously scanned the control panel, noting gauges and switches, but no key. There was a big red button with ENGINE START printed underneath it, so he pressed this. Nothing happened.

Then Andrew looked around and saw that there was a line of white water indicating the edge of a reef only a few hundred metres to port. Looking behind him, he saw that the wreck of the trawler was now on his port quarter and much closer than it had been. That set little alarm bells ringing in his head and he quickly looked around, noting the relative bearings and distances to Prescott Island and Yule Reef.

Prescott Island is nearly abeam! We are in the Challenger Channel, he thought.

The choppy, rippling waters overside confirmed that. Then realization burst on him as a very nasty shock.

We are being carried out to sea by the tide!

Chapter 33

NOT AGAIN!

"**O**h no! Not again!" Andrew cried as awful flashbacks of being swept out to the open ocean flooded his mind.

He stared wildly around him, first at the rippling current and increasingly larger waves then at the distant stone building on Prescott Island. It was visibly slipping astern and that sent another spurt of anxiety through him. Turning quickly the other way Andrew noted that the white foam along the edge of Longbow Reef was now only a hundred metres to port.

The current should keep us clear, he thought, adding a hopeful 'might!'

Then movement caught his eye and he saw it was the diver. The man was swimming hard to try to reach the reef but was still a good fifty metres from it.

He has realized what is happening as well, Andrew thought.

At that moment Carmen re-joined him. "I've put Ella in the bathroom with a towel and clean clothes," she explained. "Why haven't you started the engine?"

"No key," Andrew replied, gesturing to the empty key hole. Then his eyes were drawn back to the drama of the diver.

Carmen studied the control panel and then said, "What are you looking at?"

"That diver. He is trying to reach the reef, the same as we did," Andrew explained, pointing to the man.

For a few moments he experienced another gut clenching flashback of him and Carmen battling, and failing, to reach the reef against the pull of the outgoing tide.

"He's nearly there," Carmen commented.

Andrew nodded. "He's probably fitter than us," he said.

Carmen laughed. "That wouldn't be hard! Oh good, he's made it," she replied.

Andrew watched breathlessly as the diver clawed his way up onto the edge of the reef. As the man crawled to a kneeling position and then stood up Andrew experienced very mixed feelings. To his own distress he found he had half-wished the man to fail, to suffer the same fate he and his cronies had committed Carmen and him to. But the better part of his nature was relieved.

"Now the mongrel can be arrested and face a court," he commented.

His eyes were drawn to the wreck of the trawler which had now slid into view. The diver only had about 200 metres of reef to cross to reach the safety of the wreck.

Carmen shook her head and pointed to the wreck which was now almost abeam. "We are certainly drifting at a rate of knots," she said.

"Five at least," Andrew agreed.

By this time, they were right in the mouth of the channel and starting to meet larger wind waves. The motion of the dive boat increased and several times it rotated as back eddies and swirls caught it.

Shifting his gaze to the open sea Andrew experienced another spasm of fear. The sea looked so big and so empty! Turning quickly around he looked back up the channel. Now the rubber dingy was just a tiny dot almost lost to view over the curve of the earth.

Heavens! We've come a long way quickly, he thought.

A check of his watch showed it was only 1600hrs—only forty-five-minutes since he had been clutching the periscope of the submarine. That thought caused him to quickly scan the surrounding sea for any sign of the periscope but then he shrugged and felt foolish.

They won't be hanging around. They will be hot-footing it for home, he told himself.

Carmen pointed west. "The rubber dingy isn't heading for Prescott Island at all. It is going northwest through the Challenger Channel."

"Looks like it. He isn't even going to pick up his boss," Andrew answered. He looked to the left of the tiny dot and was just able to pick out the reef and sand of the cay and then a microscopic speck that was the Boss.

"He must be heading for the coast, trying to get away," Carmen observed.

Andrew nodded. "Looks like it. But he won't make it. He hasn't got enough fuel."

"He may not know that, or he might still think it is his best option to make a getaway. The wind should blow him ashore after a few days," Carmen replied.

The thought of spending a couple of days drifting in a tiny rubber dinghy caused Andrew more flashbacks and he shuddered. "Rather him than me."

"At least he's in a boat. We weren't," Carmen replied grimly.

Andrew looked around and noted that they were now in line with the outer edge of the reef. "We are out beyond the reef on the open sea," he said.

Carmen gave a chuckle. "Yes, but on it, not in it! That makes a big difference."

Andrew had to nod and agree but he still felt anxious. It appeared to him that their rate of drift had slowed and he said so. Then the dive boat began to rotate again as another eddy or cross-current caught them.

I wonder how far out to sea we will drift? he thought anxiously. "What will we do now?" he asked.

"First I will bandage that cut in your arm. Then I will get on the radio while you go and have a look at the engine. Maybe you can start if from down in the engine room," Carmen replied.

So she did. It was the work of a few minutes to get the First Aid kit and to place a dressing on the still dripping cut. "You might need stiches in that little brother," she commented as she secured the end of the bandage. "Now I will quickly check that Ella is alright and then get on the radio. You get down to that engine room."

Andrew nodded and turned to go, groaning at the effort and sore muscles as he did. Now he really did want to just lie down but the urgency of the situation still motivated him to move. The sight of that reef, now about half a kilometre astern, was enough.

I don't want to be shipwrecked again, he thought.

He limped across to the companionway that led down from the port side of the saloon to the lower deck. At the bottom of the steps he turned right about and went aft. There was a corridor with two cabins on each side and aft of that were two showers and two toilets and the door to the engine room.

Carmen followed and stopped at the bathroom on the port side to check on Ella. Andrew opened the door to the engine room and climbed down the five steps to stand and look at the diesel engine. It was as he remembered, all steel pipes and wires and nuts and metal things, all shining or greasy in the lamplight.

For the first time in his life Andrew felt real regret for not paying attention when he had the opportunity. He had been in engine rooms plenty of times, but only to observe or to help clean. But he had not studied the engines. He had a rough idea of the principles and main components of marine diesel engines but was quite stumped as to how to get this one to start.

For a few minutes he walked around the thing, staring at various knobs and levers and valves but it all meant very little to him. He had to admit he did not really have a clue. Biting his lip with anxiety he became aware that the motion of the boat had increased. It was rolling and bobbing about much more than he remembered.

We must be right out on the open sea now, he thought.

Unable to do more he made his way back up to the accommodation. Here he found Carmen tucking Ella into her bunk.

"Is she alright?" he asked.

Carmen gave him a bleak look and then gave a wry smile. "You have a shower and change now and I will re-do that bandage," she said.

Andrew looked past her at Ella, but she was just staring blankly at the bulkhead overhead and he suddenly felt very embarrassed and foolish. To escape from the situation, he nodded and went to the cabin he had used previously.

To his surprise he found his kitbag still there, open and obviously rifled through, but still there. Pleased with that he dug out his towel, toilet bag and clean clothes and then peeled off his wetsuit. That was huge relief and he realized he had been sweating profusely.

Making his way aft, Andrew went into the starboard bathroom and got a shock. A wild-looking, red-eyed man with a thick stubble on his peeling face was staring back at him from the mirror.

Holy mackerel! I look a wreck, he thought.

For a few minutes Andrew studied his sunburnt face and cracked lips. Then he fingered the stubble on his jaw and chin. Ever since he had started to shave two years earlier he had never gone that long without shaving and he was amazed at the length and feel of his beard stubble. It was just long enough to be moving from the prickly stage to feeling silky and flowing. He didn't know whether he liked the look or not.

I wonder if Tina will like it? he thought.

The fantasy of using it to tickle various parts of her body flashed through his mind. He managed a weak grin and decided it made him look dashing and rugged rather than just battered and poorly groomed. Still smiling he peeled off his bathers and stepped into the shower.

That hot water was bliss. For ten minutes he just soaped and soothed himself until anxiety about the boat's motion got him focused again. For a few seconds he fingered his beard and then decided not to try to shave.

No, I want Tina to see it, and anyway, sailors are allowed to have beards, he thought.

He pictured himself kissing her and rubbing the bristles on her cheek and neck and that image made him smile. After drying himself and cleaning his teeth he dressed in a dry, clean shirt and shorts and felt immeasurably better.

After a big drink of water and a visit to the toilet he made his way back to his cabin and dumped his bathers, towel and toilet gear and then Carmen removed the wet bandage and spent ten minutes putting on another clean dressing and doctoring his many cuts and scratches. Then they made their way topsides. Back in the wheelhouse Andrew noted it was 1630hrs.

Hopefully, he quickly scanned the horizon all round to check they were safe. Noting that they looked to be now about a nautical mile from the wrecks of the trawler and the *Mull of Kintyre*, he asked Carmen, "Any luck?"

"Yes. I've been onto the marine radio. They gave me another frequency and I have been talking to them, Customs I think they are," Carmen replied.

"What are they doing?"

"They know about us and say they are arranging help as quickly as they can," Carmen said.

"I wish they would hurry up," Andrew commented.

Carmen looked at him. "Feeling better?" she asked.

"Much better," replied Andrew, stroking his stubble as he did.

"You didn't shave," Carmen said.

"Sailors can have beards," Andrew answered, again stroking the stubble.

"Not navy cadets though," Carmen retorted.

Andrew shrugged and chuckled. "Yes Ma'am," he replied. Then he said, "Do you think Tina will like it?"

Carmen opened her mouth to answer then looked up as a loud roar overhead caught their attention. Both looked out and up. It was an RAAF Orion, a four-engine maritime reconnaissance aircraft.

Andrew watched it as it began to bank and circle them. "That plane is a sub hunter," he commented, his eyes noting the magnetic anomaly detector protruding from the back of the fuselage.

"I know. Good, now they can start to hunt hat sub. I.."

Whatever Carmen was going to say was cut off by the radio crackling to life. It was the aircraft calling them. Carmen sprang to pick up the microphone and replied at once.

The aircraft wanted details of the submarine. Carmen clicked the press to talk button and replied: "It is an old Soviet Russian type, a Whisky or Kilo class, diesel powered, not nuclear. It submerged near Yule Reef at about 1520 hours and proceeded northeast along the Bramble Boat Passage at periscope depth. We did not see it after that, but we presume it went east along the Challenger Channel and then out into the Coral Sea, over."

"Dive boat, that is an excellent description. Thank you, over," the operator in the aircraft replied.

"I'm a Navy Cadet Chief Petty Officer, over," Carmen answered.

"You are doing them proud C.P.O., over," came the reply.

That comment made Andrew feel really good. He nudged Carmen and said, "Tell them about the transponders,"

Carmen shook her head. "No, not on the radio. The smugglers might be listening. We put that in the letter so they should know." She turned back to the radio and called again. "There are three of the smugglers in this area. One is a diver and he is on the trawler wreck on Longbow Reef. Their boss is on the cay at Yule Reef and another is heading for the coast in a rubber dingy. There is a fourth, but we don't know where he is, over."

"Roger that dive boat. We will alert the Emergency Services and police. They are getting things moving now and should be with you soon, over," the operator replied.

"Roger, over," Carmen answered.

"We are leaving you now. We will go and hunt for this sub of yours, over."

"Roger, Good hunting, over," Carmen replied.

The aircraft signed off and then banked and turned to the east. Andrew stood next to Carmen and watched as it began to fly back and forth on an obvious search pattern. "I hope they find the mongrels," he muttered, then realized he was gritting his teeth and clenching his fists.

Carmen nodded. "So do I. Now, I will go and have a shower and change. You stay here on watch. After that I will rustle up some scran," she said.

She went below and Andrew was left in the wheelhouse. For a few minutes he looked carefully in all directions but there was no sign of any other vessel or aircraft. The searching 'Orion' vanished into the distance to the east. Feeling utterly exhausted Andrew eased himself up onto the chair at the wheel. His legs felt so rubbery that he was afraid he might collapse. But then he became anxious lest he fall asleep on watch so he slid off the chair and stood.

Oh come on! Hurry up you guys! he thought, willing the authorities to arrive.

Time began to drag. 1700hrs went by and Andrew found it hard to look towards the reef and Prescott Island as the setting sun reflected off the water and hurt his eyes.

What is taking them so long? he wondered.

In his mind he recalculated all the probable timings for the yacht to reach Townsville and for the authorities to marshal and deploy the necessary resources.

That Orion would be based at Edinburgh Air Base in South Australia. It's had time to fly all that way here and probably refuel as well. How come the local rescue chopper and police boats aren't out here by now? he wondered.

Then he noted that the wind had increased. The sea began to develop a distinct chop. Without power the dive boat began to roll and yaw uncomfortably as the wind waves pushed up a confused sea against the out-flowing tide.

This is bad news, Andrew thought. *If the wind gets too strong we will be blown back onto the reef.*

He knew that if that happened before the turn of the tide they could not hope to have the current carry them through one of the gaps. Andrew remembered reading how several sailing ships in the old days had found the reef in their lee and been carried onto it despite their best efforts to claw their way upwind.

Carmen returned, clean and fresh and wearing a new shirt and shorts. She was smiling and looking happy and had a packet of biscuits. "Have a biscuit little brother. Anything to report?"

"The wind has got up," Andrew replied.

Then he looked out to the east and felt his heart skip a beat and his stomach gave a little lurch. Since he last looked ten minutes before a line of dark clouds and rain had appeared. The whole eastern horizon had vanished in the grey, rolling mass.

Bloody hell, that looks like a real squall coming, he thought.

Pointing to it he said, "There is a real storm coming. If the rescue people don't arrive soon we could be blown back onto the reef."

Chapter 34

CARMEN TAKES COMMAND

As he looked at the advancing squall Andrew was suddenly gripped by fear. To him it appeared that the approaching storm extended from one horizon to the other.

This could get very nasty, he thought. Then his mind was swamped by frightening flashbacks and he found himself almost paralysed by fear.

Two years previously he and Carmen had endured a cyclone while marooned at the tip of Cape Bowling Green, a fourteen-kilometre-long sand spit backed by mangrove swamps. They had survived but it had been a terrifying experience. But that time they had been on land. Only the previous January he and Carmen had gone through a cyclone at sea. This time they had been on an ocean-going tug, the *Bonthorpe,* and Andrew had found that a truly terrifying experience. Now his mind just seemed to go numb at the thought of having to endure something similar yet again.

Carmen stared white faced at the approaching bad weather and then shook her head. "We had better get back into our wetsuits and find some life jackets," she said.

Andrew could only swallow and nod. When he didn't reply Carmen looked at him and then nudged him.

"Did you hear me Andrew? Go and put your wetsuit on," she said.

Again, Andrew found himself unable to move. It was as though the wall of grey rain which was now only a few nautical miles away already had him in its grip.

Carmen again nudged him. "Are you alright Andrew?" she asked.

Finally, Andrew was able to make himself move. He sucked in a deep breath and nodded. "Yeah, just scared," he croaked. "I don't really want to go through the experience of being shipwrecked again," he replied.

"We haven't been shipwrecked. We were just on a couple of wrecks," Carmen answered.

"No, not yet," Andrew agreed. With and effort he tore his gaze from the squall and turned to go below. Carmen followed. As they went down the companionway to the lower deck she added, "Anyway, it probably won't last long. Most of the squalls blow over in a few minutes."

Andrew didn't answer that. He found himself battling against another bout of anxiety, this time brought on by fear of being trapped below if the dive boat was capsized.

We might broach and roll over, he thought as he made his way into his cabin.

As quickly as he could he stripped off, not even closing his door in his anxiety and haste. Then he pulled on his bathers and began tugging on the wetsuit. As he did the dive boat began to pitch and yaw and the sound of the approaching wind reached his ears. Bile rose from his stomach as his anxiety shot up and he had to restrain himself from bolting topsides.

Then the squall struck and he wished he had as the dive boat was thrown right over onto its port beam. Andrew gasped in fright and hung on to his bunk and the door frame. For a few seconds he was so afraid the boat was going to roll that he began to pray aloud.

Then the dive boat righted itself and rolled sharply the other way before starting to bob and pitch dramatically. The light dropped to a grey gloom and through the small porthole Andrew saw that it was pouring rain outside.

Then the porthole vanished under water as the dive boat rolled again. The sight of that water swilling up right over the porthole so that Andrew found he was looking underwater again sent spasm of terror through him. For an instant the round porthole gave him a mental image of the circular windows on old fashioned brass or steel diver's helmets. Having found his own long-dead grandfather's in the wreck of the *Merinda,* along with his bones encased in a rotted canvas suit and weighted boots it was an image Andrew had often pictured. Whenever his grandfather was mentioned he pictured that circular scene as the helmet had filled with water, drowning him.

Suddenly Andrew could take it no longer. *I have to get out of here!* he thought.

Regardless of the hampering effect of having only one leg properly in the wetsuit and the other halfway in he clawed his way out into the passageway and began stumbling and staggering along towards the companionway.

Sweat beaded his forehead and made his grasping hands slippery but it was fear that drove him. At the bottom of the companionway he tripped and went down hard on one knee. Then he gasped several deep breaths and began to hop and limp up the steps. The motion of the boat was now so violent he had trouble just hanging on and he had to pause between the movements to pick his moment.

He reached the upper deck just as a large wave struck the starboard bow. The resulting motion caused him to lose his grip and he fell heavily on the deck, rolling over and ending against the door frame of the saloon. For a few seconds he lay there stunned but still terrified. Something close to panic gripped him. Then the boat rolled and pitched quickly the other way in a violent corkscrewing motion and he saw the waves through the windows on the other side.

That really frightened him, but also broke the spell. With fumbling fingers, he lay on his back and hauled at the wetsuit, swearing at every snag as he tried to pull it up over his knees and buttocks. But he managed to pull the suit on and was zipping it up when Carmen suddenly appeared at the head of the companionway.

"You alright Andrew?" she shouted.

Andrew nodded and pulled at the zip. "Just tripped," he shouted back.

"Grab a life jacket and put it on," Carmen replied.

She made her way across to one of the lockers under the nearest bench seat and hauled out a life jacket. Andrew expected her to pull it on and was surprised when she turned and made her way below, holding it in her teeth as she needed both hands to stay on her feet.

For Ella, he thought. Then a spurt of concern for his sister was balanced by admiration. *God she is brave! I wouldn't be able to do that,* he thought. But he didn't want his sister trapped below and wished she would hurry. *This tub could roll at any moment from the feel of it,* he thought.

To get a better view Andrew rolled onto his hands and knees and, picking his moment, grabbed the nearest table and hauled himself to his feet. That immediately made things better. Not only could he see but he could move with the motion of the boat. Best of all he was near the doorway and thought he had a chance of getting out if the dive boat did capsize.

He took out a life jacket and after wedging himself upright in the corner managed to put it on. Then he partially inflated it with his mouth and immediately felt much better.

At least now I will float, he thought.

In his heart he knew he was now too weak to have any chance of staying afloat and swimming using his own depleted strength.

After dragging himself forward to the wheelhouse, Andrew looked out in all directions. But all he could see was grey and dark green. The clouds rolling quickly overhead were dark grey, the rain was light grey and the sea was a mixture of whitish grey foam and murky green water. The size of the waves astonished Andrew. A few minutes before the waves had been about twenty-five centimetres in height but now they looked to be a couple of metres and building. The wind howled around the boat and spray and driving rain lashed it. There was no sign of the wrecks on Longbow Reef or of the reef itself.

But we must be being blown downwind towards the reef, he thought. The squall had come from the southeast so he deduced they would go northwest. *Or roughly that way. It will depend on the currents and their effect on the hull,* he thought.

Not knowing what counter currents or swirls there might be outside the reef he was unable to calculate whether they might be blown back into the relative safety of the Challenger Channel or straight onto the outside of one of the reefs.

We might even end up on Prescott Island, he thought.

Carmen now reappeared, pushing and lifting a scared looking Ella. Andrew moved to help and Ella was shoved into a seat in the corner of the saloon and wedged there. She looked to be mesmerized and very frightened but gave no flicker of recognition and did not speak. Andrew wished to help her mentally but was quite unable to find the right words. Instead he turned to Carmen.

"You get a lifejacket on, sis," he shouted.

Carmen did. She had her arms through one within a minute, clipping it on. "I will get on the radio and try to find out if any help is on its way. We could get blown back onto the reef if this keeps up."

Andrew nodded and glanced astern, then blanched. There was the reef, and the two wrecks! "Car! Look!" he shouted, pointing aft.

Carmen did, and Andrew saw her bite her lip and then hurry to the radio. Andrew turned to study the situation and calculated that the foaming white water on the nearest edge of the reefs was only about a nautical mile astern.

We will strike somewhere between the Mull of Kintyre and the Taiwanese trawler wreck, he decided.

That sent more chills of fear through him. His rational mind told him there were two threats. There was the challenge of surviving when the dive boat was cast onto the reef, and there was the fear of the diver.

He should be in the trawler wreck now, Andrew thought.

On balance, the danger of being smashed and then scraped across the coral reef suddenly looked to be the lesser of the two evils. Having survived that experience once, Andrew felt he might manage to do so a second time, but knowing what it would be like made him dread the ordeal.

But it is not an either-or choice, he thought anxiously. *If we survive the reef we then have to face that diver!*

And the waves were getting larger. They were now at least two metres and even though the rain was now only coming in heavy showers the wind seemed to be rising in intensity.

While he was staring out at the angry sea and the threatening reef Andrew was aware of Carmen talking on the radio. In the hope that help would soon arrive he went and listened. She was talking to a Queensland Police launch that had been sent to help them. But it was now in trouble itself from the storm and was taking shelter in the lee of the reef.

On the other side, Andrew thought, his heart skipping a beat with anxiety. *And they would be fools to try to get through in the dark.*

Because it was getting dark! Already the light had dimmed to a gloomy pall even though the rain had almost ceased. In the clearer air the white foam of the breaking waves on the outer edge of the reef stood out starkly.

And we are definitely closer, probably only half a mile, he estimated.

Once again, a wave of fear chilled him and he swallowed and bit his lip. He was about to ask Carmen what they should do when she spoke again on the radio.

"Switch to frequency four zero decimal six three, roger, over," she repeated. Her deft fingers quickly adjusted the tuning dial and she called again using the dive boat's call sign of WK47.

At once the radio crackled in reply. "Whisky Kilo Four Seven this is Australian warship *Warramunga.* We are moving to your assistance. Confirm your position, over."

Andrew felt a huge surge of relief. *Warramunga!* he thought. *A frigate. A real warship! We are saved now,* he told himself.

Carmen glanced at the soiled and stained chart on the nearby bench and then replied, "*Warramunga,* we are about two cables to the southeast of the wreck of the Taiwanese trawler on Longbow Reef. I can't give you a latitude or longitude until I get the GPS working, over."

"Whisky Kilo Four Seven, that is good enough. We should have you on radar soon. Can you confirm that estimate of two cables? Over," came the reply.

"Yes. I am a Navy Cadet Chief Petty Officer and I think that distance is about right. We are being blown towards the reef by a south-easterly wind, but I cannot accurately determine the rate of drift, over," Carmen replied.

"Is there any chance you could miss the reef and get moved into the Challenger Channel, over," the speaker asked.

Carmen shook her head and replied 'No.' Andrew silently agreed with her. The breaking waves now looked to be only a few hundred metres astern and the wreck of the trawler was now just visible through the spray and drizzle on their port quarter."

"Is your engine not working? Over."

"No. We don't know how to get it going and there is no key in the ignition, over," Carmen answered.

"Stay with the vessel, even if it goes onto the reef. We will be with you in about half an hour, over."

"Thank you. Please hurry," Carmen replied, her voice cracking into a hoarse whisper as he did.

Half an hour! Andrew thought with dismay. *It will be dark by then and we will be on the reef.*

To check this he moved to the stern and studied the distance more clearly while Carmen answered questions about their health and the state of the vessel.

She found him there a few minutes later and said, "Right little brother, let's get ready for the worst. First you tie that rifle into a couple of inflated lifejackets and find some rope to tie it to you. I don't want to end up on that wreck with nothing to defend ourselves with."

Andrew nodded agreement, feeling too battered emotionally and physically to do more. But his mind thought, *There must be more guns. I will find one for Carmen too.*

He did. He located the two loaded sub machine guns and wrapped them in a bundle as well. The lifejackets he half-inflated and then he tied them together and then secured a line with a snap catch to it so he could just hook it on.

By the time he had done that the sound of breaking surf was washing into his consciousness and he found himself repeatedly turning to stare at the line of breakers on the reef. It looked to be only a couple of hundred metres at most although it was now so dark he had trouble gauging distances. Both wrecks just looked like black lumps in the spray and haze. The wrecks were on either quarter and when he saw how close they were Andrew swallowed with fear. His mouth went dry and he then licked dry lips and found he badly needed a pee.

Having done that at the stern out of sight of the girls he went forward to the galley and had a big drink. Carmen nodded approval. "Good man. It might be a while before we get another drink," she commented. "So drink your fill."

She also had a drink and then took a cup of water to Ella, who was still hunched in the corner of the saloon.

Andrew stared out into the driving wind and spray, squinting against the cold and salty droplets, hoping fervently to get a glimpse of the approaching frigate.

Oh, where are you? his mind cried. Another glance astern did little to reassure him. *If they don't arrive soon we will be on the reef,* he thought.

Chapter 35

PROFESSIONAL SKILL

A ndrew leaned out to stare to the south and east.
The frigate must be on the seaward side of the reef. They would never risk coming through those narrow channels in these conditions, he decided.

The cold and spray drove him back inside and he overheard Carmen again on the radio. "Hurry up please. We are now only a couple of hundred metres from the reef and making sternway quite rapidly, over," she said.

"We are doing our best Whisky Kilo, over," came the reply. "We have you on radar and should be there in fifteen minutes, over."

Fifteen minutes! thought Andrew as he anxiously studied the long wall of bursting spray.

The edge of the reef now looked to be just one long, threatening line of breaking foam and he swallowed with fear and tensed, or was it flinched?, in anticipation.

For a moment he considered asking Carmen why the frigate didn't send its helicopter but after thinking about it he shook his head. "Too rough. It would be too risky," he muttered.

But it just seemed so unfair! Why hadn't a police or rescue helicopter arrived earlier in the day? Why was fate letting him down now, right at the eleventh hour?

Another look at the bursting lines of breakers did nothing to calm him. *Won't be long now. It looks to be only a hundred metres or so,* he decided.

Once again, he studied both of the wrecks, considering how to reach them and remembering with sickening apprehension the horrible struggle the last time.

The navy said stay with this boat but it is only a timber launch. It will just disintegrate when it gets slammed onto the reef, he thought.

That image caused him another swallow and more stomach-churning fear. *This is going to be bloody grim,* he thought.

To take his mind off the coming ordeal he checked that he had the bundles of weapons and First Aid and survival gear ready to throw overboard after he had clipped the rope to his life jacket.

I hope the rope doesn't get snagged in the coral, he thought, breaking into a sweat of fear despite the chill wind.

Images of being caught and pounded to death by the surf as it hammered onto the jagged coral made him tremble on top of his shivering. Again, he looked around in a sort of desperate hopefulness. And there it was, a sudden burst of white spray off to the southeast.

Is that the frigate? Andrew wondered, shielding his eyes and squinting into the driving wind and spray.

It is! he decided as he saw a solid shape lift and then drive into another wave.

"Carmen, here they are!" he screamed, pointing.

"That's not a very nautical way for a lookout to report," Carmen chided. "It should have been something like: Bridge, ship bearing green four five."

As the relief flooded through Andrew he grinned. "Yes ma'am. I mean aye, aye ma'am."

The frigate was now clearly visible, pounding and driving through the rough sea as fast as she could safely go. It was the most thrilling sight Andrew had ever seen and he cheered and then clung to the rail and watched, oblivious to the cold wind and salt spray drenching him.

But will they be in time? he wondered as he glanced astern.

Now the boiling surf was less than a hundred metres away and the noise was a deep, churning thunder that turned his bowels to water.

It was obviously going to be a race and Andrew wondered how the navy planned to rescue them. All he could do was watch and hope. The frigate came pounding in from the southeast and then rounded to about a hundred metres from them. The spray drenched warship then turned head to wind.

"Stand by to receive a boarding party," came the radio message.

"Oh, they are game!" Andrew commented, eyeing the three metre waves with anxiety.

Now he wished he had binoculars and he moved slowly and painfully back into the wheelhouse to look for some. They were there but Carmen was using them.

"They are lowering a RHIB," she commented.

Andrew knew exactly what she meant, a Rigid Hulled Inflatable Boat, seven or eight metres long and able to seat a dozen people and powered by huge outboard engines. Again, he glanced aft and now the bursting spray seemed to be right there.

"We had better get Ella outside in case we hit and roll," he suggested.

"Not yet. There is still time," Carmen replied.

"Can I have the binos please," Andrew asked, his fingers twitching with impatience.

Carmen handed the binoculars to him and he steadied them and then focused them with practised fingers. Another, smaller burst of white spray showed clearly in the lens. It was the RHIB, already in the water and appearing to bound across the waves towards them. That sight really cheered Andrew. He and Carmen had been rescued from Denham Island in January by a similar boat and he knew they were extremely seaworthy and manoeuvrable.

I don't like these people risking their lives for us, he thought anxiously as he watched the RHIB thump into a wave and get hidden by the shower of spray it threw up. Another glance aft increased his anxiety. *Fifty metres? Maybe. Oh hurry!* he thought while chewing at his fingernails.

The RHIB came skipping and thumping across the waves, the growl of its engines suddenly audible. It curved away to port and then came sweeping around in wide curve that put its bow facing into the weather. Details became visible, helmeted heads, lifejackets and mottled grey navy camouflage uniforms. Andrew felt an enormous surge of affection for the navy and grinned.

With obvious skill the RHIB was conned close alongside and then the figures were reaching out and clambering aboard. One, a Chief Petty Officer by the rank slides on his shoulder straps, nodded and shouted, "Focsle?"

"Follow me," Andrew replied.

He turned and, ignoring the pain in his thigh and buttocks, led the man through the saloon and out onto the focsle. The CPO at once braced himself against the wire railings and waved. The RHIB surged up close alongside and a line was heaved across.

The CPO grabbed at the coils and then shouted to Andrew, "Hold this."

Andrew did, clutching at both the rope and the railings to stay on his feet on the wildly pitching foredeck. In less time than it takes to tell the CPO gave a demonstration of pure professional skill by passing the end of the nylon rope through the port fairlead and then belaying it to a bollard.

Satisfied the line was secure he stood and gave a crossed arm signal. The RHIB veered away and took station twenty-five metres to port. Andrew clung on and watched but the CPO turned and gestured.

"Back inside please sir. If the tow line breaks it could kill you," he said.

Andrew nodded and slowly made his way back into the wheelhouse, followed by the CPO who was speaking into the radio he carried. When he got there Andrew found a male lieutenant and a midshipman talking to Carmen. Both wore side arms and other ratings carried Steyrs.

The lieutenant turned to Andrew. "Lieutenant Cameron, Royal Australian Navy. Who are you sir?"

"Andrew Collins, and this is my sister Carmen," Andrew replied.

The lieutenant nodded. "We have introduced each other. You two are the navy cadets, is that right?"

"Yes sir," Carmen answered.

"So, who is she?" the lieutenant asked, pointing to Ella.

Carmen again answered. "Ella Lyall. She has been very badly treated. She needs a doctor."

"She will get one as quickly as we can. The rating with her is one of our medics," the lieutenant replied.

Andrew looked and saw a female rating sitting with Ella. Two ratings more arrived, a Leading Seaman and an Ordinary Seaman. "Engine Room?" the Leading Seaman asked.

"Down there aft," Andrew replied, pointing to the companionway. The ratings turned and made their way down to the engine room.

Must be engine room people, Andrew surmised.

The lieutenant looked around and frowned. "There was a report of four men on this vessel. Where are they?"

"Not aboard," Carmen answered.

Andrew pointed to the wreck of the trawler, which was dimly visible in the darkness and spray. "I think one of them is there, we saw him climb onto the reef a couple of hours ago.

Carmen nodded. "And we saw one of them standing on the cay on Yule Reef just before sunset. He is their boss, we think."

Andrew took over. "And a third one was in a rubber dingy heading for land. He went west through the Challenger Channel just on dark." As he said this Andrew pictured the rubber dinghy trying to ride out this storm and he felt ill.

He might really have 'gone west', he thought.

"That is three. Where is the fourth?" the lieutenant asked.

That question made Andrew feel even worse. *Ella might be in terrible trouble here,* he thought. That caused him to hesitate and then he shook his head. *It will all come out,* he decided.

"He was climbing aboard with a knife in his teeth and Ella hit him with a scuba tank and he fell back into the water," he said.

Carmen obviously hadn't known this as she opened her mouth in surprise and gasped. "Andrew! What happened?"

Andrew shook his head, dread of legal consequences fuddling his brain. "There was a fight. There were two of them and the diver had a knife," he explained.

The lieutenant frowned. "So this fourth man is in the water?"

"He was the last time we saw him," Andrew replied.

"When was that?"

"About fifteen hundred hours sir," Andrew answered.

The lieutenant looked at his watch. "That is three hours ago. Where did this happen?"

Again, Andrew pointed. "We were in the channel between Yule Reef and the Feathers Reefs and since then the tide has carried us out to here."

At that he looked aft again and felt his stomach knot with fear. They were now right on the edge of the surf zone and the breaking rollers seemed bigger than the dive boat.

This is going to be touch and go! he thought, fear again making his mouth dry.

Then the dive boat gave such a lurch he would have been flung off his feet if the midshipman hadn't grabbed him. As it was, he was slewed around and slammed into the bench near the wheel and a rating who was holding it. In the process his injured thigh was wrenched and he cried out in pain. For a few seconds he staggered and clung on to stay on his feet.

What happened? he thought, although his mind actually knew.

The tow line had suddenly snapped taut. And it hadn't broken. The bow plunged sharply into the next wave and great showers of spray went up over the boat.

Andrew experienced another surge of fear but then saw that all of the navy people were standing looking quite calm. The lieutenant said in a very unruffled voice: "Take the wheel Swain. Steer to tow."

"Aye, aye sir," the Chief Petty Officer replied, spinning the tiny steering wheel in his hands to get the feel of the rudder.

For a minute or two Andrew still thought they might not make it, fearing that the tow line might snap. But it didn't and when he next looked aft he saw that they were clear of the spray zone and were punching into the waves away from the reef.

We are safe! he thought.

Then he just seemed to slump. The pain in his wound began to ache and throb and he had to grit his teeth so as not to cry out. While he stood there gripping the bench and fighting a wave of dizziness he felt strong hands grab him and he was lowered into a sitting position on one of the benches in the saloon.

"I'm alright. Look after my sister and Ella," he croaked.

"They are being looked after. We brought enough medics to look after all of you," the handsome young midshipman replied. He looked to be only a few years older than Andrew.

Andrew stared at the white midshipman's patches and thought, *That is what I want to be.* He looked up and smiled and suddenly felt safe. *The navy are here. They will look after us,* he thought.

The lieutenant looked down at where Andrew was gripping his thigh. "What happened to you? What are those rips in your wetsuit?"

"I got a spear through it," Andrew replied, his eyes watering with pain. Now he bit his lower lip in an attempt to prevent tears. Just at that moment he did not want to show weakness or cry in front of his heroes!

"Spear! When? How?" the lieutenant cried in astonishment as he bent to look more closely.

"When the smugglers first arrived. They used spear guns to kill Tristan, he was our dive master, and then they shot me. We were underwater at the time," Andrew replied.

The lieutenant called to a burly Petty Officer and pointed. "You'd better look at this Freddy. How long ago did this happen?" he queried.

"Four days? No five days ago," Andrew replied. He was trembling now and felt ashamed of his weakness.

The PO grabbed Andrew and knelt to study the torn suit. Then he shook his head. "Bloody hell! Five days! We'd better have a look at this. Get this wetsuit off young fella."

Andrew was helped out of his life jacket and then the wetsuit was peeled off. As his cuts, scratches, bruises and wounds were exposed the watching navy personnel stared in astonishment and shook their heads. The PO insisted Andrew lie on a table so he could study the wounds more easily. He spent several minutes looking and muttering to himself. Then he went and talked to the lieutenant who began talking on his radio. The PO returned and opened his First Aid satchel. Soon he was hard at work cleaning and swabbing and dabbing stinging antiseptic on the numerous minor wounds. A second rating held a torch to provide light.

"You're bloody lucky young fella," the PO commented as he probed and cleaned the spear wound.

Andrew nodded and then glanced down at the puffy red hole. The sight of pussy liquid oozing from it nauseated him. He shuddered and feared he would black out.

Then the engine burst into life and seconds later the lights came on. A rating bent to the control panel and the radar flickered into use and suddenly everything seemed alright. Under its own power the dive boat was able to steer to take the waves on her starboard bow and the pitching motion eased to a much gentler corkscrewing.

A few minutes later the CPO and another rating went out onto the focsle and cast off the tow. While lying on the table having his wounds bandaged Andrew got glimpses of the RHIB as it powered away back towards the frigate. By this time it was fully dark but the warship's riding lights were plainly visible.

The rain had stopped but not the wind. As he stared out at the dark waves and foaming whitecaps, Andrew wondered what had happened to the diver Ella had hit. To his own surprise he found he did not really care.

He has either drowned or he is drifting out here in the open ocean, he thought.

Memories of his own emotions when he and Carmen had been swept out beyond the Barrier Reef by the current caused him to shudder.

A blanket was wrapped around Andrew and he was moved into a

sitting position again. A hot drink was placed in his hand. Andrew drank it greedily, unsure if it was coffee, tea or cocoa. "What happens now?" he asked.

The midshipman smiled and shrugged. "We maintain position until this weather eases and then we either send you ashore in a helicopter or transfer you to our ship," he said.

The frigate was Andrew's instant choice, but another worry niggled at him. "But your ship can't stay here. The submarine is getting away!"

The lieutenant heard this. He moved beside the table where Carmen also sat and shook his head. "Don't worry about it! There is an Orion searching for it right now. Your safety is more important."

That was good sense but annoyed Andrew. Carmen looked anxious and asked; "What about the men?"

"They will just have to take their chances until daylight. We aren't risking a boat inside the reef in the dark in this weather," the lieutenant replied. "Now, if you feel up to it you might tell us what happened and answer a few questions."

So for the next hour Andrew and Carmen related to an incredulous officer their story. While they talked Ella was taken below and put in her bunk after being sedated. The dive boat and frigate both maintained their relative positions and heading.

"Where are we going now?" Andrew asked.

The lieutenant answered. "Nowhere much at the moment. We are maintaining position about three nautical miles east of the reef, to give us a bit of sea room and so we don't have too far to come back in the morning," he explained.

That did not suit Andrew. He wanted to be hunting the submarine but realized he had little say in what now went on. Hot food was served by a grinning rating and Andrew almost wolfed it down. Then he had to go to the toilet and felt so weak and stiff he could hardly limp and drag his way safely to the companionway. The midshipman, the PO and another rating helped him along. Carmen followed, helped by the female medic. By this time he was feeling utterly drained and he was battling to keep his eyes open.

Seeing him blinking and rubbing at his eyes the lieutenant urged them both to go to bed. "We will see to things. In the morning we can tidy things up," he said.

Andrew nodded and made his way to the companionway. The sea was till very rough but with the dive boat in the hands of such obviously competent professionals he felt quite relaxed. Slowly he made his way down to his cabin, Carmen following and being helped by the female rating. Thankfully Andrew staggered into his cabin. Easing his aching muscles he rolled onto the lower bunk and closed his eyes. The PO adjusted his pillow and covered him with a blanket. Andrew was sound asleep within minutes

* * * * *

Sometime later he woke to find himself lying on the deck. A sudden roll had deposited him there in a tangle of bed clothes. The cabin was in semi-darkness but there was a light on in the passage. A rating had been sitting in a chair in the cabin and he now took hold of Andrew. He was all apologetic as he helped Andrew up.

Clawing himself upright Andrew blinked and looked around, his heart palpitating with anxiety. Then he heard laughter.

It can't be too bad. The navy aren't worried, he thought as he experienced another sudden jolt as the dive boat shouldered its way into another big wave. *Weather hasn't abated,* he noted.

Clinging to the upper bunk he stared through the porthole. All that was visible was shades of darkness and then the darker shape of a wave washing by. It reminded Andrew of being down in the water and of their desperate battle for survival. Then he remembered the diver who might be struggling for his life out in that watery waste and he shuddered again.

Satisfied all was well Andrew allowed himself to be helped to the toilet. He gulped a glass of water and was almost carried back to the cabin as his muscles began to tremble. He lay down again and tried to relax. But his mind was now racing, dwelling on the events of the last few days and struggling to come to terms with its absolute reality and horror.

The rating became anxious and moved to feel Andrew's brow. "You've got a bit of a fever," he commented. "I'll just get you another cold drink."

He left the cabin for a few minutes and returned with a drink of cold cordial. He lifted Andrew to a half-reclining position and held the cup to his lips. Andrew gulped the drink greedily, thinking it wonderful.

Better than the fabled nectar of the Gods, he told himself.

Then the rating wiped Andrew's face with a cool, damp hand towel and Andrew trembled and felt as though his whole body was dissolving and melting. Every scratch and cut seemed to itch and his muscles ached and throbbed and his skin 'crawled'. Liquid gurgles from his stomach caused further discomfort.

But we are safe, Andrew told himself. *The navy will look after us.*

Once again, he drifted into a deep sleep. The next time he woke it was daylight. A thin bar of sunlight was slanting in through the porthole and the dive boat's motion was obviously much easier. As memory flooded back Andrew sat up.

I wonder if they have caught that submarine, he thought.

Chapter 36

LOOSE ENDS

Andrew went to sit up and at once regretted his haste. Stiff muscles protested and his head hammered. The groan he emitted attracted another rating who was on duty watching them. It was the female Leading Seaman this time. She hurried in as Andrew swung his legs off the bunk.

"Are you alright?" she asked.

"Fine," Andrew lied, his throbbing headache and shivering muscles telling him otherwise.

"You should stay in bed," the Leading Seaman chided.

"Toilet," Andrew mumbled back as he moved to stand up.

The rating moved to help him and hold him steady while his sore muscles eased. Standing on legs that felt like they were made of rubber Andrew tried to hide how weak he felt.

"How's my sister?" he asked.

"Sleeping like a baby, and so should you be," the Leading Seaman said.

"What about Ella?"

For just a fraction of a second the rating hesitated before replying. "She has had a bad time but is recovering. We will be getting her off to hospital as soon as we can," she said.

"Has the wind dropped enough?" Andrew asked, squinting to peer through the porthole.

"It is still rough but is dropping," the Leading Seaman answered.

Andrew made his way slowly and painfully out into the passageway and along it. "Is your ship still here?" he asked.

What bothered him now was being too ill to get a chance to go on the frigate when it went off to hunt the submarine.

The Leading Seaman nodded. "We are just going alongside now. We are going to transfer you all," she explained.

When Andrew had been to the toilet he made his way slowly back along the passageway and back to his cabin. Pulling the door shut he stripped off his bathers and pulled on underpants, shorts and shirt.

As he was lacing on his sneakers there was a knock on the door. "Are you alright?" the Leading Seaman called.

"Yes," Andrew called back. He stood and opened the cabin door and saw she was supporting Carmen.

The Leading Seaman pointed up. "Grab any personal gear if you can and make your way topsides," she said.

Andrew nodded. "Hi sis, how are you?" he asked Carmen.

Carmen smiled back and gave a nod of the head. "OK, what about you little brother?"

"Bit stiff and sore," Andrew admitted.

He turned and collected his kit bag and followed Carmen and the Leading Seaman up to the saloon. Now that his muscles had warmed up a bit they moved more easily and apart from some sharp pulling sensations in his wound he felt much better.

Andrew looked around at the top of the steps and saw that the rating had been right. Close to starboard was the frigate, looking impressive in the morning sun. The dive boat was moving closer into its lee.

Oh, I hope we can go on it when it hunts the sub, he thought.

Ella was brought up by two more ratings. She looked very pale and miserable but was able to walk. Andrew said hello and she gave a half-smile and nodded in reply.

"Thanks for saving me," she croaked. "You were very brave."

That made Andrew feel quite embarrassed but also very proud as he noted the quick looks the navy personnel gave him.

They know the story now, he thought.

The RHIB appeared and took station close alongside. For safety they all had to put on life jackets and that got Andrew remembering and feeling a bit anxious. Then the RHIB came alongside the dive boat and the transfer began. Stepping across into the RHIB was easy but being that close to the open ocean again caused a few flutters of apprehension.

Ella took some coaxing but made it safely and Carmen just skipped across as cool as could be. The lieutenant followed and the RHIB cast off and headed across to the frigate.

Andrew admired all this, his eyes taking in all the details of guns, radars and fittings plus all the people he could see. The RHIB was hooked on and hoisted up the ship's side and settled on its davits. Then they were helped down onto the deck.

The frigates captain, a commander, was waiting for them. "Welcome to HMAS *Warramunga*," he said shaking their hands. "I am Commander Grenville."

Andrew was thrilled and pleased. The captain said, "Doctor first, for a check-up. This is Surgeon Lieutenant Loveday. He will make sure you are alright."

They were taken to the sick bay. First it was a hot shower and Andrew took the opportunity to shave. Then they were checked over. When the doctor studied the numerous welts, cuts and scratches on Andrew's skin he shook his head. "You've been in the wars young fella," he commented.

Andrew could only nod and fight back tears of relief. Andrew had his wound examined but was pleased to learn that it was healing well.

"Just take it easy for a week or so," the doctor said.

His wounds and cuts were then redressed and he was given a set of navy camouflage overalls to wear. That pleased him enormously.

When all three had been seen to Comdr Grenville asked if they were well enough to answer a few questions. Andrew and Carmen both nodded and agreed that they were but Ella shook her head. She was helped into a bed in the sick bay while the captain led Andrew and Carmen to a very comfortably furnished briefing room.

"Have a seat please. Coffee or tea? You can have breakfast when we finish," Comdr Grenville said.

They sat and Carmen asked for Milo or cocoa. Andrew nodded and eased himself into a comfortable chair, feeling safe for the first time in a week. Several other officers seated themselves as well and the questioning began. Comdr Grenville tapped a notebook and said he had the outline from Lt Cameron.

"But I would like you to go over it again in detail please."

"But sir, shouldn't we get after the submarine?" Andrew asked.

Comdr Grenville shook his head and smiled. "No hurry. Thanks to those radio transponders you stuck on it we have its position exactly. It is only a hundred and fifty kilometres away and an Orion is circling over it as we speak. We will be on our way directly we can transfer you to a police launch."

That was a real blow to Andrew's hopes of being in at the kill. "Can't we come with you sir?" he asked.

Comdr Grenville shook his head. "Sorry. This could be dangerous if the sub has live torpedoes and besides, we could be at sea for days," he explained.

"Oh sir, that's alright, it is the Easter holidays," Andrew answered. He wanted to plead but his pride would not let him.

"From what the doctor has told me you should probably be in hospital. Besides you might miss school. We might have to chase this sub right across the Coral Sea. It could be a week or more before we get back to Australia."

"Oh, piffle to school!" Andrew cried in his disappointment. "I am going to join the navy."

"Good for you!" Comdr Grenville replied with a laugh. "But that is all the more reason why you need to be at school. What are you hoping to be?"

Andrew gazed with the eyes of adolescent hero worship at the commander and wanted to say, 'just like you', but he shrugged instead and said, "An officer sir."

"Then you need good marks. Sorry, I can tell you really want to come with us but we aren't allowed to take you. There could be combat and you are civilians and children. It would be more than my career is worth. Besides the police want to speak to you as well," Comdr Grenville replied.

Trying to mask his disappointment Andrew nodded. He could see he wasn't going to win. So he began to tell the story with Carmen adding detail. As their struggle for survival was described the faces of the five officers became more and more incredulous and then their expressions shifted to ones of frank admiration.

Comdr Grenville shook his head and said, "You two have done the most amazing job of surviving against the odds. You should be instructors on the Sea Survival Course."

Andrew blushed at the praise and wished he could be. "Will you please give our CO at TS *Endeavour* a good report on us sir?" he asked.

"With pleasure. You are both a real credit to the Navy Cadets and deserve a medal," Comdr Grenville commented.

As he said this another officer came in to report on the search. Andrew did not hear what was said but afterwards Carmen spoke up.

"Sir, have they found any of those men?' she asked.

Comdr Grenville shook his head. "No sign of anyone on Yule Reef," he replied. "They are moving to search the wrecks on Longbow Reef now."

"What about Prescott Island sir?"

"They have already searched it. Nobody there."

Andrew thought about Yule Cay and felt very anxious as horrible memories swamped him. He met Carmen's eyes and she returned a bleak, grim stare which showed she was having the same awful flashbacks. Images of the sea rising and rising until there was no dry land left and then of the darkness and the waves washing over them caused Andrew to shudder.

"When was high tide sir?" Andrew asked.

"About four this morning," an officer replied.

"And how high?"

"Nearly three metres," was the answer.

"Then he got washed away. That is why Carmen and I tried to swim to Longbow Reef because we knew we wouldn't survive a really high tide in bad weather," Andrew answered.

Again, he shuddered at the awful images that crowded his mind. But he was also bothered to find that one of the emotions he didn't feel was regret.

That mongrel tried to kill us so he got the same as he wanted us to suffer, he thought. The notion of poetic justice appealed to him.

The unmistakable sound of a helicopter reached them and Comdr Grenville glanced up. "Ah! Good. That will be the rescue chopper. It is picking up your friend. She needs to get to hospital. You can go on it if you wish or you can go back with the police launch. It is due to rendezvous with us in an hour."

Andrew was torn. What he really wanted was to go with the frigate but he accepted this was not to be. So he glanced at Carmen, who replied without hesitation: "Helicopter please sir."

That decided Andrew. He had been weighing up the relative travel times against his fear of flying over the sea but there was no way he was not going with his sister. So he nodded. They were led aft to the ship's helicopter hangar and Andrew got another shock when he realized his courage was going to be tested again: the helicopter was hovering and they would have to be winched up!

"Why doesn't it land sir?" he asked one of the officers.

"The pilot doesn't have the training for deck landings," the officer replied.

"Couldn't you take us in yours?" Andrew asked, indicating the 'Seahawk' being readied for flight just behind them.

"It is going to look for your submarine," the officer replied.

That was good news, but another niggling thought came to Andrew. "What if the submarine is in international waters, can you do anything to it then?"

Comdr Grenville answered that. "The smugglers have made the mistake of travelling in a straight line and are still in our maritime protected zone. We own about half the Coral Sea and the French own a big chunk as well and they have given us permission to chase in their waters as well."

That was all a revelation to Andrew and he realized that there must have been a lot of signal traffic and governments talking to governments even while he and Carmen were aboard the frigate. It all increased his admiration for the navy and its efficiency.

And he couldn't admit he was terrified of being winched up or that he feared flying over the ocean. After people had said he was brave all he could do was swallow and put a brave face on it!

Ella was winched up first, strapped in a stretcher. Carmen went next and then it was Andrew's turn. Clad in his overalls and a lifejacket he was led out onto the windy, heaving helicopter deck to stand with a rating who grabbed the harness when it was lowered. This was secured and Andrew could only keep a wooden grin on his face and give a thumbs-up. Then he was off the deck and dangling above the frigate.

The spurt of fear was replaced by interest in seeing the warship from above. Then he looked up and studied the hovering helicopter, his eyes slitted against the rotor downdraught. A few seconds later he was up level with it and hands grabbed him and he was swung into the cabin. Sighing with relief he was taken out of the harness and strapped into a seat.

The helicopter then turned away and headed for shore. As it did Andrew looked out and watched the frigate getting under way, white froth at its stern indicating the increase in propeller revolutions. Then the dive boat passed below, looking small and old beside the much larger warship. A few minutes later the helicopter flew across the edge of the reef. As always Andrew was struck by the change of colours; from the dark blue of the deep water to the creamy yellow and brown of the shallow water and coral reefs.

Two dark shapes came into view and Carmen nudged him and pointed. They were the wrecks of the trawler and the sailing ship. Andrew stared at them with something almost akin to affection.

They saved our lives! he thought.

Then the wrecks were far behind and the deep waters of the Challenger Channel slipped into view. Andrew saw Prescott Island clearly and noted a large white launch near it but he did not see the cay on Yule Reef.

It must be right underneath us, he decided.

Then it was half an hour of flying over the deeper waters of the sea inside the reef. As they flew shoreward at a couple of thousand feet Andrew studied the thousands of whitecaps, his eyes searching for the rubber dinghy.

I wonder if that bloke made it, he thought.

The fate of the smugglers both bothered him and made him feel bad about himself when he realized he was hoping they were all dead so he didn't have to worry about them coming to get them in the future.

Then it was a landing in Townsville with anxious parents, police, paramedics and a great cluster of news media. After an ambulance ride, a hospital check-up and a big breakfast they were taken to an interview room and questioned at length by Customs officers, Federal Police, Queensland state police and several plain clothes men whose departments weren't indicated.

Through it all Andrew fretted over the fate of the submarine. To his surprise and relief, he was told that the sub had surrendered as soon as the frigate caught up with it, which it did by mid-afternoon. It turned out that it was an old Soviet sub, stolen by a Russian 'Mafia' gang from among dozens left rusting in a remote Siberian harbour.

As for the four men none was ever seen again. The boss, Ivanoff, could not be found on Yule Cay and it was presumed he was washed off by the storm and drowned.

I hope so, Andrew thought. *He ordered me to be chucked overboard to drown. Serves the bastard right!*

Carmen asked, "What about the diver on Longbow Reef?"

"No sign of him, not on either wreck," a policeman replied.

That puzzled Andrew, but all he could decide was that the man had not made it to the wreck before the storm. Of the other diver, there was no sign. Andrew felt certain that he had had been knocked unconscious by Ella's blow to his head and that he had simply drowned and been washed away by the current, but to protect her he kept his theories to himself.

As for the man in the rubber dinghy, he was never seen again either but the next day a search aircraft located the rubber dinghy fifty nautical miles from land. It was capsized and empty. The possible fate of the man caused Andrew to shudder, but also left him relieved.

Maybe we are safe? he decided.

They were. Apart from the unpleasantness of the court case many months later, and the jealousy of peers when he and Carmen became public heroes, there was no retaliation by the gang or its masters. It was revealed that the submarine had been smuggling drugs, mostly from South America, plus guns into the Solomon Islands and Bougainville.

They also learned that the only reason the submarine took the risk of surfacing in daylight was to pick up the three men. They were major criminals who had paid big money to try to escape from Australia.

The biggest surprise of all came in the next year's Australia Day Honours Awards on January the 26th. Both Andrew and Carmen were awarded bravery medals. Andrew was awarded a Star of Courage, mostly for his rescue of Ella, and Carmen received a Bravery Medal. The presentation of these required the family to travel to Canberra the following March for them to be pinned on by the Governor General at Government House.

As both decorations could be worn on Navy Cadet uniforms they were both a source of enormous pride to both brother and sister but also caused a good deal of jealousy among their rivals and peers. Andrew didn't care.

Tina was very proud of him. She gave him a big hug and a kiss and said, "You are my hero and always have been!"

Enjoy more C.R. Cummings stories

The Air Cadets

The Navy Cadets

The Army Cadets

www.ingramcontent.com/pod-product-compliance
Lightning Source LLC
Chambersburg PA
CBHW030923260626
47169CB00002B/364